P9-CBH-371

THE THICK AND THE LEAN

THE THICK

AND THE

LEAN

a novel

CHANA PORTER

SAGA PRESS

LONDON SYDNEY **NEW YORK** TORONTO NEW DELHI

SAGA PRESS

AN IMPRINT OF SIMON & SCHUSTER, INC.

1230 AVENUE OF THE AMERICAS, NEW YORK, NEW YORK 10020

This book is a work of fiction. Any references to historical events, real people, or real places are used fictitiously. Other names, characters, places, and events are products of the author's imagination, and any resemblance to actual events or places or persons, living or dead, is entirely coincidental.

Copyright © 2023 by Chana Porter

All rights reserved, including the right to reproduce this book or portions thereof in any form whatsoever. For information, address Saga Press Subsidiary Rights Department, 1230 Avenue of the Americas, New York, NY 10020.

First Saga Press hardcover edition April 2023

SAGA PRESS and colophon are trademarks of Simon & Schuster, Inc.

For information about special discounts for bulk purchases, please contact Simon & Schuster Special Sales at 1-866-506-1949 or business@simonandschuster.com.

The Simon & Schuster Speakers Bureau can bring authors to your live event. For more information or to book an event, contact the Simon & Schuster Speakers Bureau at 1-866-248-3049 or visit our website at www.simonspeakers.com.

Interior design by Davina Mock-Maniscalco

Manufactured in China

1   3   5   7   9   10   8   6   4   2

Library of Congress Cataloging-in-Publication data has been applied for.

ISBN 978-1-6680-0019-9
ISBN 978-1-6680-0021-2 (ebook)

Quotation from *A Gentle Plea for Chaos: Reflections from an English Garden* by Mirabel Osler. Copyright © Mirabel Osler 1989.

For my mother

"And what intricacies are we led into
from the sheer chance of planting a seed in the earth?"

—Mirabel Osler, *A Gentle Plea for Chaos*

PART ONE

PART ONE

1.

Beatrice Bolano looked down at her almost empty plate. She was still hungry. Hungry in the way they warned about in church, whispered about in the girls' bathroom at school, scratched into the wall behind the Buff 'n' Go. Beatrice was hungry for taste, texture, mouthfeel. Crispy, crunchy, silky, chewy. Beatrice was hungry for juxtaposition, and she would never tell anyone as long as she lived.

There was still a small mound of rice on her plate, and next to that an even smaller mound of celery and carrots cooked together in such a way that they resembled each other. Grayish, stringy, mushy. She ate the remaining rice with a bit of vegetable mush and imagined it overlaid with lemon, butter, salt. Beatrice was comfortable with this kind of game, even in front of her parents, injecting clean, modest meals with her secret perversity. While Beatrice chewed her bland food, imagining it improved, a litany of words floated through her mind: *reduction, flambé, seared, marzipan*.

Soon Mama would go into the living room and choose a television program for the evening while Papa cleaned out the cooking pot. Feigning a headache, Beatrice excused herself from her parents to retire early. She couldn't concentrate, not on homework or television. Colors and scents and flavors she had never actually tasted, only imagined, danced through her mind. Words she knew from her secret hours lurking in chat rooms on her family computer.

Beatrice locked her bedroom door and lay down on her bed. Now that she had made her decision, she wanted to tease herself, to go slow and make it last as long as possible. It wouldn't be like the other times. No one would ever know. As if it had never happened, only a dream. It wouldn't be like that time she'd stood in the refrigerator light in Carrie Sutherland's kitchen, stuffing her face with peas and rice gruel as Carrie's mother walked in, horrified. Carrie, smirking, fist-deep into a jar of enriched vitamin syrup. Even when misbehaving, Carrie knew better than to let anyone outside her own family actually see her chew and swallow. The memory of that day still filled Beatrice with a cold, static dread every time she saw Mrs. Sutherland at church. Sometimes Beatrice felt her shame so palpably, she could almost taste it.

Her mouth watered. Her fingers twitched. Beatrice glanced at the door. The sounds of the television drifted up to her bedroom. A young man screamed out in pleasure and pain, the din interspersed with a woman's throaty laughter. It was her parents' favorite program of late, *Boy Meat*, where a gang of dominatrixes rode through the countryside on their motorcycles, torturing terrified young men. It was a city show, like most of the media they consumed. The people of Seagate enjoyed the outlandish outfits and dramatics, even though the formula of the show was tiresome. Beatrice mainly watched it for the exit interviews. The young man sat on the floor shiny with sweat and tears and body fluid, with his head resting on the lap of one of the toughest biker babes, his words dreamy and awed: "It was an experience I'll never forget—and I have the video to cherish forever!"

Beatrice took out a small wooden box from under her bed. She slid off the lid to reveal parcels of individually wrapped tissue paper. Slowly, reverently, she unwrapped the treasures she'd been collecting. One small block of cheese, a jar containing half a preserved lemon, and her prize: a small flatbread, perfectly contained in her open palms.

She had made the food herself when she was alone in her family's perfect, quiet house. Healthful, appropriate milk, strained through a fine cloth and set to curdle sinfully, the lemon pilfered from a neighbor's tree. The bread was an approximation—cornmeal, water, and salt cooked in secret on the stove that heated her bedroom. Beatrice had borrowed a clean metal tray intended for mixing paints from Papa's toolshed, his haven for endless home improvements. It had served nicely as her pan, a thick white towel stuffed in the crack of her door to muffle the aroma.

She leaned back to survey her meal.

It was all so very beautiful.

Beatrice glanced back at the door and felt the strange urge to cry. Then little Remus, her sugar glider, pressed his hot, fuzzy head into her shoulder, eyes blinking open from Beatrice's handwoven neck pouch, waking from a long nap.

Beatrice tore off a bit of the flatbread and layered it with sour lemon and sweet cheese. "Here," she whispered to the sugar glider, cupping the food in her open palm. "Eat." There was no hesitation. The food, so lovingly prepared, was devoured without a thought, and then Remus yawned, settling back into his pouch for another nap. Beatrice wiped her hands on her skirt and sighed. She didn't want to live like an animal, enslaved by mindless hunger. The church doctrine said holiness was like a ladder—or a circle, or an upward spiral, depending who was preaching. But one thing everyone agreed on was that eating pure helped you *think* pure, which in turn made you *be* pure.

Beatrice looked down at the food. For a moment, she was loath to eat at all. She knew it would feel so good, then worse than ever. She considered flushing the lot down the toilet, symbolically ridding herself of these desires so she could live a normal, productive life. Maybe if she just tried harder, it would eventually feel like she wasn't trying at all. She would simply be better—happy, like everyone else.

Just one more time, she thought. *As a purge.* One more time, and then never again.

Hands trembling, she set upon her feast like a dog, like a thief, like a chef.

The first time Beatrice had experimented with cooking, she was fourteen years old, attending her first girl-boy sleepover at their church. The pastor, Father Alvarez, corralled the teenagers into a circle after a long evening of prayers and hymns alongside his upbeat acoustic guitar. The children sat on their sleeping bags on the wooden floor, cathedral windows flooded with light from the dual full moons. The church was handsome, well-built, and unadorned, like everything else in Seagate, the flagship community of the Stecopo Corporation. Every office building, street sign, school, house, and community park was perfectly curated by Stecopo. Her parents were pioneers—city folk who had devoted their lives to the company back when Seagate was just a glossy suburban dream. The visionary Rick Tenzo had dreamt of a place where people could live together harmoniously and healthfully, with each part of their lives streamlined, beautified, purified through the power of science married with religion. It was the only life that Beatrice had ever known.

In his everyday priest robes of white and yellow, Father Alvarez resembled a bird, his nose a sharp beak, his eyes bright and round. He gave a short sermon about Bremah, the celebration of the dual full moons Lluna and Ata. He spoke reverently of their ancestors finding their way here in hot air balloons, guided by the moonslight, to be welcomed by the Free-Wah people, who were native to these lands. Esther Sima, whose mother was Free-Wah, held up her hands, murmuring, "Praise God!" at the important bits. Lately Esther had made quite a show of being religious. She also had cut her hair into bangs, covering her Free-Wah forehead ridge. While she wasn't fooling anyone, the bangs did look cute.

"We call ourselves the ALGN people, but can anyone tell me what this really means?" asked the pastor.

"All Lands Gone Now," droned the youth group.

"That's right. We came here as weary travelers, in search of solid ground. Many peoples from many different lands, all washed away in the rising tides, following the promise of the Divine Mother, the original Flesh Martyr, who discovered this land and the people here. The Free-Wah king tried to destroy her, but the faithful always rise to serve another day!" He gestured out the window to the bright circles in the sky. "The festival of Bremah is a celebration, and a solemn reminder. One day, all lands will be gone. The beauty of our two moons does not soften the forces they wreak upon our planet—earthquakes, high waves, a steadily shrinking mass of habitable land. One day, Lluna and Ata will be drawn into each other's orbits, raining destruction over us all. This could happen in a thousand years, or it could be tomorrow."

The youth group was very quiet.

"That is the promise of the Divine Mother. Through our faith, no matter what comes, we will rise again to flourish in the Forever Palace," he continued softly. "But tonight, we give thanks for this precious moment. We praise God with our bodies, with the gift of our holy love."

Then Sister Marita, a pretty young nun, gave her own speech about the privilege of them being alone together to explore sacred sex. She was hugely pregnant, and several of the boys (and some of the girls) could not stop looking at her smooth, shiny legs under her white shift. Everyone wore the same style of clothing in Seagate—loose, light fabrics, a few acceptable shades of white, yellow, and tan, the same fabrics cut into tunics, jumpsuits, shirts, and trousers. But a certain garment might look plain on one person and seem to shine on another, as if they were lit from within by a candle. Beatrice, being only fourteen, did not know if she was a candle person or not, but lately people had seemed to notice her. Mirrors were deceptive, and Mama always told her she was perfect, but Beatrice was beginning to suspect she was beautiful.

"What do we say, friends?" Sister Marita asked the youth group.

"Our bodies are divine vessels," the teenagers said in flat unison.

The chaperoned portion of the evening was beginning to wrap up. Beatrice could feel the eager anticipation in the air. Sister Marita warned the children to stick to outercourse instead of innercourse, as that was the road to becoming good lovers. "Remember, the better you get at outer sex, developing a relationship with your body, the more enjoyable inner sex will be in the future. Don't skip steps!" Most of the teens nodded seriously, but Mina Ido and Melis Peltzman looked at the ground. Everyone knew they had been having inner sex for at least four months—it was all anyone could talk about. But Sister Marita had no clue.

Then, before the pastor and Sister Marita left, Danny Walton and Michael Rodriguez began tickling each other and rolling on the floor, giggling rebelliously.

"Stick to outercourse, Danny!" called Ezra Allen, poking fun at the rolling boys. The other kids shoved and hushed them.

"Boys," Father Alvarez warned.

"Are you ready to control yourselves?" asked Sister Marita.

"You're making us wait longer!" complained Mina.

"Young ones," the pastor began slowly. "Animals cannot make love." The teenagers quieted and settled in. This was his sermon voice, with its storyteller rhythm. All they could do now was relax and listen up. "They engage in intercourse mindlessly, driven by biology. Gorillas, our closest kin, mate for one to two minutes. The females lie down and are penetrated from behind. They signal their interest in sex two to three days out of the month when they are ovulating. These same animals use tools and care for their young. They even form social circles, friendships, and hierarchies. But they do not make love. To give and receive pleasure outside of procreation is the most human act possible."

Suddenly his handsome, hawklike face looked sad. "Likewise, many animals, observed in captivity, will eat until it harms them. Some animals will gorge themselves until they die."

He winced at the moons outside, as if blanching before a judgmental God. "To be holy, you must live in a holy manner. This is our sacred task as human beings. Animal bodies with angelic souls." He gazed at them gently. "You are young and hungry to experience, to enjoy, to learn and feel it all. But be soft with yourselves and each other. Only with restraint and purity can we glimpse God."

Sister Marita touched him on the shoulder.

"Okay, that's all—we promise! We'll be upstairs if anyone needs help." Father Alvarez and Sister Marita stood up.

"One more very, very important thing," Father Alvarez said sternly, wagging his flashlight at them. "Have fun!" Then they turned off the overhead lights, chuckling, and left.

The evening started off just like all the other boy-girl parties, with all the normal games: Wobbly Bottles, Truth or Consequences, Nuns in the Bell Tower. Flora Bitman told a particularly gruesome version of the old Night Witch story, flashlight pointed up on her chin when the Night Witch lured the children into her cottage, cleaving their body parts and stirring them into her noxious brews. Eventually the boys and girls moved toward those they found attractive and split off in couples or small groups. Beatrice zeroed in on Leroy Kim. He was tall, all lanky arms and legs, and seemed to be growing faster than his mothers could keep him in new pants. Leroy was given an extra carton of milk at mealtimes to account for his raging metabolism, but Beatrice suspected that it wasn't enough.

The boy was hungry.

"Leroy," Beatrice said, pushing out her chest. "Would you like to go somewhere more private with me?"

Leroy's brown eyes grew as wide as those of a cat on the hunt. He nodded. Beatrice took him by his long, bony hand and led him away from the group.

They walked silently down a dark hallway, past the Sunday school classroom to a door painted the purest white. She pushed it open into a dark room where metal objects gleamed silver. Beatrice held a finger to her lips and turned on the light. She was surprised she didn't feel guilty about doing this in a church. But then again, she never felt bad *before* doing it, just after. She looked around; the kitchen was larger than she had expected. Its industrial oven shone with a kind of sacred internal purpose, like a potter's kiln or a surgeon's instruments. She looked down at her hands.

I'm going to make something, she thought as Leroy's wet, round mouth careened into her neck.

Leroy spoke quickly into her hair. "Do you want to be my girl-friend?"

"Yes," she murmured into his chest before gently pulling herself away. "Leroy, you look hungry. Can I feed you?"

"Um," he said, looking at the tiled floor. "I've only ever had my family's cooking. That and the nutrition packets they give us at school."

"I know that."

"But why would you want to cook?"

She groped for the words. "This is how I can show you that I like you."

"But," he protested, "we have to eat clean to be clean. To be more like the angels, who don't need to eat and are never distracted from God."

She gave him a timid kiss on the lips. "Leroy, we're together now," she said. "Maybe, someday, if we stay together, you'll come to my house for a family dinner."

He sighed, squeezing her hips. "I would be so honored, Beatrice."

She looked up at him. "But then, why wait? Aren't you hungry?"

He looked down at her bright, determined face, a half-smile playing on his lips. "Yes," he whispered.

She began riffling through the church's cabinets. All the usual suspects were here: rice, oat bran, bags of dried beans. Her hands trembled as she opened the pantry door and saw a bag of carrots, a sack of potatoes, cans of peas. Food for the pious, food for people who could not afford (or did not believe in) the tidiness of meal supplements.

Then she opened the fridge and saw it. A small drawer,

hidden behind drums of powdered milk. Beatrice opened it and gasped. Two sticks of real butter, a hard wedge of yellow cheese wrapped in parchment paper, six brown eggs, and a basket of little tomatoes. "Oh, bloody hell!" Beatrice exclaimed, covering her mouth.

"Shhh," said Leroy, laughing.

She sliced off a stocky knob of butter, then ran her greasy finger across her lips. They watched together as the yellow-white wedge began to pool and heat in the skillet.

"Is this food blessed? Who do you think it belongs to?" He inhaled deeply. "What is that smell?"

"We could bless it ourselves," said Beatrice softly. "This is our first meal of our own, after all."

"It's like we're husband and wife."

They looked down at the miracle happening in the skillet. How could such a little thing, butter over a low flame, fill the room with such a scent? Leroy tentatively put a hand on her waist as he watched her spread more butter on two thick slices of bread, then layer on many slivers of hard cheese. She placed the sandwich in the pan of heated butter, and it began to sizzle.

"Is it supposed to make that sound?"

"Just wait and see," said Beatrice confidently, but it was all bluster. She didn't know if she was burning the food; she'd never imagined it would make any kind of noise. After what felt like ages, she took a big breath and flipped the sandwich. The side was golden with butter and seared from the fire, the melted cheese crackling out of the edges onto the hot pan below. The range of colors on the toasted bread—deep, golden tan, creamy white, nutty flecks of brown . . . It was more luscious and dynamic than Beatrice's wildest imaginings.

"It's beautiful," she breathed.

"You are," Leroy said, planting another kiss on her cheek and then lingering, breath hot in her ear.

Leroy was still holding her as she sliced the sandwich in half. Bright-yellow cheese oozed out vulgarly as she pulled the halves apart. It was even more obscene than she had anticipated. She couldn't wait to take a bite.

"Oh, Lord!" Leroy licked his lips. "What do we do now?"

They joined hands. "God," said Beatrice solemnly, "bless this food and our bodies. That we might eat to serve you another day." *And please, forgive me.*

At first bite, they moaned. It was so much better than the descriptions she had read on those late-night message boards. The playful balance of textures—the crunchy, fried exterior of the bread giving way to pillowy, internal softness. They consumed her creation within seconds. But instead of the elation she expected, Beatrice felt a deep sadness overtake her.

"Oh no," said Leroy, thumbing away her tears. "Don't cry." He kissed the tip of her nose. "You were right," he whispered. "It was so, so good."

She kissed him again, more firmly this time, wrapping her arms around him. She wanted to ask, *How could something so good be wrong?* But words were too small, too bare, to contain the range of feelings ricocheting inside of her. He kissed away her tears, until her sadness was replaced by a greater longing. Leroy's mouth was nourishing, like sweet, clean water.

There was a sound at the door. Leroy and Beatrice looked at each other, filled with the same terrible thought. They did not have time to conceal what they had done.

Father Alvarez stood in the doorway in a dull white sleeping tunic, his brown hair rumpled with sleep. His usual soft, gentle expression was replaced by a look of holy rage as he stared at the stick of butter melting on the counter, the half-used block of cheese, the opened loaf of bread. Leroy dropped her from his embrace. She wrapped her arms around herself, cold.

Her father picked her up from the church sleepover in his pajamas. The walk home was very quiet. Without the usual sounds of children playing or the hum of airships, Beatrice could hear the waves below, crashing against the huge cement platform that held the Valley aloft over the water, its ingenious design keeping its citizens safe from the dangerous swells of an increasingly tempestuous sea. Their founder, Rick Tenzo, was consumed by his next big project—Seagate colonies in outer space, a dream that would take decades to realize. Walking back through this beautifully designed community, the hardworking people all asleep in their beds, made Beatrice feel even more ashamed. As if Mr. Tenzo himself were looking down from space, judging her.

In the living room, Mama sat in her bathrobe, ready with a full pot of herbal tea and three cups. After tearfully apologizing for her behavior, Beatrice curled up in her mother's lap on the couch, letting her stroke her hair. "It can be difficult, in its own way, not to have anything to rebel against," said Mama gently.

Beatrice felt lower than the ground. She could have been having fun with the other teenagers. Instead, she'd managed to get herself sent home.

"You learned an important lesson tonight," said Papa. "Keep that lesson and let the rest go."

Beatrice sat up, sniffling, and wiped her eyes. "But I feel awful!"

"Did you take your pills today?" asked Papa.

Mama stood up. "I'll go check."

Alone on the couch with her father, Beatrice felt shy. "I'll never do that again. I promise."

He waved his hand, as if pushing the thought away. "It's in the past, Beatrice. Guilt is a useless emotion."

Mama came back with a glass of water, Beatrice's pillbox, and what looked like a jewelry box, only a bit larger than Beatrice's own palm. "No wonder you're feeling bad!"

Beatrice took the small handful of pills and gulped at the water.

"Now. I was going to give this to you on your birthday," said Mama, holding out the second box. "But I think this is the perfect time."

Beatrice opened it to reveal her mother's gleaming opalescent necklace, a double moonstone she had admired ever since she could remember, on a delicate silver chain.

"The women in my family have worn this necklace for generations," said Mama. "And now it's your turn."

Papa beamed as Mama clasped the necklace around Beatrice's neck.

"Keep it under your clothes, darling," said Papa. "Don't gloat or show off what our neighbors don't have. One day, you'll give it to your daughter."

The necklace felt cold and heavy on her chest. "I'll wear it and make you proud."

"Our gorgeous girl," said her mother simply. "We are already proud."

The private meetings she was made to attend with Father Alvarez were similarly benign. First they would sit together in quiet contemplation. After about twenty minutes, he would begin to speak, gently, like softly falling rain. *God is like the sky, God is like a river. God is big and God is small, God is inside us and always around us.*

God is in everything, God exists everywhere. On and on and on and on. Sometimes she thought about his hypotonic, quiet sermons when she couldn't sleep. After their session, she'd go with a nun to sweat it out in the sauna or bounce out her feelings at the trampoline park. No one expected teenagers to do penance the way adults did, cheerfully carrying buckets of water or going on long runs with the pastor at night instead of sleeping. The young hadn't joined the community as adults and couldn't be held to the same standards.

Over the next year, Leroy would disappear for various lengths of time: a week, a handful of days, once a whole month. Of course, Beatrice had seen this happen to others before. If a classmate was slow to lose their baby fat as a teenager, they were sent on a spiritual retreat. They would come back thin, with a zealous gleam in their eyes. Some of the newly religious teenagers would talk about actually becoming Flesh Martyrs, about abstaining from food until you were taken by God back to heaven. But no one ever did it—it was all just talk. There were rumors that in the big city, wealthy families designated one of their many children to become a Flesh Martyr at birth, as a sacrifice to prove their piety. Still, these were only urban legends, like the Night Witch who stole little children for her toxic brews, or restaurants for cannibals.

One day Beatrice heard that Leroy and his moms had actually left Seagate for good. Their beautiful house was now empty, their wide, lush lawn pristine, awaiting some other lucky family to take the Kims' place.

When she turned sixteen, Beatrice explicitly lied to her parents for the first time. She told them that she was going to have a sleepover with her sometimes-lover Jaimes. Beatrice had no intention of ever spending the night with Jaimes (though he had often asked). Everyone knew the most effective way to feel the depth of God's divine love was to fall in love, as relationships were containers for spiritual development. Yet Beatrice had never felt anything close to love. She had sex as casually as if grabbing a snack—a little bit to tide her over, then off to think about other things.

Things she was definitely not supposed to be thinking about.

The walk to her destination was an hour long, but the night was fine. Tonight Beatrice was going for the first time beyond the edge of town to the borderlands, where some people lived quietly sinful lives. Her only map was a crumb of a clue from a seedy chat room, given to her by an anonymous avatar.

As she approached the end of her town, the buildings grew shabby, their appearances random—a tall, dark-gray building next to a squat white one, brown stucco next to a spire. Paint peeled, cement cracked—a stark contrast to the cheerful, unified design of Seagate.

Then she saw it. The bookstore was sandwiched between a shabby-looking traveler's motel and a pharmacy that appeared to be out of business. She could have walked by this place a million times and never glanced back at it.

It was already proper nighttime, with both moons stark in the sky, yet she couldn't bring herself to go inside. She looked up. Lluna was almost full, while Ata was a waning sliver. The next double full moon wouldn't be for years to come. Would she be in the Valley for the next full moon festival, working for Stecopo middle management like both her parents? Beatrice knew it was what she was supposed to want, but she just couldn't picture it. The moons appeared to be steady, but Beatrice knew this was an illusion—the heavenly bodies were rotating closer and closer. One day, as certain as the sun, the two would be drawn together. After millennia of courtship, Lluna and Ata would finally kiss. But only destruction would come from that lovers' embrace. One day, everything on this planet would be washed away in giant waves or shattered by falling chunks of moon dust. Nothing was permanent, not even the sky. Beatrice steeled herself and opened the door to the bookstore.

Inside, as these things so often are, was rather disappointing.

The store was musty and brightly lit, shocking in its ordinariness: protein powders, vitamin drinks, green "juices" that came dry, to be mixed with water. Nothing was fresh. By the front door, an old fridge hummed, filled with a variety of drinks and a few endurance gels. Beatrice had seen nicer versions of this type of shop in the Valley—they had smoothie bars, freshwater infusions that boasted specific pH levels or caffeine. This store was a hodgepodge of things that mimicked what people might want, but on closer inspection, every item was a cheap facsimile. Rows of sex toys of assorted shapes, colors, and sizes, but all the flimsy, synthetic kind, not the nice ones made of real leather or glass. There were rows of paperback books with lascivious covers, pulpy romances with thin plots, mysteries with more sex than intrigue, like the ones her mother read then gave away, so as to not clutter up the house. The back wall was easy-to-use bondage gear, the sort that one could set up in less than ten minutes with very little training. None of the products were particularly nice or specialized; one could find them at any drugstore. And every single object was covered with a fine film of dust.

There was someone at the counter, an unremarkable-looking older woman with sallow skin, long gray hair, and cheap wire-frame glasses. *So much for closer to angels than animals,* Beatrice thought. She had pictured a man in charge of such a place—a rakish, burly man who could not control his appetites, a scoundrel or a creep, not a lady who like herself would fit in better at a church service than the black market. One of the movies from the *Orgasm*

Wars franchise was playing on a high, small television, but the woman at the counter wasn't watching. She was thumbing through a thick book, its cover obscured.

Beatrice tried coughing to get the woman's attention, but she never looked up from her book. She held up lingerie to her body, pretending to eye it for size. Soon another woman, closer to her own mother's age, walked in. Beatrice couldn't be sure if she recognized her—she was wearing a large, floppy hat and sunglasses. The woman at the counter looked up from her book, and then back meaningfully toward Beatrice. The customer sputtered out something about needing lubricant. She bought the smallest amount available and left. Beatrice felt an expansive tenderness toward the woman, who probably had kids at home around the same age as Beatrice. Certainly, if she did, they went to her school and Beatrice at least knew their names. Maybe she was a recruiter for Seagate, like Mama, or in advertising, spreading the good word of Stecopo products, like Papa.

Curious, Beatrice picked up a chilled bottle of electrolyte-infused water and glanced at the bottom. It had passed its sell-by date two years ago. At this, the woman behind the counter raised her head.

"Uh . . ." started Beatrice, unsure how to proceed. "Do you have anything to go with this water?" She looked at her meaningfully. The woman rolled her eyes and went back to her book.

Frustrated but undeterred, Beatrice took a pile of books from the back wall and settled down in a corner. She pretended to read, but she was really just listening to the small shifting sounds inside the sleepy shop. The woman took a short personal phone call in which she inquired after someone's health. Eventually *Orgasm Wars* stopped, and a commercial for the holiday special of *Jessima McVee's Gratitude Hour* played, followed by one for a deodorant pill that made your sweat smell like cherry blossoms. Then a new program started, but Beatrice didn't recognize it. The premise sounded like another reality competition where the judges would have sex with the contestants, then rank them across intimacy, sensuality, and creativity. The city was always cranking out these kinds of shows. Father Alvarez said when you didn't have a concrete relationship to God, even your holiest of actions were farcical. In the city, unlike Seagate, sex was for sale, along with everything else. She yawned, fighting the temptation to close her eyes. Beatrice was just about ready to give up and go home when the door opened for the second time. A deep voice rang out, causing her to sit up very straight.

"Hey, Lina," a man's voice said. "I'm looking for a book about castles. Can you help me?" The words vibrated with hidden meaning. She mouthed them silently to remember.

"I just got a new shipment of books," the woman replied. "There might be something about castles. Let's check in the back."

Beatrice heard footsteps. She mouthed the words again. All was quiet. Slowly, achingly, she crept out of her nest on the floor. She approached the counter. The woman's thick book was facedown and covered in simple brown paper. She opened to the cover page.

The Kitchen Girl

a true story

by Ijo

She had never seen a book so thick, with text so fine. It didn't have any pictures. And the pages themselves felt different—the material smooth, yet slightly rough. Her fingers paused on a page, its lines spread out, like poetry.

It read:

One-half cup reserved cooking liquid
One whole cup heavy cream
Beat together until homogeneous
Truss your stewing bird
and place in large roasting pan, legs aloft
Now say a prayer to whatever gods you serve
that your meal be fit for a king.

An electric shock ran up the length of her body, starting at her feet and shooting up her spine. She shivered. Then Beatrice felt a sharp tap on her back. She turned to find the shop woman scowling at her.

Her voice was raspy, low. "I thought you might have crept out like a mouse."

"Hi, Lina," she said, trying to steady her voice, which did sound rather mouselike at the moment. She repeated the man's words in a rush: "I'mlookingforabookaboutcastlescanyouhelpme?"

The woman threw up her hands. "Okay, okay, fine. You're very persistent." She went to the front door and turned over a little sign that read ON BREAK. She locked the door.

Beatrice felt a drum thumping in her chest. She had done it. She was going to be let inside the secret room.

Instead, Lina led Beatrice to a little back room that looked like an office—an old, full-sized computer sat dusty on a desk, joined by an ink blotter with a wide pad of paper and some unopened boxes.

She motioned to Beatrice to sit. "I'll get you when I'm ready." She clicked on a small desk light. "And don't touch anything!"

Beatrice put her head down on the desk and waited. On the

television, she heard a woman discuss her easy seven-step hair-care system—the secret to long, luscious locks. Tomorrow at church, Beatrice would repent. She would ask for God's help, to be healed. And then she would truly abstain from food pleasure. She would surrender to her perfect Seagate life. She would be normal. She would be happy.

The woman opened the door. "Are you ready?"

Beatrice was frightened, suddenly, of both scenarios—that she would be disappointed, and that she might fall in love with it. She tried her best to sound confident.

"I am."

Lina led her down into a basement. Beatrice shuddered to walk below ground level, like an insect crawling into the earth. Lina entered numbers on a pad embedded into a thick metal door. The door buzzed open.

The walls were white, the wooden shelving simple. None of the displays were fancy, but the items displayed there made Beatrice feel that she had stumbled upon a cavern of riches. A wall of gleaming utensils—shiny silver spatulas, tongs, spoons of so many different sizes and depths. She reached out and touched one lightly.

"Whisk?" she asked cautiously.

Lina nodded. "Come here." She led her over to several shelves of books. Traditional Northern Free-Wah cuisine. Seafood delicacies. A manual on bread-making. *Eating Your Way through the Seasons: A Guide to Local Produce.* Cooking with herbs and flowers. A slender leaflet on homemade ice cream. She picked up *Eating Your Way through the Seasons.*

"How much?"

Lina studied her over her glasses. "These books are very rare."

"How much?" she insisted.

"Four hundred ducats."

"*What?*" cried Beatrice.

"Lower your voice. I'm not trying to fleece you, girl. How much money do you have?"

"Fifty ducats," she said, her voice hollow. Beatrice had thought for certain that fifty would be enough to buy her several items. Money was barely used in Seagate, as everything substantial was provided by Stecopo—housing, supplements, clothing, technology, medicine. Beatrice's parents gave her an allowance for visits to the greater Valley, but she had no idea how much these kinds of items cost. The idea of walking home empty-handed was too much to bear.

"I'm not running a charity here," the woman said, her voice softening.

"Please," she said. "I'll work for you! I'll do anything."

"Never tell anyone you just met that you'll do anything to get something they have. Do you understand?" She frowned as if Beatrice had offended her. It was not an expression Beatrice was used to seeing. "Here's the deal: for fifty ducats, I'll let you bring this book home for one week to copy its pages."

"Oh, thank you, thank you!"

"And then I need you to bring it back to me. In perfect condition. If you turn out to be trustworthy, maybe we can do it again." Lina looked at her steadily over her wire frames.

Beatrice reached for the book.

"Not so fast. What are you going to leave me as 'collateral'?" Her eyes sparked at the chain around Beatrice's throat—the double moonstone necklace.

"What do you mean, 'collateral'?"

"I mean, what will you give me to make sure you won't steal my book?"

"But I would never—"

"I don't know you," the woman interrupted. "Pull that out, let me see."

Beatrice took the moonstone out from under her shift.

Lina had the gall to lift the necklace from Beatrice's bosom and study it like a jewelry appraiser. "It's very nice."

Beatrice twisted the chain around her neck. "It's my mother's. And it was her mother's before that. I can't part with it."

Lina shrugged. "Fine."

"Wait!" she said. "I'll need it back."

"And I'll need the book back," said Lina, as if Beatrice were dull-witted.

Beatrice paused. "My mother's necklace is worth more than four hundred ducats." She wasn't sure about this figure, but it sounded right. "Let me keep my fifty!"

Lina shook her head. "I'm keeping the money, little mouse. You're too young to know I'm being kind."

"Fine!" She reached out to snatch the book.

Lina pulled it out of her grasp. Beatrice, grimacing, thrust her ducat bag and necklace at the woman.

"Lovely doing business with you," said Lina, admiring the necklace. Then she slipped it into a deep pocket in her dull cloak dress; it seemed to disappear entirely, swallowed up by the coarse fabric. Beatrice felt her heart sink. No book, however valuable, was worth losing her mother's heirloom.

Lina put a light hand on her shoulder. "Tut-tut, chin up. I'll give it back."

"I don't trust the promises of people I don't know."

Lina sneezed out a little laugh. "Very good. Take a little spice, for your troubles."

Beatrice stood, eyes wide, before a wall of spices in little glass jars, their colors bright and surprising—dusty red, yellow-gold, smoky brown. Little greenish seedpods. A thimble's worth of dark-orange strings.

"I can take any of these?" Beatrice reached toward the case.

"Not that one!" said Lina, gesturing to the orange strings. "Here." She took out a little scoop of the smoky brown and the yellow-gold. "Do you have food at home?" Beatrice nodded. Mama still cooked simple foods in the crockpot rather than only using food bars and meal replacements, as most Seagate families did.

Lina motioned for Beatrice to follow her back upstairs, to the bookstore proper. Reluctantly, she left the marvelous place and climbed the rickety stairs. "Take a half cup of rice and boil it in a full cup of water, covered, with three pinches of spice until tender— all the water in the pot should be absorbed. Then fluff it with a fork and salt it. If it's gummy or dry, you've done it wrong. And don't forget to rinse your rice at least six times before boiling." When they reached the main store, Lina lowered her voice, even though the door was locked and the shop was empty. "There's an easy recipe for quick preserved lemon in that book," said Lina. "Try the turmeric rice with a little preserved lemon on top. You have access to sugar? That will temper the pickle, but you can do it with only salt if necessary."

"We have plenty of sugar. My father uses it to feed the humming-birds, and Mama uses it for cocktails." She stuck her nose in the air. "And I've been preserving lemons for several months now." Although she didn't know you were supposed to wash raw rice before cooking—Mama certainly never did.

Lina raised an eyebrow. "Lucky girl, aren't you? Family jewels and sugar for birds. My, my. Now, don't stain my book." She crossed her arms. "I'll see you next week."

"Thank you," she said out of habit, because she was sure she hated this woman. "My name is—"

The woman shook her head. "We don't do names here, girl."

"But aren't you Lina?"

She smiled, revealing long, crooked teeth. Beatrice almost shuddered. No one had teeth like that in Seagate. "You can call me that. I'll call you little mouse."

Lina handed her the book, wrapped in brown paper.

Beatrice pressed it to her chest. It was hers, if only for a week.

"Oh, and little mouse?"

"Yes, ma'am?"

In the moonlight, her face looked rather ghoulish. "If you stop taking the yellow pill, your hunger will come back."

Beatrice had no idea what she meant.

2.

Reiko Rimando loaded her ducats into the slot, more than she'd ever held in her hand all at once, and with the sounds of *clink, clink, clink*, the money carried her up out of the Bastian. The Loop whirred, and its great track started moving, chugging across the sky like God's own personal train. Reiko looked out the window, and the world was new.

The Middle was spectacular. Red, green, and gold towers capped with rounded cupolas, fanciful yet regal against the bright-blue sky. The domes were embellished with cheerful stripes like a circus tent, or an overlapping lattice reminiscent of a pineapple, or in undulating ridges, as if some whimsical god had twisted the tops of these grand buildings just so.

The ride to the Middle took less than an hour. Reiko heard her station announced; hands trembling, she pressed the button on the side of the door and punched in her ticket. Paying an additional coin to exit (which she found ridiculous), she watched as an armature jutted out from the side of the train, creating a tiny, narrow staircase just for her.

The Middle was beautiful in a way that made her angry. Unlike the Bastian, there wasn't any trash in the streets, or little rivulets of water or runoff from the factories upstream. The air smelled different too, cooler on her skin and fresher in her nose. Her view of the sky was unobstructed, so Reiko could finally see the puffy white clouds, and, of course, the floating orbs Above. How expensive it must be to travel that high on the Loop, if this amount of money only took her to the Middle. She took out the electronic tablet she had borrowed from kindly Father Felix, her old computer science instructor, and pulled up the map to the university district. It was a thirty-minute walk, but luckily she didn't have much luggage. By the time she got there, she would feel ready—she hoped.

It had taken Father Felix a personal trip home to her parents in the Low Quake to explain what an all-expense-paid scholarship was, and how this was too good an opportunity to pass up. Her mother seemed suspicious, as if this man were trying con them, while her father just looked sad.

"Reiko doesn't even want to study computers. She's an artist," her mother had protested.

Father Felix nodded. "It was Reiko's latest art project that attracted their interest. She designed a very special sort of program, you see, to generate visual patterns from sound waves. Then she used these patterns to make her big paintings. But the tech behind the paintings—it was very elegant." Father Felix looked at her parents meaningfully. "The university will provide for every expense— room, board, tuition, supplies. All Reiko needs to do is show up. If she does well in her degree, she'll get an apprenticeship."

"A job?" asked her father. Reiko grimaced.

Father Felix shook his head. "Even at top firms, the apprenticeships are unpaid." Her parents blinked at him.

"My daughter will compete against other kids, wealthy kids," said Mama slowly, "to work for free?"

"It isn't like that!" began Reiko, exasperated. They didn't understand anything.

But Father Felix nodded seriously. "Yes. She'll compete to work for free. And if she does well, which she certainly will, Reiko will get an entry-level job at a top firm."

Mama spoke mournfully, as if she had been told that Reiko was ill. "She'll work twice as hard, with fewer advantages. It's a recipe for disappointment, that's what it is."

Father Felix lowered his voice to a conspiratorial whisper. "Let me tell you the average starting salary at these firms."

Mama's and Papa's eyes widened.

"As long as the school's free, I don't see how it can hurt," said Mama. She kissed Reiko's forehead ridge. "And remember, my good girl—you can always come home."

Reiko paused in a wide, grassy park to get her bearings, leaning against a great big tree. Every detail of the city was a feast for the eyes, and now her brain felt sluggish, full. The snaking paths of this park were dappled with little arched bridges, painted a bright blue. Reiko was surprised to see so many bridges, as there didn't seem to be any water nearby, except for the broad, lazy river that bisected the Middle like a winding serpent. The bridges were just there because they were beautiful, arching over gravel or grass. Reiko peered at two women in billowing, translucent dresses, their hair lacquered into towers ornamented with little jeweled birds. One woman carried a parasol, the other what looked like a giant sheaf of grain. Reiko had seen racy advertisements of women holding fruit, but never this. The soles of their knee-high lace-up boots were almost a foot thick, making them totter slowly across the little bridges. The women took turns snapping pictures of each other with their phones, in front of trees, on bridges, sometimes kissing each other, sometimes blowing kisses at the tiny screen. So far, everyone else Reiko had seen in the Middle was dressed relatively normally, in cloaks and capes and jumpsuits—nice clothes, to be sure, but nothing so fantastical. These women looked more like aliens or art objects, their faces heavily painted to suggest a mask or a baby doll. The woman with the parasol had a bright-orange square painted on her lips, while the other woman's eyes were completely encircled in blue. Reiko watched, fascinated, as one of the women lay down on the grass and lifted her skirt. Half-naked, she held out her phone with her right hand, angling it at her crotch. The other woman knelt, no longer holding the grain sheaf, and proceeded to lick her toward orgasm. Reiko looked away. She wasn't embarrassed to see people having sex—she had seen that a million times—but something about this felt wrong. The women didn't seem aroused, and there was nothing about their body language to suggest that they were lovers. The only times they kissed or touched each other was for pictures; otherwise, they just walked together like employees heading to a meeting. The woman on the ground moaned loudly, finally shouting, "Eat me! Eat me! Eat me!" then lay back as if exhausted. Her "orgasm" had taken less than two minutes to achieve. The other girl sat up, wiped her mouth, and bowed to her partner. Then she smiled into the camera, covering her mouth with her hand in a little cupping gesture. "If you liked this video, please follow our adventures by clicking the floating lips on the left! Have a beautiful day."

———

At the university gate, Reiko showed a guard her identification card. Her hands felt sweaty, despite the cool air. He glanced at his computer, found her name, and let her through with a nod. Reiko walked across the threshold and realized she was shaking. It took all of her self-control not to throw up her breakfast on the beautiful coiffed lawn. The first building was a blocky stack of levels floating off the ground. The sight was dizzying, imposing. Reiko did not want to go inside. Then she noticed that the first level was hoisted up on thick metal stilts, designed in such a way that the building appeared to hover in the air. It wasn't magical—just a neat architectural trick.

She said *I am God, and God is me* twenty-five times under her breath until the shaking stopped. Then she thought of her mother and how happy she'd be if Reiko decided she didn't want this after all and just went home so they could all eat dinner together every night. Then she walked on, head held high, and proceeded to climb the hundred small steps to enter the university compound. She could do this, she thought as she walked up, up, up. She could make something better than the options laid out before her; she could not only survive but thrive, because she was so damn smart. Her sonic program was brilliant. Father Felix took credit for molding her young mind, but her true teacher had been the Bastian, the other junk kids in the Low Quake, sifting through trash cans for hot pads and helio tape, making their own cyphers from busted-up bits of last decade's tech. She was better, not despite where she came from, but because of it.

Reiko found her dormitory, a skinny blue-gray stone building with huge turrets, and registered with a friendly older girl who said her name was Agata. Her red hair was styled up on her head like a column of fire, but her clothes were rather strange. Was she poor? Most girls in the Bastian, though their clothes were cheaply made, took fastidious care of them. This girl had giant holes in her shirt. It looked as if she had been mauled by a large animal.

"I love your bag," said Agata, gesturing to Reiko's leather

suitcase. It had been her grandfather's, and it was very well made. Grandma had mended it many times with her expert sewing.

"Family heirloom," said Reiko.

"Good taste," said Agata, winking. Agata explained how to get to her hall, and that she'd be joined by her roommate shortly, then held out a silver tube, which she said was Reiko's room key. As she walked away to find her room, Reiko couldn't shake the feeling that she was about to be stopped, that she had taken another girl's place by accident, that her scholarship was some kind of mistake. The other kids were busy being moved in by their frantic, overbearing parents, but they seemed nice enough, smiling and nodding at Reiko, a few "hellos" and short introductions over carried couches and rolling suitcases. Everyone else had furniture and things to hang on the walls, cases of vitamin-enriched water, and even flatscreen televisions. Reiko had her two bags and a mobile wallet, the first one she'd ever had, filled with the money from her scholarship. Reiko lay down on the pleasantly firm bed in her own private room. She looked at the creamy white walls, the hardwood floor, the huge, gleaming windows that she could not imagine ever leaking in rain. Reiko pulled out a roster of fascinating-sounding classes, and flyers with hours for the metalworking lab and a tech locker where she could rent equipment. She was a long way from mining junk in the Low Quake, but it was all the same. She'd find the best bits of what was on offer, then reinvent, repurpose, reimagine them into something even better. Reiko recited *I am God, and God is me* under her breath again, but she was actually praying, not meditating. *Dear God*, she thought. *You are me, and I am you. Please, help me make something larger than myself.* She gazed out the window at the lush, opulent city. *And help me to never go back to the Bastian again.*

The only sour spot for Reiko in that first semester was her randomly assigned roommate, a freshman named Terry. Terry was a mousy Middle waif who looked like a thousand other girls, with her light-brown hair in a little pointed cone. It was in vogue to style your hair as high as possible as a gesture of piety, but Reiko could never be bothered. She let her dark hair hang long and loose around her shoulders, like all the other Bastian girls at home. At first she tried making conversation with Terry, but it never went well. In fact, Terry always seemed slightly shocked to see Reiko enter their shared apartment. Terry would smile very wide, answer Reiko's questions as quickly as possible ("How was your day?" "Fine.") before quickly rushing to her bedroom and shutting the door tight.

Reiko had expected her insular roommate to loosen up once the semester got underway, but instead her behavior only grew more secretive. Unmarked boxes were delivered to their door, then quickly hidden away in Terry's room. Through the thin walls, Reiko could hear the rustling of wrappers and the crunching of their contents, all while Reiko cooked her own food in their little kitchenette. She couldn't decide if she was being rude or not, as she herself hadn't been raised in Flesh Martyrdom, but there was a kitchen, and she needed to eat. She tried to do it away from Terry, but the girl seemed to have no hobbies or friends. Other than attending class, she was always home.

Terry's room started to stink by late autumn. Perhaps she didn't even know that food had to be thrown away or it would rot. The smell drifted heavily into their common area. Terry would flee the flat anytime Reiko tried to bring up cleaning or the smell. By winter, Terry was vomiting in their shared bathroom many times a day, presumably to get thin enough to see her parents over the holiday. Reiko felt bad for her, even as she scrubbed dried vomit from the tile grout. She'd never seen the food shame of Flesh Martyrdom mess with someone's head in such an up-front and personal way, but she assumed many young girls suffered similarly. Their tech institute wasn't religious, but certainly if Terry gained any more weight, she'd be put into counseling, and if she didn't improve there, be asked to leave school. That was, if her family didn't take her out of school first. Of course, Reiko didn't learn any of this from actually talking to Terry—the girl would barely look at her. She researched extensively, as Reiko did with anything she didn't understand. One day, armed with this new knowledge, she sat down and wrote Terry a long letter. In the letter, she outlined some good resources for help and added a personal note, saying, *I know we don't know each other very well, but if there's anything I can do to help, my door is open. And if it's not, you can always knock! :)* She pushed the letter under her roommate's door and waited, feeling rather pleased with herself.

The response came back very quickly.

On the back of her letter, in red ink, it read: *GO BACK TO THE GROUND AND DIE, FREE-WAH FLOATER*

Reiko left the apartment. As she walked across the quad, she decided to go to her tech locker to work on her newest project: a heliograph that used sunlight to generate images, which, combined with her sonic program, could make something more dynamic than a mere photograph—a picture of the feeling of the moment, with lines, shapes, and colors that represented the quality of light and ambient sound, as well as capturing an image. It was absolutely brilliant. She certainly deserved to be here. Terry wasn't just some tortured girl; she was a racist bitch. In a way, Reiko was grateful. Why was she breaking her brain to be nice to someone she didn't know? Why was she scrubbing Terry's vomit from the bathroom floor? In the Bastian, if someone didn't like you, they said, *Hey, eat shit! Your mother fucks dogs.* In the Middle, things weren't so clear.

Maybe this was why she hadn't made any friends. In the Bastian, there had been kids she ran around with, but no one she would call a close friend. She loved her sister, Elena, who was two years older, but Elena had never really understood Reiko's dreams, her ambition. Elena was going steady with a Bastian boy, and everyone thought they'd be married by spring and pregnant by summer, if not before then. Mama and Papa weren't angry about this either—he had a job at a balloon factory, and that was enough. Not so for Reiko.

"Reiko," someone called. "Helloooo, Reiko? Did the moon men scramble your brain? I've been calling your name for the last five minutes!" The girl laughed, revealing a gap-toothed smile. It was Agata, the girl who'd checked her into her dorm, only this time her red hair wasn't styled in a little tower but ran loose down her back, just like that of a Bastian girl.

"Sorry, I didn't recognize you," said Reiko. "You look different with your hair down!"

"It's so much easier," said Agata, running her hands through her locks and laughing. "I don't know why I ever bothered."

Reiko studied her. Her clothes were worn and shabby, but she wore them with a kind of elegance. And she had a very fine personal tablet inlaid into a bracelet on her arm and tiny gold jewelry, hoops on her ears and rings stacked on her fingers. The gold looked real. (Reiko had developed quite an eye for metals. Gold was an excellent electrical conductor, and quite malleable too. She was attempting to source enough for her next project, a sonic cypher that could reinterpret code as sound.)

"I'm terribly bored!" said Agata. "Isn't the Middle the worst? Campus is so isolated. I haven't done anything fun in ages. Walk with me awhile?"

Reiko mimed tipping a hat. "I'd be delighted."

Laughing, Agata took her arm, and they strolled together toward the canals. "How are you finding our lovely campus, my dear Reiko? What do you do for pleasure?"

"Ah, nothing? I'm hiding from my roommate at the moment." She looked at Agata's clothes once more. Where was she from? It didn't really matter. It wasn't like Reiko could hide the fact she was Free-Wah. Her forehead ridge made that plain. "Here, read this."

She passed Agata the note. Agata's eyes bulged. "You should report her—she can't speak to you like this!"

Reiko grimaced. "I'd rather not. She's binging and purging in our rooms, and I tried to talk to her about it. She's self-destructing without my help. I don't think she'll last the school year."

"That's really sad." She cocked her head. "Don't Free-Wah people eat openly? One would think you'd be the perfect roommate for an Eater." Agata grimaced. "Sorry, did I just insult you? You're actually the first Free-Wah person I've met."

This girl was certainly not from the Bastian. "Not at all—and we do eat openly. I tried to be polite around her, of course. I tried not to cook when she was home, and I ate in my room. But our whole place stinks like rotting food. It's unsanitary! I can't live there anymore."

"Want to go do something fun?" asked Agata.

Reiko giggled. "Yes, anything!"

"Hmm, what's fun?" Agata stamped her feet. "Oh, nothing is fun here! I hate it." She turned to Reiko. "Will you take me to the Bastian? To a place you like?" Her eyes gleamed.

"I don't know. It's expensive to get on the Loop."

"Oh, I'll cover us," said Agata quickly, waving a hand. "I'm just bored out of my mind—can we go on an adventure?"

Reiko decided she didn't care where Agata was from. Being with her was a welcome relief. "Oh, hell, why not?"

———————

They looked out the window from the Loop as the train chugged across the sky. "Do you go home a lot?" asked Agata.

Reiko shook her head. "It's hard to find the time." She'd only been back to the Bastian once this year. She felt guilty, but the trip was expensive. "The first time I planned to go during the winter holidays, there were those weather warnings across the city."

"I remember that—the Loop was shut down."

"I couldn't leave. But lucky for me, Terry had already gone home for Flesh Martyr Day." Reiko raised her eyebrows. "So I decided to finally get to the bottom of the smell in our rooms."

Agata clapped her hands. "You sleuth!"

Reiko turned toward her captive audience, enjoying the telling. "I mean, I had never been in her bedroom before. I was dying to see it."

"What was it like?"

"It was really weird. Totally pristine—like, every pencil in its case, her bed neat as a pin. And it stank to high heaven." Reiko remembered there was a huge *Sky Chaser* poster next to her bed, the main dancer looking impossibly tall and thin, with a tiny waist, thighs the circumference of her ankles. "I looked everywhere for the source of the smell, but everything was tidy, normal, if not obsessively clean. Finally I opened her closet."

Agata squeezed Reiko's arm. "Omigod, omigod, omigod, what was it?!"

"Here's the really weird part. Her clothes were folded so perfectly, stored away on the upper shelf. Her dresses hung in her closet—some of them were even still in their plastic cleaning bags. But the floor . . ." Agata's eyes grew huge. "The floor of the closet was littered with rotting foodstuffs—even the moldy carcass of a roasted hen."

"You have *got* to be kidding me!" Agata squealed. "That's so putrid!"

Reiko shook her head. "As I live and breathe." She let out a long sigh. "That's when I got the idea to write the letter. I am such an idiot."

They exited the Loop in the Upper Bastian, where Reiko had previously attended Our Lady of the Starving Flesh, the best school in the Bastian. She would never take Agata to the Low Quake, where her family lived. A few weeks ago she had finally journeyed home for the spring holiday to see them (and to get away from Terry and her smells). A woman with a little girl had accosted her for money as soon as she exited the Loop, pointing to her tablet (still on loan from Father Felix). The child holding out her hand and yelling for money was too much for Reiko, who ran the rest of the way home. The beggar woman with her crying child seemed like a bad omen for her trip. Reiko had been so excited to see her family, but then it felt so strange—she was bored, mostly, with no one to talk to. Her parents and sister didn't understand anything about her classes. Papa kept asking when she was going to start making money, and Mama huffed as she reminded him it wouldn't be for many more years. Elena was already turning out a paycheck at the textile mill. Reiko bit her tongue to keep from reminding her that her yearly salary there would eventually be what Reiko, in a high-powered tech job, would make in one month's time. She had stayed only two nights, much to her family's disappointment. Then back to the Middle to suffer through Terry's hostility and vomiting. Once she was back in the dorm, she couldn't decide which was worse.

On impulse, Reiko took Agata to see *Sins of the Fruit* for a half-ducat at the Cineplex. Reiko didn't frequent the cult favorite, but Elena did, with her tough, cool friends. Agata gasped with laughter to see an old religious film reinterpreted into a campy sex romp. The audience came dressed as their favorite characters, throwing food at the screen during the eating parts. Most people came as the evil Free-Wah king who had enslaved the purehearted ALGN maiden, making her eat fruit. Reiko was nervous that Agata would find it either juvenile or offensive. She surreptitiously glanced at her new friend during the big dance number, a dozen Free-Wah kings gyrating together on the stage under the screen, smearing mango on the "innocent maiden" volunteers as the audience pelted them with grapes. Agata's eyes were aglow, her mouth in a perfect circle.

"Best day ever," Agata whispered, squeezing her hand.

Reiko felt as if she had won an award. It was a strange sensation. Back home in the Bastian, she had been praised and rewarded for her smarts at school. She'd had the relentless love of her family, always doting upon their beloved girl. But in the Middle, she constantly felt like she was running to catch up. Reiko knew she stood out. And it wasn't just her face, or her hair, or her dialect, but the very cadence of her voice, her gestures, the way she walked, a million tiny behaviors she had never noticed before traveling up. That unceasing state of self-consciousness made her feel brittle and so tired.

Reiko watched Agata watching the film, the reflected light casting shapes across her happy, open face. For the first time all semester, Reiko felt something within her unclench.

3.

On the gleaming countertop filled with vases of flowers and bowls of decorative fruit sat a pillbox with *Beatrice* inscribed on the front—little lacquered compartments for each day of the week. Today there were five pills: two pinks and one clear, which she had taken every day since she was a child, now joined by two new ones—a big white and a tiny yellow.

She heard Papa come in from outside, yard work completed, going upstairs to take a brief shower before church. Beatrice swallowed the pills, then poured her glass of nutritional shake down the drain. She heard her mother laughing from the bedroom, and her father saying if she didn't quit fooling around, they wouldn't make it on time. Then it grew rather quiet in a way that Beatrice had come to recognize. She decided to enjoy her secret breakfast in her favorite hammock in the garden. Some couples with children Beatrice's age had sex more often with outside partners than with each other. Beatrice was happy that her parents still engaged in physical love, but she had no wish to hear it.

Today's breakfast was a single juicy pear and a hard-boiled egg sprinkled with salt. The fruit had been pilfered from a tree, while the egg had been stolen from Remus's food. She bit into the light-green pear; instead of subtle floral juices, she found it tasted of ashes. She tried the egg. The salt tasted of gravel and crunched unpleasantly in her teeth, while the egg itself was flavorless rubber. She spit it out on the ground.

In the great light-filled cathedral, Mama and Papa stood surrounded by an audience from out of town. Mama wore an astonishing gown, delicately sewn satin feathers anointing her body from head to foot, as if she were a great, gorgeous bird. Lots of women and some men reached out and touched the gown, admiring its intricacy, its beauty. Beatrice resisted the urge to laugh as she watched the nuns weave through the onlookers. Solemnly they helped Mama reach her arms up so she could be stripped naked, and then covered with a light Seagate shift. Beatrice wasn't standing close enough to hear, but she knew this performance by heart. The nuns were telling Mama she was so beautiful, just by the grace of God, she didn't need to go to such lengths to display herself. Then Mama cried, pretending to be greatly purged, her face streaked prettily with tears. Papa got down on his knees in front of her and kissed her body, starting at the toes and traveling up. He was probably saying that he loved her more now than when they'd first met in the city, when she'd had a new hairstyle every week. That he loved her *because* of her simplicity, not despite it.

Mama was by far the most attractive weeper of the salespeople, which was why she was often selected for such performances. The onlookers, all potential community members who had come in from the city to experience this church service, were swept up in the drama. Some of the city folk actually took off their own outlandish garments then and there and asked to be anointed as Seagate members on the spot. Papa called this guerrilla marketing, one of his most effective tactics. Beatrice didn't like the trickery of the performance. And anyway, the word *guerrilla* always made her think of the mindless mammal, only able to have sex for one to two minutes when the female was ovulating, facedown in the dirt.

Then her parents got in line with the other Seagate adults to receive their weekly penance assignments. They'd both be accepting extra for the dress, but neither would mind. Mama and Papa were both vigorous, physical people who seemed to relish these kinds of challenges. Papa never sat still. He was always making, doing, working, be it household chores, helping a neighbor, or dreaming up new advertisements for the company. Mama seemed to barely sleep, always going on night walks with friends, or to the rec center for midnight volleyball, swimming laps or running along the boardwalk. They were vital members of the community—candle people—in an ongoing love affair with life itself. They felt real in a way that Beatrice did not.

As she made her way through the crowd, Beatrice was greeted with hugs and kisses from members of Seagate—adults calling greetings, friends from school kissing her cheeks warmly as if they hadn't just seen her yesterday. She smiled to hear the choir singing "My Lord Lifts Me Like a Hot Air Balloon," one of her favorite hymns. Her annoyance at the marketing performance and her overall sense of unease melted away. Of course she was a real person; what a ridiculous thought. The choir sounded beautiful as the sun shone through the large windows.

Beatrice waited in line to be weighed. "You're maintaining perfectly, Beatrice," said Sister Earnesta as she stepped on the scale, recording her weight for the weekly newsletter.

The three flutes sounded out, and it was time to kneel. Beatrice found a spot on the right side of the cathedral, her favorite view. She saw Mama and Papa sitting nearer to the entrance chatting with Mrs. Axel, a woman Papa had been sharing sex with for so long she was practically family.

"Blessed be!" said the great bird standing in the round, raised pulpit. It was Father Alvarez, dressed in his formal service costume, as the Flesh Martyr's hawk familiar.

"Blessed be you, and blessed be me!" the congregation called back.

Beatrice noticed a particularly striking girl near the pulpit with a tower of hair on her head, dotted with pearls. It wasn't uncommon to see teenagers from the city at Sunday service, tagging along with their parents. But something about her was special.

"Blessed be you, and me, and we. I see new faces in our holy cathedral this morning," called the great bird, gesturing with his fabric wings.

The city girl's clothes were luxurious, certainly—shiny, patterned fabrics, and cutouts revealing bare skin. Her skin was a rich, coppery brown, her neck long, her brown eyes big and wide. In short, she was beautiful, but there was no shortage of pretty girls in Seagate. There was something else about her, from her elbows to her ankles to the rounds of her cheeks, that felt different. Beatrice found herself staring, lost in thought, until the pastor's shouting jostled her out of her reverie. "Precarity!" he cried. "I myself am from the Low Quake, the poorest, most squalid part of the Bastian! Life was hard for me growing up, but it was made harder still by knowing that I could never rise up to live away from the precarious ground, unlike my neighbors in the Middle and Above." He shook his head. "But most of you are not from the Bastian, are you?" He gestured to the crowd familiarly. "Most of you are from the Middle, frustrated by the daily grind." He made a circular motion with his finger, like a wheel turning.

"Oh, the grind! Never having enough—not enough money, not enough time. Do you know that most families in the Middle don't have the savings to cover a single major emergency? I don't have to tell you about precarity." Someone in the crowd hooted loudly. "That's right, you've lived it! Now, we who choose to live in Seagate, we own nothing. And that means we have everything— together. We live together, work together, worship together, raise our children together . . ."

He gestured out to the crowd like a bandleader, and the congregation answered his call: "Here, we have more together!"

"Ooh, I like the sound of that! But there's one blessing in particular that you're all very curious about, aren't you? 'Have they done it?' you ask yourselves. Have those religious freaks in the Valley finally solved hunger?"

The crowd cawed and cheered, miming flapping wings. "Well, I'll tell you. Seagate friends, community members—you may have noticed some new pills in your pillbox today." Around her, people were smiling and clapping. Beatrice saw her parents kiss, then raise their hands in the air. The girl with the tower of hair clapped her hands in front of her face like a giddy child. "This is what we've been working for as a company, as a family of faith. With our newest supplements, we have at last solved our hunger." People around her started weeping, mixed with calls of *Praise Him!* echoing across the grand cathedral. "Yes, visitors, yes, Seagate family—the struggle is over! Yes, give thanks! Yes, praise God. Yes—" He laughed merrily, then held his wings out for silence. "Yes, everyone is welcome to this blessing. But we must remember—when a mother has more time at night to worship because she's not busy putting food on the table, those minutes are for God! When a child is not distracted during school because of a growling belly, whom do we praise? Do we praise the child? Do we praise the mother?"

"No!" shouted someone from the front.

"Do we bow down to the scientists who made these pills?"

The girl with the tower of hair shook her head emphatically.

"No!" the congregation shouted. "We praise God!"

Father Alvarez waved his arms in the air, fabric flapping. "We praise God! And when we all lose those stubborn five pounds we've been meaning to shed?" He bowed his head. "You know, I struggle too! Whom do we praise, when we see our new reflections in the mirror, unburdened by weight, by low, animalistic food? Do we make a deity out of our own image?"

"We praise God! God! God!"

The noises of celebration came together into one ghoulish din. The crowd was as wild as the winning side of a balloon race. Beatrice felt her skin flush as the blood rushed to her head. She thought of the yellow pill churning inside her, stripping away her one true desire. She swallowed, tasting bile.

———————

Beatrice brought Lina what she could, almost like a tithe to the church—five ducats from her allowance, fifteen from when she babysat for her next-door neighbors all weekend while the parents were on a hover cruise. Lina accepted the money, but still held on to her mother's necklace.

In return, Lina gave Beatrice loose copies of recipes to keep, along with tastes of precious spices for her cooking projects, a fine length of cheesecloth, and once a shiny vegetable peeler, all free of charge. The older woman was quick with suggestions for a better method to dry fruit, or a funny story from her military days of undercooking a mess of beans for the whole platoon.

"Why is food grown all over Seagate and no one notices?" asked Beatrice. They were sprawled in Lina's musty basement, taking inventory of new deliveries.

Lina pushed up her glasses. "People are trying to get right with God, and not everyone can agree on the way forward. Scriptures can be interpreted differently. Your church tried every craze under the sun—only liquids, all fruit, no processed foods. People in your parents' generation lived through all those permutations, before they decided on Food Modesty. When you leave the Valley, you'll meet all kinds of folks. Everyone does it different."

Beatrice blushed. She always got a little thrill from how easily Lina would reference a future life for her outside of Seagate.

"The Free-Wah ate openly, you know, before the rise of Flesh Martyrdom. Many still do, in their own communities. We owe all our best food culture to them." She raised her eyebrows. "That's why we have restaurants in the city. They can't be shut down because of religious freedom. But they can be driven underground, made taboo, immoral."

Beatrice gestured emphatically with a book. "But it doesn't have to be this way!"

"You know, it was that goddamn Father Alvarez who came up with Food Modesty for Seagate," spat Lina. "There is no religious reason why a carrot needs to be cooked to death, or that a pomegranate should rot on the ground, forgotten." Beatrice imagined a pomegranate falling from a tree and breaking apart on the earth, its ruby seeds spilling out. Lina was right. The bounty of the world was devastatingly simple and evident. How could something so natural be wrong? "Perfectly healthy foods, chock-full of vitamins," continued Lina. "Scriptures say to leave your belly half-empty, but they don't say food can't taste good. That's just mental gymnastics."

"Father A has always been very kind to me," Beatrice said placidly.

Lina's words cut like a knife: "That man's a monster, and you're even more of an idiot than I thought if you see him as anything else. He's ruined this town!"

They shelved in silence.

"I'm sorry, little mouse. I didn't eat enough today."

Beatrice huffed out a laugh at the poor apology. "You and everyone in Seagate for the last twenty years."

"But I don't take the pills."

"I don't take the yellow pill either." *But I'm not about to bite your head off.*

"I mean the pink pills. They're mood stabilizers." Lina noticed Beatrice's eyes widen. "Wait—don't stop taking them all at once! You'll feel terrible. Do one and a half for a week, then one for another week, then a half." Lina poked her lightly in the stomach. "Maybe stay at half. Life is hard enough. And keep taking the clear and the white—those are vitamins."

"How will I feel? Once I'm not taking the pink pills."

"Good, bad, great, terrible." She raised an eyebrow over her wire-frame glasses. "You'll feel alive." They went back to shelving in silence.

Beatrice went into a dirigible refueling station to buy a fizzy water while waiting for Lina to finish with a client. Behind the counter, next to a row of stimulants designed to keep the pilots awake for their long flights, was something called Fantasy Delight with a drawing of a mysterious seedpod on the label. She pointed to the box with trembling fingers and paid the ridiculous sum of seven ducats—money she'd been saving for Lina. She imagined the delight on Lina's face when Beatrice presented her with this precious delicacy. In the alley behind the store, she shook out one small brown pellet from the greasy box and popped it into her mouth. The first taste was sweet and deep, unlike anything she'd ever experienced. Then it was chalky, while somehow waxy, yet oily, yet crumbly. She spit it out on the street. Beatrice realized she did not care for chocolate at all.

While having a bit of innercourse with Peaton and Marty Zimmerman one afternoon, Beatrice glanced out the window and noticed a huge floppy sunflower gazing back at her. That morning she had read that sunflowers had edible seeds, and that the huge flowers themselves, when boiled whole, were as tender and delicious as an artichoke. Flustered, she excused herself from the boys to jot down in her notebook: *What is an artichoke?* in a column entitled *Questions*. The list was long. Lina answered her questions as best she could on each visit, until she grew annoyed with her little mouse and told her to stuff it.

Peaton and Marty did not invite her to their pool party the following weekend. Beatrice, after weaning herself down to only half a pink pill per day, found herself inconsolable over falling out of favor with the boys, then, just a few hours later, ecstatic over a rose blooming in the sunlight. She wrote in her notebook: *How does one harvest rose hips?* She thought back to Lina's words: *good, bad, great, terrible.* She was certainly alive.

During fitness period, Beatrice caught a flash of hair, fashioned aloft like a gleaming tower, as she ran on the school's treadmill under a banner that proclaimed EXPECT SUCCESS in yellow and white. Later that same day, while she and Melis were pleasing each other in the schoolyard during their free period, a miraculous scent wafted over. She faked her own orgasm but did not stay to help Melis climax, leaving with the poor excuse of a headache.

Beatrice followed the scent to a sturdy tree growing by the far fence. Weeks ago it had been covered in fragrant white flowers. But now its limbs hung heavy with clumps of dark-purple rounds, their flesh slightly whitish in parts, as if dusted with chalk. The fruit was sweet-smelling and dense, the ground below littered with half-rotting orbs. But they wouldn't be wasted upon the earth. They would be eaten by many animals and insects before their seeds were offered back into the ground to begin the cycle anew. Flowers turning into food. How could such beauty not be a celebration of God? Privately, Father Alvarez might say that God was here, but he didn't preach such things on the pulpit.

Then she saw her. Across the courtyard, with a group of other girls, stood the new girl from church. Today her amazing tower of hair was decorated with sparkles, the patterns on the shellacked curls reminiscent of seashells.

The new girl caught Beatrice's glance and held up her arm in greeting. From across the courtyard, Beatrice returned the gesture. She turned back toward the tree. *These are plums,* she thought suddenly as she looked up at the glossy globes of fruit, big as her closed fist. The knowledge, read somewhere and now recalled, rose in her mind like a ship opening a sail. She knelt and picked one up from the ground. *This is a plum.*

"You've become very cruel," said Ada Johnson, who was now comforting a crying Melis. Beatrice dropped the fruit. "First you abandon Jaimes, without even a word of reason, and now you're treating your old friends like . . . like—"

"Trampolines!" supplied Melis. "A quick bounce, and then you're off!" Her eyes were red and wet.

"I didn't—" began Beatrice. "I didn't think—"

"You *don't* think," interrupted Ada, "of anyone other than yourself. You'd be hard-pressed to find anyone who wishes to share sex with you now, Beatrice. You might be pretty, but you sure are mean."

The two girls stomped away. Beatrice glanced back across the courtyard, but the new girl was gone.

Beatrice wrote both Ada and Melis sincere apologies, to which they both responded in the expected gracious fashion. But Melis did not seek out her company again; nor did Ada, a sort of social captain of their group, include her in their upcoming parties, or trips to water cafés or the Saturday balloon races. Beatrice felt wounded, but she couldn't pretend they weren't right. Her single-mindedness was making her cruel.

———

Mama called for Beatrice to join her in her bedroom, where she sat applying her various face creams before bed. They looked at their reflections together in the mirror. "I have my charms," said Mama to Beatrice's reflection. "But I was never truly beautiful, even at your age. Not like you are, Bea. Maybe it's easier my way, to be good-looking without the pressures of real beauty. But I do wish I had your nose."

Her mother did this often—looked at their faces together in the mirror and compared Beatrice more favorably. She had once enjoyed it. But now it made her feel bad, and she couldn't place why.

"How is my gorgeous girl?" her mother pressed.

"I'm sad," she said to her own reflection, keeping her expression as neutral as possible. Her mother did not know she'd been avoiding the pink pills.

Mama turned to look at her directly. "About Jaimes?" Beatrice blushed. "I heard on the wind you're not seeing each other anymore."

Beatrice shook her head. How could she get advice from her mother without revealing what was really going on? "I'm scared about not finding my people," she said slowly. "The ones who understand me, who are interested in the things I'm interested in." Beatrice looked back at her own reflection. "It's not really about Jaimes," she admitted. "It never was. I guess that's the problem."

Her mother ran her hands through Beatrice's thick, dark hair. "Letting go of someone is always sad. I dated my first sweetheart for years and years, even when I didn't desire her anymore. I made her miserable—and myself miserable. I just couldn't initiate that kind of change. But you're smarter than I was at your age. Trust your instincts. You'll find your people."

"Thanks, Mama."

Remus stuck his fuzzy head out of Mama's brightly woven neck pouch.

Mama laughed, a pleasing, bell-like sound. "Guess who wants to say good night?"

———

Another weekend came with no social calls. Beatrice decided to make the most of her solitude—to pack her bag with dark, sticky prunes and wander over to one of her favorite places in Seagate, a meandering maze of short fruit trees designed for spiritual contemplation. The maze had once been quite the attraction, but the community was filled with beautiful things, and this one had gone out of vogue. It hadn't occurred to the Seagate architects that the ground would be mottled with rotting fruit many months out of the year, attracting flies.

On her way to the grove maze, Beatrice bent down to brush a bug from her ankle and almost screamed in amazement at what she saw. Bursting forth, like a finger directly from the earth, was a stalk of asparagus. She looked around. There were more dotting the grass, of various lengths and thicknesses. Her last book, thankfully, had contained a few drawings, homey little sketches of women in headscarves stirring bubbling pots around hearths, and she remembered the frilly little ridges on the head of the stalk, making it look like a skinny, malformed penis.

Could it be that asparagus grew straight out of the earth, like a finger? It had no tree, no vine, no bush?

She found, in total, thirty wild stalks of asparagus. Some were too tall and thick to be delicious. She discarded them back to the ground in the hope that they might grow again. They didn't seem to have seeds or pits—did they simply grow, like grass? But in fact, how *did* grass grow? From seeds? If she tried to transplant an asparagus stem into her own yard, would it propagate? Her father would probably mow it down, gleefully ignorant in his short tunic, humming. She could ask Lina—but suddenly she felt certain her mentor wouldn't know. The revelation brought her a spasm of pain. Her classmates hated her. She had no more friends or lovers. Besides Lina, there was nothing left for her here. And even that fount was running dry.

But elation bloomed again as she looked over her asparagus collection. Even after tossing out the big woody ones, she had about eighteen lovely stalks left. There was a fig tree somewhere in the maze. Asparagus, roasted with blistered figs? It could have been straight out of a recipe book! Beatrice wrapped her new-found treasures in a soft piece of flannel and tucked it into her sack. She wandered into the maze.

Between the rows of orange trees, she saw her. The new girl had appeared before her like a goddess rising from the earth. But yesterday's tower of hair was gone, replaced by a dense halo of natural curls. She held a large lacy fan in front of her mouth. Her top was a simple shift that appeared to be a Seagate material, but she still had on her peculiar, voluminous skirt. The shiny fabric rustled and swayed against her body in the breeze, making a crinkling sound. Beatrice felt her own breath catch in her throat.

"Hello," she said to the girl, whom she had overheard her classmates call Georgina.

"It's you," said the girl, looking up in surprise. "I've asked around about you. You're the one who doesn't like sex anymore." She kept her mouth covered with the lacy white fan.

"Who said that?" she asked carefully. Was it Jaimes? That coward. Or maybe Melis? Her chest flared with guilt.

The girl's voice was high but throaty. "You're very pretty. I can see why everyone's so mad at you."

Beatrice pinked. "They talk about me at school?"

"You're all anyone can talk about," said Georgina.

"I think you're mistaken," said Beatrice. "I think *you're* all anyone can talk about. The new girl from the big city. With the colorful skirts and tall hair. Georgina, right?"

"You know my name! How delightful." Georgina laughed, covering her mouth. Her cheeks were soft and round, like ripe fruits.

"I've been listening for it." Beatrice looked at her intently. "Why are you doing that?"

"Doing what?"

"Blocking your face with that fan."

Georgina tilted her head forward, causing her chin to double. "Where I'm from, it's considered rude to show your teeth when you laugh or smile. Like you're trying to eat someone!"

Beatrice snorted. "You must be from a silly place."

Georgina put her hands on her hips. Even her arms seemed special somehow, soft like her cheeks, with dimples above the elbow. "I bet you've never even been to the city! You don't know anything about it."

"I know enough," said Beatrice. It was hot, standing in the sun. She wiped her brow. "I know you're all Eaters who pretend not to eat. Why cover your mouth and pretend you don't have teeth? If you're going to do something, why not do it openly?"

Georgina squealed. "Oh, you're a nasty one, aren't you?"

Say what you would about Seagate, but her people had principles, even if Beatrice didn't share them. Not like these city people with their fans and jeweled hair and other nonsense, pretending they didn't eat when they clearly did. She had seen pictures of women with blackened teeth, their mouths like gaping holes.

Then Beatrice felt a stab of guilt. She was a liar too. She lied all the time, to everyone, about her cooking. That was why she had no friends. "You're right—I don't know what I'm talking about." She started down the path again, away from the girl. Georgina might be beautiful, but she was annoying.

But Georgina kept pace with her. "Of course, you're perfectly right. My parents were upset about the hypocrisy in the city too. That's why we came to the Valley. We're thinking about joining the community. Could I ask you some questions?"

"Ah, sure." Beatrice scanned the treetops. She needed to find that fig tree before sundown or she'd be out of luck.

The tall girl took Beatrice's arm in hers, swinging it slightly as they walked. Beatrice tensed at the contact of their bare arms.

"Okay, here's my first question—is everyone really this nice?"

"If you do what you're supposed to, everyone is very nice."

Georgina raised her eyebrows. "And if you don't? Do they beat you with sticks?"

"Of course not!" Beatrice couldn't help but laugh.

"I'm serious. Tell me the bad stuff."

She thought back to her parents' loving words after the grilled-cheese incident, the pastor's gentle, private sermons. "No, everyone treats you well, even when you stray from the program."

"That's a relief."

Beatrice giggled again. "Planning on being terribly disobedient?"

Georgina joined her this time, with a loud, throaty laugh. "Yes, I'd like to be entirely terrible."

They leaned against a tree, Georgina's face was dappled in the light filtered between the branches. Beatrice felt the urge to touch her cheek but did nothing. "You're going to have to give up your fancy outfits, you know."

Georgina sighed. "I'm actually looking forward to that."

"And the fan."

"I'm just waiting until I get the yellow pill," she said, tugging at her wide skirt. "You only look good in Seagate clothes if you're really a hanger, you know?"

Beatrice tilted her head. "A hanger? Like, to put clothes on?"

"Wow, even the words here are different. A hanger is someone who looks good in anything, like a model—clothes just hang off of them." She looked Beatrice up and down. "Like you."

Beatrice looked away. Georgina's gaze made her hot and uncomfortable. "Um, do you have more questions? Because I should get going."

Georgina covered her mouth again, but it didn't seem like she was laughing this time. "You're so odd."

Beatrice's nostrils flared. "Hey, you're the one who followed me! I'm just trying to get on with my day."

"Oh, very important meetings in the tree maze? Lots of business to attend to?"

Beatrice allowed Georgina to catch her eye. She really was quite beautiful. Suddenly finding the fig tree didn't seem so important. It was probably better, even, to taste asparagus for the first time in its purest form. That way when she happened upon it again, she could really understand its flavor, instead of complicating it with vinegar and figs. She would steam it, just barely, so it was still crisp. Then just a sprinkle of salt—

Georgina flicked her arm.

"Ow!"

"See that? Where did you go just now? It's like you were a million miles away. You know, everyone is saying you've broken their heart."

Beatrice couldn't decide if this made her feel hurt or proud. "Really?"

"Are you going to break mine too?" Georgina smiled, then covered her mouth with her hand.

Beatrice pulled Georgina's hand away from her face. "I want to see your teeth," she said softly. "Do you blacken them, like the girls on television?"

Their heads were unnervingly close. "Only tarts do that. You're very rude," Georgina replied.

"So everyone says." Beatrice looked at her mouth. It was full of large white teeth.

"Don't get too close, I might bite."

"You look good enough to eat," replied Beatrice wickedly.

Georgina growled theatrically, then laughed, as if shocked by her own boldness. She lifted her skirts and ran on toward the center of the maze. "Come and try!"

Beatrice, whose legs were quite a bit shorter, was panting when she finally caught up. Georgina leaned against the fig tree, but its fruits were forgotten.

"Hey, slowpoke," said Georgina. "You found me."

"I've been looking for you since I saw you in church, if I'm being honest," said Beatrice. "I like looking at you."

"Come on." Georgina laughed again, but the smile didn't reach her eyes. "You've just never seen such a fat girl in your life."

Yes, that was it—the thing she couldn't name. Georgina was thicker, rounder, than any girl or woman she had ever seen, in real life or on television. Beatrice understood, then, the peekaboo cutouts of her clothes, designed to hide her fleshier parts. But instead of her abundance looking sloppy or shameful, as she'd been taught to think, Georgina's body was wonderful—supple, soft, inviting. Sensual. But she couldn't tell Georgina that; she wouldn't hear the compliment. "I've never seen anyone dress like you before," she lied.

"That's because you're a country bumpkin," said Georgina, holding her gaze. Now was the moment. Beatrice was supposed to go to her, to kiss her. To lie with her, perhaps. If they liked each other, they could get together, eschewing other sex partners for a while. Beatrice could see it all laid out, like a map. Suddenly she didn't want it at all. It would be like all the other times—exciting at first, then terribly lonely.

Three short blasts sounded out, blaring from the center of town.

"What is that?" asked Georgina. The blasts grew louder.

"Earthquake warning—come on!" Beatrice took Georgina's

hand and led her deeper into the maze. Georgina tripped over her long skirt, then ran with it gathered in her hand.

They were within sight of the dome when the first real rumblings began. They dashed inside to huddle in the center of the room. The hut was built for spiritual contemplation, so it was empty but for a few pillows on the floor.

"We should be safe here," said Beatrice. The rumblings had already stopped. It was quiet. "Maybe it's a small one."

Then they felt it. The very foundation of Seagate started to shift and sway, the floor wobbling beneath their feet. Seagate was made for this—to move with the impact, rather than crack apart. But that didn't mean there wouldn't be destruction. Georgina stumbled, and Beatrice held her close. They huddled together, arms around each other, in the middle of the room.

Georgina stared at her, no longer smiling. "If you hadn't been with me, I might have been crushed to death by a tree. I couldn't have made it through the maze alone—"

But her words were cut off by another huge quake. Beatrice felt her heart hammering in her chest and hoped Georgina didn't think she scared too easily. The other girl's warm, slightly mineral scent all around her; her smooth, warm skin; her soft lips right next to Beatrice's face . . . Georgina was no longer otherworldly with her strange dress and her fan, but real—fleshy, animal, woman. Her nearness made Beatrice feel like her face was on fire.

The rumblings stopped. The girls still held each other in silence.

"We can let go now," said Beatrice.

"I guess so," said Georgina.

But both of them remained there, arms around each other. "You can't be too certain," said Beatrice. "The earthquakes could start again."

"Just in case," said Georgina. They grinned at each other.

"Are you going to become a community member?" Beatrice asked suddenly.

"I think so," Georgina said. "My parents are going to take the big house on Ocean Ave. It's such a dream come true."

Her heart lurched. That was Leroy's house, empty for the past two years.

"Don't you want me to join Seagate?" Georgina pressed her hand against Beatrice's lower back, causing her to flush.

"Yes," replied Beatrice, but she didn't move deeper into the embrace or stroke her or kiss her. What was the point? Everyone always ended up mad at her.

"This is normally where we would have sex," teased Georgina. "But you're the girl who doesn't like sex."

"I like sex," said Beatrice softly. *I just like food more.*

"Are you going to kiss me?" Georgina was still smiling, but her eyes had a hint of fear in them.

Beatrice touched her bare arm. It was hot and smooth and made her think of honey.

"I am," said Beatrice. The scent of Georgina undid her, floral and sweet, from some kind of beauty product she was wearing, plus the musky smell of skin and sweat underneath. "I can't help it."

"Then why do you sound so sad?"

It was such a simple, elegant question. Beatrice pulled Georgina toward her so their lips were close but not quite meeting. They were Lluna and Ata, drawing nearer in their cosmic dance. Beatrice felt, in this shining moment, powerful, like a character in a movie. Beatrice the heartbreaker. Were they really saying that about her at school? She made a decision.

"Remember," said Beatrice, looking into her eyes, "in the future. This is what it felt like, before I ever kissed you."

Then she closed the space between them and let herself be lost.

4.

"We don't have to do this if you don't want to."

After *Sins of the Fruit* at the Cineplex, Reiko had brought her by gondola to Chef Wian's place in the Upper Bastian at Agata's urging. Reiko had been dreaming of his restaurant for months, when she wasn't fantasizing about her mother's cooking. After a half-ducat to the boatman, they stood in the doorway, hesitating. Agata seemed terribly nervous, lighting cigarette after cigarette as they stood outside the nondescript awning. Agata's was the only ALGN face they had seen for blocks. Reiko kept feeling like they were going to get in trouble, like somehow their campus security would swarm into the Bastian and take them away.

Agata flicked her cigarette into the gutter. "God, you must think I'm such a baby. Yes, of course I want to. It was my idea, wasn't it?" She slapped her thigh. "Let's do it!" She pulled Reiko through the door. "They have alcohol, I hope?"

They got a private booth, and Reiko asked for two house specials. One could order other things, but everyone came here for the soup. It was a special broth, simmered for days, then stuffed full of all manner of vegetables, bits of tofu, hand-pulled noodles, and huge chunks of fried fish. The specialty of the restaurant was that you could refill your soup with broth as many times as you liked and eat steaming rice laced with chestnuts to your heart's content, all for the price of one bowl. The chef did not think anyone should go hungry. Agata ordered a large bottle of barley wine, paying for everything with her mobile wallet and a bubbly *Thank you so much!* to the server. She blushed to receive the soup, but moaned a little when she bit into the fried fish, soaked full of hot broth. She covered her mouth while she chewed, but she did eat.

"This is really good," she said, working on a bit of noodle. She was quite red now. "I've never chewed in front of anyone before."

"Not even your parents?" Reiko thought most families ate together in Flesh Martyrdom, and it was only taboo to chew and swallow outside the family.

Agata shook her head. "My folks only do liquids. And really, they're not home enough to share food with, even if they did eat." She smiled at Reiko. "I thought it would feel dirty somehow, but it doesn't. It's just good food."

Reiko beamed. "*Sei Gusian*. It means, 'Enjoy in good health.'"

"*Sei Gusian*," said Agata. "To the first interesting person I've met, possibly in my whole life."

Reiko studied her freckled, open face. "And to you." *My first friend in the Middle.*

After several bowls of soup and a whole bottle of barley wine, Agata laid her head sleepily on Reiko's shoulder.

"I'm stuffed!" giggled Agata. "That was the best meal I've ever had."

"I don't want to go back to Terry," groaned Reiko. "But I'm glad you enjoyed it."

Agata looked up at her, eyes twinkling with mischief. "Who said the night was over? We're just getting started."

Agata took her to an all-night spa. They put on robes and hit the various steam rooms, hot and cold pools, a dry sauna made of salt rock, a cold sauna made of ice. A room where the walls were gold, another where they pulsed with multicolored lights. Then Agata got a full-body scrub while Reiko read a magazine under a heat lamp. They lay on beds next to each other in the relaxation room, chatting softly as the sun came up.

"I had a group of girlfriends, you know," whispered Agata. "We did the baths together every Friday night—it was really fun for a while. But everyone's become so boring lately. Angelica only cares about being beautiful. She's getting face implants—cheeks and lips. She's already had her limbs lengthened. I think she looks ghastly. Margaret is only here in school to find a husband—can you believe that? It's like we're living in the past! And Janis and Shania keep breaking up and getting back together. It's pretty hellish to be their friend right now, at any point in their cycle. I've been so lonely this whole year." She reached out to tug lightly on Reiko's robe. "Until today."

Later, as Reiko and Agata rode the Loop back to the Middle, they watched lanterns being released into the open sky.

"They must be coming from the Valley," said Agata. "Those religious freaks."

"Hey, Agata," said Reiko, hoping she sounded more nonchalant than she felt. "About what you said, at the spa? I was lonely both at home in the Bastian and here. I've never felt welcome anywhere. Until today."

"Today was the absolute greatest." Agata's eyes grew big and wild. "So why should it end? You should move in with me! I have a really big apartment. And then you can save your money and go home whenever you want."

Reiko tried not to gasp. "Really?"

"Why not?"

Reiko shook out a shocked little laugh. "Uh, sure. Why not! When?"

She shrugged. "Now? Let's go get your stuff. It'll be better than Terrible Terry stinking up the place with her nasty shame chicken, that's for sure."

Reiko squeezed her hand as they watched the lanterns float up, up, up into the sky. She said a little prayer in her own mind. *I am God, and God is me. Thank you, God, for the gift I have just received.*

Moving in with Agata was very easy. Reiko had few belongings, and Agata was right—her apartment was palatial. There was a study with a desk that looked like it had never been used and a long, wide couch that Reiko set up as her bed. She spent the rest of the semester, when she wasn't working, getting drunk with Agata and going to spas for beauty treatments. They often capped off their long nights of drinking by soaking in the healing waters, napping under heat lamps, reading magazines, and eating flavored ice. There was never any quibbling over the bill—Agata always paid, with either a swipe of her credit card or a tap of her mobile wallet. She seemed to relish spending her parents' money.

Instead of being distracted from her studies, Reiko found that she actually worked better now that she had an outlet for fun. She went home for their three-week summer break and worked with her mother and grandmother, sewing embroidery on silk scarves, like she had done when she was a little girl. It was painstaking labor, hard on one's hands and eyes, but Reiko actually enjoyed it.

It was nice to do something repetitive and physical, knowing that it would be over in only a few weeks. She barely saw Elena, who worked at the textile mill during the day and went out to dance clubs every night. Apparently she and her beau had broken up unexpectedly. Reiko wanted to ask her how she felt, but Elena was never around to ask.

While Reiko sewed, her mind wandered expansively. One morning, working with Mama and Grandma during the brightest light, she realized what she had been missing in her sonic cypher program. The code came to her mind like a painting, fully formed. Reiko looked at the window, breathing hard. The solution and its myriad applications were probably worth good money. She wanted to tell her family, but they wouldn't understand. *I've created a piece of tech that can speak to other code languages using tonal commands,* she could say. They would comprehend the words, but they wouldn't know why it mattered. She could probably quit school now and sell her idea for a tidy sum. Leapfrog over a degree and start working right away. But she didn't know how to get in touch with the kinds of people who would hire her. And anyway, she wanted to stay with Agata, who had been writing to her every day from some island with her parents. She wrote that summer break was the worst, everyone there was boring, and she couldn't wait to be with Reiko again. Reiko, at long last, found that she didn't mind being home. It was nice to sit and chat over a sewing session with Mama and Grandma, to talk to Papa over dinner, knowing that in a few short weeks, she would be with her dear friend again.

The night of her sonic breakthrough, she decided to celebrate by joining Elena at the club. They did not get off to a good start. Elena spent two hours getting dressed while Reiko waited for her sleepily, debating whether she should just call it a night early.

When they got to the club, it was noisy and hot, overcrowded with half-dressed bodies looking to revel in excess before work the next morning. Reiko danced for a while as Elena fought with a muscular, shirtless boy near the bathroom line. Elena had thrown him over for another guy with a mustache and a silky shirt, who watched them argue while sipping a beer. Shirtless guy called her an old-fashioned Eater for refusing to date both of them, berating her until Mustache led her back to the dance floor. Later, at the club bar, a good-looking bloke bought Reiko a drink and asked her what she did. When she told him she was a tech student at a university in the Middle, he made some comment about how she should be buying *him* a drink and left her standing there alone.

Reiko wanted to go home. Elena was now kissing Mustache passionately against a wall.

"Rei—" said Elena, coming up for air. "Ethan has a house we can use. Are you ready to go?"

"You're going to another party?" She felt too tired for yet another party, but didn't want to go home disappointed. The night so far had been the opposite of fun.

Mustache continued to suck at Elena's neck. She pointed to a little huddle of guys looking at them expectantly. "We're going to go have sex, but we need more girls. They're hot, aren't they?" Then she waved to the little crowd and cheered: "Sisters! Right?!" She turned back to Reiko and slung an arm around her shoulders, jutting her hips out to the side and posing. "It's gonna be so hot."

Reiko wrinkled her nose, repulsed. Elena had barely spoken to her all night, and now this? "No thanks—I guess I'll see you at home."

Elena caught her arm. She looked like she was about to cry. "I can't go with them all by myself—it's too many boys! How could you let me do that?" She started crying in earnest, and Reiko realized Elena had at some point crossed over from fun-drunk to messy-drunk.

"Can I get you a glass of water?"

"I told Ethan there was another girl! What am I supposed to do?"

"Do whatever you want!" Reiko tried to keep her tone civil. "Or tell your boyfriend to take you somewhere alone. This has nothing to do with me."

Elena's makeup ran down her face in rough streaks. "You're such a snob. You told me you wanted to go out—sometimes you have to think of the group, Reiko! It will be fun, I promise. They're all hot—"

"I don't want to. That's my answer, and it should be enough."

"That's right. You only think about yourself."

Reiko pulled back, stunned.

Elena's face was a harsh grimace. "Go back to the Middle with your stuck-up college friends you're always messaging on your fancy tablet—you never wanted to be here anyway. You think you're too good for us."

Reiko went home alone. She never found out whether Elena did try to please all those boys herself to win the favor of her new sweetheart, or if she stood up for herself. For the rest of the break, Elena was conveniently out of the house every night and away at the textile mill all day. They didn't even say good-bye when summer break ended, and Reiko was back on the Loop once more, chugging across the sky to the Middle.

The next year, she and Agata moved into a proper two-bedroom flat. Reiko tried to explain to Agata that she didn't need her own bedroom—she was fine sleeping on that wide, comfortable couch—but Agata assured her that it just wouldn't do. On moving day, there was a flurry of men in the halls of their new dorm building in fancy business dress, with their gold slippers and felted hats, their wives in tottering, high shoes and transparent jumpsuits, fussing over their children. Agata's parents were removed, distant, as if disappointed by the student apartments, declining to sit or even drink a glass of water from the tap. Her mother kept her gloves on. Reiko was surprised to discover that she and Agata looked nothing alike. Her parents outfitted their apartment with several new appliances—a high-speed blender, a water infuser, a big black box that made coffee or tea with the push of a button. They bought furniture too, including a new plush bed for Reiko. She was saving so much of her scholarship money, she could even send a hefty amount home to her family. Agata's parents also stocked the fridge with mineral water and all sorts of infusions and supplements the likes of which Reiko had never seen. Reiko went off to the library so Agata could visit with her family in private. When she got back, Agata was alone, her eyes glazed over, wearing all of her most brightly patterned clothes, one on top of another.

"I need to fuck," she said, lighting a cigarette. "And I need to smoke about five hundred cigarettes, drink a beer, get wasted, and then fuck again. Do any of those sound good to you?"

Reiko laughed. "I'll take a beer." She looked at her watch. She had rented a booth in the metal workshop for the night, but she could stay for a little while before getting to work.

"Right, right—I forgot you're frigid!"

This was Agata's new little joke, and it was already tiresome. Reiko liked sex, in theory, but she always felt like the other person was getting the better deal. After a few lackluster evenings and one particularly boring morning, she'd decided to stop having sex until she really, really felt like it. Lately she hadn't even been having sex with herself—something she wasn't about to admit to Agata, or she'd never hear the end of it. She took Agata's beer and had a sip.

"Hey, I need that!" She struck a dramatic pose, flinging her hand over her eyes. "It's my medicine."

"Go drink one of those fancy infusions in the fridge."

"I hate that shit, you drink them." Agata got up to open another beer. "Seriously, drink as much as you want—they got me a subscription, there's more coming every month. If you don't drink them, I'll start throwing them out the window."

"That's a good idea—murder an unlucky undergrad with nutrition."

Agata took a hard swallow. "They make me want to scream. Did you see my mother's expression when she saw our bathroom? I don't think she's ever been this close to the ground before."

Well, my parents have never been this high, Reiko thought. But all families were the same, in certain ways. "My parents make me want to jump out of my skin too," she said. "Even though I love them." Just yesterday, they had all crammed together into the local community center's computer room to accept her video call. They listened with big smiles on their faces while she talked about her new classes and assignments, but they never asked her any questions. They just didn't know what to say. Elena wasn't there. Mama said it was because she was busy at the textile mill, but Reiko knew it was because she felt betrayed by Reiko for reasons she probably couldn't even name—for being smart, for leaving the Bastian, for having more options than she did. It didn't matter. She missed all of them, her grandmother especially, and yet Reiko wanted never to return. She threw an arm around Agata and gave her a squeeze. Money couldn't fix everything. No matter where you were from, families were difficult.

"Do you *have* to go back to work tonight?" asked Agata, eyes big. "I could really use the company."

It would be another couple of weeks before she could get a time slot in the metal workshop. But Agata seemed really shaken. Reiko looked at her roommate's freckled nose and almost kissed it. "Of course not," she said. "Anything you want to do, I'm ready and willing. Let's go get into trouble."

During her second semester, Reiko relaxed enough to allow herself to take one art class. She signed up to study with Elhisa, an artist who had made her name in politically charged work criticizing the Flesh Martyr Church. From their first class, Elhisa encouraged Reiko to make work about being Free-Wah, about being from the Bastian. She suggested to Reiko she might take self-portraits or make paintings of her family or the street where she grew up. When Reiko insisted that her work was abstractions, the professor assigned her to visit the local contemporary art museum. There was a current exhibition of entirely non-ALGN artists. Reiko wandered the large brick museum. As she walked, she took notes:

> An exhibit of dried flowers, in various arrangements, from boutonnieres to wreaths to an opulent overflowing vase, all dead.

After this, there were:

> Maps of how the former land masses used to look, with overlaid drawings of Free-Wah gods and goddesses.

Followed by:

> 21 black-and-white photographs of the shifting borderlands of the Ahinga people, a small ethnic tribe, neither Free-Wah nor

ALGN. Their homelands swallowed up by water, they are not natural citizens of any place.

Once Reiko dated a Bastian boy who told her she looked Ahinga. She broke up with him. It was the first time she had truly been smitten with a boy, a good-looking ALGN lad from the Low Quake, the very sort for which Reiko had a weakness, with a big laugh and mischievous eyes. He was all sunshine and roses in the beginning. But after she'd fallen for him, they would be lying in each other's arms in the park or in bed after lovemaking, and he'd say something absolutely gutting—sweetly, while playing with her hair. Things like, "You'd be so beautiful if you got your teeth fixed." When she told her mother about this, she cocked her head and said, "Reiko, no man starts out mean. Who would stay for that? They wait until you love them. He's testing you, to see how much he can get away with. When they get mean, you have to leave right away." When she broke up with him, he looked very surprised.

Reiko didn't look Ahinga, but she did plan to get her teeth fixed as soon as she had money. Ahinga people's skin had a greenish-grayish undertone, like wet stone, along with the classic Free-Wah forehead ridge. ALGN people all looked different, but their one unifying feature was that they were all ridge-less, with skin that ranged in tone from reddish to brownish to pinkish. The only thing that made them ALGN was that they were not Ahinga or Free-Wah. It was a race of exclusion, not of inclusion.

Reiko walked by an exhibit entirely of blue—blue clothes, blue paintings, blue sculptures—by an Ahinga artist with a very long name.

In the not-so-distant past, it was thought that Ahinga people had blue blood, while all other peoples had red blood, making them a different species. Modern science had disproven this as a myth, but *blue blood* was still a slur.

She sat down on a bench in the middle of the quiet museum. Reiko loved the spacious feeling in her brain from sitting in these places. Sometimes she would go to a museum and not even look at the art. She just loved soaking in the charged silence.

Before the arrival of so many ALGN peoples, Reiko's land had recognized more than two hundred different ethnic groups. Her father had explained that back then, Ahinga wasn't thought of as a different race. No one identified as Free-Wah either, but as a member of a particular ethnic group with its own specific customs and traditions. Since the arrival of ALGN people on their shores, Free-Wah had been made into a monolith, and Ahinga wasn't included. Land rights revoked and borders redrawn, most Ahinga had no papers, no agency to move about. Permanent refugees without a home. Her grandmother liked to say that though they had troubles, at least they weren't Ahinga.

She passed through a section of maps in *Shifting Territories: Perspectives on Colonial Inheritances.* One artist posited that Ahinga land rights should be restored. Their lands, some scholars and activists argued, had not been swallowed by the sea, but the maps had been redrawn, with the Ahinga displaced outside the artificial border.

A neon sign read: *The End Is Here* with the letter *H* crossed out. Next to the neon, the placard read:

> *There is no letter* H *in Free-Wah languages (of which there are many). Ere, in several dialects, can be translated as "Before"—The End Is Before. The artist reinterprets the Flesh Martyr obsession with apocalypse, so much of which has been an excuse for their occupation of these shores, to state that the*

end of their world has already happened, long ago, and we are living in their ruin. The End Is Before.

It was interesting, but Reiko didn't feel a particular connection to the material any more than visiting an exhibit filled with ALGN paintings and objects. Why wasn't Reiko allowed to just be an artist? Why did she have to be put in a context, while her classmates could create without that limitation? Why did her biography placard always have to include a picture of her face?

5.

Beatrice took Georgina to see the local theater's production of *Sky Chaser*, a fantastical retelling of the Divine Mother story: the Flesh Martyr, after defeating the evil Free-Wah king, rides a giant hawk, liberating the country from the Night Witch and her reign of darkness, spreading the light of God. The entire production took place up in the air across a series of platforms. The puppet of the hawk was over twenty-five feet long and covered with gold spangles, undulating in the sky like ripples of sunshine. The dancer who played the Flesh Martyr had trained in the capital, and rumor had it her feet hadn't touched the ground for all four years of her training. When the performance was over, nuns on the ground lit paper lanterns in intricate patterns. The lights rose together, weaving in and out of complex shapes as night fell. Stilt-walkers, dressed as all manner of birds, wove and flapped throughout the crowd as children clapped and cheered.

"Seagate is magical," whispered Georgina into Beatrice's hair.

You are magical, she wanted to say. She had never cared for theater or lights dancing in the air, not since she was a little girl.

"Ducat for your thoughts?" asked Georgina, pretending to bite her shoulder.

"Take me to bed," said Beatrice, suddenly serious. She didn't care about pretty shapes in the sky. She had to make love to Georgina, to kiss her and hold her, or she might die.

"Here?"

She shook her head. "No." She led her away from the crowds of people, the children on their parents' shoulders, everyone pointing up at the lanterns. Someone shouted, "Our holy lights are floating to the city, spreading the word of God!" The crowd cheered, and the nuns began to sing: *Arise, arise, we light the night, with the fire of the Lord.*

They walked out to the fields. They lay on the earth together like animals and rutted in the cool, hard dirt. When Beatrice came, Georgina held her until the shaking stopped. Then Beatrice cried long and hard, but wasn't sad.

"What's wrong, little one?"

Beatrice tried to find the words. "It's like I've never had sex before this." She looked up at her face. Georgina didn't say anything, just kissed her, held her until the sobbing stopped. They lay on their backs in the cool, wet grass, unencumbered and unashamed to be upon the bare ground. As the lanterns drifted up and up, merging into the city, Beatrice imagined what the city lights might be from—houses, schools, office buildings, amphitheaters. Perhaps even restaurants, Beatrice wondered, then turned over to kiss Georgina's lush mouth again.

———

Falling in love with Georgina meant falling in love with Seagate. Beatrice still cooked in secret, still copied her recipes, but her trips to Lina stopped. There just wasn't time. She did feel guilty. But whenever she planned to take the night to walk to the outskirts of town and back, she ended up accepting Georgina's invitation to frolic in the pool with other teens or to go to the movies or to drink wine at a party on someone's hot air balloon. Melis still frowned at her from across any crowded room, but otherwise her old friends welcomed her back with open arms. When Georgina would point at a particularly beautiful Seagate house, Beatrice considered it with new eyes. What if there was a tidy garden in the back for her to cultivate edible plants? And a clean, gleaming kitchen inside, like a present waiting to be opened? Her sweetheart—no, her wife— at the table in a bathrobe, drinking coffee. She even took the yellow pill, more days than not, just because it was easier.

Yet Beatrice couldn't bring herself to go into Leroy's former house. She waved hello to Georgina's parents at church and saw them beam with pride when Georgina turned in her city clothes, at last, for a dust-colored tunic as the congregation clapped and cheered. Georgina was a candle person who made those simple Seagate clothes shine with an easy inner radiance. Sometimes Beatrice was so happy she felt like she could die and ascend to heaven right then. But she still remembered what it felt like in the church kitchen to cook for someone, to enjoy food with them. Whenever she couldn't sleep, she'd imagined Leroy holding her after they both had eaten that grilled-cheese sandwich. Only then could she rest. Now her dream lover wasn't Leroy or some faceless person. In her fantasies, it was Georgina who ate her food and gazed at her with love. But she didn't invite Georgina to her house or ask if she could spend the night.

One sunny Saturday, Georgina invited Beatrice to accompany her to the mall for a bit of holiday shopping. Outside the bounds of Seagate proper, the Valley's mall was the place where Seagate residents mixed with most of the outside world. The air was cold and the sun was bright as they glided over the town in a small hot air balloon. They had missed the public airship, which came only every ninety minutes, and neither girl had the ducats to hire a personal one, which was more precise and certainly faster. They opted for a free student balloonist who needed to build up hours to apply for his commercial license. Even the bumpy ride felt romantic, though the balloonist almost skewered them on a church steeple during takeoff. It took him half a dozen tries to park on the mall's landing strip. They thanked him for the ride and walked away quickly before bursting into laughter.

"We would have gotten here about the same time if we'd waited for the airship," whispered Georgina as they giggled toward the mall entrance. They glanced back. The boy was still struggling to tie the balloon down. "I hope it doesn't float away!"

"I hope it does. I hope it starts a new life, far away from him!"

Georgina rewarded her lover with her loud laugh, and Beatrice felt pleasantly satiated. "Fly free, balloon!" Beatrice shouted to the boy. "Fly off to a better world!" Georgina covered Beatrice's mouth with her hand, and the girls brought their smiling faces together. "Maybe I should learn how to pilot a balloon," murmured Beatrice. "Fly us both far away from here."

"What would we do then?" asked Georgina, pressing a kiss to her bottom lip.

"Whatever we want."

They walked along the rows of stores, shelves loaded down with frivolous niceties in bright holiday displays. Beatrice squeezed her sweetheart's hand, pointing to a particularly festive array of tiny spoons designed to remove hard-to-reach earwax, next to long, tapered candles and a huge bag of bath salts. *Holidays Are a Time for Self-Love*, read the accompanying sign in a florid, looping script. An expansive feeling blossomed inside her as she looked at the beautiful, useless objects in the holiday display and realized that she wanted nothing except what she already had.

Georgina looked up from her shopping list. "You're somewhere else again," she said. "What's going on in that pretty head of yours?"

"Just feeling grateful," said Beatrice. "And blessed."

"I haven't even given you your present yet."

"Haven't you, though?" *This is what happiness feels like,* she thought, holding her hand over her chest. *This is happiness.*

After a few hours of shopping, Georgina excused herself to the restroom. Beatrice waited outside the women's room for a few minutes, then thought better of it and decided to relieve herself too. Entering the restroom, she was surprised to find Georgina sliding coins into the bathroom food supplement dispenser labeled STECOPO CARES in bright, blinking letters.

Georgina turned sharply, as if caught stealing. The food bar clunked down, waiting to be claimed in the open basin. "Sorry! I'll be quick, I promise." She went inside one of the stalls and closed the door.

Beatrice heard the sound of the wrapper rustling.

"I have a high metabolism," explained Georgina. "I've been feeling faint for the last hour."

"I don't have an issue with you eating," said Beatrice. "Quite the opposite, actually."

"Easy for you to say!" Beatrice heard her swallow. "You're one of those girls who never needs to eat."

At this mention of food, an older nun who had just entered the bathroom looked scandalized, and immediately turned and left.

Beatrice laughed. "You just scared off a nun!"

"Oops," said Georgina. She exited the stall, brushing her hands on her legs. Beatrice took her place in the stall, did her business, and flushed the toilet. The little trash can next to the toilet was filled with bar wrappers.

As they continued their trek through the mall, Beatrice could feel that something between them had changed, but she didn't know how to reverse it. She noticed a woman with a gleaming tower of hair, her dress tight and shiny, getting her nails done at the salon.

"Do you miss your old clothes?"

Georgina looked at her sharply. "Why would you say that?"

"Just curious."

"Of course not," she said tightly. "I don't need to display myself like that ever again." She squeezed Beatrice's hand. "Sorry . . . I let my blood sugar get too low, and now I'm embarrassed."

Beatrice kissed her cheek. "I'm sorry! I'm really not trying to make you feel bad."

"I feel faint if I don't have at least one meal replacement every four hours." She cringed. "Sometimes two." She looked at Beatrice plaintively. "The pill stops my hunger, but I still get shaky if I don't eat. But I'm shedding weight, so my doctor isn't worried." Beatrice had noticed. She still found her beautiful, but Georgina was starting to look like every other girl in Seagate—thin, a bit washed-out. "Every time we're together, I go into the bathroom to have a meal supplement. Gross, I know." Georgina kept smiling, yet she looked scared. "If I eat less than a thousand calories a day, I get cross-eyed in the afternoon. But I don't enjoy them!"

"Hey," said Beatrice, turning to face her. "I really, really don't mind."

She pouted prettily. "I wish I could be like you."

"I eat," said Beatrice slowly.

"Well, not when we're together," said Georgina.

"I mean . . . I don't have a problem with eating. I love the way you look, and the fact that you eat."

"Yeah, right. Ew!" She made sloppy, fake eating sounds. "*Nom nom nom nom nom.* You like this, Beatrice?" She rubbed her belly. "Come here, little girl, I'm a cannibal!"

"Stop it!" Beatrice shrieked, but she couldn't even pretend to be mad. She giggled as Georgina mouthed at her neck. "Hey! Come on. Don't you have more shopping to do?" Beatrice had barely bought anything, but Georgina had purchased countless trinkets for herself and her family. Beatrice couldn't see a reason for any of it. City people just did things differently.

Georgina spun Beatrice toward her. This time her smile reached her eyes. "Actually, I have a better idea."

Georgina lead Beatrice to the sex court. They waited fifteen minutes for a clean, private comfort station to be available, but it was worth it to be alone and unhurried. They lay together on the thin mattress, not even bothering to take off their clothes. Beatrice had the bumps right now in any case, so they were sticking to hands-only activities until the rash went away. She didn't mind. Kissing Georgina, lying with her, feeling her weight on top of her, all of these had become a second oxygen to Beatrice, her orgasms a happy afterthought. She had to know if Georgina felt the same way. She put her hand on her lover's chest, right above her heart.

Beatrice formed her question carefully. "If you were on a runaway hot air balloon, where would you go?" She took a deep breath. "If you could go anywhere and do anything in the whole world, and no one could tell you no. What would you do?"

"Hmm." Georgina pressed a kiss to Beatrice's head. "I've never told anyone this, but before we came to Seagate, I wanted to live in the countryside. To keep all kinds of different animals. To care for them, study them." She looked steadily at Beatrice. "Does that surprise you?"

"I also . . . want things I'm not supposed to." She fell silent for a long moment, thinking of the woman in the floppy hat in Lina's store and all the other secret appointments she never saw. She suddenly missed Lina dearly. "I think they're more common than we realize," she whispered into Georgina's chest. "Secrets." Beatrice propped up on her elbows. "There's really nothing about the city that you miss?"

"In the city, it's just . . . everyone is always judging everyone else. I thought you were judging me just now, and you were only asking an honest question. It's like everyone needs to show that they're better, to stand out with their clothes, their hair, their houses. Some people need to show they're more religious, and they make a big fuss of only drinking liquids and never chewing. But most people are hypocrites. Preach one thing and do another."

Beatrice thought back to the hidden larder in the church's kitchen. How many more secret pantries were there in Seagate? How many in the rest of the world? She'd never know. How to measure all the world's shame!

"In the city . . . do people really eat meals in public for pleasure?"

Georgina gasped. "Of course not! Even the Free-Wah don't eat in public anymore. There's always rumors of restaurants, but I never went to one or knew anyone who did. The city is not the den of sin you think it is. But . . . people aren't unified the way they are in Seagate. They're not working together toward a common goal. I don't see why anyone would want to live there if they could live here."

"Spend another few years here, then tell me that again."

"You're bored with Seagate?"

"Bored? I was out of my mind until you showed up!" Beatrice felt an idea forming hazily in her mind, sparkling like a jewel. "But what if there's another place, someplace that isn't Seagate and isn't the city, a place where you could keep and study animals, and I could also . . . live as I wish."

"And what secret way of life might that be, dear one?" Georgina's tone was light, and her eyes were closed, as if she were falling asleep.

"Botany," Beatrice said suddenly. The half-lie made her feel drunk and light. "I want to grow plants and trees, to garden, to study the natural world." She looked into her lover's eyes, which were now wide open. "I haven't told anyone."

"You're my absolute twin," Georgina whispered. "We're the same!" She squeezed Beatrice's hand. "What if we moved somewhere new together? A place for your plants and my animals? It would be perfect!"

Beatrice's next words spilled out in a jumble. "Do you want to come over for Martyr Day with my parents?"

"Wow, yes! I would be honored to sit at your family table," said Georgina, sealing the acceptance with another kiss. It was really happening. The words *I love you* were on the tip of Beatrice's tongue. As they lay in that comfort station, listening to the couples in identical suites having loud, languorous sex, Beatrice made a plan. After the ritual, she would show Georgina her private collection of recipes. She would tell her about her obsession with food, her shameful incident in the church kitchen, and her quest to prepare and consume the most exquisite dishes in the world. She would tell her about Lina, about the bookstore, about her mother's necklace. She would reveal herself completely to her one true love, becoming naked in a way she had never been before. They would sit at her family table as sweethearts, and then sleep in each other's arms. Their future was an open road, and they would walk it together.

6.

Reiko was busy finishing a project for Professor Echel's theory of mass computation class when an upsetting message came into her student account. It was a bill for the semester. The amount of ducats for lab fees, tuition, and room and board was so staggering that Reiko felt momentarily dislodged from reality. The people around her were paying this much to be here? People like Agata, with her shabby clothes and her wealthy parents, who never even did the reading for class? Reiko wasn't worried about the bill itself—she was certain that this was an error on the administration's part. Her academic performance was flawless, so there was no way her scholarship was being revoked. But the principle of it bothered her. Half of the kids in her classes didn't even work hard—they were always getting extensions on assignments, skating by with the least effort possible. It seemed to Reiko that, like Agata, their getting a diploma was some kind of deal they had with their families, and they didn't really care if they learned anything as long as they received their degree. Of course, if these were the people she'd be competing against for jobs when she was ready to enter the workforce, she couldn't be too bitter about it. But Reiko didn't have any connections with the best firms or labs, so she'd need to make the grade just to get a foot in the door. She suspected some of these little scions would just stride into those positions, and then continue to be rewarded by life for their mediocrity. It just wasn't fair.

Well, baby, she thought, *who said life was fair?* She walked down the gleaming marble hallway to speak with the registrar. She waved as she passed Professor Bruin, her comp teacher, who looked about the same age as Elena. And yet she was pushing forty, with two degrees and a world-class apprenticeship under her belt. Middle women didn't age the same as Bastian women. Under Agata's influence, Reiko's skin had never looked better. She glanced up at the floating orbs above. Rumors were that the women up there were so modified, they barely looked like people at all.

After her meeting with the registrar, Reiko ran to the art building. Elhisa was in her office, drinking a cup of tea and staring out the window.

"Reiko! What a surprise. You never come in for office hours."

Her lips began to tremble. She explained the whole noise in a rush. They were taking away her scholarship.

Elhisa shook her head. "Listen, I'm glad this is happening. I've been meaning to have this conversation with you. You're very talented. But you're not going to be an artist if you keep going in tech. I'll help you prepare a dossier—switch to Art and Design, with me. You can keep taking your tech classes—they're a part of your practice. But you're an *artist*, Reiko. You can feel it in your bones, can't you?"

Reiko nodded slowly. "I do feel it," she said. Then she cringed. The artist's path was so uncertain. And art supplies were expensive, as was studio space. And there was no guarantee of a cushy salary at the end. Did she want to gamble with her future like that? Who did this woman think she was, to congratulate her for losing her scholarship, for getting into crushing debt? She thought about her sonic cypher. The applications for that level of tech were endless. Maybe she really should quit school, sell the idea, and try to land herself a job at an elite firm without a degree. Could that even happen?

Elhisa was still talking, but Reiko was only half listening. "You need to focus on what makes you unique. With your talent and life story, there isn't anything holding you back. Did you go see that show I told you about?"

"I did."

"Exceptional, wasn't it? Those maps! Beautiful, impactful, clever. I think you could make something like that. Art that makes people think about their relationship to power."

"But my work is abstractions, based on math. On algorithms—"

"You're only twenty—don't limit yourself! Look," she said, pointing to a calendar hanging on her wall. "Next month is Women's Celebration Month, and then, in four months' time, it's Free-Wah Appreciation Month. It's too tight to do anything for Women's Celebration this year, but I could get you a spot for Free-Wah Appreciation Month. Not a solo exhibition, of course, but in a group show. At a museum, Reiko! You're actually quite lucky."

Reiko couldn't figure out if Elhisa was saying she was lucky to be a woman *and* a minority *and* a poor person, or that she was lucky to have such a benevolent mentor.

"You probably think I'm conniving," Elhisa said. "Disingenuous. But I want to give this to you straight. It's actually very exciting—we just need to be practical!"

It wasn't even Elhisa's fault. She probably waited all year for Women's Celebration Month. Reiko met her gaze. "I have to make myself a commodity if I want to be bought."

She waited for Elhisa to disagree with her. But the words never came. "Think it over," the professor said flatly. "You have everything it takes to be a successful artist. You're even good-looking. You could have it all laid out at your feet."

Reiko frowned. "Why do my looks matter?"

"Beauty makes everything easier," Elhisa said. Suddenly she looked tired. "Or so I imagine—I never had the burden of beauty in my youth. I wasn't pretty or even particularly thin. No one liked looking at me while I yelled at them about equality, which makes all the difference. But now I'm on every womanist panel, in every lecture series, every group show. Maybe if I'm lucky, I'll have a retrospective of my work at a well-thought-of museum when I'm eighty. You can either be young and beautiful, or you can work forever in anonymity, while all your male peers get famous, get the prize teaching jobs, get solo shows, get awards. Then, when you're an old woman, if you've somehow kept going and you're very, very lucky, the world bows down at your feet."

"You're not exactly talking me into being an artist," she said slowly.

"I don't think anyone in the world can tell you what to do, Reiko. Thanks for coming in." Her tone sounded final, like a door closing.

"Elhisa," she said gently. "I think you should burn it all down."

"And record the whole thing—that would make a great piece. I would be very famous in prison. At least for a little while." Reiko got up to leave. "Reiko?"

"Yes?"

"Please leave the door open." She gestured vaguely to the empty room. "Office hours." Then she went back to looking out the window.

7.

"She's very punctual," said Papa inanely at the sound of the door-bell. "That's a good sign!"

"Alberto," said Mama, laughing. "What does that tell us?"

"Well, timeliness is a virtue." He grinned at Beatrice. "She's all right in my book, kiddo!"

"Dad!" whispered Beatrice. "Stop it!"

"Stop what?" he whispered back.

"Um," said Beatrice. Being so enthusiastic? So easy to please? Making bad jokes, and often? She squeezed her father's hand. "Nothing," she replied. "I'm just being terrible." She motioned for her mother to sit. "Relax. I'll get the door." Beatrice took off her apron and smoothed her hair, checking her reflection once again in the hallway mirror. Then she opened the door to Georgina holding a bouquet of creamy white lilies. Beatrice took a mental picture of this moment: Georgina, framed in the doorway, her dark skin aglow with lamplight, holding a bouquet of flowers like a bride.

"Happy Martyr Day!" she said, holding out the flowers. "These are for your parents, from mine!" Beatrice accepted the bouquet with a grin.

"Happy Martyr Day," replied Beatrice, taking in Georgina's long dress and hair in thick braids around her head like a crown. This girl meant business.

After introductions, they enacted the Ascension ceremony, one of Beatrice's favorite rituals since she was a little girl. As Georgina was their guest, Mama offered for her to wear the crown of candles, symbolizing the Divine Mother ascending to heaven to reside with God after defeating the Free-Wah king. Beatrice smiled when she realized that Georgina must have suspected this might happen— could that be why she had braided her hair? Papa sang "Holy Night, Mother's Night" in his rich baritone while Mama played the tambourine, joining in on the *sha-la-las*. Beatrice clapped along, her heart overflowing to see her beautiful girlfriend, face lit by the crown of candles, twirling between her mother and father in song. They were a perfect family.

When the ritual was finished, Beatrice left Georgina with her parents to make small talk at the table. For the first time, Beatrice had insisted that she cook the family meal, to symbolize her coming into adulthood with all its temptations and responsibilities. This had led to a little fight with Mama and Papa, who understood she was trying to show off for her new sweetheart but did not wish for their daughter to rush into anything before it was necessary. Beatrice reasoned that she was growing up and needed to be trusted with such things. Wistfully, her parents had agreed.

Beatrice brought in the plates just as Georgina was laughing her loud, wonderful laugh at one of Papa's better jokes.

Mama looked down at what Beatrice had placed before her. "Beatrice," she asked carefully. "What is this?"

"Forgive me, Mama, Papa, Georgina. This is my first time

preparing a meal for the family, so I suspect it will be rather strange."

Mama laughed uncomfortably. "Well, thank goodness for supplements!"

"Hear! Hear!" said Georgina, and she pushed at the plate in a gesture of derision.

The meal was all the usual things Beatrice had eaten since she was a child—rice enriched with vitamins, beans, and an assortment of acceptable vegetables. But Beatrice had soaked the dried beans overnight so they'd be plump and tender when she slow-boiled them, along with perfectly diced carrots, onions, and celery. The natural flavor of the vegetables had been released by a quick pan sear, keeping their outside flesh crisp while they slow-cooked in the beans. Then the rice was mounded in an elegant dome on each plate. Instead of straining the beans from their broth, she'd ladled the soupy mix on top of each rice mound, before flavoring it with salt. The natural sweetness of the onions and carrots had been released by the slow-cooking, and the celery provided a slightly acidic counterpoint to the rich bean stew. She didn't dare add any oil or secret spices, but otherwise she had used most of the tricks up her sleeve. It was, in short, delicious.

"Beatrice, thank you for your labor," said Papa, laying a hand on her arm. He looked at her seriously. "I hope you understand now how graceful your mother is in the kitchen. Her cooking looks like it takes no work at all! Now, let us pray." They all joined hands. On this night, Papa's typically short, casual prayer was long, borrowing liberally from last Sunday's sermon. Beatrice wondered if this was for Georgina's benefit. "God," he began, "please forgive us for what we are about to do. We are so lucky to be given human minds, which can discern animalistic desires from more angelic endeavors. Perhaps one day we will be like the angels, never needing to partake in nourishment to continue thriving." His eyes grew glassy and thoughtful. "Or might we be blessed to evolve like the noble plant, able to survive solely from the sun's gentle rays! That would be terrific. But until that time comes, oh Lord, we humble ourselves before you, to chew and swallow, to digest and shit, and then do it all over again, like the hungry animals we still are. The lot of humankind is to have angel souls trapped in hungry, animal flesh." He blinked. "It's quite the paradox. So please forgive our baseness and allow us to receive nourishment, despite our shame, so we might live to serve you another day."

"Amen," the women chorused. "Amen!"

Georgina said very little over dinner. She kept covering her mouth while chewing, then remembering herself, lowering her hand in an attempt to treat Beatrice's family as if they were her own. Beatrice saw this struggle between modesty and familiarity and appreciated her effort. The meal was over rather quickly. Beatrice wanted seconds, but she didn't dare go for more. Once the food was eaten, Papa took the dirty plates away. They sat together in the family room, sipping from long flutes of sacrament wine—a sweet, mellow beverage, slightly fizzy, and low in alcohol, perfect for teenagers.

"Georgina," said Papa genially, "I've been working on some new slogans for the company as we move to expand our campaign. I thought, since you're a former city girl, I could run them by you?"

Georgina squeezed Beatrice's knee. "Of course!"

Papa cleared his throat. "Okay, be gentle—I'm not ready to face the boardroom just yet. You know our community slogan right now is—"

" 'Seagate: Join us and have more!' " exclaimed Georgina, holding up her arms.

"Right!" said Papa. "That one is polling very well. But some people don't even connect Seagate to Stecopo, our business arm, so we're thinking of rebranding. Right now, our slogan is—"

" 'Stecopo,' " the women finished, " 'the family company!' "

"Why, this is my favorite focus group. All lookers too." Papa grinned. "Okay, the storms are getting worse in the city, right? So what about: 'In these times, who will protect you against the oncoming storm? We'll be your safety net. Stecopo: The caring company!' "

"I like it!" Georgina paused. "Maybe it's a little long?"

"Indeed," sighed Papa.

"I always thought it should be 'Stecopo: When your company is your family,' " said Mama, gesturing with her wineglass. " 'The family company' sounds like it's just one family that started a company." She sipped. "Which I suppose is true of Mr. Tenzo, but it's not as if he's lounging in Seagate, swimming laps in our community pool!"

Georgina nodded. "My parents came here to have more time, send me to better schools, and live in a beautiful neighborhood. And for the yellow pill, of course."

Papa wrinkled his eyebrows, as he did whenever he was thinking. " 'Stecopo: Saving you time, so you can spend it with your family!' " He paused. "Or: 'Stecopo: Solving hunger through science!' "

"Yes! Don't lead with the scary stuff, like the storms," said Mama. "Focus on the positive! Not what's bad about the city, but what's good about Seagate!"

Beatrice's tone was dry. " 'Stecopo: You are what you don't eat!' "

The room grew very quiet.

"Ah, just kidding," said Beatrice. "Stupid joke."

Papa looked at her curiously. "It's edgy. Really makes you stand up and take notice. 'You are what you DON'T eat.'" His brow wrinkled further. "I don't like it. . . . But I can't help saying it!" He chewed his lip. "It can't be the main campaign. It only appeals to one demographic—people who are interested in the yellow pill. But it could be one of the new slogans. Targeted marketing!"

"If I'd seen that in the city, I would've been really intrigued," offered Georgina.

Mama shook her head. "Do we want the company associated with eating, though?" she asked. "It should be a positive slogan, something that makes you feel good!"

But Papa and Georgina were already sold. " 'Stecopo,' " they said in unison. " 'You are what you don't eat!' "

"I have chills!" Papa stood to grab the whiteboard Mama used to keep track of household chores. "For the ad, there's a slim woman smiling with her happy family behind her."

"And it's a little bit sexy, maybe," said Georgina. "Like one of those ads with the women caressing flowers—"

"She's holding a lemon," said Papa, writing furiously. "But she doesn't eat it or even hold it near her mouth. She doesn't need it. It's just beautiful, the way she is. And that's perfect, because yellow is the color of the pill. Plus, the clean scent of lemon can represent cleanliness of the flesh and soul—"

"What if she's looking out at the ocean?" asked Georgina. "The wind on her face, birds in the sky. She's so light, she could practically float up to heaven."

Papa nodded. "Beatrice, could you stand up for a minute?"

Beatrice put down her wine flute. Her initial joy at her parents getting along so well with Georgina had morphed into annoyance. Why couldn't they talk about something else?

She plastered a smile on her face. "Like this?"

Georgina stood and styled a few of Beatrice's strands of hair away from her face. "Turn to face the window," she said. "Here, wait!" She ran into the kitchen and grabbed a lemon from the decorative bowl. "There—hold it up. Imagine you're looking at the sea. Now look back at me."

Papa took out his phone and started recording.

"Am I in the frame?" asked Georgina.

"No, you're good." His voice was low, concentrated. "Now, Beatrice. Do just what Georgina said, please. You're at the seaside, looking out over the platform to the sea below. Hawks circling above you. Keep holding out the lemon. . . . Now look back at me."

"'Stecopo,'" she said jokily, voice warbling. "'You are what you don't eat!'"

Georgina moved behind Papa. "Try again. Look at me."

Beatrice coughed. "Sorry, okay." She visualized the sea, then turned back, not toward the camera but right behind it, to Georgina. Her love, standing in her living room, next to her parents. Her chest flared with feeling. "'Stecopo, you are what you don't eat.'" She gazed into Georgina's eyes. "'Come to Seagate, and live in love.'"

For a long moment, everyone was quiet.

Beatrice raised her eyebrows. "Like that?"

"Yes," said her father firmly. "I think we have something." He clapped Georgina on the back. "Lady, I think you have a future in marketing!"

Her mother stood. "Okay, enough. Girls, go have fun!" she said, pulling Papa by the sleeve. "We've taken up enough of your time. Wine's on the counter, if you'd like a refill." She turned to Georgina and hugged her. "I'm so happy you've joined us. You make a lovely Martyr Day Queen."

Beatrice took Georgina by the hand and walked her upstairs.

Georgina sat down on her bed. "So this is where you sleep at night!" She held open her arms.

Beatrice didn't move into her embrace. Another girl would have shown a new lover her bedroom ages ago. But this was her secret haven, where she copied her recipes by candlelight and dried fruit on her windowsill. "Georgina," she began. "I thought we could talk for a while?"

"Sure," said Georgina, smiling at a picture of Beatrice at the seaside, taken with her parents when she was little. "Let's talk."

Beatrice took a deep breath—but a knock sounded at the door. It was Mama in her swimsuit, grinning like an imbecile. Beatrice wanted to yell, *Get out!* But she sat still, staring daggers at her instead.

"A little friend wanted to say hello," she said, taking Remus, still in his pouch, off from around her own neck and giving him to Georgina. "Can you watch him while we're out?"

"Yes, please!" Georgina squealed with delight. "So adorable."

"Of course, Mama." *Now go!*

Mama mouthed something that looked like *I like her* to Beatrice from behind Georgina before sashaying out of the room. Now that the ritual was over, her parents would be joining friends in the community pool to praise God with their bodies.

The girls were alone.

"You're so lucky you have a sugar glider!" exclaimed Georgina.

"Just ask the community board for one," Beatrice said absentmindedly as she fiddled with the bedspread.

Georgina kissed the little animal gently on his head. "You have to be a community member for a lot longer than we have to get a pet," she said. "But that's just another thing to look forward to, isn't it?" She scratched his little body and cooed, "Who's a baby? You are!"

Something inside Beatrice unclenched. This was Georgina, *her* Georgina, the Georgina who also had forbidden desires, who also wanted to forge her own path. She would understand.

"Georgina, remember when you told me about your dream of living with animals?" Georgina nodded. "I want to tell you something about me. Something important." Beatrice put her hand on her heart. "Because I love you, Georgina. And I think you might love me too."

"I do! I do love you." Georgina put the sugar glider gently back into his pouch and leaned in to kiss her.

Beatrice pulled away. "Wait. I'm so happy you feel like that too. But . . . I want you to know me. Really know me."

Georgina blinked. "Of course."

"What did you think of the meal I made for you tonight?"

Georgina wrapped her arms around Beatrice, kissing the top of her head. "Don't worry. We'll just use supplements." She kissed her hair again, sniffing. "Your family is very sweet. I hope I'm making a good impression."

Beatrice untangled herself from Georgina's arms. "Georgina, what did you think of the, um, presentation?"

She waved her hand in the air. "Well, it wasn't very modest. But like you said, it was your first time. And I'll make enough money to get us supplements if we ever move to the city, or we can stay in Seagate and Stecopo will take care of us. So we won't have to worry about it!"

Beatrice shook her head. She tried again from another angle. "Look, Georgina. Two, almost three years ago, I was at a church sleepover with Leroy—Leroy Kim. He left Seagate."

Her big eyes grew wide. "I've heard about the Kims. They used to live in our house. They must've done something really bad. Did his parents steal from Stecopo? Is that why they were kicked out of Seagate?"

"Maybe his mothers took him away because they were worried about him. He kept going on those retreats to lose weight." Beatrice looked up at her pleadingly. "Do you see what I mean?"

Georgina paused. "I sometimes forget you haven't lived anywhere else. No one leaves Seagate voluntarily, Beatrice. My parents thought long and hard before coming here—they had to give all their savings to the church, and any future earnings too." She gestured around the room vaguely. "It takes money to live on the outside. It's not like Leroy's parents could sell their house to start over. They were definitely kicked out." She shook her head. "But you were saying, you were at a church sleepover?" She grinned. "Did you let him stick it in you too early? You naughty girl!"

Beatrice's mouth went dry, but she forged on. "We snuck into the church kitchen. All of the usual things were there—rice, dried beans, powdered milk. Then I saw it." She took a deep breath. "There was a secret larder." Beatrice remembered how it felt when she found it, like stumbling upon a cavern of jewels. "Fresh bread, real butter, sharp cheese." Tiny ripe tomatoes with frilly green stems.

"That's so crazy! Did you ever find out who the food belonged to?"

"What? No—"

"I mean, it has to be one of the sisters, right?" Her dark eyes grew big. "Do you think it could be Father Alvarez?" she whispered. "That's twisted."

"No, Georgina—that's not the point." Beatrice bit her lip. "Oh, damn it, I'm muddling it all up! Wait." She got down off the bed and slid a box out from underneath its frame. "I'll show you." Beatrice pulled the lid off the box and took off the decoys she had placed on top, the old toys, past history tests. She took out her notebooks, smoothing the covers like she was touching a lover's arm.

"I'm not sure what I'm looking at," Georgina said.

"This is who I am," said Beatrice, handing her one of the notebooks. Georgina's forehead creased. "If we were to take a hot air balloon ride anywhere, I'd want to find a place where I could be a chef. A real chef, in a restaurant, where people would come to taste my recipes."

"You did the right thing by showing me these, Beatrice."

"I did?"

Georgina squeezed her hand. "God, if anything, this just makes me love you more!"

She let out a huge sigh. "It does?"

Georgina kissed her forehead. "Do you know how stressful it is to have fallen in love with Ms. Perfect? I never understood why you'd want to be with someone like me." Georgina flipped through the notebook, Beatrice's meticulously copied version of *Eating Your Way through the Seasons*. Never had she worked on something with so much attention, with so much care. Georgina looked at the pages, her mouth falling open—they were dog-eared and annotated, the margins darkened with scribbled notes and half-baked recipes.

"I love you," said Georgina, looking into Beatrice's eyes. "I love you, Beatrice." Then she reached into the book and started ripping the pages out. The sound was unbelievable.

Beatrice managed to stifle most of her scream, covering her mouth. "It's just like what we were talking about," Georgina said as she destroyed nearly a year of work. The torn pages fell to the floor like leaves. "I think most adults have some kind of secret larder. My mother did. She was like you, before we came to Seagate—obsessed with food. She would ingest unclean, immodest food in secret several times a day. She told me that before the yellow pill, she would go to sleep thinking about food and wake up planning her next meal." After all of the pages had been pulled out, she began picking up the fallen sheets and tearing them anew—over and over and over again into clumsy confetti. "It never stops! If you give in to these desires, they take over your whole world. You can't do it once, or even twice. You'll be enslaved by your hunger, always waiting for your next meal." She stopped ripping, her task complete, then gently scratched Remus's head. "Like an animal."

Georgina, noticing that Beatrice had gone pale and slack-mouthed, smoothed her hair as if she were a child. The beautiful handmade cookbook lay in tatters on the floor. "There, there," she said. Her voice was cloying, the sugar coating of a bitter pill. "Take a deep breath." Georgina kissed her forehead. "That was the hard part. But it's over now."

"It is?" choked out Beatrice.

"Yes," breathed Georgina, wiping away Beatrice's tears. "It's going to be so easy to stop. This is what I love about life in Seagate, Beatrice. I've been thinking about it ever since you asked me at the mall. I don't think I'll ever get bored here. This place is designed for people to be comfortable, and to be happy. And I want those things—I want to be happy." She looked at her seriously, brown eyes unblinking. "Do you want to be happy?"

"Of course."

"Well, silly, that's that. That's why the yellow pill is so amazing! It's not your fault you gave in to temptation. If you'd had the yellow pill when you found that food in the church kitchen, you wouldn't have been tempted at all." She straightened up and reached into her pocket. "Come here. Let me give you your gift." Georgina took out a small velvet box and handed it to Beatrice. "Go ahead, open it."

Hands shaking, Beatrice opened the soft box. Inside was a small silver ring, beautifully delicate, with a yellow-gold stone in the middle. Two hands clasped over the stone. It was a purity ring, the hands over the stone meant to symbolize a promise of two lovers to keep each other pure in thought, word, and deed. This purity promise was a step toward marriage—a serious gift. Beatrice turned the ring to see there was an inscription on the inside of the band. It read, *Beatrice—your love lifts me like a hot air balloon.*

A storm of conflicting emotions raged inside of her. An hour ago, this gift would have meant the world to her. But now the sight of the ring chilled her. Beatrice closed the box and placed it on her nightstand.

Georgina's eyes were even more luminous and beautiful as they filled with tears. "I love you, Beatrice. We don't need to find a new place or remake the world—we can stay right here in Seagate."

Beatrice looked at the floor. "I had some counseling from the pastor. It didn't do much. I take the yellow pill." *Sometimes. But I don't want to,* she almost added.

Georgina shook her head. "No—you don't have to stress about it. It's so easy, Bea." Beatrice focused on her large white teeth, gleaming like fresh-fallen snow. "There's a new type of yellow pill coming out. My parents told me about it. Everyone's going to get it. It isn't a pill at all—that's the genius part! It's an implant— it goes into your arm. Like the way the boys have surgical birth control. You won't have to think about it ever again."

Beatrice's hands and feet grew cold. "A surgical yellow pill?"

"Isn't it wonderful?" Georgina let out her booming, beautiful laugh. "God, you know—I'm so happy this happened. You were so perfect before, almost untouchable. I felt queasy before every date, I was so nervous to see you." Georgina kissed her deeply and sweetly, and Beatrice, despite her upset, felt arousal swirling in her stomach, the heat pooling between her thighs. "But you're the same as me, aren't you?" Georgina peppered Beatrice's face with kisses, her plush mouth roving over her neck. It felt so good and so bad.

Beatrice tried to keep her voice light and steady. "What about the people in Seagate who don't want the implant?"

Georgina tipped her head just slightly and narrowed her eyes, looking for a moment like a serpent about to strike. "I don't see why those people belong here."

Beatrice felt the room rotate and sway. She needed to get away—from Georgina, from Seagate, from everything. "I think you're right," she said quickly. "I need help. I'll tell my parents, and we'll go get the implant."

"I'm so happy to hear you say that." Georgina held out one hand, her other on her heart. She looked, in that moment, like the dancer from *Sky Chaser*, posed and unnatural.

"I'm all tired out from the ceremony tonight, though. Let's figure out the details tomorrow? I'm going to go to sleep early."

Georgina paused. "Did you like your present?"

Beatrice took the ring out and slipped it on her finger. "It's perfect," she said. "I almost forgot!" She held out a brightly colored bag, stuffed with tissue paper. Georgina accepted it and pulled out her gift—a beautiful abalone hair fastener accented with mother-of-pearl.

"Oh, Beatrice," she cried. "It's far too fine!" Then she kissed her, and clasped her close again. Beatrice had spent all the money she had been saving for Lina on this gift. She knew that Georgina, the city girl, would expect something lavish. But her real present wasn't anything money could buy. Beatrice had been planning to ask Georgina to spend the night, to sleep with her in her own bed. Now she couldn't wait for her to leave.

"I love you, Beatrice. All I want is for us to be together, happy and healthy!"

"And without appetite," said Beatrice, quoting scripture.

Georgina stood up, satisfied, clutching the comb. "I'll see you tomorrow." In the half-dark of her bedroom, Georgina towering over her, the girl Beatrice had loved seemed suddenly malevolent.

8.

From the sounds of it, Agata was busy entertaining her latest lover. Reiko bit her lip to keep from screaming. She was so mad and so damn tired. It had just started to feel like she belonged somewhere. She needed to talk to someone, but even if she could arrange a call with her family, they wouldn't understand half of the things she had to say.

A litany of Bastian curses raced through her mind—*go fuck a goat, you son of a nun, I'll shit in your milk, you've got assholes for eyes!* "Burn it all down!" she yelled, punching one of Agata's decorative sofa pillows.

"Rei-Rei?" Agata called from her bedroom. "Everything okay out there?"

Reiko tried to make her voice sound normal. "I'm fine!"

"No, sweetie, she doesn't want to join us," she heard Agata say with a laugh. "Reiko doesn't like sex!"

"Maybe she would if she tried it with me," answered a deeper voice.

"No, I don't think so," Agata retorted coyly. "You're a pretty selfish lover!" This was followed by more giggling and thumping and the sound of something like a lamp falling over. Reiko lay on the couch and closed her eyes. She just needed to think. She needed more time.

Agata walked into the living room, mostly naked, her silken floral-print robe open, face flushed and hair wild. "What is it?" she asked, frowning. "You look like you've seen a ghost. Is it your grandma?" Reiko groaned and sat up. She had poured her heart out to Aggie two nights ago over a bottle of wine about her grandmother's declining health. Agata closed her robe and sat beside her.

"They're taking my scholarship away." She felt too tired, suddenly, to even weep. "And they said it wasn't my performance—my grades are perfect. They said they just don't have the funding. The registrar thinks I should take out a loan, then try for the scholarship again next semester."

Agata began rolling a cigarette. "Those nattering Middle thieves," she said mildly. "They did this to Marjorie last year—do you know her? They gave her some kind of excuse, like she had too many credits. She's been taking loans for the last two semesters."

"She never got her scholarship back?" Reiko did know Marjorie; they competed for top grades in Syphoning Systemics. She was an excellent student.

Agata held the skinny cigarette to her lips and lit it. "No, Rei—they don't give anyone anything once they take it away, not that I've ever heard, anyway. I think it's a scheme. Your classes won't transfer to another institution, and you've already invested so much time and effort. So you go into debt." She moved to the window to blow the smoke into the quad. "Could be worse, of course. Most kids here will leave so deep in debt, they won't see a ducat back for years and years." She gestured toward the bedroom. "Poor

Peter is already eighty thousand in the hole, and he's not even a very good student." She shrugged. "But money is imaginary anyway, or so they tell me in The Shape of Commerce."

"But that's ridiculous! He won't get a job at a top-paying firm, not if his grades aren't up to it. He'll be paying off this degree for the rest of his life!"

Agata took a deep inhale and considered. "You're right, of course. There are loads of people with better grades and connections. But what's the alternative, not to get a degree? Then he's really done for, isn't he?" She tapped the end of her cigarette into a glass ashtray. "He could always give up and go live in Seagate. No debt then."

Reiko chewed her lip. "Those other kids who aren't on scholarship—I thought they all came from money."

Agata sniffed derisively. "Not here in the Middle. Not *real* money, anyway."

"I don't understand." Everyone around her took so much for granted—their pristine school supplies, their fashionable clothes, their new textbooks (which they barely opened). "Why do they all act like they have money?"

But Agata just laughed, a light, high sound like a balloon lifting. "Oh, sweetie. There's money, and then there's *money*." She gestured toward the bedroom. "Peter's mother is a dentist. Cynthia, down the hall? Her father is a lawyer. Angela, next door—her parents own a small chain of pharmacies." Reiko nodded. All these jobs sounded lucrative. Agata looked at Reiko over her wire-frame glasses. "Do you know what my parents do?"

Reiko imagined something impressive-sounding, like brain surgeon or physicist or even parliament official. "Tell me."

Agata smiled an ugly smile. "My parents don't have jobs, Reiko. Neither of them has ever worked a day in their lives. And that keeps them very, very busy." She snorted. "My mother didn't even do the work of giving birth to me. I'm a surrogate baby."

"You're from Above?"

"Guilty."

"But . . . why aren't you there?"

Agata looked almost proud. "Because my grades are shit. My parents had to donate a *lot* of money to even get me here." Reiko studied her friend with new eyes. The torn, shabby clothes, the shaded glasses, the unkempt hair, the rolled cigarettes—she was slumming it in the very same place where Reiko was struggling so hard to look like she belonged. It didn't matter if Agata got good grades. Eventually she would inherit her family's money. She would get married, not to someone like Peter, someone who had to work his way up the hierarchy in some Middle corporation, earning a new pip on his collar every year if he was lucky. Agata would marry money to match hers. Agata frowned at her cigarette, which had gone out, and relit it. "But don't worry too much about it," she said, puffing. "Your grades are stellar, and you're sharp as a knife. You're going to land a great position and work your little guts out, up, up, up the ladder, and then you'll have it made in the Middle shade."

Reiko did some rough math. The gobsmacking number she'd seen on her tuition bill today was only for one semester. She had several more to go, and then, with luck, two years of an unpaid apprenticeship to look forward to. The debt would be staggering. Reiko shook her head. "Goddamn it," she said. "My parents were right. What a grift."

Peter, a tall boy with long hair, exited the bedroom stark naked and stood in the living room with hands on his hips. "Are you coming back or what?"

Agata slung an arm around Reiko. "Sorry. My Reiko needs me."

Peter, obviously annoyed, turned to go find his clothes. Reiko softened. Agata really did care about her. Above or not, she was a good friend. She felt her mind calm. She'd figure out another way. Not becoming an artist—that felt too unpredictable. She'd make a lot of money, then make art to please herself, not as some Free-Wah flavor of the week. But she couldn't leave just yet. She put her head on Agata's shoulder. She couldn't leave her Aggie.

"Can we go to the spa tonight?" asked Reiko. "I really need to think."

"Definitely." Agata pressed a quick kiss to the side of Reiko's head. "Let me just finish up with Peter over here," she said, taking off her robe. "Then I'm all yours!"

"Aggie—" she began.

"I know." Agata ran to get her purse. "But we're in the middle of a complicated scene. We should be done in a couple of hours. Don't stress. How about you take my card and get started without me?"

Reiko stood frozen as Agata pushed the glossy black credit card into her slack hand.

"Aggie, no," she said softly, putting the card down on the counter.

"Oh, you're right," she said, grabbing her purse again. "They might ask for a signature." She took out her mobile wallet and practically threw it in front of Reiko. Then she heard the all too familiar words, said in the exact same way, that Agata spoke to every shopgirl, every spa attendant, every doorman or valet or bartender of any place they patronized together.

"Thank you so much!" Agata chirped, then ran back into the bedroom and closed the door.

Softly, but growing louder with each passing moment, the little moans started up again from the next room. Reiko paced the living room, feeling sick and gut-punched, rejected by Agata, by Elena, by the university, by the Middle, by the whole world. Should she stay here and take on the debt for a chance at a bright future in computer science? How could she face her family? And if everyone was mortgaging their future on expensive education in the hopes of landing a high-paying job, then the market would be very crowded indeed. She was a top student, but there were others here who were as excellent. And this was just one program at one university. What about the other kids from colleges she didn't even know about? Maybe she would never make her money back. Reiko looked around the apartment. It was filled with Agata's belongings. Agata had a whole rack of high-quality designer dresses that she never wore, eschewing her Above threads for thrift-store finds and vintage boots. An anger snaked up from the pit of her insides, a terrifying, secret rage. She was no longer angry at the registrar or out-of-touch Elhisa. She was angry at Agata. At all of the lazy Above and Middle kids clogging up her university with their sloth, fucking full-time and studying as an intermittent hobby. Reiko looked down at Agata's credit card. It was so small, yet so powerful, the solid black like falling into a void. This object that opened every door. Agata never worried about anything—money smoothed her life into a dreamy decadence with no consequences. And she was generous with Reiko, but suddenly that generosity made her furious. Why should Reiko, who worked so hard and was so goddamn smart, have to leech off of someone like Agata, who just happened to be born Above? If people got rich based on how hard they worked, then Mama should be a millionaire, Papa swimming in jewels. Grandma should reside in a castle.

Reiko was seized by an idea, but it was hazy, ill-formed, more like a mirage. The vision in her mind was a swollen tick, sucking on the leg of some unsuspecting animal. She took out her sonic cypher and attached it to both Agata's mobile wallet and her own. She watched her creation spit out streams of numbers and ratios; after a few minutes, she saw Agata's wallet unlock and flash green, as if Reiko had punched in the passcode. She took a long, deep breath. The two devices were speaking to each other now, through her universal translator. It was just like she had imagined, but never for this purpose. With the press of a few simple commands, Reiko linked the two unlocked accounts, just to see if she could. She trembled—it was so easy. She looked at the routing number. This was the account from which all the money poured. But would it be possible to modify the mobile wallet accounts so they would both appear on Reiko's but not on Agata's, like a one-way mirror? She made a quick patch of new code and restarted both devices.

Reiko grabbed a beer from the fridge and sat down on the couch, her body lightly humming. Finally, after what felt like a very long minute, her viewscreen turned on again. She peered at her screen into Agata's bank account. Breathing hard, she got up and checked Agata's mobile wallet—there was only one account on the screen. She returned it to her roommate's purse and sat back down on the couch.

Reiko looked through Agata's account from the privacy of her own screen. She wasn't planning to steal anything; she was just curious. Oh, the stupid things this girl bought. Sometimes she went to the water café two or three times a day when their fridge was full of the exact same infusions. Expensive record collections, books she didn't read, art supplies she didn't use, concerts and trips and shopping galore, massages, teeth whitening, hair treatments. It took a lot of money to look this poor. There was a transfer of funds every month on a set schedule. And no matter what Agata spent, her cup was refilled to the same level. As she sat and sipped her beer, Reiko felt a little tendril touching Agata's account. And it would still be touching her while they studied and laughed and drank bad wine together. If she did steal from her, Agata wouldn't even notice. Suddenly Reiko felt the unfamiliar pull of deep arousal. She took another swallow of cold beer and unbuttoned her pants.

Reiko slid her hand past her underwear to discover that she was wet. Slowly she stroked her swollen sex to the sounds of Agata and Peter in the next room. She wasn't pretending she was Peter or Agata. She was something else, a third thing—an entity all around them, like smoke or fog. Like God. Reiko climaxed long and hard, her leg shaking, her expression as if she were in great pain.

9.

Lina answered the door in her nightclothes. In the lamplight, she looked rather old. "What's wrong?"

Beatrice, hastily packed knapsack at her side, flung herself into Lina's arms and cried. The whole story poured forth in teary rambles—Georgina, falling in love, her rejection of Beatrice's cooking, destroying her beloved handwritten recipe book.

Lina looked up and down the deserted street, clicked her tongue, then pulled her inside. "Stupid girl," she said. "Come on."

Beatrice followed her, not into the bookstore but upstairs to her own apartment, which Lina had never taken her to before. The kettle was already boiling.

As they held their steaming cups, Lina looked at her seriously over her wire-frame glasses. "Little mouse," she said, "my condolences for your broken heart. But you're a fiery one. You'll fall in love many times before the moons collide."

"I'm such a fool."

"You're living in the Devil's Butthole!" she shouted. "Your world is the size of a peanut on this already shrinking planet! The land is disappearing as it is, so we're living practically on top of each other. Why make your world even smaller?" Lina looked her straight in the eye. "There's another place for you." She straightened up, proudly puffing out her chest. "A place where you can learn how to cook, if you still want that."

Beatrice gasped. "Where?"

Lina looked at Beatrice in her usual way, like she was an idiot. "In the city, of course." She drained her mug. "I can't answer any more of your questions. At first, when you stopped coming around so much, I thought you were staying away so as to not hurt my poor feelings. I know I can't help you much nowadays." She coughed. "But lately I had wondered if you'd been found out and sent away."

Beatrice wrinkled her nose. "Sent where?"

"You think you're so special? There are others like you. You've had classmates disappear for ages, haven't you? For these so-called retreats?"

Beatrice nodded. After Leroy, she'd noticed it all the time. Adults had their versions of these retreats as well. She'd had neighbors who seemed to spend more time away in "self-reflection" than at home.

Lina leaned in close. "They stuff you in a zeppelin and carry you away," she said. "To starve you and sweat you out in the sauna. To brainwash you. Force you to take the yellow pill. Or," she said, her voice dropping, "I've heard on the wind that there's a new implant."

"My parents wouldn't do that. . . . Would they?" Lina sounded like she was talking about the Night Witch or restaurants for cannibals. If Beatrice hadn't just heard about the surgical yellow pill herself, she would have dismissed these ramblings as conspiracy theory. She hung her head. "Lina, can you ever forgive me?"

Lina flapped a hand at her, a gesture Beatrice now knew meant she was embarrassed, her attempt to shoo away the feelings. "You silly goose! Are you hungry? Let me make you some food."

While Lina cooked, Beatrice looked around the apartment. It was shabby but well-kept, with a threadbare floral couch, a wooden dinner table with matching chairs, and a giant, ancient-looking television. The screen was off, but string music played from the old speaker. It sounded as if it were coming from far away. She studied a bookcase crammed with a wide array of books the likes of which she had never seen—ones with incredibly fine text and no pictures. Not recipe books, but more akin to the novels her mother read. She spotted the thick, musty book that Lina had been reading the first time Beatrice entered her store. She took it down from the shelf.

"*The Kitchen Girl*," she said aloud.

"Written over a thousand years ago," said Lina from the next room. "It's real paper, you see, from trees! Not the textile byproduct we use nowadays."

"What is it?"

Lina came out to the table, holding two steaming bowls of food. "It's a lot of different things. A recipe book, for one. But also a diary and a love story." She smiled, as if pleased with herself. "And owning a copy is in itself illegal." She set the bowls on the table and motioned for Beatrice to sit.

Beatrice squinted. "An illegal book? I've never heard of such a thing." Even the wares in the bookstore, while very taboo, were not illegal. There was no penalty for owning such things except for social disgrace.

"Eat while it's hot."

The meal was simple—a perfectly soft-boiled egg, its insides like a little sun, over sautéed greens and some kind of nutty, fluffy grain. It was delicious.

Beatrice looked at her friend for a long moment.

"What, you don't like it?"

"All these months together, we've talked for days about food but never cooked it for each other." She pushed at the grains with her fork. "Georgina shared my family meal today." Beatrice laughed sadly. "Before today, I'd never shared food with anyone other than Mama and Papa. And now two people outside my family have seen me eat!"

"You need to think about what you want. You can't stay here with me, little mouse. And anyway, I have nothing more to teach you." Lina took off her glasses and rubbed her eyes. "This old army cook is tapped dry."

"I never told you," Beatrice said softly. "I found asparagus growing out by the tree maze. Straight from the earth, like a finger." She had never cooked those precious stems. They'd sat in the bottom of her bag, forgotten, until she found them more than a week later, slimy with rot. In falling in love with Georgina, she realized, she had betrayed herself.

"Oh yes," said Lina, blinking thoughtfully. "The Valley used to be quite the producer of crops, including asparagus."

"But why are they still there?"

"Seeds blow, little mouse. That's their nature. Try as the company might to control them, they will travel, eaten by a bird and expelled, or carried by the wind and the rain."

"I'm sorry I was gone for so long," started Beatrice. "You mean so much to me—"

Lina waved her hand. "Far be it for me to begrudge a young person falling in love." She stood abruptly. "I need to make a call."

As Lina murmured to someone in the kitchen, Beatrice let her eyes drift back to the bookshelf. Next to several other knickknacks was a framed picture of a girl at her high school graduation, wearing a sash and holding flowers. She looked like Lina.

Lina came back from the kitchen looking tense.

"Is this you?" asked Beatrice, pointing to the photograph. "You look beautiful."

She shook her head. "That's my daughter, Risa. She's a pretty one—like you. I never had the burden of beauty."

"My mother says the same thing to me." Why did all these women think being beautiful was a bad thing? She'd always thought just the opposite. "Where's your daughter now?"

"She's in the Valley, but not in Seagate. A neighboring town."

"It's nice that you're so close."

Lina sat across from Beatrice, her tone curt. "It's not nice. We don't speak. Or rather, she doesn't speak to me. Do you understand? Because of who I am. How I live." Lina took her hand. "We have to make some choices. Now, little mouse." Lina looked at Beatrice over her wire-frame glasses. "There's a place you can go to learn the art of cooking. You will be warm and fed and safe." Her mentor's watery, pale-blue eyes bored into hers. "Do you want that?"

"It's all I want in this world."

Lina's brows knit in agitation. "But you could wait a year. Keep your head down and leave Seagate freely when you turn eighteen. What do you think of that?"

So much could happen in a year! "What if they make me get the implant?" She gestured to her mostly empty bowl. "What if I can never enjoy food again?"

Lina glanced at her sideways. "The birth-control implant only works for ten years—maybe it's like that, not permanent. Or perhaps you could get it removed."

Beatrice shook her head. The resolve that had formed within

her became an invisible armor around her chest. She was always going to leave Seagate. She had been in the process of leaving for years. "I'm ready, Lina."

"Are you ready to leave tonight?"

"Yes. Tonight."

Lina let out a big sigh. "All right, then." She pushed up her glasses. "Brave girl. I lied when I said I had nothing left to teach you. Before you go, let me show you how to cook an egg." Beatrice followed Lina into the kitchen.

Two hours later, Beatrice had learned how to fry, then poach, then soft-boil an egg, before the lesson was interrupted by a sharp knock at the door below.

"Some say there are a hundred different ways to cook an egg, but we're out of time." Lina looked at her watch. "Are you ready to travel, little seed, to parts yet unknown?" Her eyes grew glassy and soft. "If I were younger, I'd come with you."

Beatrice felt her heart jump into her throat. "Oh, please come with me!"

Lina shook her head. "My place is here." She took her by the shoulders. "This is your adventure."

After a moment, Beatrice bent to pick up her small bag and threw it over her shoulder, hands trembling. Leaving Lina, especially after abandoning her so callously for Georgina, seemed like too much to bear. There were so many things she wanted to ask her, to tell her. "I'll write to you," she said. "I'll call!"

"It's best if you don't. Here. This belongs to you." Lina pressed something cold into Beatrice's hand. She opened her palm. It was her mother's necklace. "Keep that hidden."

The bell rang.

"My real name is Beatrice," she whispered.

"My name is, and has always been, Lina," said the bookshop

lady. She gave Beatrice a rough squeeze. "After you turn eighteen, look me up. They can't get you then; you'll be an adult. Wait—" Lina crossed to the bookshelf and took down her copy of *The Kitchen Girl.* "It's yours now. Take it." Lina kissed her forehead. "Savor and enjoy it—it's my gift to you. And keep it hidden! I know you know how."

Beatrice accepted the book and offered Lina her other hand. The women walked downstairs together. The man in the foyer was short, round, and balding, with tan, unctuous skin and a large mustache. Papa would have described him as a used hot air balloon salesman. Beatrice looked closer at his face and realized he must be Free-Wah—there was a ridge on his upper forehead.

"This is Walter," Lina said. "He's going to look out for you from now on."

The man presented her with papers. "Ms. Tabitha Green, lovely to meet you! Here are your birth certificate and travel papers. It was kind of you to visit your aunt in the Valley, but now we must get home to the Middle." He glanced at the watch on his wrist. "Ladies, time is of the essence."

Beatrice turned to Lina. "Thank you," she said simply.

"Make me proud, Tabitha," she said with her crooked smile. "Now get out of here. I need my beauty sleep." Beatrice turned away, but not before she caught the gesture of Lina taking off her glasses to wipe her eyes.

The other passengers on the airship were businesspeople and practiced travelers, from the looks of it—none of them gazed out the windows or seemed impressed by the polished silver zeppelin with its shiny molded seats. A bored-looking guard checked their papers and gave Beatrice's new travel pass a stamp without a second glance.

Beatrice pressed her face to the glass. Her town looked very small from above, the winding rows of neat identical houses laid out like dominos by some careful hand. She quickly gave up looking for her school, her house, and all the places where she and Georgina had ever made love, distracted by the glittering lights coming into view ahead.

"So that's the big city," whispered Beatrice at the towers crushed together all along the waterfront. She had seen this view from afar many times on hover cruises with her family. It certainly hadn't looked like much.

The man called Walter snorted, then spoke in a low voice. "That's the Bastian, where the poor folk live. They're practically below sea level. See? They travel by boat."

Beatrice squinted at the shoreline, wondering about the neighborhood where Father Alvarez had grown up. A figure navigated the dark canal in a small, narrow boat. It looked like he was delivering newspapers. Walter pointed beyond the water to hills in the distance. "And you can't see it now, but way out there is farmland, soybean country, where Ahinga farmers grow most of the city's food." Beatrice looked back. Her whole town suddenly looked small and dim, with few lights. It was only slightly brighter than the farmland, and much smaller. "There," whispered Walter, pointing up toward higher ground, far above. New levels of the city appeared before them as the dirigible rose higher, streets and buildings appearing to float, as if suspended on a huge platform in the air. "You see that big patch of green? That's a park close to my street. That's where we're going. The Middle, for good, hardworking entrepreneurs like me, and now you, Ms. Green."

The towers of the city, in all their colorful glory, were illuminated by a bevy of lights, everything as clear as if it were day. As the dirigible drew closer to the ground, Beatrice was delighted to see the lovely rows of townhouses with their high, majestic stoops of marble and stone, the streets lined with trees. But the houses were unique, not all the same color and material like in Seagate. They seemed to delight in their difference. Under a streetlamp, Beatrice could make out a tall woman strolling in a bright, open cape, her breasts smooth and gleaming in the lamplight, nipples removed, just like someone on television. Father Alvarez would preach about this kind of rich city woman who modified herself to pretend she was closer to angel than animal. Women who did not give birth or lactate, whose breasts had no function, only form. Father A had preached that body modification as a substitute for prayer and penance was a shortcut, like ingesting a big meal and then throwing it up.

"That must be a very wealthy neighborhood," she said.

"Oh, child," he said. "Look up."

Beatrice pushed her face closer to the window and looked up to the sky above. There she saw the transparent gleaming orbs, spiraling higher and higher, like helium balloons. It was impossible to tell how large they were, as they seemed both impossibly close and desperately far away, extending up endlessly into the night sky.

"What are those?" Beatrice asked.

"That's Above," he said. "Where the truly rich live."

Beatrice tried to keep her voice even. "So there really is a place where people never touch the ground, like angels?"

Walter laughed without mirth. "I don't know about angels," he said. "But they certainly loom over us."

10.

Reiko went to an upscale bar on the first floor of a hotel. Agata had taken her here once before—it was a place she liked when in a certain mood, away from the noise of the university. It was frequented by students and businessmen alike. They made very strong cocktails. Reiko sat at the bar, body still humming. She had brought her own mobile wallet, but now there was another account below hers, staring at Reiko, daring her to use it. She ordered her drink from the bartender and chose the secondary account—Agata's—from the tiny screen. Then she held her wallet up to the sensor and waited. It was accepted with a low beep. She looked at the screen and saw the charge of her expensive cocktail.

Reiko sipped at her drink thirstily. It had been too easy. One press of a button, and now she was a thief. It didn't matter that Agata would buy her this drink—that she had given Reiko her mobile wallet, in fact, and told her to put things on it. Reiko had left Agata's wallet in her purse on the counter, next to a note that read *GONE OUT TO FUCK, DRINK A BEER, SMOKE 500 CIGARETTES, DRINK ANOTHER BEER—R.*

She hoped that repeating Agata's words from the night with her parents would make her feel bad, but Reiko doubted she'd even remember. Because Agata wasn't a good friend, she realized. She was a selfish friend posing as a good one, just like she was a rich hack posing as artsy and poor. Reiko looked around the bar at the students trying to act posh, the businessmen faking lost youth. She ached to see into their accounts, beneath the veil of social propriety of the Middle.

"Ducat for your thoughts?"

Reiko turned toward the voice. A young businessman sat at the bar in his felted hat and satin robe. He had only a few pips on his collar—she didn't understand what they all represented, but he couldn't be all that rich. "You should watch out for the Night Witch," he said with a smile. "You look young enough to be eaten."

Reiko rolled her eyes. "I'm having a rough night," she said. "Would you please let me wallow in peace?"

"Of course. Just answer me this: What does a big bear do on a frozen pond?"

Her mouth twitched. "What?"

"It breaks the ice!"

Reiko laughed despite the ridiculous, overused pickup line. There was a warmth about him, and his eyes were kind.

"Okay, I'll let you wallow. Have a good night."

She turned her body toward his. "Actually, how bad you are at this is distracting me from my misery."

He motioned for the bartender. "So glad I can be of service. Can I get you a drink?"

She hesitated. He looked about thirty, but Reiko wasn't always good at guessing ages in the Middle.

"If you feel like talking about your night, I'm a pretty good listener."

She studied his plain, friendly face. "I'll be the judge of that."

Reiko's first boyfriend had been a kid named John who was friends with her cousin. They couldn't have been more than twelve years old. One day at school, she heard a rumor that John liked her. The following day, she heard a rumor he had asked her out. And the day after that, she heard that she had said yes. So for three weeks, Reiko was boyfriend-girlfriend with John. He bought her costume jewelry and they kissed twice in her cousin's basement.

Reiko let this stranger buy her a drink, then another after that. She talked to him for a long while, the strength of the cocktails making her warm and chatty. She didn't mention her new sonic cypher, but other than that, she didn't leave much out. She talked to the man at the bar about her terrible fight with Elena, her short-lived tech scholarship, Agata, and how she felt trapped and misunderstood all the time, like there was no place for her. Not on the ground or in the Middle. He listened well, peppering her monologue with insightful questions and making sympathetic sounds in the right places.

The memory of John was a silly one, but the pattern it had set in motion hadn't changed. People pursued Reiko, and she either let herself be carried along by the river of their desire or shunted them if they were unacceptable to her. But she never sought out lovers, because she didn't understand the shape of her own longing.

When he put his hand on her knee and said he had a room at the hotel, she nodded. She wanted to keep talking. She was still wet from her orgasm earlier that evening, and her body felt loose and ready. It would feel nice, to be kissed, to be held, to share a bed with a sympathetic stranger. Reiko went upstairs, sat on the bed, and waited.

The Kitchen Girl

a true story

by Ijo

Before the year of our Lord, when we still kept time by the moons, I was born in a little town by the sea, so small that a bird flying by would miss us. Father was a rice farmer, and Mother was a free diver with hearty lungs and an ear-to-ear smile. She'd regularly come up from the bottom of the ocean with treasures to trade and eat. Father was quieter but just as kind, riding along the gentle waves in his handmade craft and tending to the deepwater rice.

My aunt was a keeper of the old knowledge, a healer, while my uncle ran a kitchen in the middle of town. All my parents' spoils were sent there—the rice of course, but also the scallops and herring, pike and flounder, clams and oysters, and the occasional jellyfish to be stewed or pickled for salad. We spent long, balmy evenings as a family collecting our fishing lines and emptying our nets, as though we were simply opening our palms to receive. Our gifts from the sea were bountiful, and though life was modest in our seaside village, we felt as rich as kings.

Of course, we had never met a king. The few stories we heard of a young princess's impending marriage or a king's foolhardy quest, well—they seemed to us like fairy tales, not stories about real people who could ever affect us or our way of life.

Later I would come to learn a great deal about court intrigue, and certainly more about kings and queens than any poor girl in a fishing village ever had. But that's getting ahead of my story.

It was Uncle who taught me the trade of cooking, and Auntie

who taught me about our plant guardians of both food and medicine. I was born in the middle, one girl among three boys, on a full Blood moon with a Hunter crescent, so I was marked as special. My two older brothers took after my father, as was our way, and became rice farmers and fishermen. I was supposed to follow in the footsteps of my mother, while the youngest of four, whatever sex, was meant for the monastery. Yet my family could never get me out of the kitchen. People said I shucked oysters until my hands were raw at only four years old. Having known many young children now myself, and having worked in kitchens for years, I doubt this story is true. My family was also known for telling marvelously flexible tales, meant more to delight than to inform, or to convey a spiritual truth rather than a literal one. I do remember kneading dough until my arms were thick and fine with muscles. I churned butter from our sweet little goat Ida's fresh milk, and when I grew old enough, Auntie let me go with her to tend the sick in our village and assist her in making poultices and tinctures. Mother and Father were happy, easygoing sorts, so no one sought to pry a child away from what was clearly her true passion. They let me work in Uncle's kitchen, learning all manner of recipes, and my youngest sibling, Eusa, elected to become a free diver to fulfill my mother's place in the village. He was then termed an Ansanga, meaning a man with the soul of a woman—a high compliment. Our family was very blessed.

But this is not a fairy tale, dear reader. We always had waves in our waters during the rainy season, which would destroy Father's crops, so he had to plant anew after the monsoons had ceased. It was no worry for my father—he fished in those seasons, and when he couldn't fish, he mended nets. We were no strangers to tsunamis and floods, and we knew that one day a wave would come that would best our little village. But what were we to do? We were people of the sea. We were not afraid; we loved and respected the sea like our great mother. We sang songs about what to do when the big wave came, how the men should take their boats far, far out into the flat sea before it happened, following the clues from their animal friends. Songs about how the women and children should run to the highest and driest place they could find. We sang these anthems as children, as we played with rocks and traded shells, "When it arrives, do not hesitate! Run so high, run so high! Do not collect the fish on the beach. . . ."

That wave came when I was in the high forest, gathering mushrooms for Uncle's famous fisherman's stew. It was a special dish in honor of my father's birthday, which was in three days. The mushrooms would be simmered very slowly with special herbs for those three days, creating a rich, unctuous broth. Finally, the fruits of the third day's catch would be steamed right before serving and added at the last moment to the broth. Sticky fermented balls of cassava would be presented on the side to soak up the delicious gravy. My mouth waters as I write this—I must be careful not to drip and run my ink! It has been many years since I last tasted such gravy, and perhaps I will not taste it again before I die. I am an old woman now and do not have many meals left in this world. I don't cook so much anymore, but I eat very often, at least in my memory. Now I close my eyes and feel the rich, earthy broth running down my throat.

All those years ago, on the occasion of my father's thirty-fifth birthday, my family never had the chance to eat this delicacy. Father did not see his next birthday, nor did any of my other friends or relatives. My entire village was washed away in the wave. My mother and brothers did not run fast enough. My father's boats, and all the boats in the harbor that day, did not make it out far enough. They were dashed upon the rocks.

In that instant, I became an orphan. My home was gone—my family, my friends. All I had were the clothes on my back and my knowledge of cooking. I knew no other options than to survive on the stories I had heard, bits of knowledge carried by the odd traveler passing through our little town. *The castle is under the three stars bunched together on the horizon like a bud of a flower.* And so, I turned away from the cruel sea, the great mother who had betrayed me, away from the only life I had ever known. I walked a mountain pass and traversed the deep, dark forest. I traveled alone by foot to the castle to seek my fortune, or at least to find respite from certain death alone in the woods. I was fifteen years old.

PART TWO

1.

"Here's your first mistake."

Beatrice rubbed her eyes. It was too early in the morning for Margot. The spiky-haired head chef sounded almost pleased to point out Beatrice's failings.

"Yes, Chef?" she answered weakly.

She folded her arms across her bulky chest. "Look at that trash can. What do you see?"

"Potato peels." Beatrice rubbed her sore hands. "You asked me to peel potatoes. And I did." *One hundred of them. All morning.*

"But you know there's no food waste in my kitchen," said Margot. "I don't know about where you come from, but here, food matters. It's expensive, it's risky to grow, and it's hard to source. So, what are you going to do about it?"

"Next time—"

"No, not next time. *Now.* You're going to pick out all of the potato peels, every single one, and wash them well. And remember— clean water is also a resource, and also something we pay for. Don't overuse it." She sniffed at the trash, thick with slimy beef shanks that had arrived at the restaurant already rotten. "But don't under-use it either."

"Use it perfectly, got it." Beatrice wasn't used to having to ration and heat her water for bathing as well. She had run out this morning yet again. Her fingers were blistered and calloused from weeks of chopping and peeling, her arms tired from stirring and churning. And she hadn't even made a real recipe yet. Margot first trained her apprentices in knife skills and prep work, and each time Beatrice thought she'd mastered a dice or learned a more efficient way to break down cilantro, she was shaken to find she had blundered into another mistake.

Erek, the other apprentice, a lanky, pallid boy, all knees and elbows, cleared his throat meaningfully. He was younger than Beatrice but had been with Margot longer and seemed comfortable with her bullishness.

"Good work otherwise," Margot said gruffly. "When you're done with the peels, make a stock with them."

"Yes, Chef," she said heavily. Margot should've taken the Stecopo seminar How to Motivate Employees (without the Promise of Bonuses or Better Pay). All she'd let Beatrice do for months was chop vegetables, wash dishes, scrub the floors, and make stock. Beatrice shouldn't have thrown the peels away—she should have known better. It was just that potato peels were so . . . ugly, she'd assumed they would be bad to eat. It was difficult to get in the habit of saving things that would certainly have been trash in Seagate.

"Chef Margot, do you have something else to say?" prompted Erek gently.

"Oh, right. We've decided that you're ready," said Margot. "For our meeting today, come up with at least five ideas for potatoes, Tabitha. Be ready in two hours." Margot left the kitchen.

"Yes, Chef!" Beatrice called after her, eyes gleaming. She had never been invited to share ideas at one of their planning meetings before. Whatever the delivery brought, they had to use. This time, it was more potatoes than their root cellar could handle. "Thanks," she whispered to Erek, elbowing him gently in the side.

"Here," he said, pulling up a stool in front of the trash can. "I'll help you sort this out."

Beatrice shook her head. "No, it's my mess. But thank you for sticking up for me."

"She doesn't realize how she sounds. Margot was trained by some old guy at a soup restaurant who didn't let her even chop vegetables for a year. In her mind, she's easy on us!" With his high-pitched, silly laugh trailing behind him, Erek left her alone in the kitchen to deal with her potato skins.

Beatrice sniffed the garbage. In Seagate, no one had ever raised their voice at her or punished her or made her interact with trash. After an hour of picking, sorting, and washing, Beatrice looked at the huge mound of clean potato skins. Time to prepare another stock. She had made plenty this week from onion peels, celery tops, apple cores, woody overgrown zucchinis, a head of broccoli that had gone to seed. The first thing Margot made her do every time they got a shipment was comb through all of the produce and take out what was already unfit for consumption, which at times was a third of what they received. It was disheartening, all that waste, but Margot assured her that stock was an incredibly important ingredient, so the food was never really wasted unless it was rank indeed.

Beatrice took a pat of precious butter and melted it into a deep pot. She chopped an onion in the perfect dice, then dumped it into the melted butter. She fried the onion till it was fragrant but not browned, then added about half of her potato peels. She let them cook down until they were soft, along with a bay leaf and a good pinch of salt. Beatrice added the celery-onion stock she'd made last week, along with a generous swirl of cream. Seasoning with salt and pepper, she added the entire pot to the blender in batches, processing until smooth.

Beatrice tasted her creation and considered. It was missing something. She set the soup to cool and ran out of their row house on Delany Lane, into the street, and down the hill toward the public park. There, along the hedges, she found what she was looking for: soft, fuzzy green leaves with a slight silvery hue. She stripped several stems of their leaves and ran back toward the house, holding her findings in her clean apron.

Margot was on the front porch, her pale, round face looking rather red, hands clenched at her sides.

Margot didn't say a word until they were inside the house. "I was coming to get you for the meeting. But I see you've been having a meeting all by yourself!"

Beatrice stiffened. "I only used the peels," she said. "I promise."

"You're making things very difficult!" shouted Margot.

Beatrice tried not to smile. Margot puffed up like a bird when she got mad. She was scary, but also a little ridiculous.

"I only used the free ingredients," she said gently.

Margot blinked at the pot. "Is that so?"

"Plus one bay leaf, a pat of butter, and about a cup of cream."

Margot peered at her apron. "What's that?"

"Sage. I found it growing outside." Beatrice smiled sweetly. "May I serve you some soup, Chef?"

"At the meeting," Margot grumbled. She stomped into the dining room, muttering about chaos and anarchy and the chain of command.

Beatrice heated a generous slick of oil in a wide pan and fried her freshly washed sage leaves. They crisped up nicely, as she hoped they would. She then crisped up a few of the remaining potato peels as an additional garnish, for texture. In a sudden flurry of inspiration, she opened a jar of pickled apples, an experiment from last season's overflow. She rinsed a few to get rid of the excess vinegar, patted them dry, then minced the apple into a fine relish. She carried the soup pot into the dining room.

Walter, wearing a voluminous orange velour tracksuit that reminded Beatrice of a puppet from a children's show, sat at the table next to Erek, drinking coffee. They were uncharacteristically silent as Beatrice served small bowls of potato peel soup, topped with fried sage, twirls of fried potato skin, and pickled apples.

For a long moment, only the sounds of contented slurping filled the dining room. Then Walter spoke.

"So, potatoes," he started mildly, uncapping his pen. "Our cellar overfloweth! Who wants to go first?"

"I've been reading about a traditional Northern Free-Wah preparation of fermented potato," started Margot.

Erek groaned. Margot's answer to everything was to pickle it.

"But today, I believe Tabitha wants to start," she continued. "She certainly has a lot to contribute."

Was no one going to say anything about her soup? She thought it was lovely and well-balanced. "Uh, yes. Thank you." Beatrice thought about standing up but decided against it. "Potato pancakes topped with beef stew and sour cream! Shepherd's pie with a mashed potato topping. Potato hash with seasonal vegetables. Potato dumplings," she added, "with herbs and butter. Or with tomato gravy, that would be delicious, or floating in a light broth."

"That's three separate ideas, then variations on dumplings," said Margot. "What else've you got?"

"Well," said Beatrice, gesturing to the table, "potato peel soup, with fried sage and pickled apples."

"I like it," said Erek quietly.

Margot looked at her carefully. "Give me more," she said firmly. "And not just mashed potato."

"Sure," said Beatrice. "What about potatoes in small, crunchy cubes, roasted with spices and fat, or oven-fried with lemon, or in a cold salad with pickled vegetables, celery, and hard-boiled eggs?"

Erek applauded. "Well, she took all of my answers! Except chowder. Everyone loves a good fish chowder, don't they?"

"Delicious!" declared Walter, writing it all down as fast as he could. "Perfect on a chilly night." He always agreed with Erek.

"What is it you're not saying?" pressed Margot. "You've been holding out on me."

Beatrice wanted to scream, *I've been holding out on you because you never let me do any real cooking!* Instead, she took a deep breath and replied mildly, "I've been thinking about our issues, how it's hard to get a steady supply of flour and good cream." Sometimes their sources just mysteriously dried up—they could go for weeks without a shipment of flour, or eggs, or cream, or some other staple they normally depended on. Then, when all hope was lost and dessert was fruit compote yet again, the flour suddenly came back, or eggs reappeared, too many to enjoy, and they souffléed everything, savory and sweet. "I know you said no mash, but could mashed potato be a substitute for cream? In desserts, I mean."

Margot frowned in a way that meant she was thinking. "Mashed potatoes," she mused. "They do have a silky mouthfeel and full body, when whipped properly."

Walter, who was always interested in saving money, banged the table with his large fist. "Desserts from potato, that's genius!"

"We'd still need flour," said Erek thoughtfully. "And some dairy, in most things. Otherwise, you'd get a gummy mess. But I could set up a cheesecake, I reckon, with half potato, half dairy.

Truffles," he said, eyes dreamy, for he had quite the sweet tooth, "with potato instead of cream. A fluffy apple cake, sweetened mostly with applesauce . . ." They always had more fruit than they knew what to do with. "It's worth trying, certainly."

"Decadent desserts for a fraction of the price." Walter nodded. "That helps our bottom line!" The last bit he sang out with a flourish: "Saves us moneeey!" Beatrice suppressed a laugh.

"Fruitcake," added Margot. "Write that down, Walter. It'll keep for ages with good brandy or rum."

Erek laughed. "Margot has figured out a way to pickle cake!"

"Ice cream?" asked Beatrice. "Would it set?"

"Potato ice cream!" shouted Walter. "Brilliant!"

This time, Beatrice couldn't hold in her laughter. Walter was no longer the mysterious stranger who had whisked her away from Lina's in the dead of night—he was rather silly, a gentle administrator and a highly unfortunate dresser who prided himself on his long, greasy mustache and immaculately polished shoes.

Erek gesticulated with his spoon. "But when it melts, will it taste too strange? I always think people who wait for their ice cream to melt before eating it are a little sick in the head, but"—he looked up at the ceiling—"they are out there."

"We'll need to experiment," said Margot with the terse clip of a general. "That much is certain." The restaurant was open to the public Thursdays through Saturdays, and only for dinner. It had seemed like lots of time to learn, prep, and plan when Beatrice first came to their little cooking school, but she'd quickly realized that there were enough jobs for at least twice that number of people. Even when she burned the bread and Erek underwashed the greens, there was a high demand for a restaurant where people could sit and eat together without privacy screens or separation booths.

"We're starting Operation Dessert Potato," exclaimed Walter. "Remember the ground rules, people! Small batches! Write down your experiments as you go. Measure, for God's sake."

"Walter's right—it's no good if it's delicious and we can't remember how to reproduce it. The best part is," Margot said, looking excitedly at her companions, "we can mince and dehydrate potatoes in bulk. We could continue substituting dried, flaked potatoes in our desserts all season long, and no one will be the wiser!" Both Erek and Beatrice shuddered at the words *mince* and *bulk*— they knew who would get that lovely job.

Walter lifted his soup spoon, triumphant. "To Tabitha!" he shouted.

Erek raised his bowl, then drank from it. "Hear! Hear!"

"To Tabitha," said Margot. Beatrice pinked. "Now, go get prepped. We're serving this soup tonight. Add in more whole chunks of potato—people don't come here for purée, they want to chew. You'll need to make it, while you do all of your other work." Margot stood up. "You certainly like making things hard for yourself."

"Yes, Chef," Beatrice called after her. "Thank you, Chef!"

Margot walked out, and Erek and Walter patted her on the back. "Good girl," said Walter. "What a show!"

"When you served that soup, I thought she was going to murder you," said Erek brightly.

Beatrice couldn't stop smiling. "I can't believe we're putting my recipe on the menu tonight," she squealed. "I cooked!"

Erek grinned. "Welcome to the fun part, Tabitha. You made it!"

———

That night their patrons stayed until well past one in the morning, demanding soup and bread, wine and cheese. Beatrice's easy confidence cracked like an egg. She burned her hand when her oven mitt slipped as she was taking out some overdone pumpkin seeds. She struggled to remember what orders were for which table and who needed them first. She left table four waiting for their salads for over thirty minutes while she labored over piping perfect whipped-cream flowers on an apple tart. She rushed her potato peel soup, and it wasn't as savory this time. She almost cried from disappointment at the flatness of the flavors, the complete ordinariness of her once-wonderful creation. Lost in self-doubt and misery, Beatrice forgot that the stove was still on. She scorched the bottom of the soup pot.

Margot came to Beatrice's station, her nostrils flaring. "It burned," she said. It wasn't a question. Beatrice felt her eyes grow large with tears. She couldn't trust herself to speak. "Don't stir it," Margot grunted. "You'll dredge up the burned bits." The chef took out a large empty pot and carefully poured the soup in. Then she dipped in a spoon and tasted it thoughtfully. She squeezed in one whole lemon's worth of juice, then added red pepper flakes and a few more hearty cranks of black pepper. On the menu, next to the soup offering, she wrote the words *Smoky lemon potato soup, with apple and sage.*

"You're serving it anyway?" cried Beatrice. "But it's burned!"

Margot rolled her eyes. "Taste it." Beatrice grabbed a spoon and tasted. It was a different soup, certainly, from the one she had labored over so lovingly, but it wasn't bad. This version was perhaps even better than her own bland re-creation of the original soup. She bowed her head. "Listen," Margot said. "Working in a kitchen is equal parts inspiration, perspiration, and improvisation. Even if you hadn't let the bottom burn, it wasn't as good as the first time, was it? You have to be able to repeat your successes, again and again. Take notes! Sometimes you won't have time to taste and adjust, taste and adjust. We'll get a rush, and Walter will be the one caramelizing the onions. You need to be able to give over control, to delegate."

Beatrice wiped her eyes. "Like you're doing now."

"Now go wash your hands. You're getting snot all over my kitchen."

Beatrice wanted to thank her, not just for fixing the soup, but for everything—for taking her in when she had nowhere to go, for teaching her. But table seven needed all new plates, because they'd decided to fuck on top of the entrées instead of eating them, and now they were hungry. Beatrice yawned. She would sleep well tonight.

Later that night, as Beatrice arranged the bins of compost and trash to be sorted, some compost fell on her shoe. It landed in such a way that a sprinkling of coffee grounds and a slice of wet banana peel slipped right where her sock met her ankle with a dreadful squish. She groaned. Yet, kneeling on the ground to pick the sludge out of her sock, Beatrice felt a strange glowing in her chest, as if someone had turned a light on. This was what she wanted to do. This was how she wished to spend all her days and nights. The dirt, the grime, the frustration—it was all more than worth it. Every bit of it, even the annoyance of curdling a sauce, the pain of burning her hand, every single trial was worth it. Margot, so full of piss and vinegar, was worth it. So was Walter, all bluster and tomfoolery, and slow but sweet Erek. Because each of them was working toward the same goal—to make exceptional food in a place where all people were welcome to eat. Her eyes welled with happy tears. Then Margot yelled at her to shake her ass, and she stood, picked up the rest of the trash and compost, and hauled it to the bins outside. The feeling was still there, the one of perfect rightness, as she breathed in the night, stars and moons glowing overhead. Then she heard it.

"Hey, Fatty!" some guy, presumably ambling home from the pub, called to her from across the street. "*Pssst*," he hissed, then followed it up with, "Hey, Fatty, good night!" before disappearing around the corner, laughing.

Beatrice looked down at her body. No one had ever used such a word to describe her before. Stung and deflated, she went back inside.

Margot cooked a "family dinner" most days before service began, turning the meal into a lesson in real time. She would give a gruff little speech about the techniques used in her typically simple but very satisfying dishes. For today's supper, Margot had re-created a traditional Free-Wah soup her mentor had been famous for in his restaurant in the Upper Bastian. A broth simmered slowly for several days, full to the brim of various leftover bits of meats, ends of carrots, celery innards, rinds and stems and garlic husks. Eventually the broth was strained, and huge amounts of cabbage, wild onion, and soft soybean hunks were added back in, as well as hand-pulled noodles, light yet delightfully chewy. What made the soup quite special, however, was that its main ingredient was huge filets of fried fish.

"Before refrigeration," said Margot, serving up several bowls, "you could either salt your fish or fry it to keep it fresh longer." She raised an eyebrow at Erek. "Not everything needs to be pickled." Beatrice bit into the fish and groaned. It had become a tasty sponge for the broth, each bite still crunchy, yet swollen with soup. The fish tangled with cabbage and bits of tofu, circled by ribbons of fresh, springy noodles and floating black garlic. Each bite was uniquely delicious and distinct from the next as the flavors kept building, changing, complicating. It was the most exciting thing

Beatrice had ever eaten. "Tomorrow, Erek and Tabitha, I want you in the kitchen bright and early. We're making noodles—some to serve fresh, others to dry for the weeks ahead. It will be a long day, so prepare accordingly. We'll be setting up the next round of black garlic as well."

The slow-preserved garlic was tar-black, complex yet mellow, and tasted almost syrupy, like balsamic vinegar. From her reading, Beatrice had learned that it took almost three weeks to prepare and made the whole room smell like heaven. "I can't wait to learn how to do that!"

Margot looked at her seriously, but her eyes twinkled in a way that Beatrice had come to learn meant she was pleased. "Things will get messy. Dress prepared to be covered in flour."

Erek slurped his soup. "I could eat noodles every day and die happy."

Walter nodded. "Indeed. Margot, my compliments to the chef! And the fish is tender yet still oh-so-crispy. Iiiiiimpressive!" he sang out, long and loud, brandishing his spoon.

"It was many years of study before I was able to make these noodles. I was very proud when Chef Wian decided to teach me."

"May I have some more?" asked Beatrice.

"All the real cooking happens below the Middle." Margot, now fully grinning, ladled her another bowl. "I'll give you a book of this style of Free-Wah cuisine, Tabitha. You're ready for it." It was perhaps the nicest thing Margot had ever said to her.

Beatrice pushed back from the table and placed a hand on her stomach, satisfied. Then she frowned, grabbing at the excess flesh she found there. Shame spread inside of her, thick and hot as melted wax. She excused herself to the restroom. Standing over the toilet, she could hear the nuns' voices in her head, announcing her weight for all to hear. How many pounds had she gained since coming to the underground restaurant? Twenty? Thirty? More?

Fatty.

She shook her head. No matter. She knew what she needed to do. Hunching over, Beatrice slipped her fingers into her throat and pressed down.

The soup didn't taste very good coming back up. When she had thrown up so much she was only tasting bile, Beatrice wiped down the toilet twice (she was often the one who had to clean it anyway). She exited the stall to find Margot standing by the sink with her arms crossed.

"If you're going to eat the food I make for you," she said slowly, "you are never to do that again. Do you understand me? You never have to finish your plate or go for more, but you will *not* throw up my food."

"But—" started Beatrice.

"No," said Margot, crossing toward her. There was something sharp, almost pleading in her eyes. "Don't you understand? You think you've run away from all that, but you haven't. Not until you stop doing this bullshit." Margot wetted a paper towel and passed it to Beatrice. "As long as you punish yourself for having a body, it doesn't matter where you go. You could fly to the moons and not be free." She narrowed her eyes. "Clean up." She left the bathroom.

Beatrice wiped her eyes and mouth. Later that evening, as they worked silently together at the chopping station, Margot grated fresh ginger into a mug with a sprig of mint, then topped it with boiling water. She gave the tisane to Beatrice without a word. Beatrice's stomach, which had been churning, was very grateful. They never spoke of it again.

———

Beatrice looked at herself in the flimsy full-length mirror leaning against the bedroom wall. It was undeniable—she was no longer thin. She could practically hear the man on the street—his hiss, his derisive jeer. *Fatty.* The one dress she'd brought with her from Seagate was stuffed in a drawer. Walter had taken Beatrice to a clothing store where everything was garish and brightly patterned, in line with his taste, but Beatrice had managed to find a few simpler garments there. Alone in her little bed, she sometimes ran her hands over her body like a lover, thinking about touching soft Georgina or some other faceless person who wore their weight like a gorgeous cloak. But when she looked in the mirror, she no longer found herself beautiful. Why was it that she could be attracted to a larger body on someone else, but not accept it for herself? The voices in her head said she was impure, lazy, disgusting. She used to be pretty, they said, and she'd thrown it all away. Some days she made plans to eat only enough to taste her creations, but her body demanded more. She worked hard all day, six days a week, with no pills to mellow out her moods or abate her hunger. If she kept gaining weight at this rate, her own parents wouldn't recognize her if she passed them on the street.

And yet, she lived in a new kind of paradise. Margot brought Beatrice bags of books with only a sharp look and a grunt for an explanation—books on baking, fermentation, cooking with local herbs, even a slim treatise on foraging in urban centers. Glorious books she didn't have to copy and return—books to study, to keep stacked by her bedside, to thumb through in the morning as she woke up with her coffee, or to put her to sleep at night to fragrant, delicious dreams. She decided to focus on the good and let go of the rest, as Papa would advise. Beatrice covered her bedroom mirror with a sheet, blocking out her own reflection.

———

On one particularly long evening, a raucous group of about ten finely dressed persons turned their multicourse meal into a proper orgy, fucking and sucking as the salads were cleared away and the main course was about to be served. Margot grabbed a half-open bottle of wine from the counter, filled her slim tobacco pipe, and started for the back door. Then she hesitated for a moment, turned back, and gave a single motion for Beatrice to follow.

They stood out back by the trash cans. It was cold enough to see their breath. "If Walter thinks I'm going to let those people lick my soufflé off of each other's butts, he's in for a rude awakening. I won't serve them." Margot took a swig from the bottle. "It's unprofessional and unsanitary. Even more than usual." Then she passed the wine to Beatrice. "Nothing to say? Or are you shocked that I'm drinking on the job? I can never tell with you."

Beatrice took a short swig from the bottle and passed it back. "Walter won't try to stop them?"

"He might, if just to sell them a private room. That man only cares about his bottom line." She took a hard swallow. "This is the one place where sex is supposed to be off the menu. The one place in the whole goddamn city! They won't even let us have that."

Backlit by the streetlight, the tiny light-blond hairs along the side of Margot's well-defined jaw were visible. Beatrice found her attractive, in a stout, rough way, with her crew cut and her thick neck. "Do you have a lover, Margot?" She imagined Margot going for long motorcycle rides in the countryside with an equally tough-looking woman. Or maybe she was into men, stuffing wimpy-looking ones into her sidecar, like on *Boy Meat*.

Margot looked at Beatrice like she had said something rude, which was strange, because it was such an ordinary question. "Let's get back to work." They went inside to assemble and dress the salads for table four. Beatrice saw Walter lead a conga line of half-dressed men and women down the hall toward the private dining room. So he'd managed to corral them away from the other patrons after all. Walter slapped a man's pert behind as they danced off, then poked his sweaty head into the kitchen.

"I've sequestered the cannibals!" he cried. Then his tone sobered. "I'll be their waiter for the evening. Don't let Erek near those people—they might try to eat him!" Then he laughed his wild laugh, hoisted the lamb tagine overhead, and strode back into the dining room, singing a wordless, warbling tune over the din of voices.

———

There were strange holdovers from her Seagate days. When she had been living with Walter for about six months, he took her and Erek for doctor's visits and teeth cleanings. The mild doctor said she was in perfect health and suggested Beatrice take a multivitamin, especially for bone health. Shaken, she went home and got into bed, pulled the covers up, and stayed there until it was time for work the next morning. It felt so silly to spiral just because a doctor told her to take a vitamin. But it was so much easier to live in absolutes— Seagate bad, city good. Food good, vitamins bad.

But the city itself was a strange mélange of beauty and ugliness. It was common here to see a person in filthy rags asleep in front of a gorgeous building. The first time Beatrice saw this, she stopped walking with Erek to ask if they needed help. Erek looked at her as if she had grown a second head before ushering her along.

Garbage was stacked on the street for regular pickup, but sometimes it was overlooked by overwhelmed city workers, or the collectors were on strike, or a storm had taken out transportation, until it stank and attracted flies and occasionally spilled out onto the sidewalk.

Most of the women she'd met here seemed normal, like Margot—confident and self-assured, whether they wore clothes straight out of Seagate or see-through gossamer jumpsuits and five-inch heels. But almost every night there would be some woman in the restaurant dripping with jewelry, hair in a high tower, breasts bare and without nipples, who smiled more than spoke and tittered like a child, even though she was certainly an adult. Their dates were always businessmen in gold frocks and felted hats, without exception older. It made no sense to Beatrice. How could someone purport to worship the Divine Mother, then turn around to treat women as objects? How could any self-respecting woman allow herself to be paraded around like a doll? Erek even told her that some of the women they saw on the street in fantastical garb were nuns for nightly hire, a strange perversion of the blessed communion between clergy and parishioners. Beatrice found this monstrous.

But each night in her dreams, Beatrice was always back in Seagate. Some of these dreams were like the world's most benign nightmares. In them, Beatrice found herself sitting on the couch with her parents, listening to their calm murmur of conversation, the television low and familiar in the background. Then she would jolt into half-consciousness—*I need to leave this place. How did I end up back here?* She would awake in a cold sweat, scanning the room to remind herself of how far she had come. Her books, her few articles of clothing. Her freedom.

But the more pleasant the dreams of Seagate, the greater the pain upon waking. Sometimes they featured the sounds of the sea, the wide-open spaces. She missed the feeling of a church service—that warm, holy certainty. She sometimes heard murmurs of interest in Seagate from those who patronized the restaurant. Their eyes were open about what was at stake—the yellow pill and new implant, not having to worry anymore about anything, not even hunger. It was approached almost like a silly game you played with friends at a slumber party. If you could live in paradise but you had to give up something essential, would you do it? What would you trade to live an easy life?

On the TV, two very different-looking women stood together on a stage, facing a panel of judges. One was nude, with long natural hair and a fresh, clean face, while the other wore the most outlandish garb Beatrice had ever seen—a series of translucent hoops around her body that moved with her, a cape of dark feathers, and, inexplicably, a full-face mask of silver sequins. The nude, barefaced woman spoke earnestly into the camera.

"I'm here because I believe in my intimacy. I believe it's the most profound way to connect to God. When the judges share sex with me, they feel that intention. I'm not putting on a show. There aren't sparklers, there isn't a dance routine. Vivica," she said, gesturing to the woman in the bizarre costume, "has a completely different approach from mine. And I'm not putting her down. Both are valid. My sex is a form of prayer." She smiled winningly at the judges. "And that is why I'm going to be the World's Best Lover."

Beatrice found herself rooting for the Seagate-type girl, then asked Erek to change the station.

Erek nodded. "These shows are so formulaic! I swear, there hasn't been any good reality TV in twenty years." He clicked through a couple dozen channels. "Anyway," he said brightly, taking a sip of coffee. "As I was saying, I'm lucky. It's much easier for me than for you. My dad died and my mum gave me up, so I don't have to worry about anyone being mad at me for cooking."

They were in the den, the little room on the third floor of the house that contained a gloriously ratty couch and a television old enough to rival Lina's set. Beatrice, who couldn't keep out of the kitchen even on her day off, had decided to experiment with sweet potato cinnamon rolls, which made for a lovely breakfast spread on the chipped coffee table. The rain was coming down in droves, the wind blowing shingles off the roof. Even the Loop had closed down for a weather advisory. But she couldn't complain, not when there were fresh warm buns topped with orange icing sugar and a pot of piping-hot coffee. Beatrice had just finished sharing her sob story of Georgina (leaving out all details that could connect her to Seagate or her former life) when Erek surprised her by mentioning that he was an orphan of a kind. This made Beatrice feel foolish for her melodramatic story. At least both her parents were alive, as far as she knew.

Erek flipped on a rerun of *Looking Good, Grandma!*, a reality series where grandmothers—and the occasional grandfather— re-created nude photographs from their younger years. In this episode, the grandmother, Mary Jane, explained to her grandkids how she'd taken these pictures for her first real love, a soldier who never made it back from the war.

"I'm sorry about your dad," Beatrice said gently. "And your mom too, in a different way."

He picked at his breakfast. "She was one of those women where everything she ate was sucked out of her bum. Constantly getting colonics. Made it rather unpleasant to share a household. I'm right lucky I had Walter to take me in." On the television screen, Mary Jane went to the beauty salon to have her nails painted, hair and makeup done up to match the style of the photographs. The stylist told a ribald joke, and she laughed. Erek took a big bite. "Walter's my uncle, you know," he said, his mouth full.

Beatrice almost choked on her roll. "What?"

He swallowed. "Yep. Without him, I would be quite the sob

story." Now that he mentioned it, there was a resemblance between Erek and Walter—or would be if Walter were younger, leaner, taller, not so hairy, and significantly more snaggletoothed. They were both a bit unfortunate-looking, in different ways. She tried not to stare at Erek's forehead seeking the telltale Free-Wah ridge by his hairline. If it was there, it was very slight.

"So Walter is your father's brother?"

Erek shook his head. "Nah, he's my mother's uncle. My mother's bum uncle, to be specific, the one she always warned me about. I was never allowed to be in a room alone with Walter, much less visit him at his house of ill repute. So mark my surprise when she left town and he picked up the pieces. Honestly, my first few weeks here, I was terrified. I thought he was going to butcher me and serve me to the highest-paying customer!"

Beatrice scoffed. "That's ridiculous."

Erek looked at her sideways with his gray, watery eyes. "That's what people like to say about us, Tabitha. That we're so obsessed with food, we'll consume anything, people included. Get used to it now, 'cause you'll be hearing the rumor a lot."

Beatrice placed the sweet bun down on her plate, repulsed. "Reminds me of the stories of the Night Witch."

Erek frowned. "Some of the guests are just here for the thrill. To see if we really serve people." He shrugged. "Not most of them. But a few."

"Maybe we should only serve vegetables," Beatrice said with a laugh.

But Erek only looked pensive. "Not a bad idea. Hard to get reliable meat deliveries anyway." Last week's shipment of ground meat had been putrid, gray green, and growing fuzz. That night, they'd had to scramble to find something to serve at all.

Onscreen, Mary Jane took off her robe. Her naked body was

dusted with a sparkling powder. She smiled coquettishly at the camera while the host clapped and cheered: *Looking good, Grandma!*

"I'm glad you told me Walter's your uncle. I've seen him put his hand on your shoulder so many times, I was starting to think you were sleeping together."

"Gross." He wrinkled his nose. "I don't know about where you're from, but here, that kind of age gap isn't permitted." Erek was always cautious in referencing anything from Beatrice's life before the restaurant. Now she wondered if Walter had told him not to bring it up.

She'd never considered that some of the same Seagate taboos applied in the restaurant. "Most other things I was taught were wrong at home are right here," she replied, shrugging.

"Even if he wasn't ancient—have you seen the way he dresses? His mustache?" He seemed mildly offended. "Anyway, I prefer girls. I keep trying to have it on with mates, because it's friendly and easy and nice, but then they get feelings for me and I just want to play video games. Doesn't seem fair." He shook his head. "Girls, though! I don't get them at all. It's like they're a different species." He took another bite. "You like girls, mainly?" He squinted at her. "Maybe you can explain them to me."

"I don't know," she said. She thought of how it had felt to be held by Leroy Kim. "Both, I think. But the main thing I need is someone who accepts my cooking."

"You're in the right place for that," he said.

"I'm working my arse off! Who has the time?" She flicked him on the nose. "And sorry, kid, but you're too young." He was a full three years younger than Beatrice.

He giggled. "I didn't mean me! People come into the restaurant all the time."

Lately Beatrice had developed a schoolgirl crush on the head chef, but she wasn't about to tell Erek that. Margot was the best—and only—woman chef she had ever met. Of course Beatrice wanted her attention, her praise, her love. But Margot ruined her fantasy every time she opened her mouth to criticize Beatrice for dicing when she said to mince or not fully utilizing every ingredient. "Can you imagine? Tabitha!" she barked, attempting to imitate Margot's exacting speech. "Let's consummate our relationship! First you must wash your body exactly as I say and clip your toenails from left to right. Here, I will demonstrate!"

Erek laughed until he had to wipe tears from his eyes. "That's too good! But don't even think about it. Margot doesn't have sex."

"She's frigid?" Beatrice asked, frowning. "Really? But she's so passionate!" She shook her head. "I don't believe you."

"Believe me or not, it's true."

"That's so sad," said Beatrice.

"Well . . . perhaps it isn't," said Erek. "That's the thing about our religion. My mum—you know, she ran away with her preacher. He said it was good for her, to forget she had a child, because God wanted her to focus on the immaterial—having given birth was too animal. How can that be right, but our restaurant wrong?"

"What do I know? I'm the poster child for everything my church taught us not to do." She'd meant it as a joke, but it came out sounding melancholy. Maybe she really would never see her parents again.

"Cheer up, Tabitha! We love you. All of us, even Margot in her way. Everything has been better since you got here."

Somehow this made her feel worse. Erek's life had been hard, harder than hers, and he never complained. Some days she didn't feel lovable at all. Besides, he didn't really know her. He didn't even know Beatrice's real name.

The photo shoot over, Mary Jane sat in front of a roaring fire with her grandkids. She showed them the pictures from her youth and the ones they'd re-created with the camera crew. They all shed a tear for her fallen soldier love. *Looking good, Grandma,* her granddaughter said, the words tender this time.

"Erek, if you still feel like that a year from now, tell me again."

He held out his hand to shake, and she took it. "Okay, weirdo. In a year, I'll tell you I love you."

The program ended, and the next round of commercials began. Beatrice's hometown, filmed from above, filled the screen. The perfect houses, the gleaming, window-filled church, the mazes of fruit trees. A melodious voice murmured, *Work, bills, keeping up with your home—isn't it all so much to manage? What if there was a simpler way, a leaner way, to go through life? With Stecopo,* the voice promised, *all of your needs are taken care of.*

"Change the channel!" cried Beatrice as a happy family waved from a hover cruise. Then there was a wide shot of a thin, beautiful girl, head turned out toward the sea, a single lemon held aloft in her palm. She turned to the camera and smiled. Beatrice froze.

Come to Seagate and live in love, she said.

Erek stopped with the clicker held out, transfixed by the screen. "Tabitha," he whispered. "That girl looks like you."

My first week working in the castle, the old woman made me reach with bare hands into a huge pot of boiling water to pull out still-shrieking lobsters. This was to "toughen my hands" so I might be of use to her in the kitchen. She seemed to draw pleasure from my torture. I had never experienced such malice. But my body was numb from grief, the instant loss of all I had ever known, so her jabs and barbs, be they spoken or physical, did not fully reach me. In retrospect, if she had been kind to me in the midst of my agony, I might have gone mad. Instead she became my adversary. Having a villain focused my grief, burning it into a clarifying rage. I became very quiet. I was no longer the happy, innocent girl of my village, but a serpent, lying in wait to strike. The old woman had some tricks to teach me in the art of cooking, and I learned them, quickly and well. Then I planned to get rid of her.

I learned how to create a centerpiece worthy of royalty. Our little village had no use for the eating of land animals—they were much better served to us, with our limited space, as workers, producing milk and eggs. From her, I learned how to kill and prepare all manner of fowl, how to roast a suckling pig in a pit in the earth until it fell apart with only the touch of a fork. I learned how to make a goat taste not of game but of spice, how to stew a bull after his breeding days had passed. The dishes were opulently styled in our kitchen, yet nothing was wasted, and I begrudgingly appreciated the old woman's thrift. As I observed her, I learned who the other players were in our little drama—the stablemen, the scullery maids, the gardeners, the boisterous young pages who often sneaked into the kitchen for an extra feeding. Our kitchens were the center of the castle's employ, the meeting ground for gossip. People fell in love over bread baskets and traded in secrets as they traded in spices. My world was very small. Our kitchen, the stables, the gardens—all were along the far wing of the castle, a half-mile walk from where the actual royalty slept, ate, read, and strolled.

For years, I never saw a member of the royal caste.

I am now an old woman myself and have no reason to lie. Most of the persons I am writing about in this record are already deceased, and I will soon be joining them. I have nothing to hide, and only relief to gain from telling the truth.

Reader, hear me with an open heart—I am not proud of the story I am about to tell you. But my own survival was at stake. When I was seventeen years old, I set out to become a murderess.

That night, my life changed forever.

I had been secretly preparing a noxious stew—savory-smelling, intensely piquant and sharp, as these were among the old cook's favorite flavors, and deadly if consumed in a moderate portion. She wasn't a big eater, but if I could get the better part of a cup in her, the old woman would sicken and die within a day as the poison wormed its way through her blood.

I didn't have much of a mind for politics back then, which demonstrates how little I understood about the world and my place in it. The intricacies of the ruling class did not concern me; they were simply the heavenly bodies around which our small lives rotated. I thought the head cook was my queen, that kitchen my territory. I would learn, that very night, how far this was from the truth. I was never separate from my masters.

As my stew bubbled away pleasantly on the range, I set about finishing the last of my duties. I went down into the root cellar to find some tubers, alliums, and other aromatics to chop in preparation for a feast that was to take place in three days' time. I didn't know the occasion of this particular celebration. Such feasts, for even the most minor holidays, were common, as our land was plentiful. This was part of how the king, even whilst traveling on his quests, kept in favor among his constituents. There was always a festival to look forward to, and our kitchen, which mainly fed the minor noblemen and working folk of the castle, was only one of many kitchens working in tandem throughout the grounds to prepare the feasts for all the king's subjects.

As I returned with my vegetables, there was a figure standing at the range, right over my deadly stew. He was holding a spoon and chewing happily. I rushed over and slapped the spoon out of his hand. I did not think, only acted. Then, and only then, did I realize that he was not a simple gardener or stableman, as I had grown accustomed to seeing about our kitchen (and whose hands, once or twice, I had slapped away from freshly sliced apple or cheese in partial jest), but a knight. I could tell by his bearing—I had seen them about the castle, looking regal and rigid, some with greased curls and even painted lips.

This knight looked dusty, as if he had just come in from the road, having ridden hard for many days. But there was no doubt about it—he was my better. I cringed deeply, looking at the decoration on his collar, the medals on his tunic, some kind of special crest. I knew little of such things, but wondered if he was a particularly high-ranking knight, perhaps some kind of general, though he looked young for such an important station. I squeaked out a brief begging of forgiveness and expected very much to be hit or even flogged. Then I noticed his eyes. They were a wonderful gold-green-speckled brown that seemed to shift in the light, reminding me of the pools of my fishing village in the places where seawater met fresh. Estuaries, I believe they are called.

He did not raise his hand to strike me, nor his voice to reprimand me. He laughed, showing even white teeth—teeth so perfect, I thought they must be fake. (Later I was shocked to learn they were real.)

"Little Mother," he said, using the formal variation as a sign of respect. I blushed, to have one above me address me so. "Is there some food in the kitchen I might partake of? I have just come in from the road and am very hungry."

It was mighty odd he wasn't in the knights' kitchen, which was certainly bustling with lads demanding meat and soup and bread, but I was not one to argue with my betters.

"I fear that soup has gone off," I said, curtsying. "I was only concerned for your health—please, forgive me! How much, pray, did you sup?"

"Only a taste," he said, his eyes gleaming. "It was delicious."

I blushed deeply. "If Master craves a sour soup, sit and I will make one for you."

"Please," he said, "there's no need to address me so formally, Little Mother. I would be honored to eat whatever you prepare."

Quickly I drew together a plate of bread and butter, pickles, raw radishes, apple slices, and sharp yellow cheese.

"Enjoy this while you wait," I said, employing the more intimate "you" form, instead of the formal one. He appeared pleased and sat at the counter. I took some pickled cabbage from its vat and joined it with a new stock I had mellowing on the range. I busied myself with alliums. He seemed to enjoy watching me work, chatting with me in a relaxed manner as if I were still a village girl chasing crabs and he was idling by the docks, sitting in the sun. We spoke of nothing important—"Is your job difficult?" he asked. "Do you enjoy cooking? What are you preparing?" and so on.

"There's wine in that barrel," I said, pointing to the cask, "and mugs in the cupboard, if you fancy something stronger than tea."

He poured a small cup for me too. (It wasn't half as strong as the stuff you lot drink these days—water wasn't always good to drink, so most everyone drank watered-down wine or tea, either enjoyed hot or left to steep with pungent herbs and served cool.)

Here's how to make this simple soup. It is humble, yet powerful, dear reader, so take care when you serve it. Some palates, I believe, crave a certain kind of complexity—they need sourness, the intensity of strong flavors. Once I served my knight this sour peasant soup, my life changed forever. I took a half cup each of these vegetables, already cleaned and chopped in preparation: leeks, carrots, parsnips, celery, and onions, and set them to brown in a deep pan with butter, adding garlic once the onions were translucent and the parsnip half-soft. I rummaged through the larder and found cooked potatoes from dinner, chopped them roughly, but did not add them. After the vegetables were fragrant and tender, I poured in three quarts of bone stock, mostly turkey and lamb, and let them cook down. Here, after cooking, the old cook would strain out the vegetables and add the potatoes to the pure broth, but I found that silly. I looked at my knight, eating carefully crafted bites of his bread and cheese, then bread and butter with pickle, then bread and apple and cheese, then radish and butter. It was as if he had never tasted such things. He caught my eye looking and smiled, once again revealing those perfect teeth.

"I can't tell you how grateful I am to have food such as this!" His cheeks dimpled pleasantly when he smiled.

I began grating sour pickles. "Food isn't very good on the road, I suspect," I replied.

He quirked his head, looking at me peculiarly. "What's your name?"

"Ijo," I said. "I'm the kitchen girl."

"Your dialect," he said, gesturing to his own mouth. "Are you from Ketell Province?"

I felt tears spring to my eyes upon hearing mention of my home. "Yes," I said. "A small fishing village in Ketell."

"Your home is a beautiful place."

I smiled and brushed a tear from my eye. "Forgive me—I'm making your soup saltier! My home was washed away in a big wave. My whole village." His eyes were so serious, so kind. "I'm the only one left."

"Then you are very important," he said softly. "You are the keeper of a noble tradition." I tasted the soup for salt and pepper, grateful to turn away from his gentle gaze. After seasoning, I added heaps of grated sour pickles and a full cup of cream. I stirred the pot.

"In my village," I said, ladling out a bowl of soup, "we would serve this half the year with herring, cured in salt and vinegar. Now *that's* a sour soup!"

I garnished it with fresh dill, and more black pepper. Then I put the bowl in front of him and saw his eyes light up like a little boy's, but he did not eat.

"If you are not too busy," he said humbly, "I'd be very honored if you would sit and talk with me."

I poured another bowl of soup and sat across from him.

"Ahhh," he groaned, taking a big bite. "I had a nurse, when I was little. She would make sour pickle soup in the wettest time of winter, when the snow had stopped and it was no longer beautiful. 'Now,' she would say, 'it's time for sour pickle soup.' After eating such a piquant bowl, my appetite would come back for all the usual things I had to eat. I haven't enjoyed it in a long time."

"What's this festival in honor of?" I asked, suddenly shy.

"Do they not let you out of the kitchen?" He laughed at my expense, but his eyes remained kind. "The wayward king is back," he explained, "from his foolhardy quest. He has brought back with him a bride from a faraway but powerful land. Their marriage will secure an important alliance between our two nations."

"Does he love her?" I asked. "How strange, to marry for a political alliance!"

"He doesn't know her," he said slowly. "But I don't imagine it will ever be a love match."

"Poor king! Is she very ugly?"

He shook his head. "She's like a being from another planet. She is mild and kind, and she doesn't look like us at all."

"People say our king is very handsome," I said. "So that must be a disappointment."

To this, he said nothing, but his cheeks grew quite pink.

I raised my wine in a toast. "To the success of your mission, and in honor of your safe homecoming! *Sei Gusian.*"

Smiling widely again with those beautiful teeth, he drank to my health, my ancestors, and this fine bowl of soup. "*Sei Gusian.*"

It was getting rather late. Noticing my fatigue, my valiant knight washed all of my dishes as I finished my preparations for tomorrow's feast. After our work was complete, he spoke again.

"Aren't you going to throw the soup away? The one that has spoiled," he said suddenly.

I froze. I couldn't think of an excuse to keep it.

"Yes," I said. "I'll pour it out, but not with the slop. I don't want it to harm the pigs. I'll take it out into the muck."

"It's heavy," he said, frowning. "And it's dark outside, barely any moons tonight. I'll take it there for you."

"No," I protested. "You've already done so much! It is my responsibility—"

"No," he said firmly, and I wondered suddenly if he perhaps understood more than I realized. "I will dispose of it."

I could have cried. I knew, in that moment, that my plans had been thwarted by this strange man, so gentle in his attentions. He was the first person to be kind to me in years, and in that kindness, I rediscovered a part of myself. I could not kill the old woman. I was stuck with her. All at once, I felt tired to the bone.

"Ijo," he said, "I would like to visit you again. And to try more of your cooking, especially your family recipes. May I?"

I nodded, my heart lightening.

He stood up and brushed his lap free of crumbs, grinning that boyish smile again. "I have not enjoyed a meal so thoroughly for a long time."

"Well, I'm glad my cooking is better than field rations."

He looked at me like I was speaking a different language again, and I wondered if my parrying of his compliment had offended him. Then he held out his hand, which I noticed was very, very clean—much cleaner than that of any stableman or groundsman I had ever spied in the kitchen. Keeping his distance, he lightly touched the inside of my wrist. His fingertip was rough, and it made my own skin, which I'd never thought much about, feel so soft and smooth in comparison. No man outside my own family had ever touched me there. He held his finger there for a moment, looking directly into my eyes. I was embarrassed, yet I couldn't bring myself to break his gaze. My knees grew weak, my feet tingled, and my face flushed redder still.

"You are like the rain after a drought," he said softly. Then he took his hand away, bowed low, and left, carrying the vat of poisoned soup.

I ran off to my humble bed, which was really nothing more than a pile of rags in the far corner of a forgotten room behind the kitchen's fireplace. It was warm there, which was what mattered, for the stone was very cold in every season, even in summer. I lay awake, though I felt how tired my body was. I had made a friend. The thought insulated me from my despair about the old woman. I fell asleep, imagining him watching over me with his quiet, deep gaze. *He is sitting on the edge of my bed,* I thought. *He is looking at my face. My ears, my cheek, my neck, my chin. He is looking at my mouth, my eyelashes. He is watching over me.*

MENU FOR A WAYWARD KING, HOME FROM A FOOLHARDY MISSION

Millet porridge with grilled clams

Whole roasted sea bream

Braised ox on a bed of turnips and potatoes

Steamed young greens in garlic

Pickled cabbage and mushrooms in vinegar

Platter of peaches, plums, apricots, dates, chestnuts, hazelnuts, pears, sweet crabapples, persimmons, melon, cherries, oranges, and tangerines

2.

One fine afternoon, as Reiko strolled through the Hills, where the Middle lapped at the feet of the lowest part of Above, she noticed a particularly splendid home. It was sandwiched between an upscale cobbler and a businessmen's tailor, yet it stood apart from its neighbors by appearing to float a good ten feet from the ground. It was, of course, suspended by an intricate lattice of thin metal beams, artfully arranged in such a way that the palatial home appeared to be hovering against the bright-blue sky, rising up from its surrounding gardens like the high bloom of a sunflower. Reiko was seized by an intuition as she appreciated its fine design—this was the place of her next mark.

I am God, and God is me.

The wrought-iron railing of the spiral staircase connected the street to the bright-yellow front door, shining in the sky like a cheerful painted sun. Reiko noticed that the home was in beautiful shape, the door freshly painted and pristine, while the lower grounds were rather unkempt. The hedge of lavender encircling the ground beneath the floating mansion was quite uneven on one side, while little tufts of weeds were sprouting through the sparsely mulched flower garden.

Reiko looked down at her clothes. She was wearing a simple gray shift dress. That was lucky. It was rather expensive, one of those minimalist garments she'd paid dearly for, but it would suit her purpose well enough. Reiko took out a pair of reading glasses and set them on the end of her nose. She removed all her jewelry, carefully placing her delicate silver and gold bracelets, her large opal ring, and her amber hair comb into a small silk bag before tucking that into her purse. Then she wiped off her lipstick and loosed her hair from its crown braid. She mussed it slightly, then tied it back at the nape of her neck in an unflattering low bun. Finally, Reiko slouched. It was the easiest way to make yourself look bad, as her grandmother had liked to say when she was alive, rapping Reiko on the back to sit up straighter with a wink and a grin.

Just as Reiko rang the doorbell, she remembered her very expensive handbag.

A tall, muscular woman with a rough pink face opened the door. She was in a maid's uniform, the plain white muslin just sheer enough to see her undergarments, and she looked rather weary. She didn't seem the type to sink a paycheck on a purse, or to even covet one. "May I help you?" the woman asked. Her voice was surprisingly soft and high for such a large person. Reiko hitched the bag up higher on her shoulder as a test. The woman didn't clock it, and Reiko knew she was safe. Besides, she could always say it was a fake.

"Good afternoon, ma'am," said Reiko, with a bit of a bow. "I'm looking for work, if I can find it. Cleaning, cooking, gardening—I can do it all. Are the masters of the house in?"

The woman bit her lip, looking suddenly like she might cry. "I don't think—" she began.

"Linka!" a croaky voice called out from deep inside the house. "Who is that at the door?"

Linka winced. "There is a person here who says she can help us with the garden," she called back toward the voice.

"Send her in!"

Linka stepped aside, allowing Reiko to cross the threshold of the musty house.

She looked around. The house must once have been magnificent, yet it was now dim and ill-kempt, its floors dusty, the windows streaked with dried rain. When she turned back, Linka was nowhere to be seen. Frowning, Reiko followed the sounds of coughing down the gilded hall, each corner and table crammed with expensive little knickknacks about fifty years out of fashion, frozen in quaint tableaux and thick with dust. She stepped into a large, pristine parlor. In the center stood a firm, perfectly white sofa that looked as if it had never been sat upon, surrounded by overstuffed chairs in a small arc. Reiko turned in a full circle before she realized the room was empty.

"In here!" the voice called again. She followed the sound to a little light-brown wood door at the far side of the posh parlor. The door was so small, she had to bow slightly to get through it. Reiko was not very tall, and she now felt as if she had traveled into a fairy realm. Beyond the door, she finally found the source of the voice.

The scene was like something out of a picture she'd watch at the cineplex for a half-ducat. A very small, rather bent old woman was ensconced by a roaring blaze in the fireplace, the room stiflingly hot, even though outside the afternoon was quite warm. She sat on a once-fine but now worn loveseat, its velvet crushed to death, with a steaming tray of tea beside her. The woman was coiffed and powdered, dripping with lace and furs and far too many jewels. Her eyebrows were drawn on quite heavily above eyes blue-white with cataracts, and her lipstick was bright but uneven. Her hands trembled significantly as she supped both broth and tea from short, delicate mugs before clattering them back down on their saucers.

"So you've found me at last," she said in a raspy whisper, then coughed violently for a full minute. Once the spasm ended, her voice was much clearer and louder. "Do sit!" The woman looked quite near death, but Reiko suspected she was the type to hover for ages without surrendering to the abyss, as her own grandmother had done for so many years. "This old house," the woman continued rather loudly. "I have trouble keeping up with it since the death of my husband. You say you're a gardener?" The woman blinked at her.

Reiko perched on the edge of a chair and looked at the floor, improvising a little story for her audience of one. "Yes, ma'am," she said demurely but loudly, as she suspected this woman was hard of hearing. "Someday I'll go to university and become a certified master gardener, but first I need to earn my school fees."

The woman nodded vigorously. A good start. "Of course, of course. And call me Clarissa, my dear. University is a wonderful goal! Simply wonderful."

Reiko nodded, adding a bit of flesh to the bone of her character. "Yes, and I'd also like to send a portion of my pay home to my brothers and sisters in the Bastian each week."

The old woman loved this, it was clear by her expression. "The Bastian, you say? Oh my!"

"Yes," she responded, ready to lay it on thicker. From the looks of her home, Clarissa wasn't a fan of subtlety. "Things have been a bit rough at home since Mama died." Reiko said a little mental prayer to absolve herself—*I love you, Mama! Please know I don't ever want you to die—I'm just lying to this old bat to steal her money. I am God, and God is me.*

The woman clucked her tongue. "Such a shame, such a shame." She sat up straighter. "Why, you haven't lost your father too, have you?" The old woman looked at her from the corners of her eyes, her face absolutely still. "You're not . . . an orphan, are you, my dear?" she asked, her tone strangely light.

Reiko had learned one thing from her marks in her early days of grifting. People told you very clearly who they were and, more importantly, who they wanted you to be. It wasn't mind-reading. One simply had to pay attention. Reiko took in the way Clarissa almost held her breath and squinted while she waited for Reiko's response. She was performing in a play—they both had their parts and took their cues from each other.

Reiko nodded solemnly, and the old woman's cheeks flushed as her eyes grew wide. "Yes, Ms. Clarissa," she stage whispered. "I'm an orphan, working to support my brothers and sisters. Both my parents died in a fire in the textile factory a few years ago. It was in all the papers." At this, Clarissa leaned back in her chair as if she might faint, and Reiko knew she was in.

"Oh my, oh my, oh my," said the old woman, reviving herself with a sip of broth. "Well, you see, I have a tendency to . . . collect orphans. My Rory and I, we always wanted children, but things don't work out the way we plan, do they?"

Here Reiko decided to look sad but resilient, remembering dear old dead Mum and Dad. "No, ma'am, they certainly do not."

"Please—do call me Clarissa!" She cleared her throat and moistened her lips on her teacup. "Now, while we cannot arrange our lives like a tidy little garden, I do believe that things work out for the best in a grand sort of way, perhaps even more beautifully than we ever could have planned or even imagined. You see, my entire staff are my family. Linka, who you met at the door, gruff as she is, has been with me for over fourteen years." She yelled out toward the kitchen or wherever Linka was hiding: "And we don't mind your sour little moods, do we, Linka?" She shook her head. "No! Because that's what families do. They stick together, through thick and thin." Clarissa looked her square in the face. "Now, my dear. What is your name?"

Reiko surprised herself with her answer. "Elena."

"Elena! Lovely. Elena, I would be very interested in supporting your endeavors. The only thing I ask is that you stay here, on the grounds with me. I'm an old woman and I can't go out and visit people very often. It's important to me that I have people around me, people to talk to, people who will notice if I've fallen on the bathroom floor and can't get back up!" She laughed again, until she started coughing.

Reiko nodded demurely. "That would be just fine, Ms. Clarissa. You see, the commute from the Bastian is rather far, and quite dear in terms of ducats."

Clarissa's eyes grew wide. "Oh my, yes, that would be a terrible commute." There was a long silence. Reiko felt the question Clarissa wanted to ask, but she couldn't decide if it would be rude or not.

Reiko gave her what she wanted. "I've been commuting, you see, with barely enough time left in the day to sleep before starting it all over again. My health is suffering. I would be very grateful to stay put for a while."

Clarissa sucked in her breath. "You brave, brave dear. Commuting all that way every day, studying and doing all of your classes, *and* supporting your brothers and sisters? Why, you have to work twice as hard as the other students at the university, don't you?"

Reiko blinked, realizing that this woman had conflated her expressed dream of becoming a student with actually *being* a student, and she was going to have to shift her story to accommodate this new twist. She'd figure it out. "I don't know about all that, ma'am, but I am excited to settle in one place for a while." She smiled, but with her lips closed to hide her perfect teeth.

The old woman's eyes gleamed, and Reiko felt the evidence of her success as clearly as if someone had rung a bell. This woman loved the idea of struggling, student-orphan Reiko, and this first impression would carry her far. She wouldn't even have to be a good gardener. She just needed to be demure and make sure to pepper their conversations with a few sentimental details. Of course, *too* much of a sob story would make even the most well-intentioned rich woman feel exhausted and guilty. One needed a lighter touch for this kind of grift.

The old woman called for Jono, an ancient-looking, very tall cook, to "feed this young woman up right" before sending her back home to the Bastian to pack. Reiko was taken aback at seeing a man doing the cooking, but this household *was* rather odd. After she'd eaten her disgusting protein-enriched gruel behind a privacy screen, Reiko shook hands with Clarissa and went home to pack her things. As she walked toward the Loop, Reiko's plan appeared in her mind as clearly as a well-drawn map. She'd return with a beat-up-looking suitcase, some inconspicuous clothing. She'd also bring her disguises, and her handmade tech, all the tools she needed to thieve. But this wouldn't be a common dip, a little skim off the top, a few thousand ducats that no one would even notice. This woman was old, hard of hearing, and losing her vision, and her staff of poor, dear, elderly "orphans" clearly hated her. No more small change from the loutish men she met at uptown bars, with their fancy business dresses and lies about their wives. This money would be a real and mighty foot in the door to Above. Then Reiko would kick the goddamn door down and take her rightful place at the top.

She settled into a routine quickly. A bit of light cleaning, then a few hours of the day spent in the garden. Reiko enjoyed the physical work, keeping her mind free. The old woman, when she wasn't downstairs in her parlor, kept to her bedroom on the sixth floor, using a lift to travel between. In her explorations of the grand house, Reiko found a room filled with what looked like Free-Wah artifacts, more fitting for a museum than a forgotten, dusty room in a rich woman's house. It seemed that Clarissa and her husband were collectors of other traditions' sacred objects, not just orphans. She clicked her tongue. Even one of these pieces would fetch a tidy sum on the black market, but it wasn't worth the risk. She needed to be thoughtful about this job, bide her time. She picked up a copy of an old book, sat down in an armchair, and opened it.

The Kitchen Girl
a true story
by Ijo

She smoothed the lovely cream pages, their edges browned with age. There were so few Free-Wah books available in print, and Reiko had never seen such an old edition. On real paper too. She felt she had to liberate this one, so sad and alone on the high shelf of Clarissa's musty study, and secreted it back with her to her room.

Certainly, no one would notice.

Reiko stared at the bartender polishing cut-crystal glasses, their intricate patterns reflecting the soft light as he turned them this way and that. Cocktail in hand, mellow music playing, Reiko allowed her mind to grow fuzzy and soft. She had been at Clarissa's for just over a month. Her biggest chore was supping copious tea and broth with the woman as she talked about her husband and the old days, all while pressing Reiko for details of her poor Bastian life. It was a different kind of labor from gardening, but a labor nonetheless. Reiko tried to keep all the details fabricated, but every so often she'd be in the thick of relating a sob story and realize that she was indeed talking about her own family. Though the players were different and the settings changed, the struggle remained the same. Her family *was* poor, and that meant they were less safe than Clarissa would ever be.

That was the great grift of poverty. Death and disease slinked about, looking for a crack in the armor, waiting to worm inside. Not to say that Clarissa didn't have her own problems—various illnesses from when she was young, an uncle who was too fond of drink. But the problems were hers, and her resources were like knights in a vast army, championing her at every turn. Each time Reiko stumbled upon another of Clarissa's accounts, tied up in this or that, like stocks that the woman had forgotten about or perhaps never known of in the first place, she would look at the number and think, *This sum would change my family's life.*

Reiko did send home money. At some point after she'd quit college, she had decided on a figure and kept to it. Her family received 15 percent of everything she made, no matter what. They'd never asked for money. Sometimes she would probe Elena for news of someone's health, hear a terrible story (a doctor who didn't listen, an insurance company who'd cheated them), and she would send home a bit more. They never mentioned the money she sent, but she knew they were grateful. Reiko often imagined how happy they would be when she sent them 15 percent of what she would take from Clarissa. Like winning the lottery.

So far, the setup hadn't proven difficult. Linka lived in a servants' bungalow at the back of the estate with her wife, Rita, a seamstress who worked in Upper Mansfield, across the river. Linka kept herself scarce, running the house with a sour, faraway expression— all duty, no joy. The ancient cook, Jono, was also losing his vision but wouldn't admit it. (Reiko often found her few solid suppers still frozen in the middle or with their centers completely raw.) He lived on the first floor of the house in a bedroom converted from a former drawing room, for he was so old even managing the helio-lift by the central staircase proved too daunting. There was a young orphan girl of eleven, Sabrina, who did the pressing and the dusting in the evenings between her days at a religious school. Reiko tried her best to avoid Sabrina, as she had no wish to develop any sort of bond with the girl. She needed to focus on the task at hand. With gruff Linka rarely anywhere to be seen, Jono keeping to the first floor, and Sabrina in school for most the day, Reiko found ample opportunity to sleuth into Clarissa's accounts. Only the deeper she explored bank statements and accordion folders stuffed with bonds, the more elusive the root of the money was; she found instead a rhizomatic, creeping stalk that snaked and bloomed into hidden offshore accounts and plentiful portfolios, more numerous than Reiko had imagined. She could have dipped and run at any moment, taking a bigger prize than she'd ever thought possible in a single grift. But the more she discovered about Clarissa's secreted monies, the more she wanted to take and take and take and take. This was the big one.

The old woman wasn't an issue—she could barely find her socks, much less protect her own coin. But someone must be paying attention to that kind of money—a family member, perhaps, or a former business partner, or an accountant who knew an opportunity when they saw one. Reiko had to play her hand very carefully, make her move thoroughly and completely, then move on. Make the dip and leave—it was always the same process, whether the job was to skim off the top of some businessman's bank account or to take this old woman to the cleaners.

Reiko settled in at the bar, all cozy with a cocktail, to read *The Kitchen Girl*, covered with a pulpy jacket from a bestseller. Little Ijo, finally through the forest, had made it to the castle. She begged for a place in a kitchen, but the head cook was rather evil, making her sleep on rags on the floor like an animal. Ijo was planning to murder her, which Reiko found exciting but extreme. Why not just get a different job? She'd walked into the castle with nothing; why not walk somewhere else? Apparently she could live in the forest like a squirrel.

"I'd like to buy you a drink, if that's all right." Reiko looked up from her book, annoyed at the interruption. No doubt some highly modified, chiseled Adonis looking for a quick bounce.

A distinctively handsome man gazed back at her, leaning against the bar, his head cocked to one side. Reiko was momentarily taken aback by the confident, lazy gaze, as if he were already staring at her from a pillow.

"Well," she said, "we'll see."

He smiled at being appraised so frankly, revealing deep dimples in both cheeks. She sipped her cocktail and looked him up and down like she really was considering it, scrunching up her nose. Reiko was surprised by how playful she was being with a perfect stranger. Yet the longer she eyed him, the clearer two things became: First, he didn't look like anyone she knew. Second, she really liked looking at him.

Reiko placed his age around forty-five, with a tan face like he had spent long hours in the sun and light-blue eyes that shone out intensely from his darker skin. He could have been younger and lived a rather hard life, or older and kept himself in good order. She suspected the latter, as was the habit of the rich. His face was a little craggy, which she liked (she hated the feminine style of Middle men who used too many bone extensions and cheek lifters to become smooth and sculptural as marble statues), and when he smiled, he revealed long, slightly yellowed teeth. This face, so full of character, was paired with the fancy business uniform of the ultra-rich—the long sashed gown, the gold slippers, the felted hat with two distinct plumes. She looked at his wide lapel and saw he had more than a few pips on his collar—he was a citizen of Above, floating down to the Middle on business. In Reiko's experience (which was considerable), this level of businessman was normally rather pale and doughy-faced from long hours at the office. But the suntan conjured the image of an island vacation. Maybe even a private island? Perhaps he was the wealthy son of a tycoon: all of the titles, none of the responsibilities. Whatever his story, those pockets were deep.

"Well, my lady," he said, flashing those dimples. "Do I pass the mustard?"

Reiko giggled at the food entendre. "I already have a drink," she said, gesturing to her cocktail. "How about I buy you one?" She motioned to the bartender, and the man grinned wider. Reiko felt the spiral of arousal swirl in her low belly. She was going to land a mark tonight.

Reiko had already quite enjoyed her one day off from Clarissa, with a visit to the spa for a full-body scrub, oatmeal lavender facial, and fruit acid skin peel before changing into a very expensive little black dress and exquisite orange lacquered heels. She'd left the spa to get a very pricey dinner at a private dining room above a juice bar touting smoothie diets and twenty-one-day liver cleanses, where if one knew how to ask, one could order off a secret menu of solid food. Cocooned in her privacy stall, Reiko had eaten spicy rice noodles with fish cake, slow-braised mackerel with white rice, and house pickles, all washed down with a cold beer. It was almost as good as something she'd have in the Bastian, but not quite. Fermentation was an important aspect of Free-Wah cuisine, but the mackerel had been heavily seasoned, Reiko suspected, not due to technique but because it wasn't fresh. That was, thus far, her grand disappointment with leaving the ground—the food was better below, where no one cared if anyone saw them cooking or eating.

Scrubbed, beautified, and reasonably well fed, she'd planned on one magnificent cocktail (maybe two) at this beautiful lounge, reading a few chapters, then going to bed at the upstairs hotel to be refreshed for another day at her long, fat con. Meeting this handsome stranger might conjure a rather different evening, but Reiko didn't mind. It had been a long time since she'd really enjoyed herself with a mark, and her instincts told her, loud and clear, that he would show her a good time. There was just something about him—the way he stood with an easygoing confidence that made him gleam as if he had just been polished. He ordered his drink, and she made a showy gesture of paying with her mobile wallet, which made him laugh again, a loud bark of a laugh that delighted her. This was a great trick she'd learned in her earliest days of fishing. She did it with almost everyone—insist on paying for something first, and they would never let her buy another thing again. This way she'd never be treated like she owed them anything. Otherwise, a beautiful young woman who expected the man to pay for everything might be treated like a nun for hire, which she'd learned the hard way when she was younger.

Regardless, of course, she would rob them.

They sat together on a little couch and sipped greedily from their cocktails. He said his name was Alexander, then told her about all the normal things—his high-powered placement at an international firm, his private airship, his home Above. Reiko waited for things to get interesting, but that spark never returned. Of course he'd be like every other mark she'd grifted, with their wives, their surrogates, their expense accounts, their meandering stories about their college days, their anxiety over the next great promotion. There was something distinctive about him that made her sit up a little taller and lean in a little closer, but maybe it was just that she found him attractive. It didn't matter. She spun her normal nonsense about being a daughter of the elite who was "exploring her options," which was code for playing around until she settled down. Tonight's character was Agata, the girl who would run wild until her parents told her it was time to get married. Another businessman, noticing the vast swath of pips on Alexander's collar, tried to chat them up. She sat back, preparing to find an elegant way to exit. Talking business with some Above fops was not how she wished to spend her one night off. But instead of making nice, Alexander growled at the other man to leave him and his lady companion alone.

Reiko leaned in, pressed a hand on his knee, and asked him if he'd like to join her in her room upstairs. His eyes widened, and for a moment he looked almost frightened. Then he nodded and stood without a word. She took his hand, which was very warm and surprisingly calloused. It felt wonderful. She felt the spiral of desire once more and led him up to the room she had rented for the night. The image in her mind was of a panther stalking its prey.

They didn't talk very much at all after that.

He started kissing her as soon as they got into the room. His kisses were warm and direct and ingenious, snaking his big tongue into her mouth in a way that she might find disgusting with another man. Something about him was comfortingly animal, like he was hungry for her, and his desire made her feel like a pet and a jewel and a good thing to eat, all at once. She found herself without her dress rather quickly, those big, rough hands kneading and squeezing her thighs, her stomach flipping over in anticipation. Reiko reclined on the bed. Then he just looked at her.

"Aren't you lovely, Agata," he said in a low voice and what almost sounded like a Bastian accent. The whole time he disrobed, he kept his eyes on hers. Every other businessman she had lain with pristinely folded his clothes in a neat little stack, but he tore off his garments, kicking his gold shoes across the room in a way that made her squeal. His chest was broad and dense with curly hair, which thrilled her anew, for most men were waxed and smooth, like all the women she knew, in order to be closer to angels than animals.

"Are you ready for me?" he asked. She leaned back again, this time spreading her legs and shutting her eyes, waiting for him to take his place. But he didn't move. She opened her eyes and saw him looking at her again in a way that mystified her. "C'mere," he said, holding out his hand. She took it, confused, as he helped her up to stand. Then he sat on the edge of the bed, naked and erect, and, never taking his eyes off her, impaled her onto him.

Reiko was astonished by the sounds she was hearing. Deep moans were being wrenched from her own body, as if they belonged to another person. Then she was yelling, she was swearing. There was no room for performance, no space for fakery. Then Alexander was yelling, he was swearing, and they grunted and moved and shook together, a cacophonous chorus of two. Reiko came in a short, triumphant shout, and he followed suit quickly, as if his orgasm held a kind of fealty to hers.

Then she paused, breathless and slick with both their sweat. A huge wave of sadness crashed through her, a tsunami of grief, for this was the only time in her life she had felt such things, and it was only a grift. Suddenly Reiko felt like she was the one being robbed.

Reiko didn't meet his eyes. "I'm taking a shower," she said.

His voice was soft. "Do you want company?"

She shook her head. "I'll be quick."

Reiko spent a long time in the bathroom, letting the warm water soothe her. She felt strangely heartbroken. She wanted him to leave. Reiko longed for the night she was supposed to have had, with her book in bed by herself before midnight. When she finally exited the bathroom, he was already asleep, just as she'd hoped, releasing long sighs from his back like a great bear. Reiko slid in next to him and waited, forcing herself to stay awake until he had fallen deeper into dreaming. While she waited, she thought about every boy she had ever half loved. There had only been a few, mostly from the Bastian—rough boys, loud boys, boys who didn't understand Reiko or her dreams but knew how to make her laugh. There had been no one to hold her interest at school, and after that, well, she hadn't really dated. She had only grifted.

She studied his profile in the dark. It looked as if his nose had been broken, perhaps more than once. A skiing accident, or maybe he'd been a boxer at school? She didn't need this man's money. She had her tendrils in plenty of other people's accounts. She never took too much money from one account, which was the beauty of the program—no one ever noticed that they were spending twice as much as they normally did on water infusions, or whatever other little luxury they barely thought about. It was enough to keep her in the Middle without another means of income, enough to afford a designer handbag once in a while and not a lot else. But soon enough, she'd be living high off of Clarissa's unconscious largess, perhaps for the rest of her life. So why rob this man? She had simply met a man at a bar and found him attractive. She had brought

Alexander upstairs because she wanted to have sex with him—nothing more. She hadn't ever been more attracted to the man than to the act of stealing from him, a development that made her queasy. He shifted in his sleep, moving his big body closer to hers. He felt warm and deliciously solid, and she resisted the urge to lay her hand on his barrel chest and go to sleep.

Normally she waited longer, but it was late, and she was tired, and tomorrow was another day of pretending to be a servant. This was the time. Silently she crept out of bed. She took out her sonic cypher, now much more sophisticated than the rudimentary tool she'd used for opening Agata's accounts. She found his cylindrical briefcase and took it into the bathroom with her tool kit. There she used her tuning router program (with a silencer, of course) to find and break the phonic code of his briefcase. It unlocked for her easily. Reiko was surprised to see his briefcase was rather bare, with no important papers or even a phone or tablet. There was only a single mobile wallet inside, but that would suit her purposes fine. She connected her cypher on one end, then frowned to realize she was already inside the account—he either kept it unlocked, which was very unlikely, or he used the same code as another one of her marks.

She did a deeper dive than normal. Nowadays Reiko used a program she'd devised to find the top five most common charges and duplicate them on the mark's bill for the coming months. That money was funneled back to her. But tonight she scrolled through manually because, well, she was interested. She saw the charge for a night at the hotel, and drinks. And then she saw the meal at the restaurant where she had eaten in the financial district, and her spa treatments—including tip. A slow, creeping cold started at her feet and traveled up. She scrolled down further to find every purchase she herself had made over the last period, and all those from the other accounts that fed back into hers like tributaries. Before she could think, before she could speak, there was a warm hand on the back of her neck. She turned and saw him, flabbergasted, eyes bulging, and for a brief moment she wondered if he would hit her. Then he smiled, like a dog—no, like a shark. He crouched next to her on the cold tile floor, wearing only the hotel robe, and she was still nude. Her mind was a shifting kaleidoscope of emotions—shock, disbelief, fear, and doubt, and then a strange, airy delight, like discovering she had won the lottery without having bought a ticket.

He gently touched her cheek, as if checking to make sure she was real. He said softly, with wonder and awe, "You're a thief."

"*You're* a thief," she repeated back at him. Then she leaned to close the space between them and kissed him.

Their next round of lovemaking was very different, but just as marvelous—slower, more tender. Afterward, Reiko didn't feel like crying. But she also couldn't tell if it was over—he kept kissing her and kissing her, her armpits, her shoulders, mapping secret freckles, tonguing the edge of her ear. She lay on the bed and let herself be kissed, laughing again at the wonderful strangeness of the world, until she did cry from joy. *This is what happiness feels like,* she thought, her hand over her own heart. *This is happiness.*

———

"Tell me about the first time you did this."

Reiko smiled in the dark. His great big head was on her breast, and she ran her fingers through his curly hair. "Storytime, is it?" She pressed a kiss to his head. "I was in my second year of college. I had just learned that my scholarship was being taken away by a mousy man in the registrar's office with a weedy little mustache. I remember how he looked, shuffling papers, fingers twitching, playing with the sleeves of his purple frock. He couldn't keep still. Now I wonder if he was guilty—he knew they'd been out to devour me all along. I was crying about losing my scholarship, really breaking down, snot running down my nose and everything—and then I realized that shiteater was staring at my legs!"

He chuckled softly. "My poor lamb. What a shiteater!" Then he looked up at her again. "What's your real name?"

Reiko gave his shoulder a squeeze. In his sleepiness, his Low Quake accent was coming out thick and strong. He sounded like a neighborhood boy. "Reiko."

"That's a mighty fine name, Reiko."

"What's your name?"

"Keith."

Reiko had learned how to suppress her own accent when she was only a little girl, by parroting the beautiful women and men speaking in the broad, rounded accent of Above on the big screen. Only when she spoke to her family did she feel the old speech patterns coming back. Grandma's funeral was the last time she had set foot on the ground. That had been over two years ago.

"How old are you?"

He stroked her side. "Well, my ID says I'm a highly respectable, well-kept forty-nine."

Her heart beat in her chest. "How old are you really?"

"I'll be thirty-seven in the spring, sweetheart." He shifted up to look at her. "How old are you?"

Reiko felt her eyes grow humid with tears. "I tell most people I'm nineteen. But I'm twenty-six next month." *We're the same,* she thought. *You're just like me.*

"You're my twin," he murmured, peppering her skin with more kisses. "My absolute mirror image. I want to hear the rest of the story."

"Ah," she said. "Well, that was the night of my first grift. I dipped my roommate, a rich girl from Above." Reiko felt a coil of something like regret surge up from her belly. She missed Agata, certainly. After her, marks were never so personal—Reiko made sure of that.

"You seduced your roommate?" Keith asked sleepily.

Reiko shook her head. "No, I've never been a lover of my own sex, not even for a con." She wanted to tell him everything, but the words felt heavy, cumbersome in her mouth. Where to start? "I did it in two parts. I realized I could steal from Agata, and it turned me on. I hadn't felt that in a long time, or maybe ever. Later that night, I couldn't sleep. I went to a local bar with students and some working folks. Businessmen went there occasionally, looking for college girls. I sat alone at the bar . . ."

"Ah, I see. You have a type." He looked up at her. "Was he more handsome than me? Taller?"

"You're so vain!" She squeezed him tight. *No,* she thought, *none of those men were even half as beautiful as you.* "He was quite plain. He seemed a good bit older at the time, but looking back, I realize he was barely older than I am now. Isn't that funny?" He made a soft little sound of agreement. "He asked to buy me a drink, and I let him. And we talked—we really talked. I was so raw that night, I told him everything! Told him about losing my scholarship and my sister at the textile mill, about how I didn't want that life. I even told him I was from the Bastian. I was upset, confused, I felt so alone." The weight of Keith's head on her chest grew heavier. He was falling asleep in her arms. She'd finish the story, whether he was listening or not, enjoying the sound of her own voice in the dark room, his steady breathing. "He wasn't good-looking, but he was a good listener. As soon as we were on the bed in the hotel, though, it was like he was a different person."

His voice was deeper, husky with sleep. "Tell me."

Reiko kissed his hair, delighted to discover she wasn't talking to herself. "Well, I had liked him because he was a good listener. But suddenly there was no communication happening at all. It was like being made love to by a sleepwalker. I almost said something."

"Did you want to tell him to stop?"

"I wanted to tell him to start!" She laughed at her own joke, which delighted her all the more. It normally took her much longer with a person to let any humor in. "But afterward, the man from the bar seemed to return. He was chatty and warm. He kissed my cheek . . . then asked me if I'd like to have something to eat." She paused. "Will it bother you if I talk about this?"

Keith shrugged. "There are no fancy juice bars or smoothie fasts in the Low Quake." He looked at her. "But I don't have to tell you that, right? I ate like everyone else ate. And if we didn't eat, we'd actually starve, not just pretend to starve to get closer to God, or get our meals sucked out our butts like—"

She put a hand on his delightfully hairy chest. "Like some of the women you've lain with, in your businessman frock?"

He grinned. "Indeed. But on with your story."

Her stomach swirled with warmth. "I told him I was hungry and would join him for a meal. There was a refrigerator in the room for beverages. He asked if I would set the table for us, like we were husband and wife."

"I think I know where this is going . . ."

"Inside the refrigerator was a cold feast. Crab legs, oysters on the half shell, small sweet clams. Salty caviar, to be served with crepes and cream. We used the hotel iron to heat up the crepes." They were both still half-dressed, giggling as they "cooked" the crepes on the ironing board. "Sliced pink duck breast with cherry compote. A salad of endive and pear. A chocolate tasting." A basket of bread, hiding on the counter under a cloth, revealed with a magician's flair. "I could go on! All this to say, it was very opulent."

"What did you do with it?" He wrinkled his nose. "He didn't make you sit in it, did he? Or pelt your naked body with crab legs from across the room?"

She laughed. "No, but I've seen stranger things since. Back then, I had no idea about anything. We just ate and chatted. Opened another bottle of wine. It was lovely. And then the meal was over, and he seemed sad. He grew very quiet. I remember that after our dinner, I wanted to lie down again, I was so full! But he stood, even though it was four in the morning, and began to get dressed. I was so confused—I thought I had done something wrong."

"Oh, love—"

"And finally I asked him why he wasn't tired—"

His voice was soft. "Brave girl."

"He said, 'I can't afford any more, you're bleeding me dry!'" Reiko blushed. She remembered how his face appeared to change in the dim lamplight, no longer like an older, worldly man, but a petulant boy. "And then he pressed several hundred ducats into my hands and said that I was a very beautiful girl, and that he hoped that I really did enroll in school one day. Then he handed me my shoes and pushed me into the hallway, half-nude." The story hung in the air for a long moment. Then Keith started laughing, really laughing, in a wild uproar, kicking his legs about the fine cool sheets. "Don't laugh at my humiliation!" Then she joined him. "Oh, fine—it *is* funny."

When he laughed, he seemed even younger. "He thought you were a nun for hire. Oh, wow!"

Reiko kissed his hair again. "Who knows what he thought," she whispered. "I realized that night that it didn't matter. People were going to see me in a certain way and fit my face to whatever story they wanted. So why not make money off of it?"

"You're a bloody genius, is what you are," he said sleepily into her hair. Her heart felt buoyant and light, as if it could float into the night sky like a runaway airship. At that moment, Reiko knew she already loved him. She didn't even know his last name.

I did not catch a glimpse of the returned king, nor did I see his new wife from that faraway land. All the fragments of conversations I overhead seemed to agree that they were a strange match—he so handsome, she thin and pale, with a strangely smooth head, no ridge at all, like an egg. Rumors abounded about her odd customs to petition the god she served. I paid these outlandish stories little heed.

Weeks passed, and my life was much the same—cooking, cleaning, feuding with the old woman, sleeping on rags. In the late spring, my knight came back. He knelt on the ground and took my hand, apologized for staying away for so long. I was so happy to see him, but I mistrusted the feeling. He would surely leave as soon as he came, like before, and I would be alone again. But all through that spring, summer, and into autumn, again and again, my knight came to visit me, to learn about my life previous to Castle Mora, and, of course, to enjoy my recipes.

I learned that his name was Henray, and that he had never really known his mother—she died when he was a baby. His father was a good man, but overly burdened, and Henray's rearing had been left mostly to nursemaids and schoolteachers. At some point during this period, my living conditions improved—one day I returned to my little hovel, my pile of rags, to find it all gone. Had I been demoted by the old woman to sleep on the bare floor, like a dog? But then a scullery maid led me to my own little room with a proper bed, a table, a chair. Having a bed was a luxury not afforded to me since I'd left my village, and truly, I had never had a room of my own, with a door that I might close or even lock, in my entire life.

Cooking for Henray filled me with joy. When I prepared a meal for him, only for him, especially one of my village's recipes—that was when I felt most like myself. I often stayed up later than I ought, chatting with him, sleeping only three or four hours before rising to do it all again the next day. I wasn't tired; I was young, I was energetic.

I was falling in love.

By winter, I thought of him constantly. One day the following spring, when I had the morning to myself, I went hunting in the neighboring woods for mushrooms. I hadn't foraged for mushrooms for pleasure—only for survival, when I traveled to the castle with only the stars to guide my way—not since the day the wave had come and changed my life forever. But instead of feeling sad mushroom-picking that day, I felt a calm, quiet joy, like the way my mind would sometimes feel after staring at the sea. I missed my parents, my siblings, my aunt, and especially my uncle. I missed the food we would make together, the stories we would share, our lives in tune with the seasons. Meeting Henray had revealed an ache that I had been carrying inside me all these years. It felt lighter, now, to share my past with someone dear.

And oh, was he dear. Henray insisted that he do all the dishes from our meals together. *I don't want to create more work for you, Little Mother,* he would say. I grew angry when he was gone for too long, envious of the compatriots who got to see him, to speak to him in the daytime, as he could see me only at night. I wondered, in my little room, my single bed, if he was alone as I was, or if there was a woman keeping him warm.

The mushroom soup would need to cook down, slow and low, for three days until the broth was ready, the fresh fish added at the very last moment in cooking. I was now friendly with the fishmonger, so I could select a few choice morsels—a fine, flaky whitefish, two small lobsters, oysters, clams of several varieties. I had never taken such agency over the kitchen, and I didn't know how the old woman would respond.

By some miracle, or a blessing from the gods, the old woman sickened on the second day of my broth-making, and she kept away until she was well. The night the soup was ready, my Henray came to see me, bearing a small gift, as he often did now when he visited. This time, it was a box of sweetened fruits on delicate colored paper. It was the finest object I had ever possessed, from the beautiful carved wooden box to the paper inside to the exotic fruits like bright sugared jewels. Inside, however, among the fruits was a real pearl, set in a surround of gold.

"No," I said, pushing the box away. "It's far too fine!"

He laughed. "Little Mother, I procured it for you to celebrate one year since our meeting. You are my pearl from the ocean."

I huffed. "Well, I made you a soup, but now it will seem rather poor in comparison." I felt my face grow hot, as if I might cry. "I might as well throw it away in the muck!"

"Ijo," he said softly. "I did not mean to embarrass you. I'm sorry." He put a finger to my cheek and wiped away a tear. "May I try the soup, please?"

I served it silently. The smell was all around us, heavy and rich as wet leaves, complex, earthy, intoxicating. I put the bowl and spoon in front of him like an offering.

His nostrils flared, and when he looked up at me, there was fire in his eyes.

"What is this?" he whispered.

"Three-day mushroom soup with seafood," I said, puzzled by his tone.

His eyes narrowed, and he sighed as if he was angry, then took up his spoon like it was a knife, stabbing at the bowl. He swallowed, groaned, then let the spoon clatter down on the table.

"Henray," I asked, fear stirring within me, "do you not like it?"

He stood then and walked over to me. I don't think he had ever been so close, so powerfully near. I felt the disparity in our heights— no longer was his friendly face looking over at me from the kitchen counter. Henray loomed over me.

"What do you want from me," he said softly. I could feel the heat coming off him in waves.

I knew what I wanted.

"I want to be with you," I said. "Not just in the kitchen. And I want to cook for you. I want to talk to you, and—"

"Do you wish to be close to me? For your days and your nights?"

He was so very near.

"Yes," I said.

That was enough. He gathered me up in his arms.

My first kiss was like returning to the ocean: warm, thrilling, yet somehow familiar. I trusted, yet it felt dangerous, like I was being carried away by the current. His heart beat fast, like mine. We swam together.

Henray kissed me in the kitchen, long and sweet, standing up against the counter, and then, after a few moments, nestled me against the wall. He kept pulling back to look at me, to see my face, the flush in my cheeks, my half-closed eyes, then kissing me anew. At the time, I didn't know any better—I thought perhaps all men kissed like that. Only later did I realize he was checking, so very fastidiously, that I was equally happy in our embrace. He did not wish to paw at the kitchen girl while she waited for it to be over.

I was so naïve. I thought kissing was the end of our investigations. A whole continent to explore, and I had no other destination in mind. But then he leaned against me with the full length of his body, and I felt an electric charge from the bottom of my feet shooting up into my spine. Unthinkingly, I ground my body back into his, panting into his mouth. He gripped me at the hips, and then pulled away again. His mouth was a firm line, his brow furrowed. He no longer resembled my gentle friend of so many late-night chats.

I leaned my face in toward him again, for another kiss. But he paused.

"Ijo," he murmured. "I don't know if you're ready."

"I'm ready," I said, wishing for more. "Kiss me!"

He pushed his head into my neck. I stroked his hair, unsure of what was happening. "Then I'm not sure if I'm ready."

"Forgive me," I whispered into his hair. But I still did not know what I had done wrong.

He lifted his head and kissed me, again and again. This time he did not pull away for a long while. When we finally separated, breathless, the soup was rather cold. I did not mind.

I heated it up again without speaking and motioned for him to sit. He poured us both a glass of wine, as was now our habit. I gave myself a bowl as well and, suddenly ravenous, a slice of crusty bread and butter.

He grinned to see me eat.

We enjoyed our soups in silence. The taste of the slow-cooked mushrooms, the memory of Henray's mouth on mine, his body pressing me against the wall—something within me had unlocked.

"It was my father's thirty-fifth birthday," I said. "I had three siblings—Hadir, gentle and tall, like a sunflower, who was quiet and loved to walk in the woods, always so kind to animals. Bijo, my name-twin, could not have been more different in affect from Hadir. His laugh was so loud, you could hear it anywhere in the village, like a great, braying goat. He was always ready with a joke, a story, a song. And Eusa, our special diver, who made us feel as though all the oysters in our ocean had pearls. I was the middle child, and only remarkable because of my love of cooking. All of them were better people than me—smarter, kinder, quick to laugh, quicker to forgive. I was fifteen when the big wave came. Nothing was left of us except me."

I wiped my face and was surprised to find it as wet as if I'd been swimming.

"It's amazing you survived," he said. "That you found your way here." He held me in his arms. "To me. No one has ever treated me like you do. You are so dear to me," said Henray slowly, looking into my eyes. "I want to keep you. But I'm afraid of what will change. Do you understand? I want to go to bed with you at night and wake up with you in the morning. Not once," he added quickly, "but for many moons to come. Forever, if you'll have me."

I felt as if my heart's desires were being offered to me on a plate. But I did not understand what was being asked of me, or what I was agreeing to. Had I, my life might have turned out very differently.

"Yes," I breathed. "Henray, I'm yours."

After more embraces and promises of affection, Henray told me to go to sleep while he washed the dishes. He said he needed to be alone, to think. I floated back to my room, feeling like my mouth was new, my hands were new, my face, and certainly my body, all anointed by the power of his kisses and the weight of his hands. In my little bed, I reached down to touch between my legs and found another ocean. I pressed my fingers to the softest spot, whispering his name. *Henray, Henray, Henray . . .*

Dear reader, it must surprise you that I was not thinking of marriage. In my village, couples did not formally wed. They partnered together, had children, ran a household, but their households were often many more than two people—in my house, I lived with my parents, my brothers, my uncle and auntie, my paternal grandparents, and some cousins from a neighboring village who were training with my mother to be divers. Thinking back, I do not know whether these "cousins" were actually blood relatives—they wished to be divers, and we took them in. Who wasn't a cousin, in some way or another? The sea was our mother, and we lived from her benevolence. I do not know if my parents ever had a marriage ceremony. There were certainly no papers signed, no official seals or announcements. Just two people who had decided to make their lives together. I did not expect this from Henray, nor was I looking to extract the promise of forever. I did want to be with him in the morning and at night. I was also very young and did not think much about the future, which rushes toward us at all times, severe and certain as a hawk in its dive.

MENU FOR A GRAND SEDUCTION (WITHOUT KNOWING IT)

Three-day mushroom soup,
combined with a temper tantrum and unwashed hair.

Serve hot, tear-stained, and reeking of fish.

3.

Margot, Beatrice, and Erek sat in the dining room while a very angry Walter paced in front of them, stroking his greasy mustache. On the table before them were five servings of the previous night's main course, all untouched.

"Last night," began Walter, "for the first time in as long as I can remember, we had a loss instead of a profit. And not by a little— we made less than half of our usual! I fear this has lost us several longtime customers as well. My restaurant is no place for political statements, nor art pieces. This is a place of *business*."

Erek looked as though he was about to cry. Walter sighed and put an arm on his shoulders. "I'm simply saying, this kind of thing will send us all to the poorhouse. Do you understand?"

"I don't," said Beatrice. "Erek made a gorgeous dish." She glanced over at one of the beautiful birds, made out of celery, several types of mushrooms, and a fanned lemon-slice tail, plus "eggs" of carved turnips. "Perhaps not as flavorsome as it could have been, but—"

Erek hung his head.

"No, Erek, listen—with a few tweaks, it would make a first-rate main course." She squinted at Margot. "We've often served a dish not up to our standards, and it's always gobbled up. I don't see what the fuss is—"

"Tabitha, did I say you could speak? This is not a planning meeting." Walter squeezed his forehead, deepening its ridge. "Now," he said, brushing off his jacket, "Erek and I are due at church. Tabitha, would you like to join us? Of course, you are free to do whatever you wish with your day off."

She repressed a shudder. Walter and Erek attended some food-positive Free-Wah church. No matter what its name or purpose, she couldn't imagine ever setting foot in a church again. "No thanks," she said gruffly.

"Suit yourself. As head chef, Margot is responsible for the fiasco last night. She will stay and turn this mess of mushrooms into something we can sell. Erek, let's go." Walter hoisted his umbrella over his shoulder and guided Erek out the door with a flourish.

Margot gathered the platters and began to bring them into the kitchen, grumbling all the while. But when Beatrice put on her apron to join her, she crossed her arms.

"Not your problem."

"I'm happy to help—I don't have anything else to do."

Margot raised an eyebrow. "You should get some hobbies."

"I don't understand why Walter's so mad! We've failed with risks before. We're a small team. Our food sources are unreliable! And Erek and I are still learning! Isn't that the whole point?"

Margot sighed. "This is one of the few places in the Middle where you can eat without privacy screens. Some folks want to pretend to be cannibals, so we serve them some unrecognizable meat, stewed or braised or roasted." She rolled up her sleeves. "Other people just want a hearty meal and a glass of wine without having to hide their faces. Yes, what we served last night was beautiful. But it tasted like mush. If you serve a vegetable-forward dish, it better be amazing." She rolled up her sleeves. "Or folks will send it back. They risk a lot in coming here; we have to make it worth it."

"Then we have to figure out how to find better ingredients—"

Margot glared at her. "That isn't your problem." She pushed her out of the kitchen with a grunt. "Go be a teenager!"

Beatrice wandered the quiet city. It wasn't Walter's fault that their supply chains were so unreliable, that everyone in the city pretended not to eat and then pounded on their door at night. But she'd come to the city to learn how to cook, not to playact cannibalism for anyone who paid. It was demeaning. Dozens of little moments came flooding back to her, but especially Margot storming out into the alley to smoke out her frustrations after another table of rude, naked guests smeared food onto each other.

After days, the rain had stopped and the sky was gray. Rather than making the landscape drab, the bleak sky accentuated bright colors, the wetness giving the whole world a kind of luster. Potted plants tangled together in merry crowds on windowsills. A breeze made the trees lining the boulevard wave hello. Beatrice loved her neighborhood on Delany Lane. She now knew the restaurant was in a residential section on the edge of the Middle, hovering just above the Bastian, not too far from the arts district. There was a nice mix of Free-Wah and ALGN folk in the neighborhood, and while no one made a show of eating in public, every so often Beatrice would pass a huskier stranger or see someone carrying a brown paper package under one arm and realize it was probably a loaf of bread. She stayed away from the financial district— the bright, shiny office buildings with juice bars and cycling studios at the bottom, billboards for cleanses and colonics and even weight-loss surgery at the top. Several of the buildings had Stecopo's name in tall, monolithic lettering.

Beatrice wandered around the perimeter of the park. There was a man by the entrance, gazing at her.

"Hello," he said. He looked about twenty—light skin, brown eyes, blond hair. "You look so familiar! Do I know you?"

She studied his face, wondering if he had been to the restaurant. She couldn't place him. "I don't think so."

"Well, I'm Thom."

"Nice to meet you. Tabitha."

He put on a stern voice. "Shouldn't you be in church, young lady?"

She thought back to something that Father Alvarez had said to her during one of their private counseling sessions after the grilled-cheese incident. "How could God be in church and not here in the park as well?"

"I love that." When he smiled, his face went from ordinary to handsome.

How long had it been since she'd flirted with someone? Certainly not since moving to the city. "Anyway," she said with raised eyebrows, "I'm too fat for church."

"I think you're lovely." He looked at her body frankly. "Maybe we can have our own service."

At this, her cunt gave a mighty kick. Beatrice had been so busy cooking, she hadn't had sex in months. "All right," she said, unbuttoning her coat. She took him by the hand and led him deeper into the park.

They found a private spot by a tall oak tree. She pressed her back against the bark, and he came to her. The man hitched a hand into her knickers while the other ran across her left breast. "Ooh, that's nice," he said, kissing the side of her face. She almost turned her head to meet his lips, then remembered that kissing on the mouth wasn't done in these kinds of encounters (or so it appeared on television). Beatrice had never had sex with someone she didn't already know from Seagate. As he moved his mouth down to her neck and caressed her, she wondered if he would try some city technique she didn't know. So far, he was like the other boys she had lain with—energetic, easy to please, though perhaps chattier than most. He kept exclaiming over different parts of her body: her breasts, her thighs. Beatrice had never had sex as a fat girl before, and his hands wouldn't let her forget that her body had changed. He kept returning to her fleshiest parts, finding and squeezing her ass, her belly. She had certainly never seen anything like that on television. At one point, while he was activating her with his fingers, he even whispered, "Oh, I just love a plump maiden—I hope you don't mind me saying!"

"I don't," she said, deciding that the time for outercourse had passed. She turned around and hiked up her skirt. "I like a plump maiden too."

"You're a rare bird, aren't you?" He rolled on a prophylactic, then, pulling her underwear to the side, entered her, keeping the fabric around her hips. Yet she kept hearing the words of that drunk arsehole in her mind—*Fatty. Fatty, good night, Fatty,* as she looked down at the dimples in her knees, the squish of her pale thighs. She couldn't shake the words away. The man grabbed at the fleshiest part of her hips and moaned, her ass shaking with the force of his thrusts, his breath hot and joyful in her ear. *Yes, Fatty,* thought Beatrice. *That's right, you glorious, beautiful Fatty.* Beatrice cried out, ascending almost immediately. The man held on to her panties like a lasso. It had been too long since she had been touched, and everything around her seemed hopelessly erotic—the tree bark, the grass, the dim twin moons in the morning sky, the spires of buildings, the buds of flowers. She held the tree and shuddered. Beatrice came with a shout, then relaxed into revelry, allowing herself to be kissed, grabbed, complimented.

While he was exclaiming over her body, calling certain parts tight and small, others big and luscious, all in a hazy, joyous jumble, she noticed the most beautiful thing growing up from a crack in the sidewalk. But instead of running toward it, the way she would have in Seagate, she let him finish, just to be polite.

"That was downright marvelous," he said afterward, kissing her cheek. "Can we do that again sometime?"

She hesitated. Should she invite him to the restaurant for a meal? Then he looked at her again, this time with eyes narrowed. "Ah! I know where I know you from. Has anyone ever told you that you look like the Stecopo girl?"

Her nostrils flared. "Yes, I've heard it before."

"So lovely to meet you, Tabitha. Hope to see you around!" He tightened his belt, blew her a kiss, and left.

Beatrice knelt on the concrete to caress the tender weed. Its small, waxy green leaves were connected to a light, wiry stem, flopping and sprawling over the sidewalk. She pulled up several by the roots, brushing off dirt clumps, before tucking the little plants into her coat pocket. Beatrice ran all the way home with her prize.

And then she saw it.

A slip of bright-orange paper, tucked under the corner of their doormat. Someone, in a shaky hand, had scrawled on it:

JUST BECAUSE IT'S LEGAL, DOESN'T MEAN IT'S RIGHT

She looked around, heart hammering in her chest, but there was no one on the street. Someone was watching them—but who?

When she got back to the kitchen, she was disappointed to

find Margot gone, and last night's leftovers turned into meatballs. "Hey, Lina," she said to no one. "I thought I'd just call you for a chat. How are things?"

She turned on the stovetop burner and held the note to the flame. It caught and curled instantly. Beatrice put it out in the sink, rinsing the little burnt flecks of paper down the drain. "Lina," she said to herself, as if her old mentor were present, "every day I move between the happiest I've ever felt and the worst I've ever felt. Sometimes more than once a day! I'm like a yo-yo." She washed her prize—what the foraging book called purslane—in the sink, along with a whole onion. Chopped together with a good squeeze of lemon and salt, it would make a satisfying salad, topped with a globular poached egg. "I wish you could come for a visit. Call me little mouse, berate me, that kind of thing." Beatrice tasted the salad and made improvements. Less salt—purslane was naturally salty—white pepper, a touch more oil. "Chef Margot thinks I need some hobbies." The poached egg made a bright sauce for the dish. Paired with a piece of her warm, puffy flatbread, the meal would feel rounded, complete. "Not fair, is it? Back in Seagate, my only hobby was cooking."

Beatrice had set a table for three when Walter and Erek returned from church. She had already cried twice in the bathroom that afternoon—over the note, over the man in the park recognizing her from the Stecopo ad, over her parents, over everything, over nothing. She felt purged from all the crying and excited for her next sales pitch. It was what they had taught her at school—*you don't sell Stecopo products, you sell personal success.* She smoothed her hair and smiled at her audience.

"Allow me." She poured three glasses of water from the carafe, joining Walter and Erek at the table. "This is purslane, a green that grows wild in even inhospitable environments. It's incredibly rich in calcium, potassium, and vitamin A." They looked at her as if she were speaking another language, but she pushed on. "Spring is almost here! And there's a bounty outside our doorstep for anyone willing to look. That's the first part of the plan—to forage for wild ingredients. This salad is made from greens I found in the park." *Breathe,* she thought, shoulders back, spine tall. "Walter, the main problem with the vegetables last night was their quality. With a little space and care, our cuisine could be much improved by an influx of fresh ingredients."

He did not look impressed. She almost faltered, but she'd already made it this far. "I'm asking for permission to start a garden. I'll do all the work myself, of course."

At this, he hooked an eyebrow.

"Walter, imagine! What if twenty percent of our food costs went out the window? Or even thirty? What that could do for your bottom line?"

He sighed melodramatically.

"I only ask"—here Walter groaned, chewing noisily—"I only ask for your contacts, so I may be sent seeds."

"All right, then," he said finally, wiping his food-speckled chin. "I suppose it's my turn, but I feel like I'm caught in a marketing seminar in my own bloody house, so I'll summarize." He took a sip of water. "With habitable land shrinking by the year, he who controls the land controls the people. Now don't look at me with those eyes—I'll let you propagate some plants and rummage around the city like a common squirrel." Then he looked at her very gravely. "But you will not bring the great eye of the public to my door." She thought of the note, now ashes, but said nothing. Walter continued without missing a beat. "You may grow things on the third floor, in the spare room, under the skylight. You'll need heat lamps and soil and fertilizer, lots of water, plus all man-

ner of other things you aren't anticipating. It is far more complicated than ordering a few seeds. But it's a good idea, if an ambitious
one, and I will support it."

Beatrice beamed. "Thank you, sir! You won't regret it."

"But if I wake up and there's a field of corn in our alley, I will
chuck you out on the street. Do you hear me? I won't let you risk
what we've built here." He looked at her carefully. "Do you hear
me, whatever-your-name-is?"

He had never before alluded to her life prior to the restaurant,
nor the papers he'd secured for her escape in the night.

"Yes," she said quietly. "I understand."

There were some early successes. Salad greens, sprouts, cherry tomatoes, barrels of fresh herbs. Plants that were easy to cultivate and
hard to kill. Margot, in her all-knowing, taught Beatrice how to
grow an avocado tree from a pit, and likewise how to propagate
ginger from the root. Her wanders through the city grew very productive as the spring deepened. Chickweed, lovage, sorrel, lamb's
ear. Grape leaves liberated from a decorative arbor in the dead of
night. Beatrice sewed deep pockets into all of her clothes.

In a park close to the row house, plantain, violets, clover, and
dandelion greens cropped up under the elm trees. Beatrice's father
used to give her a half-ducat to uproot the dandelions from their
yard, before their bushy spores floated all over. Her whole life, there
had been so much food around her that she had never noticed. She
thought back to that miraculous plum tree in the schoolyard.

Roses blossomed, their hips and buds harvested, pounded into
tea, or candied with sugar and eaten with creamy pudding. Sting-
ing nettles grew in abundance by the airstrip out past the edge of
the city. Beatrice harvested massive handfuls of the prickly, painful

green while wearing gloves. (She learned that the hard way.) Later that evening at the restaurant, the green of the day would be the nettle, boiled and drained, then salted and sautéed in oil. The delicate green was a marriage between the flavor of cucumber and the texture of baby spinach.

Quickly their greenhouse spread out, first into the hallway and then into Beatrice's room, where she lined her windowsill with edible flowers. Because Beatrice had almost no belongings, the room finally felt properly full, as if she had gotten several dozen new, quiet roommates. She lay in her little bed at night, breathing in the rich oxygen from the baby plants, imagining her own breath feeding their secret, hidden mouths in return. *What do plants dream about?* she wondered as she drifted to sleep. Beatrice's own dreams were scattered and vague. Georgina's laugh. Her strong, bare back. A ripe peach, dripping. Her mother's voice coming from far away, as if from underwater. She awoke in the middle of the night and looked out her window. The moons were high in the sky, poking out from behind the domed, tiered skyscrapers that held the richest citizens, like a child playing hide-and-seek. Against the night sky, the silver orbs of the high-rises floated ever upward in space, the black beams between them nearly invisible in the darkness. Beatrice couldn't imagine the lives of those floating Above, ethereal beings who would never soil their feet on the earth below, closer to angels than to animals. Perhaps they truly were without appetite. But how could God dwell more in a silver zeppelin or a closed habitat orb than in the perfect green of a tender leaf? *Let them have their mechanized heaven,* she thought. She plucked a small orange nasturtium from her windowsill and popped it into her mouth. With the spicy taste of the flower still on her tongue, Beatrice fell back asleep.

Two men stood outside the back door to pick up their large to-go order. Typically the restaurant didn't do takeaway, as much of its appeal was people eating together without privacy screens. But the order was a very big one, perhaps for an event, and Walter assumed they had rented their own venue. Sometimes Free-Wah families used restaurant food, packed up in hot steam trays, for a baby shower or even a wedding. Beatrice loved cooking for events—imagining proud parents, forks and knives scraping on plates, children asking for second helpings. It gave her a sense of satisfaction she'd never known existed.

The men kept looking up and down the street. They handed Erek the envelope of bills so he could count them. Beatrice began bringing the trays of food out to their trolley.

"Stupid me, I forgot a tip," said the man, gesturing with a twenty-piece note. "Allow me to tuck him in?" He took the envelope out of Erek's hands and placed the tip money inside to join the rest. Then the man put the whole envelope back in his own inside jacket pocket and looked at them squarely.

"Tabitha," said Erek softly. "Go inside."

"But I'm not done yet."

"Margot!" Erek called. "Walter! Code red!"

"Now, now," said the man, patting his lower jacket. "None of that."

His friend took the handle of the trolley, and they walked briskly up the street with half the food and all the money, receding into the mist.

Fog had come in from the harbor and made the night steamy. For a moment, Beatrice stared after them in confusion. "What?" she began, her mind a jumble of noise. "How?"

"We were just robbed," said Erek curtly. Walter emerged a second later, wiping his sweaty head with a dishcloth. "There you are!"

"Those folks with the big order?" he asked mildly. "They seemed off on the phone. Are you all right? Did they have a gun?"

"We're fine," said Erek. "Maybe? One man patted his jacket, but that was it. I'm sorry, Walter."

"Tut-tut," Walter said, lighting his pipe. "*You're* not the one who robbed me."

"Shit, fucking shit," said Margot, joining them, wielding a chef's knife. "Goddamn it! Again?"

"Again," said Erek glumly.

"Well, call the police!" exclaimed Beatrice. "What's everyone standing around for?"

"Yes, that's an excellent way to triple our losses," said Walter dryly. "Let's call the police."

Margot went back inside for a moment. When she returned, she'd replaced the knife with her pipe and joined Walter in smoking.

"But we've been robbed!" cried Beatrice. "What am I missing?"

Walter put a big hand on her shoulder. "The police won't do anything but ask for a bribe—or, if they're the upright sort, they'll find a way to fine us for having a bathroom without the proper square footage, or some other nonsense. The authorities don't like Eaters, Free-Wah or otherwise. They aren't on our side."

She thought of that stupid note. "But we're not doing anything illegal!" But her voice was higher this time, childlike and less convincing, even to her.

———

Margot entered the kitchen silently, holding her helmet under one arm and a large parcel under the other. Beatrice had grown accustomed to the nuances of Margot's stoic expression. A slight frown at the mouth meant she was holding in either a sharp remark or a witty joke. But tonight she looked openly tense and grim.

"Am I about to be fired?" joked Beatrice. "Margot, what's in the box?"

Margot put down the helmet, then withdrew a folded piece of paper from her jacket pocket and handed it to Beatrice. It was a Missing Persons flyer. There was Beatrice—her younger, thinner self, smiling up at the camera, an anonymous hotline number at the bottom.

Beatrice crumpled up the piece of paper, wrinkling and distorting her own face. "Where did you get this?"

"In my neighborhood." Margot lived way on the other end of the Middle. "There was a whole mess of them. Plastered all over— walls, lampposts, anywhere they could stick them. But I kept my eyes peeled on my trip here. I haven't seen any nearby. They're barking up the wrong tree." Margot set her unopened parcel on the counter.

Suddenly Beatrice couldn't breathe. She felt like an overgrown plant crammed in a tiny pot.

Margot sat Beatrice down on a kitchen stool. She held out a snip of basil. "Chew," she said. Beatrice obeyed, and the sharp flavor spread over her tongue. Her breath returned to her.

"I'm going to tell you a story," said Margot. "I was born up there." She pointed out the window to the tallest of the floating orbs hovering over the city. "At the table of the richest. My family had eight children." Beatrice sat speechless. Only the very, very wealthy could reproduce limitlessly, using a parade of surrogates. "I was the youngest girl. When I was fourteen years old, I realized my place in the family dynasty: I was the designated Flesh Martyr."

"They starved you?"

Margot shook her head. "The stories you hear are mostly metaphors, Beatrice. They point to an emotional truth, not a literal one. My parents would never have come out and said that they wanted me to starve myself. But they *did* say it, in a million ways, big and small. I was raised to be thin—so thin I could disappear. To survive off of light and air, off of crumbs. And if it made me sick, so be it. If my bones grew brittle and weak, so be it. If my period stopped, so be it. If I died, I died living as I should. Quietly, politely. An ornamental body." Margot put her hand on Beatrice's shoulder. "We're taught that the most important thing we can contribute to the world is our beauty, our thinness. This saps our energy, our brainpower, our internal fight. It makes us feel crazy, as if our bodies are enemies, our own minds cannot be trusted. We cannot take on the world for we are too busy battling ourselves."

"So you ran away? Like me."

Margot sniffed. "You could say that. Hey, open this. It's for you."

Beatrice pulled the thick cardboard packaging apart to reveal a stocky little lemon tree, barely more than a foot tall. Yet already on one of its spindly branches grew a globular lemon.

"It's young," said Margot, hanging her jacket on a hook. "But how splendid it could become, if we gave it time to grow?"

Beatrice threw herself into Margot's arms, her head against the head chef's wide chest.

"It's all right," Margot whispered fiercely. "You're not going anywhere."

Beatrice looked up at her, eyes glistening with unshed tears, and leaned in to kiss her.

Margot gripped her shoulders and moved her away. "Tell me what you have for me," she muttered, turning back toward the stove.

"Sorry, I know I shouldn't have done that," Beatrice said quietly. "We'll wait until I'm eighteen—"

"I'm only going to say this once." Margot looked at her

straight-on. "That is not what I'm offering you. What I'm offering is something different. Now, what do you have for me?"

Beatrice wiped her eyes, the sting of rejection alien and confusing. "Tables two and seven need salads. Five wants your sorrel soup. Roasted mutton with wild mushrooms for three and six."

Margot tied on her apron. "Let's get started."

Beatrice's crumpled face smiled up at them from the compost bin until it was covered with wet tea leaves. Later it would be joined by a burned Bundt cake Beatrice had forgotten to take out of the oven, so badly scorched it couldn't even be salvaged for bread pudding. Margot scolded her for her negligence. Beatrice couldn't decide if being treated as if nothing had happened made her feel better or worse. She got back to work.

———

That night, Beatrice made the mistake of typing "Stecopo girl" into the search bar on the house computer. She wasn't sure what she was looking for—a statement, perhaps, from the company, some clue as to why her parents would do such a thing. Instead, she found her image had been doctored and duplicated on a dozen different platforms by people outside of Seagate who just wanted a laugh. The lemon in Beatrice's hand was replaced by a chicken, a dildo, a plunger. She even found a giant lemon standing by the seaside, holding a tiny Beatrice.

Instead of computer or television for solace, she returned again to the book, feeling as if this girl from over a thousand years ago understood her the way no one else could.

Gentle reader, the book warned, *take heed of this very important lesson—it's vital for you to name exactly what you want.*

Beatrice had done that all those months ago, with Lina. She

had named exactly what she wanted—a place to learn how to cook—and she had gotten it. She had told Walter she wanted to cultivate and forage fresh ingredients, and she had gotten it. What did she want now? To speak to Lina, to see her parents again. To not waste this rare, sparkling opportunity she had been given to follow her passion. To fall in love again, this time with someone who understood her cooking. But sometimes that all felt about as possible as stepping back in time to have a cup of tea in Ijo's parlor.

———

Erek ran over, his basket overflowing. "Beatrice! Is this edible?" After the flyers, Beatrice had asked him to use her real name, at least when they were alone. He had taken to wandering the woods with Beatrice ("for your protection," he would say) as she hunted for wild mushrooms: morels, chanterelles, hen of the woods. He nearly poisoned himself every trip.

"That's hemlock. Don't eat it—you'll die."

"Oh," he said. "How about this?" He showed her a handful of berries.

"Those are gooseberries!" she exclaimed. "Show me where? We'll make jam. Nice find."

He poked through his basket. "And these?"

She stopped in her tracks. "Where did you find these?"

He pointed south. "There's a whole tree of them!"

"Yes," she said, laughing, visions of walnuts, raw and roasted, puréed and candied, dancing through her mind. "Yes, we can eat that." She paused, looking at her friend dappled with sunshine. "Hey, Erek?"

"Yes?"

She grinned. "You're like the brother I never had. I love you."

"You're ahead of schedule! It hasn't been a year yet."

"Felt silly to wait." The truth was, she missed her parents, she missed Lina, she missed the easy love of her childhood, like a hot-water tap that never ran cold. But she couldn't imagine ever going back.

They walked together back to the restaurant arm in arm. Everything suddenly seemed beautiful—the sky, the fresh air, the trees, the people walking on the street to church or school in their fine Middle clothes. A regular at the restaurant, a woman she knew as Ms. V, waved at her and Erek from across the street.

First Beatrice thought it was a trick of the light. As they approached the door of the restaurant, their home, their safe haven on Delany Lane, she let out a thin, audible cry when she realized the door was splattered in thick red paint. It dribbled down the steps, like sauce or blood. There was no note.

G entle reader, take heed of this very important lesson—it's vital for you to name exactly what you want. The asking in itself is a magic spell. Make sure your words are quite specific.

The old woman returned from her convalescence, but still no sign of my Henray. I was in the kitchen preparing the evening meal, tying together a rack of lamb with twine for a slow roast over a bed of chestnuts. The old woman came in and stared at me from across the room.

"You viper," she said softly. "I should have stamped you out while I had the chance."

I was used to such talk from her. She was a bitter old hag. "Pardon me, Chef?" I asked blandly. "Is there something you require?"

"You have been removed from your position," she said. "I'll have to find a new kitchen girl. And she won't be half as good as you." She snorted. "Maybe I should get two silly girls who can do the work of one. As long as they can keep their legs closed!"

She had called me a whore, a trollop, a tart, all manner of foul words for women of loose morals, so many times over the years that they no longer stung. But her other words frightened me. "Chef?" I asked. "I've been . . . removed?"

She looked at me very seriously. "You've been summoned to the main castle. You will no longer live here, but reside in those walls." She shook her head. "A word of advice—keep your wits about you, girl!" Then she cupped my chin with her gnarled, wrinkled hand.

"I'm glad I don't have the burden of beauty," she said softly. "I hope you're not devoured by the wolves." She looked at me sympathetically, as if she had just been told I was terminally ill. "A shame. You were becoming a very good cook."

Now I was frightened. I returned to my room to find there was a lady waiting for me there. She was very tall and very beautiful, with broad, regal shoulders and a head of dark, glossy curls. My mother had always taught me to look past whatever someone was wearing, their outward beauty, and study their eyes. This was what had first guided me to Henray—the kindness present in those depths. This woman, dressed like a queen, had a steely, flinty gaze. She was impenetrable. I remembered what the old woman had said about the wolves while I looked at her shawl, which appeared to be made of animal tails.

"Gather your things," she said nonchalantly. I'd had only my basket with me when I was foraging for mushrooms in my village on that fated day—my one remnant from home, from my old life. In the basket, I now placed my hair ribbons, one set of coarse underclothes, woolen socks, a few sachets of herbs and spices, and, of course, the wooden sweets box from Henray, with the secret pearl inside.

She tittered at my paltry possessions. "Come, little one. Take your treasures and come with me."

I would have engaged her in questions, had I not been so frightened. We walked out of the servants' quarters, the only place in the castle I knew, past the stables, past the knights fencing in the yard. I looked for Henray among them but I did not find him there. She nodded and even winked at several knights, and I understood that she must not be a princess, even though she was so richly dressed, but some kind of lady-in-waiting. We walked through a courtyard lined with fruit trees, flowering branches abuzz with bees and blossoms. The sun was high, the sky was blue, and I began to feel my dread overtaken by excitement. I wasn't sure where I was going, but I trusted Henray and his pledge for us to be together. I knew he didn't live in the servants' quarters. We walked on, toward a glittering dome at the center of the grounds—the main palace. In the resplendent green, peacocks swanned about with their opulent cloaks of feathers, pheasants ran to and fro, and flowers selected for their color and variety swirled in complex patterns across the great lawn. We followed a man rolling a cask of wine through a servants' entrance. This immediately made me relax. I was being taken to perhaps another kitchen, away from the old woman, or to become a lady-in-waiting. We walked quickly through gilded halls until we reached a large chamber, the richest of its kind I had ever seen, decorated in gold and red and green, inlaid with mother-of-pearl. She led me deeper into the chamber, to a room with a giant tub in the middle, filled with steaming, fragrant water. Here, she told me to strip. She took off her fur collar and pushed up the sleeves of her silk dress. I couldn't believe my eyes—this fine lady meant to bathe me.

"Do you know how to read?" she asked, as she poured water over my head.

"No, ma'am."

I knew my letters, but had no use for reading or writing. Here, for some reason, I half curtsied as best I could in the bathtub. Then, much to my surprise, she proceeded to speak to me in my own dialect.

"Can you play an instrument?"

"No, ma'am," I said.

"Needlepoint or sewing? Any of the kind arts?"

"Just cooking," I said, blanching. I felt suddenly cold. Would I be sent back?

She took my shoulders in her hands and turned me toward her. "We have a lot of work to do," she said, looking deep into my eyes. "Do you understand?"

I paused, afraid to speak foolishly. "Am I meant to be some kind of lady?"

She nodded. "You have been summoned to court. Obviously, you cannot be here as yourself. We will give you a new name and new origins. You must stay in these rooms until your training is complete. It might take a year, perhaps more. Do you understand?"

I could barely formulate words; my mind felt thick and hot.

"Your old life is over, Ijo. You will live in the palace now. You will eat the finest foods, and sleep on the softest linens. I will train you to speak properly, to read and write, to attend court functions, to be a lady. It will be hard at first, but in time, your days will be your own."

She said nothing of my nights.

Then she washed my hair with a sweet-smelling soap and scrubbed my back. "Oh, go ahead and cry," she murmured. "I'm Pilar."

I nodded, then burst into tears. I didn't understand what was happening to me or what kinds of questions to ask. I knew I was being lifted up in station, but for what purpose? Pilar helped me out of the bath, and I shivered. She wrapped me in a fur robe to keep warm, put satin slippers on my feet, then led me back into the great gold-and-green room. She opened a closet to reveal dozens of fine silk gowns. She held up one after another: yellow silk, a blue-and-white ombré, then the darkest forest green.

"Green, I think," she said, studying my face. She dressed me in creamy silk underclothes, finer than anything I had ever touched. Then she wrapped me in the green gown, tying it on the side in a loose bow, rather than the formal style in front or back.

This should have been a clue to the purpose of my new life. My dress was being tied simply, instead of with the hooks and fasteners of a proper lady. It was designed to be untied easily, by the hands of a clumsy man. It was the same green as the pattern on the walls; it complemented the sheets, the lamps, the curtains.

I had been decorated to match the room.

Next she shellacked my hair with oil and coiled it into a soft, high knot. Then she painted my lips with a small, fine brush—a bright coral that set off my eyes. Around my throat she tied a jewel of amber, with a matching hair comb affixed to my hair. My eyes were lightly surrounded by kohl. I did not realize that my makeup was being kept very simple at the request of my powerful new benefactor.

"Please," I said softly, looking at a girl I no longer recognized in the mirror. "Tell me—when can I see Henray?"

She wrinkled her brow, puzzled. "I don't know who that is," she said, "but, Ijo, you have been promised to the king. You will wait for him in these chambers. You have caught his attention. He wishes to keep you." She looked at me as if my shock was distasteful. "You should know you're very lucky."

I don't remember breaking down, only her sweet smell all around me, holding me as I sobbed. Then eventually she left me alone on the island of the bed, floating, as if lost at sea. I stared at the great bronze door, the room filled with beautiful objects. How had I stumbled into such a fine prison?

Later I awoke from a half-sleep to see a fire roaring in the furnace and a table set next to the grand window (which overlooked a very pleasant cherry blossom tree, just past its bloom). I smelled food, and my stomach betrayed me. I crept over to the table to see a variety of covered dishes, all very lavish, and a stout candle that had been lit. Relief flooded me when I discovered that it had been set for one.

I thought about running away—to the knights' quarters, perhaps, in hopes of finding Henray. But at this point, I feared for his life and what would happen if we angered the king. I poured myself a glass of wine from a carafe and took a small swallow. It was much mellower than the stuff from the great cask in the servants' kitchen. A series of flavors danced on my tongue. I opened the first dish with anticipation and saw a pleasing presentation of hen over rice, cooked in a kind of nut gravy, topped with rose petals and pistachios. I had never eaten rose petals (my aunt would use their essence in salves, extracted by steaming) and did not know if they were edible or for decoration. Cautiously I took a bite and found the rose petal pleasing, its texture velvety on my tongue.

I next opened a smaller vessel, which contained an exquisite crystal bowl of several honey balls rolled in sesame, a familiar dessert of which I was already fond. Finally I uncovered the last course, a hammered pot of silver metal. It was sour pickle soup. Comforted, I ate my fill with bread and butter and drank another glass of wine, until my head felt woozy. Then I lay down, not on the bed but in front of the fire, and fell again into a restless sleep.

4.

Love softened Reiko. Even Clarissa noticed her mood lighten. The weeks followed in a beautiful haze, where every action she took toward completing her plan was enhanced by a vision of the future—a life with Keith. *Keith and I will live in a floating house on a hill,* she thought, washing dishes from Clarissa's endless, all-day tea. *Keith and I will travel, Keith and I will have a garden, we'll plant wisteria and roses, our children will sit under the boughs of elm trees. They will never know what it is to be poor.*

The desire to have Keith's child surprised her. In the past, she had thought of pregnancy as an unfortunate virus you could get if you weren't careful. Yet now she would be proud to walk down the street, her belly large, for everyone to see. It wouldn't be like being a Bastian wife—tired, overworked, old before her time. Two proper people, husband and wife, with one child as a natural birth, the rest from surrogates, as was the custom in the upper Middle. They would say things like, *Shall we summer abroad?* And the children would learn how to play instruments; they would see plays and read fine literature, all the things that Reiko never did as a child, with her dashing, handsome husband beside her in his businessman's frock and pirate smile.

———

Reiko felt love around her like a fine mist, walking with Keith in a cute little commercial district of the Middle, between the university sector and the river neighborhoods. They strolled idly together, hand in hand in the sunlight, pausing when a display struck Reiko's fancy. Normally they didn't last very long before climbing into bed, but today they'd decided to behave like a normal couple, not a pair of thieves who only saw each other once a week. They spooned in front of a window display of pretty glass-blown jewelry—a bit whimsical for Reiko's taste, but she admired the little amber leaves and spun-glass flowers set as pendants, earrings, and rings. They looked charming in the afternoon sun.

Keith wrapped his arms around her tight, his low voice vibrating in her ear. "Which one do you like best?"

"Red roses for love." She kissed him, and they walked on.

Reiko and Keith decided to do a bit of whatever they might do by themselves, then meet up in the early evening. Reiko got a facial, a body scrub, and a massage (her skin-care routine had been suffering, her attention distracted by this new relationship), while Keith went for a beer at a local pub to catch a bit of the day's balloon race. It gave her a pang to spend any of her precious free time away from Keith, but she savored this feeling of normalcy. She longed for him so much throughout the week—sneaking glances at her phone for a sweet message, a little joke, a naughty picture—that each day they got to spend together was almost panicked with joy. The anticipation was exhausting.

Refreshed from her spa treatment, Reiko strolled back to the hotel feeling buoyant, swinging a posh little shopping bag at her side. She had picked up several little serums and hydrating face masks from the spa, plus a few extra to send home to Elena. Reiko hadn't yet told Keith the entirety of her plan to grift Clarissa, only that it was a big job and she was putting the pieces together. The well of Clarissa's money ran so deep that, aside from the 15 percent to her parents, Reiko was planning to leave a tidy sum for her sister. A nice little chunk could give Elena security in her old age. Then Reiko would feel truly at ease to live as she wished. Elena might be a feral little beast, but she loved her.

Reiko was humming one of her grandmother's old songs when she put the hotel key in the door and the light turned green. She was looking forward to drinking tea and reading *The Kitchen Girl* in the plush hotel bed. Ijo was concocting a special stew for her love, Henray the knight. As she expected, Keith wasn't there yet, but Reiko immediately noticed evidence of him—the red rose pendant lay glinting on the white pillow, linked through a gold chain. *Red roses for love.* She held it to the light and peered through it, the room made soft and pink. Reiko put it on and admired the red curving glass against her pale neck in the mirror. The necklace was overly romantic, not her taste at all, and she loved it. Then she noticed five or so jars of different face creams on the dresser, quite expensive brands, some of which had been used on her at the spa. But when she opened a jar of geranium night cream to smell it, she was shocked to find it was not only unsealed but half used, with the traces of other people's fingers still outlined in the thick, viscid cream. She sat on the bed, touching her hand to the necklace at her throat. The necklace had not come in a bag, lightly wrapped in paper, or in a sweet little jewelry box lined in velvet. It had been lying out on the pillow, just like it had been in the display.

Keith had stolen them. Stolen them for her—expensive things, things that he was right to assume she would like. She knew he was a thief, just as he knew she was a thief, and she couldn't decide why this bothered her. There was a brutality to it that chafed her. That first night, when Keith caught her dipping, he'd thought she was stealing his mobile wallet, like he'd stolen hers. But Reiko had been attempting to embed a little tendril into his account, artfully skimming for as long as she maintained the connection. Reiko had dozens of these little tributaries feeding into the river of her personal account. Small amounts, innocuous-looking charges—invisible, safe, and smart.

She didn't pull from Agata's accounts anymore (it felt malicious, somehow, to steal from an old friend when she didn't need to), but she still found herself looking through her friend's bank account some nights when she was a little lonely. *Oh, look, Aggie went to the opera, Aggie went to the juice bar, Aggie's at the seaside, Aggie's on a hover cruise.* Reiko had decided that when she got her money (a.k.a. Clarissa's money), she would contact Agata. They would meet again, on her terms: with Reiko not as a poor, struggling student or a thief, but as an equal. They would be friends who drank wine while their children played in the yard. Reiko opened the jars of creams and lotions one by one. A few were actually new. Keith probably hadn't realized that half the time, he was swiping her a present that had been used by a dozen or more other people. His sloppiness pained her. It just didn't fit the image she had of the floating house on the hill, the lovely garden, the well-behaved children with the manners and gestures of the elite. Would Keith be standing there, next to her and Aggie, laughing? She had found his businessman persona exceedingly dull. Staying high up meant a life of passing, of smoothed-over accents and impeccable false backstories. Reiko was suddenly exhausted. Was there nowhere in the world they could be happy together?

Then the key turned in the lock and Keith entered, his whole face lighting up at the sight of her sitting on the bed, wearing the necklace.

"My lovelamb," he exclaimed in his Low Quake brogue. "It's a goddamn miracle every time I see you." Then he knelt on the floor, took off her narrow shoes, and kissed her feet.

"I'm all sweaty, hold on!" She giggled, halfheartedly trying to push him away.

"Would you deny me my prize?" he growled, then pretended to eat her feet until she collapsed on the bed, laughing. Reiko felt herself going pink, growing silly and soft and unable to find fault with him at all. She tossed her unease away.

———————

"*Menu for a Mistress's Breakfast,*" Reiko read aloud as she stroked Keith's hair. "*Fresh bread, chocolate, butter, and jam. Strong tea. Talk in bed about everything and nothing, feel as if you might die from happiness, until he has to go back to his wife.*"

"It's clever," said Keith, his head in her lap. "I see why you like it. Sexy too."

They were lounging together on a blanket in the park under a statue of a horse and its rider. They had drunk almost a full bottle of red, and somewhere between her first and her third glass, Reiko had gone from feeling loose and warm to melancholy and maudlin.

"Do you want to keep reading?"

She closed the book. "I feel like Ijo. Like I might die from happiness, until you have to go back to your wife. There's just never enough time!" She pouted. "I look forward to this all week, and then every minute we're together, I'm anxious."

"You're not my mistress, darling, and I'm not married. What can I do?"

"It's just, I want to go to the cinema with you, go dancing and lounge in bed all day. I want to cook you dinner and watch you eat it." At this, he sat up and tried to kiss her, but she kept going. "I want to sleep in your arms. I want to talk all night. There's so much to do, this isn't enough—"

"It's not forever, love. You'll finish this job, and we'll be together," he said, running his hand over her forehead ridge and then kissing it.

"It's just so hard," she sniffed.

"Then be with me," he said softly.

"I *am* with you," she said abruptly. They had never discussed monogamy. "I'm yours, Keith. I've never been anyone's before, and I'm yours."

"Then marry me," he said into her hair. "Be my mistress and my wife. Be my everything."

She turned to face him. "Excuse me?"

He flashed his pirate grin and made a show of performing the traditional proposal ritual—the arcing flaps, the head turns. Several people in the park saw this and cheered.

"Marry me, Reiko, queen of my heart! Be mine."

"Yes," she said, touching his cheeks. "Yes!"

"All right, then, *wife*!" He kissed her deeply. "Stay here, I'm getting us bubbly." He untangled himself from her arms, and she felt a chill.

"Keith, I'm cold!"

He turned to salute her in acknowledgment before taking off in a sprint. She laughed and gripped her arms. She looked up at the statue of the horse and rider. She didn't know who the rider was or what battle this statue was meant to commemorate. She didn't want to know. This would always be their spot, hers and Keith's, where they had decided to spend the rest of their lives together.

The minutes ticked by, and Keith still wasn't back. Impatient and giddy, she took out her phone and video-called her parents.

"Mama," she said, smiling into the phone. "Point the camera down, please! I'm seeing up your nose."

Her mother scowled at the viewscreen. "Like this?"

"Yes, that's good."

"You're outside? Why are you out on the street?" She squinted into the camera. "Have you been crying?"

"I was just having a glass of wine outside with my boyfriend, Mama. Is Dad there?" She wanted to say Elena's name but felt too shy. "I have news, I want to tell you all—"

"I'm here!" Papa blundered into view, then angled the camera up at the ceiling. "Hi, my beautiful girl!"

"Hi, Daddy! Can you point the camera back at your faces, please?"

"We love this tablet you got for us, darling. It's so wonderful! But our successful daughter shouldn't spend her money on gifts for her old parents—"

"You guys, listen to me!" They went quiet, and suddenly she felt nervous. "I'm getting married."

Her mother's eyes bulged. "To who?"

"To my boyfriend, Keith." She had barely mentioned him before today.

Her father spoke slowly. "That's wonderful, Reiko. When you know, you know."

Elena's pretty face poked into the viewscreen. "Rei, did I hear that right? You're getting married?"

"She is!" Keith appeared behind her like a magician, holding roses, a sweating bottle of bubbly, and a brand-new, luxurious silver coat. He slipped it on her shoulders without a word. On the viewscreen, Elena's eyebrows raised up practically to her scalp. "Hello,

I'm Keith! And I love your daughter very much." He bowed, smiling, his Low Quake accent blazing. "May I have your blessing?"

Her parents gasped, eyes teary. "Yes!" cried Papa.

"This is so exciting!" cried Mama. "When can you visit?"

"Soon," said Keith, kissing Reiko's head. "But first I have to take her dancing and to the cinema." They popped the bubbly and toasted, her parents and Elena holding mugs of tea.

"*Sei Gusian!*" cried Mama.

"*Sei Gusian!*" cried Papa.

"*Sei Gusian!*" cried Elena. "Reiko," she said over her mug, "I have a good feeling about this one."

I awoke to the feeling of being lifted from the floor and placed on the bed. I felt my dress open from the side. I squeezed my eyes shut and trembled. Then I was being kissed lightly on the face and eyelids, the soft rasp of a man's beard on my face. He was saying my name: *Ijo, Ijo, Ijo, Ijo.*

I opened my eyes, and there was Henray.

I clasped him very tightly. "Come, we must leave this place," I whispered.

He looked at me, eyes full of desire. "How beautiful you are," he said.

"We must leave, before the king catches us!" I slapped his arm lightly, as I had done so many times before when he annoyed me.

"Ijo, please forgive me." He sounded almost ashamed. "I thought you knew."

"Knew what?"

"I thought we were playing a game. Ijo . . ." He rubbed the cloth of the bedspread between his fingers. "I am the king."

I bit my lip, confused. "You're . . . the king?"

He nodded.

My mind swirled. Henray, *my* Henray, was the king? "But . . . aren't you married?"

He nodded. "These quarters will be yours."

It took me a long time to remember how to speak.

"For how long," I said shortly.

"Ijo?"

"How long am I yours, Henray? Until you've grown bored of me?" I felt my face flush with fury, and that all-consuming feeling overtook me: the one when I know I should stop talking but cannot. "How many other girls do you have in this castle? Do you visit us one by one, like a bee to flowers?" Blinded by rage and pain, I began hitting the man I had thought was my knight. "I don't even know your name!"

He didn't move to stop my blows, just accepted them until I collapsed, sobbing. "What have you done?" I asked, voice breaking.

"Ijo," he said softly. Very slowly, he brought my hand to his lips. "Listen to me. Being with you has been the happiest period of my life. I thought these feelings were lost to me, surrendered into duty and responsibility. I thought ease was gone, tenderness gone, levity gone! But in your kitchen, I could feel again. Please—I know I can make you happy. I know we have something special and good. Will you let me try to make you happy? Because I love you, Ijo. I know you love me too." At this, he bowed before me, placing his forehead on the bed in supplication, as if I were a queen and he was awaiting my pronouncement.

Reader, I admit, my first instinct was: *Off with his head.*

It was as though I were in the midst of a waking dream, only I could not tell if it was pleasant or a nightmare. I removed myself from the bed and stood to look out the window, my open dress trailing me like a cape. How it burned to hear the words I had been craving for so long, in such a cruel context. The beautiful tree outside my window glowed in the moonslight, as if lit from within.

"How dare you tell me what I feel," I said bitterly. "Clearly, I am a fool who knows nothing. And whom did I love? Not a man—a fabrication!"

"Every word I told you was true."

"And all those words you didn't tell me?"

He hung his head. "Please, Ijo. This is our chance. We can be together. Here, in these rooms. We can create our own world."

To my young mind, it was as though my former adversary, the old cook, had been supplanted by the most powerful woman in the country. "But what about the queen? Your *wife*."

He shook his head. "It's normal where she's from to have many lovers. She will not harm you. She will welcome you in court."

The queen, lovers? I strained to imagine it. Rumors said she barely spoke and spent most days in quiet contemplation.

He noticed my expression. "She is abstinent in all things of the flesh." He looked at me, eyes so open and pleading. "I am yours, only yours, in body, mind, and spirit. That is my pledge to you."

I was silent a long moment. I crossed over to him and stood next to the bed. He seemed so young, so lost. Based on whispers I had heard in the castle, that year he had turned twenty-four years old. "I have always liked your spirit," I said, touching his cheek. "Your best attribute."

And we both knew I had forgiven him.

He wrapped his arms around me, huddling to my chest like a child. "I'm sorry," he cried into the green silk of the dress.

I smoothed his thick hair. "It's all right," I hushed him. "What should I call you?"

"Please, continue to call me Henray. It's my nickname from childhood."

I pulled out of his embrace, sat next to him on the bed, and dried his eyes. "Henray, my world cannot be these four walls. Even if you wish it, and we both wish to be together."

He followed my gaze to the large bronze door.

"What can I give you?" he asked. "Anything you desire, name it, it will be yours."

"A garden," I said suddenly, thinking of my uncle's little plot of land back in our village. I could finally have something that was mine to create.

He stroked my hair. "You will have a world of gardens."

"Can you . . . spend the night?" I asked.

"This night, and so many others, except for when I am called away from the castle." He put his hand over my heart. "Will you take me as yours, Ijo?"

I reached out and flicked his arm. "Sour pickle soup, I should have known." His eyes drifted down to the bare skin above the silk of my chemise. My heart felt raw and weary. "Not yet," I said. "Not tonight."

He nodded and kissed me on the cheek. "May I sleep here with you?"

"Yes, help me out of all of this." He delicately removed my hair comb, as if he were my lady-in-waiting, then hung my dress on the back of a chair. Then Henray brought over a warm dish of water and delicately rubbed off my kohl with a soft cloth before kissing my bare face.

"What am I to you officially?" I asked, once we lay beside each other in bed. "After my year of training is complete, and I am presented in court—who will I be?"

He paused. "I had to choose a surrogate for the queen. She will not reproduce herself—it's against her beliefs." He thumbed a gentle finger on my bottom lip. "So you are my real wife, Little Mother. We are married. This is our house, and in it, we can live however we wish."

"Surrogate," I repeated, the word unfamiliar, like a stone in my mouth. The weight seemed to lessen when I kissed him, and we lay there, forehead to forehead, until we fell asleep in each other's arms, a luxury I had never experienced.

MENU FOR A MISTRESS'S BREAKFAST

Fresh bread, chocolate, butter, and jam

Strong tea

Talk in bed about everything and nothing,
feel as if you might die from happiness,
until he has to go back to his wife.

5.

Beatrice's eighteenth birthday sneaked up on her. It was a hot Tuesday in the late autumn. The first thing she did was call Lina on the house phone. She could tell Lina was happy to hear from her, even if she spoke with her usual spikiness and volunteered almost nothing about her own life. Beatrice talked about her work in the restaurant: all the new skills she was learning, silly Erek and terse Margot and warbling Walter, while Lina occasionally grunted "That's good" or "Well, I'm glad."

"Oh, Lina," she said when it was time to hang up. "I've been wanting to ask you this for months. Why is that book you gave me..." She paused. It seemed unwise to say anything specific about an illegal cookbook over the phone. "I love it, but it's pretty tame. I can't imagine what all the fuss is about." Open mention of cooking was certainly taboo, but one could find worse things in late-night chat forums. In comparison, *The Kitchen Girl* was barely illicit.

"I'm not a goddamn world religion scholar," Lina said roughly. "Happy birthday, little mouse. Call me again soon."

Margot came in early and baked a chocolate cake. Beatrice

decided not to tell Margot she didn't care for chocolate. It was a difficult ingredient to source, so she was touched by the gesture, though those gritty air depot chocolates would always leave an unpleasant memory.

Margot sliced up the cake at their 4 P.M. "family supper." Beatrice plunged her fork through the tender cake and took a bite, and nearly dropped her fork in surprise. The flavor was as smoky and complex as coffee, as rich and unctuous as nut butter. As she ate, Beatrice felt the chocolate become a doorway, a tunnel. She discovered base notes of berries and toffee. Burnt sugar, fresh cream. And a trace of mint? What magic was this?

"You all right, Beatrice?" asked Erek.

She nodded. "I've never had real chocolate before."

Margot had a little wrinkle at the bridge of her nose, which meant she was pleased. "Finish your cake," she said.

Erek set up the traditional semicircle of eighteen short candles, while Walter sang a very long version of "Make a Wish, It's Your Birthday." Beatrice, weighing more than she ever had, felt so light, as if she might float off with too sudden a movement. *They're my family,* she thought as Margot yelled at her to blow out the candles already, or she'd fetch the fire extinguisher. *I love them.*

Walter pressed a wrapped package toward Beatrice. "It's from all of us," he said.

"This isn't really a birthday present," said Margot. "Just something you've earned."

Beatrice opened the package. Gleaming before her was powerful, heavy silver. A chef's knife.

Before the restaurant was open, Beatrice heard Walter usher in a customer asking to speak to the young woman apprentice. She took off her apron, fluffed her hair, and went to meet her fan. Beatrice approached the table. "Hello there," she said to an older man in a broad fedora, studying the menu.

She smiled to realize that, for the first time, she could use her own name without fearing repercussions. "I'm Beatrice. Do you know what you'd like this evening?"

"What would you recommend?"

"The chili is a crowd-pleaser," she said carefully, "but the pasta is exquisite." As their vegetable dishes grew more intricate and delicious, they regularly outsold the meat options, much to Walter's surprise.

"I would be honored to eat whatever you bring me." The man looked up. It was Father Alvarez, wearing street clothes.

She felt the shame, hot and hard and terrible in her stomach. Then she remembered the hidden larder in the church's kitchen—the fine cheese, the butter, the tomatoes, the bread. *You're just like me, except you're a liar,* she thought.

He looked up at her with wide, solemn eyes. Then she saw the thick stack of flyers on the table. Her own face stared back at her. *Have you seen this girl?* the poster asked.

"Stay here," said Beatrice. She went to the kitchen and plated the pasta special—handmade noodles with small roasted eggplant and seared radicchio, tossed together with a pesto of basil, mint, and pumpkin seeds, completed by a side of foraged greens cooked with garlic. She loaded up a full tray and carried it to his table. But he didn't make a move for the food, nor did he open his mouth to speak. She sat down across from him and nudged his plate.

"Eat," she said. "I made it just for you." Beatrice didn't realize it was true until she'd said the words. She'd been working this hard so she could make something so good that even someone from her prior life couldn't deny its worth.

Father Alvarez began to eat, making his way through the pasta, the side of greens. He paused only to sigh into his plate and wipe his brow. She had never seen him wear anything other than priest garb. The experience was disorienting and surreal, as if Beatrice's dreams had followed her from sleep into the dining room.

When his plate was clear, he spoke. "This was the best meal I've ever had."

Though it was what she'd wanted to hear, his words brought her no pleasure. His voice sounded faded, like a garment washed so many times its patterns were indistinct.

"You're the one hanging the flyers around the city."

"Yes, with your parents and your friend Georgina and several others from the church. Yesterday was our last visit." He gazed at her with bright eyes. "Everyone else has gone home."

"Why was yesterday the last visit?" Part of her felt wounded by this.

"You're eighteen today, Beatrice. Had you been found before this, you would have been taken to a place for people . . ." He hesitated. "People like us. Do you understand?"

Her stomach turned. "Is that what you wanted for me? To have me kidnapped and brainwashed? Starved half to death?"

He shook his head once. "No."

Then she realized. There had been so many flyers, but never around the restaurant. Her eyes widened. "You knew where I was all along, didn't you?" She glanced at the door. The patrons had begun to trickle in. Several people waved hello to her. She looked back to the pastor. "You led them away from me."

He grimaced. "I should have done more to help you."

They sat in silence for a long moment. "Why are they still using my image in the Seagate advertisements? And how can I stop it?"

He shook his head. "You can't. The release was signed by your parents, and in any case, Stecopo owns everything in Seagate."

Beatrice cringed. She thought back to her childhood bedroom— the knickknacks, the photographs. All of that belonged to Stecopo?

"As for why, I suspect your parents thought the campaign might convince you to come home."

She leaned closer. "When I was caught cooking in the church kitchen, my parents made me go see you for private counseling. Do you remember?"

"Of course."

"You didn't scold or berate me. You spoke in general terms— *God is the sky, God is all around us, God is within us.* I didn't feel judged by God, because I didn't feel separate from him. That gave me the strength to find a place I belonged. Because I didn't feel unloved by God." She put her hand on his. "Thank you for that, Father."

"Please, call me Ferdinand. I'm not a Father anymore." He looked down at his clothes. "I have always struggled with a profound lack of imagination. Perhaps that's why I spent my life attempting to concretize a relationship with the invisible, to build the necessary muscles for faith." He stroked the tablecloth absentmindedly with his thumb. "I hope God is kinder than I was taught."

"I believe God is as kind as the one you preached."

His face no longer looked boyish. It seemed as though he had aged thirty years since she had last seen him. "I'm glad I could help you, in some small way, to find a path to a life you deserve." He smiled at her. "Happy birthday, Beatrice."

"Will you do something for me?"

He nodded.

She took off the double moonstone necklace she always wore under her blouse. "Can you return this to my mother? I've kept it too long. Tell them . . ." She paused, blinking back tears. "Tell them if they want to know me, I'm ready to show them who I am. Tell them where to find me."

He hugged her good-bye. His body felt so frail in her arms, as if he had hollow bones, like a bird.

The phone call came on an unremarkable afternoon.

Beatrice was in the backyard, trying to wrangle the garden she'd devised from dirt and cement, hidden from the neighbors by tarps arranged on a clothesline. Working with little pots inside was certainly easier to manage than the great outdoors. The soil was rocky and sandy, dearly in need of fertilizer. Her pie pumpkins weren't thriving, instead growing small and mealy. There were other unexpected frustrations. The plants that were doing well, such as her tomato varietals, attracted creatures in the night that would nibble at them. She'd learned to plant them interspersed with strong-smelling herbs like thyme and lavender to ward off the critters. It turned out that mint, however, overran anything it was next to—she had to place slabs of stone around the plant to cut off its growth, which only half helped. She wouldn't make that mistake again next season.

Beatrice crouched frowning at the beetles infesting her lovely purple potato plants, picking the docile pests off one by one and tossing them in a tin can of soapy water. The demands of her fledgling garden had taken her away from the kitchen more than she liked, but the satisfaction of cooking with fresh ingredients was second to none. Luckily, there was a new apprentice, an Ahinga boy named Cedric, who had appeared quietly in the night, much like Beatrice. She could hear Margot now, explaining to him the difference between a mince and a dice. Beatrice grinned. Poor guy—it would be months before he did anything but peel and chop. But Margot was right. You couldn't rush the basics.

"Hey, Beatrice!" yelled Erek from inside. "You got a call on the house phone."

Beatrice stood and brushed off her loose cotton pants, stained at the knees with dirt and grass. It might be one of her seed suppliers, informing her of a new available shipment. Or it could be Lina. Beatrice had hoped to hear from Father Alvarez again, but had received no word from him since her birthday.

She picked up the phone. "Hello?"

A man's voice crackled onto the line. "Beatrice?" It was her father—he sounded old. "Is that really you?"

Beatrice watched Erek come into the dining room. He and Cedric were starting to set up for the evening crowd. Cedric had been born with a condition that affected his spine, which meant some days he walked with crutches, others with a cane, and occasionally used a wheelchair. He had a cane today, and he held on to a chair while using it to joust with Erek, who was brandishing a spatula.

"Yes, it's me." She listened to the sounds of muffled crying from the other end of the phone, mixed with the sounds of the boys laughing in the dining room. "Papa?" she asked. "Is Mama there too? Is she with you?"

"You're—" he choked. "You're safe? There in the Middle?" She looked around the restaurant. Margot walked out to the garden with an empty woven basket, nodding to Beatrice. Erek and Cedric folded napkins into the shape of swans, then flew the birds into each other, furiously cawing.

Lately she wondered if Cedric was growing sweet on Erek. She hoped Erek wouldn't break his heart without trying, as he had with all those boys on the rugby team.

"Yes," she said into the mouthpiece. "I'm safe in the Middle." Her voice grew firmer. "And I'm happier than I've ever been."

The sobbing returned on the other end. Margot came inside with her basket full of clippings of fresh herbs. Beatrice felt herself grow annoyed. "Papa," she said. "Did you get the necklace? Where's Mom?"

He breathed loudly. "She's here. But she, ah, can't come to the phone."

"Is she sick? Hurt?"

Her father's tone softened. "Oh, no, she's watching television."

"She can't come to the phone because she's watching television?"

"This was . . . a lot for her to take in," said her father. "Especially after what just happened."

Beatrice twisted the phone cord in her hand. "Do you want to come see me? See where I work?" She hesitated. "I would love to cook for you."

There was silence on the other end for a long moment. Then her father spoke, all warmth drained from his voice. "I shouldn't have to explain to you why that isn't possible."

She listened to her father crying softly, mingled with the background television noise. "Papa—what do you mean, 'after what just happened'?"

"Father Alvarez is dead." He had quieted to almost a whisper. "He threw himself off one of those high-rise hotels in the city. He sent us the moonstone first."

"Father Alvarez is dead?" she said numbly. She remembered his frail body in her arms. His resolute words: *I'm not a Father anymore.*

The whisper grew plaintive, as if coming from a hostage who

was scared to be overheard. "Would you come visit us sometime? Come see me and your mother?"

She imagined coming home as a fat girl. Breaking their image of her that showed up on every television screen. "I'm a different person now, Papa. I'm not thin, and I won't be ever again."

The pause was barely detectable. "We'll figure it out. Just come home, Beatrice."

"Okay," she said softly. "For a visit. I've wanted to, so many times."

For a moment, he sounded exactly how she remembered him—jolly, vital, young. "That's wonderful! I'll send you the address. When can you come? Tomorrow?"

She blinked. "The address? Did you move?"

"No, silly," said her father. "For the clinic. We'll get you all fixed up, and then you can come home."

Even after a long moment, no words came to her. Something inside her had broken open.

"Hello?" asked her father. "Beatrice? Are you still there?"

"No," said Beatrice, her voice soft but firm. "If you don't accept me as I am, you don't get me. You don't get to change me to suit your, your—" She lost the thread. It didn't matter. She heard her voice raise and she couldn't control it. "Don't you understand? If I stayed there with you, I'd be like Father Alvarez. Living a lie until it killed me."

Her father's voice pitched low, a familiar tone of mild disappointment. "Oh, sweetheart, don't be so dramatic."

The words erupted from the deepest part of her stomach. "I'm dramatic? Your pastor is dead!"

Sobbing returned on the other end of the line.

"I have to go now," she said, hands shaking. "They need me in the kitchen."

He inhaled sharply at her words, as if she had sworn at him. Beatrice didn't know if she had spoken so boldly because she was angry—angry at his tears, how they robbed her of her own— or simply because it was true. She had to get into the shower before the dinner rush. Their simplest words now carried different definitions. How could she have imagined ever going home again?

Her father huffed out a wobbly little laugh. "Oh, Beatrice. Please—"

"Give my best to Mama," she said, ready to hang up. "I hope her show is good."

"There's more I want to say to you!" he said. "But I . . . I don't know how."

"Well," she said, "you've got my address. You can write me a letter." She looked at her reflection in the window. The girl in the glass stared back. She reached out, touching her fingertips to her own reflection.

Beatrice hung up the phone. From across the dining room, Cedric leaned on his cane and gazed at her deeply, as if straight into her soul. She blushed and wondered how much he had overheard.

"Do you want help setting the tables?" she asked.

He shook his head. "Nah, I've got it." He resumed placing silverware next to plates. When he spoke next, his voice was gentle. "You can set the table for them, but you can't make them sit."

She studied his face. He could be anywhere between seventeen and thirty. She had never gotten to know an Ahinga person before. Beatrice wiped her eyes. "Are you close with your parents?"

He paused. "I'll tell you another time," he said. "Our guests will be arriving soon."

Beatrice climbed the stairs, then surveyed the restaurant, her little kingdom, from the top. They'd be coming through the doors soon, the wild weirdos who came from all walks of life, to taste, to eat, to feel alive. The words she wished she'd had said to her father flowed through her with a fiery clarity. *People like you killed Father Alvarez. You, and Mama, and everyone I loved as a child with your suffocating shame. You're devoted to worshipping a woman who died a thousand years ago, but there are real Flesh Martyrs here now! They're your friends and neighbors and clergy.* Beatrice felt her throat tighten. *And your children.* She shook her head. *The Divine Mother died for a cause. What's the use of all our suffering?*

In her bedroom, Beatrice turned toward the full-length mirror. It was still covered with a dusty sheet. She pulled it off and looked at herself. Beatrice took off her clothes. She stood naked in front of the mirror. *This body,* she thought. These arms stirred and carried. These hands chopped and minced. These strong shoulders. These capable thighs. These wide hips. This belly that moved with her, that *was* her. This body was not decorative, it was not slight, it was not willowy, it was not thin. This body took up space, this body made things. This body was her home.

"I owe you an apology," she said into the mirror, her eyes streaming with tears. The water felt good on her face: warm salt, like the ocean.

It was in a garden that I first glimpsed her. She dressed humbly, in dun-colored robes. I might have mistaken her for a servant, if not for the crown on her head. When she turned, I could see she held a hawk on her outstretched forearm. But unlike the stable master, the queen wore no heavy gloves or sleeves of leather to protect her arms. She then gave a high-pitched call, and the bird flew away into the bright sunshine.

I took the opportunity to study her. Her strange, smooth forehead, her pale skin. The queen returned my gaze. Her eyes, so bright, seemed lit from within by vestal fire. I was held there, in her looking. Later I would learn this was not particular to me or to this moment—with the queen, there was an absolute clarity to her attention. Then she held up her hand in greeting, and gave me a slight bow. I returned the gesture, bowing deeply. When she raised her arm, I could see even from some feet away that she was bleeding.

"Why does the queen hurt herself?" I asked Henray that same night, as I lay in his arms. We had just made love in my favorite style, moving so gently that each bit of friction brought on wave after wave of ecstasy. I didn't know it then, but I was already one month pregnant with our first child. I should have known. My nipples were so sore that night, I didn't let him near my breasts. The queasiness would come to me a few mornings after and stay with me until late into my gestation.

"She uses the body to release the body," he murmured into my hair. "The pain is a ladder. Or that's how I've heard her phrase it."

I thought of her bright, zealous eyes, the blood dripping down her pale arm in little red rivers. "Does she frighten you?" The question felt small and sharp—a needle in the pillow of the night.

"Fear is like salt," he said quietly. "A little is always helpful. Too much ruins the pot."

6.

Reiko stood in Clarissa's garden, pruning the rhododendron. It was late afternoon on a Sunday. Jono was still at church, as he was quite religious, while stern Linka was at home with her wife, preparing their Sunday meal. Clarissa lay dozing in front of the fire in her tiny parlor, resting fitfully after the day's ablutions at church.

Reiko's phone buzzed. She brushed the dirt from her hands and reached into her oversized handbag. She had taken to carrying all of her important possessions around the massive estate in her handbag—her phone, her mobile wallet, her smaller thieving tools (in case Linka got nosy), and *The Kitchen Girl*. There was a message from Elena: a snapshot of several swaths of shiny, garish fabric.

For the table settings . . .

What color??

Reiko laughed in the fragrant, buzzing garden. "None of them!" But dutifully, she typed back:

> All so pretty!!

> You should choose

> You have the whole scheme in mind

The reply came an instant later.

> Ok I'll take care of it!!!

> BEST WEDDING PLANNER EVER

> How lucky are you???

All of which was followed by a video clip of a baby blowing a kiss. Reiko laughed and sent her back a clip of a pig on its hind legs, bowing deeply in gratitude. Wonders never ceased. Reiko engaged to a man, and a Bastian man at that, had finally proved to her sister that she could, indeed, be normal. For the first time in perhaps her entire life, her family had something to talk to her about: the wedding. Flowers, color schemes, venue, music. At first she enjoyed being the center of attention. She chose the invitations, then the dress, the dresses of her attending ladies, Keith's outfit, on and on.

Keith had been agreeable at every step of the process. He had no parents (the orphan of Clarissa's dreams, as a child he had bounced around from cousins to grandparents and finally to an orphanage) and seemed to soak up every aspect of Reiko's noisy family. Their precious days together were no longer spent in hotels, but at her parents' house, arranging a wedding. Now, when Clarissa said something innocuous like, "Have a good time visiting your family, dear!" Reiko was disturbed to find this true. She was visiting her poor family in the Bastian, with her Low Quake man at her side, traveling to and fro on her father's boat, and she loved it.

Perhaps Keith loved it even more. He loved sleeping next to her in her little childhood bed, listening to her sister and father tell stories about Reiko as a girl, watching her mother cook and serve food without shame or guile. Reiko enjoyed this new intimacy, but the weeks of wedding planning grew interminable. It seemed the more big decisions she made, the more small, insignificant details emerged. For the reception, did she want the candelabra to have rounded or oblong bulbs? Reiko found herself being asked this question while sitting with Elena and Mama in the nicest venue in the Upper Bastian, an entire display case of marginally differently shaped lightbulbs in her lap.

"Can I just show up and get married?"

Instead of being offended, Elena and Mama smirked at each other, then quickly promised to handle the rest of the details. Reiko kissed them, thanked them, and took them to lunch. Perhaps they had been pushing her to give up control all along. She didn't mind. Reiko was excited to be married to Keith, to have a house, to fall asleep with him every night and wake up with him again every morning, but she had never fantasized about a wedding. Truly, she had never imagined herself getting married at all.

After her chores were done, the rest of the day was hers to do with as she wished. Reiko thought she might read outside, catching the last of the afternoon light before it got too buggy. Her phone buzzed again. "Just pick whatever you bloody want!" she muttered. Grinning, she saw it wasn't a message from Elena at all, but from Keith.

> Are you alone in the house?

Reiko smiled, allowing a sultry feeling to come over her. She quickly typed back:

> Why, yes. What are you going to do with me?

> How long will you be alone?

> All night long, my lion.

This had been their recent game. She would describe where she was, what she was wearing, and he would write back in detail a lurid act he would perform with unimaginable ardor on their next day together. Or sometimes he would give her instructions, which she found thrilling, like *Show me a picture of those fine pretty breasts*.

Reiko put away her gardening tools and cleaned up, humming along to the song in her earphones (an old Wah-Pop band from the Bastian that she would never let anyone catch her listening to), checking her phone every minute or so for another message from Keith. But there was nothing. Reiko took off her headphones and let out a mighty yawn. She surveyed her progress, the garden aglow with late-afternoon sun. Work was over, and she felt a surge of pride. To her surprise, Reiko enjoyed keeping the garden. She had gotten to the section on gardening in *The Kitchen Girl*, and the descriptions were intoxicating—lush cloisters, tasteful enclosures, romantic grottoes. The canals of Reiko's childhood home were no place for gardens—too unsteady to plant anything of substance. In the Bastian, gardens were gaudy geraniums and common pansies in pots and pitchers, next to an old coffee can with holes drilled in the bottom, stuffed with dirt, and seeded with chives, sat upon someone's stoop. When she and Keith found their home, Reiko mused, she would make sure it had space for a lush garden that would grow with them over the years.

Reiko stretched, excited to start her leisurely afternoon. Should she read *The Kitchen Girl* in the backyard, or perhaps naked in bed, after a long soak in the tub? She entered the house from the back patio. First, to the kitchen, to poke around in the larder before Jono returned to feed her something unappetizing.

And then she heard it. A long jangle, followed by a scrape and a very quiet grunt. Still holding her large purse, Reiko went to the main foyer.

A man she had never seen before was setting down a long black bag on the handwoven rug. The precious little knickknacks from Clarissa's stuffed shelves lay all around him, beside a flatscreen television. Before she could scream or form words like *May I help you?* Keith appeared beside him, grinning. He was holding a showy, rather ugly lamp that Reiko recognized from the east sitting room. They were both dressed in black, caps and all, as if they'd been cast as burglars in a school play.

"Oh, good, you found us!" Keith strode over to her, giving her a quick kiss on the cheek. "Let's get this show on the road. We'll hit the upstairs next, and then do the parlors. Tell me—where's the safe?"

Reiko couldn't make sense of what she saw. "Why—why are you here?"

"I'm liberating you, my lamb. Enough is enough. This is Bernard. Bernard, this is my old lady! Isn't she fine?"

The man nodded, and took out a professional-looking toolbox from the bag. "Let's get to work."

For a long moment, all Reiko could do was stand in the foyer. "Keith . . ." she whispered. "What are you doing?"

His handsome face became a puzzle. "Robbin'," he said, as if she were slow.

She had too many objections, her mind a thicket of insults and accusations, but she chose the most urgent. "You *idiot*," she hissed. "Clarissa's still here—"

"Elena!" Clarissa's voice called from the far parlor. "Who are you talking to?"

Bernard gave a sneer and rolled his eyes, as if his colleague was regularly incompetent. "You said this place was empty!"

"You have to leave!" said Reiko, shoving Keith, hard, toward the door. "Go now!"

"Oi—" said Bernard. And then he took out a gun, cocked the trigger, and looked around.

"Bernard," cautioned Keith.

"Elena?" called Clarissa. "Do you need me?"

"No, ma'am!" Reiko called, her voice high and tight. "It's just a package delivery. Stay put and I'll bring you some broth."

Keith looked almost ashamed. "All right, let's go."

Bernard trembled, his hand on the pistol. "But it's just one old lady," he said, his voice petulant. "There's loads here to get!"

"Nah, come on." But Keith didn't leave. He began to methodically pack up all of the things at his feet.

"Keith, you imbecile—" whispered Reiko. Her head felt so hot, as if coated in flames. How dare he try to steal her grift? And so sloppily at that! "You have to leave, right *now*." But Keith looked to Bernard, then defiantly grabbed the hideous lamp.

In that moment, Sabrina came through the door with her school case in tow. Reiko remembered—she'd been at some kind of math club that met on the weekends, home in time to relax before dinner. What a stupid, stupid plan! Sabrina looked at Keith and Bernard, and at Reiko, at their black clothes and their tools, and so many household objects at their feet, and then she started to scream loudly, a single piercing sound like an alarm. "Get out, get out, get out!" screamed Reiko, hitting Keith, over and over, with her large, heavy purse. If they were smart, the two of them would play it like a botched robbery, Reiko cast as the poor screaming maid. Bernard raised the pistol toward little Sabrina, whose mouth shut tight like a door slamming closed.

"I wasn't expecting any packages," said Clarissa, tottering in from the far room, just over to Reiko's side. "Do we have any more broth?"

A gun fired, a sound so large and loud Reiko felt assaulted by the noise alone. She covered her ears, but was confused by a sharp, hot-needle sensation in her left gut. Then she was too surprised to scream. Reiko looked down at her semitranslucent maid uniform, red seeping out across her belly. Keith screamed, however, long and loud, like a child. And then he did the stupidest thing he had done all day. He fell to his knees and cried, "Oh, Reiko, oh, Reiko, oh, Reiko, my love," before picking her up and half dragging, half carrying her out the door into the too-bright sun.

PART THREE

1.

When Claudia awoke in her lavish apartment on the ninety-ninth floor of Felicity Towers, she could tell that Martin wanted to fuck. It wasn't anything he said or did. It was just a quality to his gaze, the way he cleared his throat. Claudia wanted to take a piss, drink a cup of strong coffee, and eat one of those amazing tiny blueberry scones Sergio baked just for her. But she didn't do any of those things. She crawled into the lap of her man and got to work.

While earlier than normal for a weekday morning, their coupling was otherwise ordinary in every way. The same thing every day for the past two years, while she lived with Martin in the luxury suite of the poshest residential tower Above had to offer. Up, down, the three formal positions, the secret thing Martin wouldn't admit that he liked, and then the big finish. But this morning, during the transition from second to third position, Martin started to talk.

"You don't even like this, do you?" Martin said. "I get up to go to my job, but before that, you have to do *your* job, which is getting me off and pretending to like it. You're so bored of me, of this, of us. You can't even pretend to enjoy yourself anymore."

"Martin!" she exclaimed. The opening tremors of the first legitimate orgasm she'd had in weeks climbed through her. "Don't stop!" They finished together, looking into each other's eyes with mutual distaste and open lust. Then, still gripped by aftershocks and damp with bodily fluids, they stumbled to the meditation turret. Martin led them in the breathing exercises his newest teacher had sold him, followed by their own custom chants. Claudia's orgasm had cleared space in her mind to focus on the immaterial, a calm brightness opening up. She could sense the energetic channel from the base of her pelvis up the length of her spine, lights dancing behind her eyes. He had never admitted the true nature of their relationship until now. When their twenty-two minutes of meditation had elapsed, she opened her eyes. Martin looked the same— his bovine eyes, the small round mouth that made her think of a baby.

She briefly caressed his knee and left the turret. "That was something new," she said, pressing a button inlaid in her bracelet. "Aggie, morning meal version four." The highest-ranking butler in Felicity Towers, Sergio, would be coming with breakfast by the time she was clean. Her flat stomach rumbled in anticipation. In her private waste chambers, she used the warm bidet to rinse off their intermingled sexual fluids. The basin of the toilet bowl was filled three times a day with fresh rose petals. She always enjoyed glancing at them before flushing them away. Then Claudia entered the larger wet room, covered from floor to ceiling in blue and gold tiles, to draw her morning bath.

Martin came up behind her and kissed her neck. "I thought we should reprise Mr. Flick and his secretary, Mrs. G. They don't get to come out and play nearly enough. Who's my favorite secretary? Who's my perfect little slut?"

For a moment, she couldn't bring herself to respond. The first time she'd come in months, and he'd been playing a character, not seeing into her heart. Then she giggled and said in a sultry voice, "I hope I get to work for you again soon, Mr. Flick."

Martin slapped her bare behind, then walked toward his closet to get dressed for the day. Claudia tested the water temperature. She got into the rounded tub and sank down, down, down to the bottom. Curled into a ball, she imagined herself as an anchor at the floor of the sea, heavy and unmoving as fish swam in bright groups overhead. She held quiet until the feelings passed. It didn't matter that he didn't see her, she reminded herself. She didn't want to be seen. She bobbed up to the surface, flinging her hair back like a mermaid.

Martin had put on his tie and now was back at his vanity, applying aftershave. He spoke in a low, constant murmur about mergers and meetings, the Stecopo agreement, what time she could expect him home. Early on living with Martin, Claudia had realized that only about 20 percent of the time was she expected to respond to him.

"We have that thing next Saturday," she reminded him as she dried off. "Don't forget, my little dummy." Martin nodded, ordering his phone to mark it on his calendar. Then Sergio came up with a tray of their nutritionally balanced oat gruel and superfruit smoothie. He bowed deeply with a quick wink to Claudia and left. She and Martin drank their coffee—his black, hers with a droplet of coconut cream because she was a naughty girl. Then Martin kissed her ardently good-bye, doubtless proud of himself for being such an inventive lover. "I love you," she said sweetly. "Bring that nasty ass home to me in one piece." This was a trick she had learned early on as a hustler. If she was too sweet to her mark, they never really trusted her. The teasing and inane pet names relaxed any suspicions they might have.

He kissed her on the nose, then went off to do his work, making sure his pharmaceutical company suffered no consequences before the law. Claudia looked around the palatial apartment. She had a good nine hours before she had to playact at being in love with Martin again. The day was hers.

The first thing Claudia did after Martin left for work was start her day over. It made her real life, her interior life, a little bit shorter, but her day was never as perfect without a solid restart.

"Aggie, blackout curtains. Twenty-minute timer." Claudia went back to sleep in the large, firm bed. In her life with Martin, she slept on the right half of the bed, curled on her side like a child. In her own life, Claudia slept on her back like a starfish in the middle of the mattress, her legs and arms spread wide. When the light, cheery programmed birdsong signaled her to wake up, she pleasured herself sleepily, pressing the wetness between her legs as though it was just evidence of a good dream. Ijo, in that green dress, waiting on the bed, like a present to be unwrapped.

In her fantasy, she wasn't Ijo, nor was she the king. She hovered outside the situation like a little deity, observing. After her climax, she sat in the little turret for eight minutes, the bare minimum for daily meditation. Claudia didn't use any designer chants or breathing exercises; she just sat as she'd been taught as a child, inwardly repeating the mantra *I am God, and God is me; I am God, and God is me; I am God, and God is me*, until the black space between thoughts opened up like fertile, hidden soil. Then she leaped up to boil water for chrysanthemum tea.

"Aggie, Claudia morning meal." She took a hot, vigorous shower, scrubbing her body in long, circular motions just like the spa attendant had shown her, to keep her flesh high and tight. She turned on all the different showerheads, blasting water from various directions. For the last five minutes, she pressed the steam button and selected a eucalyptus oil for the day. As her pores soaked in the fresh-smelling steam, Claudia sang a song her grandmother used to sing as she did her embroidery work. Then Sergio rang with her real breakfast.

Sergio always surprised her with something special from the high-rise's kitchen. Today it was a tiny cranberry muffin, barely bigger than her thumb, glazed with a hard little helmet of lemon frosting, next to a perfectly soft-boiled egg and little batons of seeded toast for dipping, followed by a crystal goblet of perfectly ripe fruits, all beginning with the letter *p*: peaches, pluots, pomegranate seeds, and persimmons. Sergio loved playing these little games with her private meals. Tomorrow he might bring her "bacon and eggs" fashioned out of carved fruit, with real bacon and eggs cut into the shapes of flowers or even birds. In her silky gray robe with hair still wet from the shower, Claudia poured tea for herself and Sergio as they sat out on the balcony together, gossiping about the other residents. The Engleses' pleasure party in the garden dome had gotten out of hand again; someone had broken an arm and threatened to sue the building. Mr. Fruithill's newest health regimen was more akin to a pyramid scheme; he was conscripting the waitstaff to sell vitamins while they worked. Her closest downstairs neighbor, Mrs. Bauldstrad, kept cloning her little fluffy white dogs when the eldest got sick. She was now on the eighth iteration. Could she even believe it? Claudia laughed and said she couldn't. Sergio was so firmly Middle that the antics of

Felicity Towers were the most ridiculous he had seen. The problems he dealt with were like those on a television program: slightly madcap and solved in under thirty minutes.

Claudia scooted her chair closer, slipping her small feet into his lap. "Please and thank you?"

He laughed, massaging one strong digit at a time into her arch. "Does that feel good?"

"Oh yes," she groaned.

"Claudia, my love." His genteel voice was thoughtful and serious. "There's something I need to say to you." Sergio's family had paid handsomely to have his bones extended, his face sculpted with plates through various surgeries. It was a look popular among the elite serving class—Middle folks who had made themselves beautiful enough for upward-facing jobs were always in demand.

"Yes, my dear?"

Sergio's call button sounded out in three bright tones, summoning him back to his duties. "Ah," he said. "We're star-crossed again. Until next time." He kissed her fingertips and made her promise to stay beautiful. Claudia laughed and waved good-bye. It was her kitten laugh: coy, light, and flirtatious, reserved for men who preferred other men.

Claudia wasn't naturally the world's greatest beauty, which she had once worked very hard to counter with makeup and angles, avoiding certain kinds of light. But over time, she'd realized her slightly imperfect face worked in her favor. Very rich men were naturally suspicious of perfection in a partner, and she had no wish to look like a high-class servant, available to the highest bidder. Now she only worked hard to appear young and fresh. The older she got, the more work this required. This morning, she applied her kombu and moss face mask to keep her pores small and complexion even. She drank Beauty Broth™ in three big gulps, its concoction of boiled beef bones, fish scales, lemon, and a variety of medicinal-grade herbs and mushrooms distilled into a tonic designed to keep her face young, her hair shiny, her nails strong, her bowels regular, and her belly flat. The bottles were twenty ducats apiece. Claudia drank one every day. When she first came to live with Martin, she had noticed the other women carrying it around as a status symbol, like a handbag. Their bottles had bold black-and-white-striped labels with no logo. Martin had wanted to know what all the fuss was about, this drink that every woman except for his was swilling. He'd bought her thirty bottles to start. Now she had a special little refrigerator just for her Beauty Broth™, replenished monthly by the high-rise staff. With each bottle, Claudia swallowed what her grandmother would have earned in three hours. She went from being squeamish about the money to a serious BB convert in less than a month. Her skin, hair, and nails looked healthier than they had when she was twenty-three, and her digestion was a dream. After she drained the bottle, she brushed her teeth, then painted them with a whitening polish. Claudia asked her personal assistant program, Aggie, to put on some opera, passing through several selections before finding the right atmosphere. She rinsed off the face mask, then blotted with pure rose water and green tea toner. She applied a powerful aloe facial gel to hydrate her skin and maintain a dewy glow. Then she moisturized with a blend of borage, raspberry seed, and evening primrose oils, followed by a skin barrier serum with added sunscreen. After the mask, the toner, the gel, the moisturizer, and the serum, Claudia's skin looked perfectly even, luminous, and well-toned.

Years ago, a visit to the plastic surgeon had smoothed out her forehead ridge, but otherwise, she remained uncut and all-natural.

The surgeon had tried to talk her into all kinds of procedures as she was going under, but Claudia was grateful, in retrospect, that she'd held firm. Fashions had changed, and now the younger crowd were keeping their nipples. Those who had gotten them removed looked old and square, like newscasters, or worse, like servants living Above. It was best to remain subtle and flexible and not to stand out.

She dipped a small bristly brush into a tiny jar filled with waxy cream. She scrubbed the tiny brush onto her lips in vigorous little circles. The sugar cream buffed and exfoliated her lips, plumping and deepening their natural color. It also added a very slight gloss. Claudia expertly applied the barest trace of mascara, then filled in her eyebrows lightly. She painted her short, oval nails with clear polish. Finally she smothered her entire body with lotion. She studied herself in the mirror. She looked like she had just woken up and was naturally lovely, by the grace of God.

Claudia consulted her closet, though *closet* was an inaccurate word for the adjoining apartment that held all of Claudia's beautiful things. She had rooms of dresses, shoes, purses, and capes. A personal turret of floor-to-ceiling mirrors for applying makeup and drawing the stray hairs out from her chin, her nipples, the sides of her face. Martin called it "Claudia's world." In the beginning, she had spent hours playing dress-up, considering which side was her best. But now the luxurious items barely distracted her. She pulled on a long-sleeved black silk gown, buttery soft and diaphanous, then cinched the waist tight with a red silk ribbon. Her nipples pushed into the sheer fabric, creating two little tents. She piled her dark hair into a messy bun at the very top of her head, pulling out strands to frame her face. Casual, elegant, just pretty enough to be real. Claudia painted the corners of her eyes with smoky liner. Any day now, Martin would propose. Never had she found such an affluent mark who was so gentle, so easy to please. She wrapped a fur cowl around her neck and considered herself in the mirror. Who would she be today? Claudia pulled on a wire-frame monocle. A poet? A sculptor? A semiretired dancer? The girl in the glass stared back, waiting.

Claudia went to the museum. Today she was pretending to be an art student from an elite Above family. Claudia entered the curving white building that reminded her of the inside of a seashell. The exhibit on the second floor was simply called *BLUE*. Of course, there was no first floor at all, just stairs that took you to a higher plane. Claudia walked into *BLUE* and was immediately stared down at by portraits of Free-Wah kings on a rich blue background. On a low glass table lay secret personal maps of the city crafted by a woman artist, all on deep-blue handmade paper hammered with accents of gold. Her maps were next to a blue book of ancient ALGN poetry that praised God like a lover. She passed oil paintings of the sea during a storm, a calm harbor with the usual boat, a spindly blue dock perched over a broad river. There was a display of chipped pottery called "Heads of a Queen or Goddess"; an ancient chess set, blue with age; a statuette of a sitting lion in teal. Claudia learned that the glazed ceramic style called *faience* was made by ground quartz combined with alkali. She recorded this in her journal, then looked around. Perhaps, to an observer, it might seem like she was writing a poem. Perhaps she was. She wrote down the words:

A right eye from an anthropoid coffin
obsidian, crystalline, blue glass.

Then she studied a collection of perfectly maintained bowls from the thirteenth century. Bowls for tea, for washing brushes, a brazier for incense. They contained secret knowledge about how to stay intact in a perilous world. She recorded their descriptions in her little black notebook. A spherical jar with double handles, a ribbed censer, a squat vase. Tomorrow she would wear blue all day: blue clothes, blue lipstick, blue gloves. She would meditate on water, on its density and turbulence, on the sky on a clear, lovely day.

She thought of more art pieces to create as she walked to the museum's small water café. Perhaps Claudia would wait for the seasons to turn before taking out her favorite red handbag, then stuff it with leaves, like autumn gems. She'd spread the leaves out on Martin's bed and roll in them, naked and laughing. A fall witch. She'd wear gray and brown all winter long, sticks and stones, dirt and sky. Then she'd carry a bright-orange parasol through the dead of winter to mock the season. In spring, she'd be as pink as a newly green bud. A rose containing ever-smaller roses.

She looked at the museum wall. This specific shade of cream made her brain feel so quiet. Floating above it all, like steam, like a cloud, untethered and light. Claudia ordered a blue water infusion and asked for it to be served in a blue bowl. The café was crowded for a weekday. A group of girls posed with their brightly colored waters, taking pictures of each other in a flurry of chatter and activity. They trilled orders at their virtual assistants, computer programs called Trisha or Tonya or Frieda or Melissa, but none were as sophisticated as her Aggie, of that she was sure. These Above girls documented everything on their phones: their meta-meals, their fucks, their clothes and grooming activities. They made Claudia tired, but they weren't so different from her. Their lives were also art projects, but while they found and cultivated their audience, Claudia labored alone.

They were the daughters of the rich, making their way through the wilds of social media as lifestyle emblems. They lived fabulously inconsequential lives—they were born rich and they would die rich. Their children, if they had them, would be rich like their parents and grandparents. Around her, the shopgirls, baristas, and museum guards stood stoically, waiting to be needed. They were happy, lucky, to be employed Above, but they did not live here. They knew it, and everyone who looked at them knew it too.

Claudia found a chair by the long window and turned to sit facing the outside sculpture garden. She could hear the murmur of voices in the café behind her. To her left, two middle-aged women discussed washing their babies in tap water. Was boiling enough to disinfect, or must one only use bottled? She tuned them out, allowing the voices to merge into a low hum. This made the feeling intensify: a pleasurable sense of wellness, of connectedness, enveloped her as the café buzzed around her like a hive of bees. She thought about her perfectly unlined face. The lines would come, no matter what tonics she drank, or how many creams she applied. Small and soft at first, around her eyes, her mouth. She would get older. Perhaps a deep furrow would appear in her forehead one day, without her consent. A bit of skin would wobble from her neck. Her upper arms would sag. Her nail beds would grow brittle and dry. Spots would appear on the skin of her hands. Who would she be then?

Claudia felt her imagination falter. She had never truly imagined living past fifty. Mama had aged swiftly, then died as an old woman before her time. Her grandmother, it seemed, had been born old, then stayed that way for a century, the weight of the world on her bent back.

Claudia imagined forty thousand suns appearing in the sky, one by one. Hot, dense, and radiant. The brightness would be terrible, astonishing. She would be eaten by the light. She saw it all in radiant color.

After her visualization was over, Claudia imagined that she did marry Martin. She saw herself kneeling at the altar, smiling her feline smile, wearing the most marvelous gown. And then what? Who would she be? No longer a grifter, just a wife. Serene, untouchable, beyond reproach.

"Aggie," she murmured into her bracelet, "have wedding dress catalogues waiting for me at home."

Claudia left the museum to walk to the botanical gardens. She loved the plants and trees suspended in the air and often imagined the Martyr's version of heaven, the Forever Palace, very similar. Claudia's own faith had no conception of heaven, but she still appreciated the aesthetic of a floating paradise in the clouds. On her best days, her secret life in the clouds was a sort of Forever Palace, when Martin was away at work or on a business trip. Claudia continued her meditation on the color blue as she walked to the gardens. There was a little boy drinking from a blue bottle. His mother had blue flowers on her yellow scarf. A lazy blimp ambled by, advertising a new nightclub in jewel-tone turquoise. Today the sky was a light blue, punctuated with round, puffy clouds. Her life was the art project, and it didn't matter if her audience was in on it. All that mattered was her own commitment to the practice. She imagined a retrospective of her life's work: the period when she was living with the old woman in the Middle Hills, her university days, her humble beginnings as a credit thief. Every meaningless exchange that had brought her here today, to this very moment, when she felt light and free, at home in her body and easy in her mind. She inhaled. She was in control of her own life. Claudia decided she would marry Martin when he asked.

He would probably propose on her birthday in front of a towering, illicit cake and all of their friends, most of whom she despised. After the semicircle of candles was blown out, the cake would be wheeled away, back into the kitchen to be sliced, then given to each guest as a parting gift to enjoy in the privacy of their own homes. Claudia imagined herself standing in front of the cake and the crowd. She would have on a real smile, thinking of the apartment, the view of the earth below, her rooms filled with beautiful things, days of pure leisure. Only a fool doesn't notice when they're happy.

Right outside the botanical gardens stood a woman in a rough-looking coat passing out pamphlets. Claudia could imagine what was on them: something about poor children or saving marine life. She had grown up with this kind of cheap political stuff all over the Bastian; there was always someone organizing for something, tabling or canvassing with petitions, signs, and placards. She had never seen the likes of it Above, other than a gaggle of bored old ladies petitioning to have the calendar adjusted, as the gravitation of the moons extended the daylight hours with each passing year. Claudia quickened her pace to walk past the woman, who held out a pamphlet.

"Miss," she said urgently. "Are you aware that the waters have risen over five inches in the last quarter? Whole neighborhoods below have been flooded, belongings and homes washed away." The woman went on about the lack of government support, her voice rising higher and higher as Claudia rushed away to the gardens without a backward glance.

She walked through the huge, thick arc of grapevines, bare and spindly. Claudia unbuttoned her coat and allowed the sunlight to warm her exposed throat. Everyone knew the waters were rising. Even the staunchest deniers could feel that each day was warmer than the last on record. But Claudia knew better than to allow a stranger to stir her emotions into a panic. She watched as a respectable mother, or perhaps a live-in surrogate, and her two small children picnicked together on the large green lawn. Claudia sat on a curved stone bench that faced a statue of a nude goddess. The statue was so old that the goddess was downright plump, with a curved belly and broad gray hips. It no doubt predated the first Flesh Martyr, the noble Queen who gave up her physical form after liberating the kingdom from the evil Free-Wah king, or so said scripture. Claudia knew that this wasn't historically accurate, a discrepancy that would have deeply upset her when she was young. It had taken her years to realize that facts didn't matter. In the end, it was all storytelling.

Claudia meditated on the Forever Palace while she sat on the stone bench in the sun. The stone was cold, and the sun was warm on her throat. There was no need to be frightened of the rising seas, the increasingly frequent storms. It had been five years since Claudia had let her feet touch the true ground, to attend her mother's funeral. And if she let Martin marry her, she would never have to touch the earth again. The endless events that led up to the wedding—lavishly curated parties for preengagement and engagement, a getaway weekend for his friends, then one for her friends (who, other than Sergio, were only Martin's female relatives and wives of his associates)—these would be like an obstacle course, the final push of her ultimate performance, until life in the sky was hers forever.

There were a few things about life Above that irritated her, but she tried not to dwell on them. For one thing, Felicity Towers had its share of design flaws. While they were in no danger from the storms, it remained impractical to have a building of such an impossible height, no matter if it was "the best high-rise in the world," as its advertising touted. Money couldn't bend the laws of physics. On particularly blustery days, being on the top floor of Felicity

Towers felt like sailing on a rollicking ship. Over time, the slight shifts from the wind had misaligned some of the more subtle mechanics of the building. Once Claudia had put a lemon rind down the garbage disposal, and the resulting noise was like a bomb going off. The residents complained constantly to the eager staff of their mechanical problems. But most of Claudia's neighbors were never home. Those empty apartments were owned by shell companies, as a simple way to stow or even launder money. Martin's company, Rivirslow, owned several apartments in Felicity Towers; it was how he'd gotten the idea to move in there.

Claudia looked at the woman playing with her two children on the lawn. From the ease of gestures and the children's close familiarity with her, she seemed to be a surrogate, not a proper mother. After they were married, Martin's seed would be carried by a tall, lean surrogate who would tend to their children's care while Claudia focused on heaven. The more money he amassed, the more children they could produce this way. Secretly, Claudia enjoyed the idea of having a baby, her own little person. But a true Above woman would never debase herself that way.

Suddenly Claudia felt tired. Too tired to contemplate the color blue, too tired to go shopping. Her life was laid out before her like a well-marked trail. All she needed to do was stay the course. She decided to go home early. Perhaps Sergio would come upstairs to the apartment and massage her feet again. She was surprised to see the woman with the pamphlets still outside the gardens.

She thrust her flimsy pamphlet at Claudia once more, but this time her words were much more personal. "I bet you've never even set foot on the ground," she said. "You don't know what it's like down there. Whole streets being washed away! Parents rowing their children to school in boats. Even the Middle is experiencing—"

"I'm afraid I don't have time for boat rides," said Claudia. "I'm an art student, you see. This is a particularly stressful point in my semester—"

"You're just full of feces," said the horrible woman. "We could all be washed away by the Great Wave, and you wouldn't even blink, would you? You don't care about anyone below." Claudia imagined her sister, her father, her cousins and aunts and uncles, all drowning, crying out for her to help them, to get them to higher ground. She shook the thought away.

The woman was still ranting—"companies in cahoots with the government, profiting off our misery! What's next—will Stecopo buy the moons, the water, the air, the sky?"

Who had let this woman in here? But before she could threaten to summon the police, she was distracted by the blinging of sirens. She turned toward the sound. Would they ask for a statement from Claudia? Would that cause trouble for Martin? Breath quickening, Claudia turned back toward the woman and her booth. But they were both gone, as if she had only imagined them in the shifting light.

2.

Claudia got home from the botanical gardens with plenty of time to prepare for her next performance. The apartment had been beautifully restored in her time away—breakfast cleared, dishes returned to cabinets, beds made with the sheets turned down, any stray water droplets in the bathroom wiped away. Martin's shirts, back from the cleaners, hung in their plastic bags like ghosts. There were fresh flowers in every vase, and the floor-to-ceiling windows sparkled with cleanliness. Five thick, glossy bridal magazines were fanned out on a coffee table. Claudia hid them away in a drawer. Not for Martin's eyes, not yet. Tomorrow morning, she and Sergio would sit together on the balcony with the magazines, scrutinizing bodices and trains and lengths of veil. He could guide her through all that was expected. A wedding dress for Martin's set was never just that—there was the ceremony dress, the reception dress, then at least a third costume change for dancing, plus outfits for all the surrounding events. So much could go wrong. She changed out of her chic art student ensemble and lightly washed herself, then picked up a fragrant, warm towel, one of many that stayed fresh and toasty all day long in their built-in warming cabinet. As Claudia dried herself, she imagined she was wiping away her interaction with that unfortunate woman.

"Aggie, music program nine, please." Relaxing flute music began to play. There had always been floods. That Middling do-gooder wanted to yell about the Bastian like she knew what their lives were like. She knew *nothing*. There was no evidence that the flooding was worse now than it had been when Claudia was a child. And no one had petitioned to save her—she'd had to do it herself. She pulled on a sheer red jumpsuit that Martin loved on her, made from the softest cashmere, and buttoned it all the way up to her chin. Then she selected a simple emerald choker, which wound three times around her neck. She had chosen the necklace herself, but was forced to ask Martin's permission before spending such an exorbitant amount. The asking almost ruined the necklace for her altogether, even now. She looked at the jewels in the mirror and sighed. It could never be a necklace for her real life, the one that belonged only to her. It would forever be for Martin. At the beginning of their relationship, this didn't bother her. Now she wasn't so sure.

She had never planned to marry Martin. He was a high-profile corporate lawyer brokering the biggest deals Above, and he was a mark, like all men were to Claudia. He was an affluent rube, easy prey. Yet anytime she decided she had amassed enough of his fortune that it was time to cut and run, he would do something so lovely, so generous, it made her almost forget she was stealing from him. Martin gave her diamonds like some men gave flowers. His sexual tastes were orthodox and reliable; he was gentle. When he was stressed at work, he never took out his frustrations on her. He truly liked hearing her talk. They both enjoyed music and quiet evenings at home more than crowds and parties. Many pleasant evenings had been spent together in bed, reading side by side on lush, plump pillows. Living with Martin had taught her so much about the good life. She had finally slowed down enough to actually enjoy it.

But if she married Martin, she would no longer be a grifter, outsmarting rich men by the skin of her teeth. She would be just another elegant trophy wife, who had thrown her lot in with a man willing to take care of her. She didn't love him. But many other Above wives looked at their husbands with daggers in their eyes. Perhaps all relationships were transactional, at least up on this high-floating tier, so far from her childhood home.

"Aggie, music off. TV on." A big-screen television emerged from the wall. She scrolled through the familiar programs and advertisements, then picked a channel arbitrarily and allowed the murmur of conversation to take her away from her own mind. Claudia lubricated herself lightly, just in case Martin wasn't satisfied from the morning. She dabbed a bit of rose oil on the hollow of her throat, her wrists, and the space between her breasts. On the television, she overhead a woman crying, saying her daughter had been lost to a cult. "I spent years of my life trying to get away from Seagate," she said, her voice warbling. "I would have been better off letting people there think I had died."

"Aggie, TV off and away." Claudia wetted her swimming cap and hung it to dry in the master bathroom. Then she waited for her mark, sitting on the divan just so, angled toward the window with her good side in profile. She held her tablet and pressed the icon labeled GARDEN STORY. Years ago she had digitized *The Kitchen Girl* so she could access it anywhere without worry. For all she could glean using the proper channels, and with Aggie searching the dark web, hers was the only digital copy in existence. She realized lazily as she read that she did want Martin to approach her with ardor. She would close her eyes and think of Henray, enjoying the attentions of Martin's uninspired but reliable lovemaking.

Martin came home with two rowdy associates. His firm had won the Stecopo agreement, and the boys were looking to celebrate.

Claudia felt naked. *I've grown soft,* she thought. She was wearing an outfit for sumptuous relaxing with her man, not for boisterous entertaining. She had imagined the two of them might enjoy a massage at the spa, then a sound bath before bed. She loved these quiet, luxurious activities with Martin, where she could pretend he was anyone. Now she was unexpectedly playing hostess.

Martin's tiny mouth was glossy from fried foods, his eyes already red from drink. The men rummaged through the refrigerator, taking out cod jelly, a terrine of liver pâté and olive mousse, a mound of gin-infused aspic, and an assortment of tiny silver spoons. The elite tended to shirk the doctrines about not eating in public by stretching what the scriptures meant by "liquid," creating not-quite-solid concoctions that Claudia found nauseating. Some of these so-called delicacies, like the gin-infused aspic, would get you drunk while they filled you up. Claudia brought out a very nice bottle of bubbly from the refrigerated case.

"Let's celebrate!" She popped the cork, and everyone cheered, raising their drink flutes aloft.

"We're all bloody rich!" said one of the men. Without their wives present, she had trouble telling the businessmen apart. Claudia couldn't remember if he was Mr. Peterson or Mr. Muelber, so she deemed him Sweaty Neck.

"I'll drink to that!" Claudia said, playing the requisite bimbo. "Now, what's this about Stecopo?"

"We're celebrating a few different things, my love—we don't want to bore you." Martin pulled her onto his lap. "They've just passed a bill in our favor—a sort of deregulation, so it'll be easier to do business. And we've finally closed the deal with Stecopo, who will use our pharmaceuticals in their new projects. It's all very well timed."

"No coincidence there," said Sweaty Neck, elbowing Martin. "There's such a big revolving door between Stecopo's executive board and the government, I can barely keep track of who works where."

"Stecopo might be doing food supplements now, but they used to be a chemical company," said the other man, whom Claudia labeled No Neck. "That marketing community of theirs in the Valley is ingenious."

Sweaty Neck held out his arm in a poor attempt to look beguiling. "Come to Seagate, and live in love," he crooned.

Everyone laughed. Claudia kept her eyes wide and innocent. "I heard people in the park today talking about deregulation. They didn't seem happy about it!"

"Oh yes, well, get used to that," said Sweaty Neck. "The common man is frightened of progress. But technology is the key to solving the world's biggest problems. It can all be used for bad or good—genetic engineering is just a scary term for something that's been done in some form or another for thousands of years. Farmers have always selected the hardiest crops, the fastest-growing varietals—"

Martin patted her thigh. "Please, forgive our shop talk! To put it plainly, Stecopo has figured out a way to make pesticide-resistant crops, so their seeds are treated and the weeds are killed without harming the plant. It's brilliant, and it's going to feed a lot more people with a lot less work. Some farmers didn't like this, they took Stecopo to court, and they lost."

"See, *this* is why Martin closes the deal!" Sweaty Neck patted him on the back. "Plain as parchment, so understandable."

"So you're going to end world hunger?" Claudia put a hand on her hip. "I didn't know you were a humanitarian, darling!" All three men laughed, and Martin excused himself to the restroom.

"Here's the thing." Sweaty Neck took a spoon of aspic and placed it to one side of the plate. "By merging with Stecopo, Rivirslow will create these flood relief packages for the poor people below. That's where our payday comes in." He scooped off another spoonful of aspic and dotted it around the plate, then another, and another. "See? Little communities, safe and sound from the rising waters! With everything they could ever need, all in the same place!" Sweaty Neck took a final spoonful of aspic and devoured it.

"They don't seem terribly safe now," said Claudia dryly.

"I have a better idea," said No Neck. He looked at her and patted his lap. "Why don't you sit in this nice chair, little lady? I've got something to give you. It's a big sort of present, but I bet you can take it."

"I'm afraid Martin is the only one who gives me that sort of present," said Claudia sweetly. "But I'm sure yours is very grand indeed."

"You don't even want to take a look?"

Sweaty Neck rolled his eyes. "Good Lord, can we have one evening that you don't wax poetic about your cock?"

Claudia rewarded him with a smile and decided that Sweaty Neck was her favorite. He seemed genuinely interested in engaging her in conversation instead of just trying to get it on.

Martin came back from the bathroom, wiping his hands on his pants. He got sloppy when he drank—he'd forget to use a towel or leave the toilet seat up. Sometimes she'd come into the kitchen to find the refrigerator door left open and the cabinets ajar, like he was a child. It deeply irritated her. But he rarely indulged, except in these kinds of business situations, as was expected. She considered herself lucky that he did not hold his liquor well and, in turn, develop a dependency, like so many Above citizens. Claudia knew some women who mainly lunched on wine, and men whose hands shook until they got their afternoon cocktail.

"Martin, is this true? Are you and Claudia monogamous?" asked No Neck, his eyes bulging.

Martin kissed her cheek. "My Claudia likes to enjoy my favors alone—she's a very special sort. I, of course, share sex with others when I feel so moved. That's just her way!"

Claudia stood so he could take his seat, then reclaimed his lap. "Once you've had the best, you don't need the rest," she teased. Martin blushed.

"How quaint! Just how many sexual partners have you enjoyed, dear Claudia?" asked No Neck, rolling her name around in his mouth as if it were an olive pit. He swallowed a large spoonful of aspic.

"Eleven," she said lightly, and lowered her head, though she did not smile at all.

"Incredible!" Sweaty Neck shook his head. "I had eleven lovers by the time I entered college."

"Fascinating," said No Neck. "But with so few partners, how can you use your body to move up to God?"

Claudia took this as her invitation to show that she had claws. "Are you saying you want to save my soul?" she asked teasingly. He squirmed, which made the other man laugh. She looked at Martin; his eyes were slightly unfocused. "But as for sexual activity . . . We make up for it with quantity, don't we, my dear? Perhaps other girls need to take on lovers because they don't have a man at home giving it to them morning, noon, and night!"

The men chortled and slapped the table. Martin's dull eyes sparkled for a moment with drink and pleasure. He kissed the side of her face once more and gave her upper arms a squeeze. She had done well. Claudia felt something warm inside her breast, something adjacent to love.

This was why he had brought them home to celebrate their new account, or merger, or whatever the Stecopo agreement was. Another wife or partner would have dutifully sucked them all off between putting out more gelatin molds. But not Claudia. Claudia was mysterious, in her sheer red jumpsuit and sparkling green collar. Martin had something the other men didn't have access to, and all Claudia had to do was be as aloof as she wished.

"Speaking of women who won't give me what I want," No Neck said, "I went to the most amusing restaurant the other day in the Middle. I have half a mind to take you there tonight."

"With those pretend cannibals?" asked Sweaty Neck, wrinkling his nose. "How gauche!"

"No, no—it's all vegetables, in fact, and truly something. There's a young lady there who is quite the chef. Her cuisine was beyond expectations, if not overly generous in portion size!" He cupped his hands in front of his chest in a gesture to indicate a big bosom. The men laughed. "Oh, oh! How do you fuck a fat girl?"

"How?" cried Martin, already breathless with laughter before the punch line. Claudia felt herself tense. How he repulsed her sometimes.

"You roll her in flour and go for the wet spot!"

Martin snorted and gasped, choked by his own amusement. Claudia sprang up, putting on her most threatening shark smile, and walked to the kitchen. There she leaned against the refrigerator door, savoring its coolness. Her mother and grandmother sat in the corner of her mind, looking at her quizzically. They would never understand her life now, what was expected and inferred, the barrage of judgments every way she turned. Suddenly she longed for Sergio: his genteel presence, his easy warmth. "Aggie, call Sergio."

"Hello?" he answered. His voice was low and rough, as if he had been sleeping.

"I'm sorry to disturb you, Serge. I need to order a meal for Martin and his friends. I know I should have called the kitchen, but I just wanted to hear your voice. Can we have the sea bream porridge with extra condiments? That should be fine."

"Oh, Claudia," he murmured. "I wanted to hear your voice too." His voice pitched low and urgent. "Can you get away? Meet me on the roof deck?"

Happy shouting rang out from the living room. Martin wouldn't get to sleep until very late, but he would certainly be drunk enough soon for her to do whatever she pleased. "I'm not sure," she said slowly. "He has guests, and I'm supposed to entertain them." Sergio was silent for a long moment. "Oh, not like that!" said Claudia. "I just have to stay, at least for a while, until they're too drunk to notice my absence."

"I need to speak to you." His voice was so serious, unlike that of her dashing, playful friend. It must be important.

She concocted an excuse to leave. "All right. I'll see you on the roof deck soon."

"See you soon," he breathed, then disconnected the line.

Claudia walked back into the dining area. "Darling," she whispered into Martin's ear. "The concierge isn't responding. I'll go downstairs and place our order myself." She lowered her volume even more, but put on a girlish voice. "But please, steer our guests away from our bathroom. My swimming cap is there, and the place is sopping wet!"

Martin fingered her black hair. "You had a good swim, my mermaid?"

She nodded, and he kissed her again tenderly, keeping his plump lips closed. Claudia felt the stirrings of affection yet again. "You're my crown jewel," he said, quietly enough that only she could hear.

Claudia smiled a real smile, though a small one. It climbed up her face, all the way past her eyes, even causing her forehead to slightly crinkle. She made her way to the door. "Oh, and Claudia," Martin called out behind her. "Can you see if Nessa is free for the evening? I can't leave my brothers without their release!"

Alone in the silent hallway, Claudia cringed. "Aggie, Nessa is requested for entertainment in the penthouse. Party of three." A pang of hurt swirled through her. They didn't really want her there anyway, not if she wasn't going to fuck them. Martin loved showing off her modesty, but that didn't mean he and his friends would go without for a night. She reminded herself again that Martin was not her boyfriend—he was a mark. "Aggie, can you believe these men? They say they believe in the spiritual superiority of women, and yet they take every opportunity to ejaculate into a woman below them in station." Claudia had programmed Aggie not to respond to these kinds of statements; the robotic voice speaking back to her just underlined her loneliness. It was so much better to pretend to be hearing one side of a phone call. She sighed. "No, you're right. I'm being judgmental." Perhaps Nessa liked being passed around in the middle of her shift. Maybe it broke up the monotony of folding towels, or whatever else she did at Felicity Towers?

Or perhaps Nessa pities me, she thought as she walked down the long golden hallway, *because I have to sleep with Martin every night, and she gets to do as she pleases at the end of the workday.* Claudia entered the elevator. Perhaps she should find a new mark. Someone with a little less money, someone it would be easy to leave. A simple job, to clear her mind. She pushed away errant thoughts of Keith—his laugh, his smile, how his simplest touch made her whole body feel warm. She had held real love in her hands for only a few months. There was no equal to the feeling of going to sleep and waking up with someone you loved. But that was the trick of it. It could just happen, if you weren't careful, whether the person was worthy or not. Love was, perhaps, the greatest grift of all.

———————

The roof deck was a splendid profusion of plants and plush furniture, a few hand-selected sculptures, a charming water feature next to her meditation cushions. There was an outdoor pool on the lower floors, but she rarely used it—she enjoyed her privacy too much. Claudia leaned out on the railing and savored the balmy air. Both moons were but a whisper tonight, giving the sky a seldom enjoyed darkness. Claudia used *I am God, and God is me; I am God, and God is me* to reconnect to her breath. Sometimes she wished for Martin to be just a bit more ill-fitting as a partner— older, uglier, more crude in word and deed. Then she could detest him all the time, even when he did something endearing, and not just during his most thoughtless acts. But as it was, the thought of leaving Felicity Towers, all her beautiful clothes, and, yes, even Martin's loving, puppyish gaze from across a candlelit table was too much to bear. Now that she was calm, Claudia realized that she was upset because he didn't care to celebrate with her after he got his big promotion. Her idealized version of Martin would have come home with a bottle of bubbly and taken her out to a special evening, just the two of them. But did she really wish to have more of his attention? Nessa was upstairs now, receiving her share of those attentions. Claudia shuddered.

She felt a soft touch on her shoulder. Claudia turned to find

Sergio, looking handsome and serious in the gentle moonslight, like a figure from a romance novel.

"Darling!" He embraced her, leaning in much closer than usual, burying his face in her hair.

"Hello, dear," she said, pulling back. "What's the matter? You had me worried."

"I just needed to see you," he said, never letting go of her hands.

"Well, now you're seeing me. So dish!"

Sergio leaned over and kissed her cheek. He kissed her other cheek. He kissed her forehead, her nose. Then he hovered his mouth in front of her lips. Claudia kept smiling statically, her expression locked into place. Sighing, he took her hand and held it to his lips.

"Serge," she said, pulling her hand away. "What's going on?"

"I love you," he said. "Let's get away from here."

"Quit playing and be serious. What's gotten you so upset?"

"Oh, Claudia, I can't stand it. Wait . . . here." He took out a small container and pressed it into her hands.

"Ooh! For me?" It appeared to be a slice of cake.

"Cardamom citrus coffee cake. There's a woman in the Middle who's been making the most incredible creations." He looked at her seriously. "Perhaps we can go there one day soon for dinner. Would you like that?"

Claudia wrinkled her nose. "As a rule, I try to stay well above sea level." She opened the container and took a bite of cake. "Oh, wow, this is delicious. Well, I suppose I could make an exception." She winked at him. "Just this once, for you."

"Oh, Claudia!" He threw his frame around her much smaller body. "Do you think Martin knows?"

Claudia paused, her blood running cold. "Knows what?"

Sergio sighed. "I thought I'd stay at Felicity for the rest of my life, but that doesn't matter now. I was asleep, in purgatory, before I met you."

"Serge—"

"We could stay with my family for a few weeks while we get settled. They have a nice little room above the garage—it's like a separate apartment, really. I know it's not the lifestyle you're used to, but that won't matter, not when we can finally be together. My parents are going to love you! I've already told them so much about you. Not everything, of course. But we won't have to hide anymore, and that's the most important thing."

Claudia felt the ground shift and sway under her feet. "What is this? Are you rehearsing a play?"

He sighed melodramatically. "Listen, I enjoy our usual repartee, I really do. But I can't wait another moment." He placed her hand on his bulging groin. She pulled it away, stunned by his crudeness. "Can we leave tonight? It's rash, I know. But we have to leave all this behind us before Martin finds out."

"I'm sorry, Serge—do you think we've been having some kind of affair?"

Sergio froze, staring at her. After a long moment, he put his head in his hands. Claudia was afraid he might weep or collapse onto the floor.

"Hey, hold on." She touched his shoulder. "One day we'll laugh about this together, I promise."

Sergio moved away from her, taking out a violet cigarette and lighting it. He paced back and forth, taking a couple of long drags in silence. Finally he murmured, "Nessa warned me, but I wouldn't listen."

Bile crept up into her mouth. "What did Nessa say?"

He turned to her, his sharp features highlighted in the moonslight. "She said you were a Bastian brat, a Floater. She said you didn't understand the implications of what you were doing, not for a moment."

Claudia felt outside her own body, as if she were viewing the scene from above. "You don't know anything about me," she whispered.

He threw up his hands. "Then tell me! That's all I've ever wanted since I met you."

She shook her head. "No."

He reached out to her. "Please, I'm sorry, my love, forgive me—"

Claudia moved away from his touch. He had been quick to call her foul names, then chase them with florid words of love. But he was right—she'd assumed Sergio accepted her as his better and would never dare think of her as within his reach. She hadn't realized what she had been doing, not at all. "I need to get back to Martin."

"Claudia—please!" His voice was sharp and pleading. "Don't go."

She ran from his words, from his scrambling grasp. She knew that there was nothing she could say. Another *no* would be met with more vitriol. But anything that sounded like *yes*, and he would try to possess her, to consume her, just like Martin, just like every person she had ever lain with. To all of them, she was a commodity. Except for Keith. Sweet, murderously stupid Keith.

At least with Martin, the perks of such a possession were far, far greater than with someone like Sergio. She paused by the glass elevator and rubbed her arms, looking at her reflection. She looked cold, windswept. So Nessa had realized she was from the Bastian. How many others knew? She hoped the orgy would be over soon. She couldn't bear to be in the room with that woman, not now, not ever again. How could she have been so stupid?

When Claudia got back to the apartment, blessedly, Nessa and the men were nowhere to be seen. Claudia threw away all of the aspics and fruit molds, poured the half-drunk bottles down the sink. She couldn't even bring herself to call a staff member to tidy. She felt exposed, as if Sergio had peeled off her skin and she was walking around inside out. What had the rest of the staff been whispering about her? How could she keep living at Felicity Towers if everyone knew where she was from? A million little things she had said or done came roaring back through her memory. All those breakfasts together—Sergio's intent gaze as she devoured the food he brought her, pressing her feet into his lap. Claudia shuddered. There was nothing like feeling she was too old and wise to make this kind of mistake, only to realize she had been making it so spectacularly and for so long.

There was a knock at the door, and her heart jumped at the sound. She peered through the peephole. It was only Miguel, standing with a tureen of sea bream porridge and dozens of condiments—puréed garlic, cilantro paste, a slurry of onion and scallion, red chili oil. Heart still pounding, she opened the door, but made no move to let him inside.

"The party has moved on," she said. "I'm afraid there's no one here to eat this lovely meal. Would you take it back to the kitchens and enjoy it with your friends?"

Miguel's face revealed nothing. "Wouldn't you like it, miss?"

"I have no appetite tonight. Please, take it and enjoy." She started to close the door, then hesitated. "Wait!" Claudia went to the temperature-controlled wine rack. She pulled Martin's prized bottle of Salon Blanc de Blancs down from the top shelf, feeling a little thrill to give away something so precious, to punish him simply for existing. "This will pair very well." He accepted the bottle without a word and left.

Claudia went to bed spread out like a starfish. As she was falling asleep, she imagined she lived alone in the Middle in a modest one-bedroom apartment. Something spacious with good light. There, she could sleep like this every night, keep her own hours, eat whatever she pleased, whenever she pleased. She could do things that brought her joy but didn't cost huge sums of money. Wake up each morning and decide which way to flow. Claudia imagined herself dressed all in gray, walking to an open-air market on a sunny day. She'd buy a bouquet of bright, simple flowers. Go home and put them in a vase. Make herself a cup of tea. Read whatever she wanted. She'd grow old like this, finding pleasure in rosebuds, in cups of chamomile.

Over the years, Claudia had kept thinking she would make art when she was settled, when she had enough time, enough money. Now she had both, but couldn't force herself to bring paint to paper. The last time she had been in an art supply store, looking at a display of various brushes, Claudia had felt suffused with dread. She'd left the store in a cold sweat, buying nothing.

It was almost morning again by the time Martin joined Claudia in bed. He smelled thick and hot, like spices and hard liquor. She shifted away from his weight, curling in on herself. When she found sleep again, Claudia dreamt of the ocean rising, rising up to consume the whole world. *So silly*, she thought as people struggled and cried out for higher ground. *Don't they know that life is better at the bottom of the ocean?* Better than up in the air, that was for sure.

3.

When Claudia awoke, it was to the sound of Martin vomiting in the guest bathroom. It was very polite of him to choose that one instead of hers. Claudia filed that under the column *Reasons to Marry Martin*. She looked over at the clock by the bed. It was 5:45 A.M. She pulled on her robe. She ordered Martin some dry toast and ginger tea to settle his stomach. Then she sat in the meditation tower, but she did not visualize or chant, just allowed her thoughts to drift by like passing clouds. It was Miguel who came up a little later with the tray. She suspected that Sergio wouldn't be setting foot in the apartment again. Miguel was silent as he poured her coffee. He didn't add one lump of sugar and a dollop of coconut cream the way Sergio would have, just left a little jug of milk and a ramekin of sugar on the tray. He left without a word. Claudia decided she wished to see none of the staff of Felicity Towers. "Aggie, cancel my personal trainer. And no further maid or concierge service today. Do not disturb."

Martin, still groggy, smiled at the tea and toast. "My little nursemaid." He blushed. "We celebrated a bit too well last night."

"Can you go into work late? Surely they wouldn't mind."

Martin shook his head. "There's more to do now than ever." He squeezed her hand. "I'm going to be at the office for longer hours in the coming weeks. You'll have to amuse yourself a bit more." He kissed her nose thoughtfully. "But not tonight. Tonight is just for you and me. I thought about you all evening, Claudia. I hope you weren't too lonely."

"I missed you." Claudia tilted her head. "You know I'm not as comfortable a host as some women."

Martin pulled Claudia onto his lap. "That's one of the many reasons I love you." He kissed her neck. "You're mine, mine, mine." He gave her a squeeze, then pushed her off his lap lightly. "Ah, I have to go! No rest for the wicked."

"Martin?" Claudia's eyes lit up. "Can I redecorate the apartment?"

"Yes, I'm getting tired of, what's this called?" He tapped the wall beside him.

Claudia giggled. "Milky quartz."

"I can't wait to see what you think up next, my genius girl." He kissed her good-bye. In his gold slippers, his work dress, and his satin coat and broad felt hat, Martin almost looked like a grown man instead of a giant baby. No doubt he would be teased mercilessly by his inferiors for his overindulgence the night before. But his foolery would be rewarded: a good old boy who worked hard and played harder. Another man would have taken the day off, but not Martin. He sealed the deal, stayed up all night, and went in hungover to file the paperwork.

Around ten o'clock, Miguel returned with her second breakfast. She did not remember ordering it, but Claudia awoke from her second sleep very hungry, and it smelled divine. Fried lemony

potatoes, a salmon croquette the size of her palm, and a bright little salad. A carafe of fresh-squeezed grapefruit juice and a pot of
Darjeeling tea sat next to the plate. There was a vase on the tray,
containing a single pink rose. With a sinking feeling in her stomach, Claudia realized this food was from Sergio.

"Miguel! Did you enjoy the porridge and the wine last night?"

He didn't smile. "I don't eat animals or drink alcohol. But the
others enjoyed it very much. They give their thanks to you."

"Oh," said Claudia. She hadn't considered that he might have
dietary restrictions, religious or otherwise. "Miguel, I want you to
tell the person who made this that I threw it in the trash. Can you
do that for me?"

He shrugged. "I can."

Claudia sat down and smothered a thick white sauce over the
potatoes and salmon. She tore off a big bite with her fork and was
about to raise it to her lips when she noticed Miguel was still
standing by the doorway, watching her intently. She cringed. The
staff must be talking about her, the slut upstairs who would let anyone watch her eat. "That will be all, Miguel. And don't forget—"

"You threw it in the trash." He let himself out.

Claudia pushed her plate away. Life with Martin was making
her weak. She hadn't even considered that Sergio might be interested in her. He'd never even kissed her. Only, thinking back on it,
he had. Sergio had kissed her cheek, her fingertips, her temples.
Once he'd sat on her bed and brushed her hair glossy with a hundred even strokes. And the foot rubs! Damn these effeminate Middle men with their cheek lifts and manicures. How was Claudia
supposed to know he'd wanted her in such a way? It seemed bizarre
to her that a man would go through such an elaborate courtship
before expressing his interest—she'd been so sure he preferred

other men! Though it pained her, she took the beautiful plate of food and threw it in the trash, then placed the trash can in the hallway outside the apartment door.

Claudia went into her clothing chamber to dress and was surprised to find that the maid had not been there to tidy. Her clothes were strewn about, her makeup jumbled on the dresser. Even her beloved black cashmere dress lay in a heap on the floor. Then she remembered—*Do not disturb*. As she hung up the dress herself, she found that the pamphlet from the hysterical woman was still in the pocket. She sat on her stiff velvet chair and began to read.

The text was too fine and the language strangely punctuated, but Claudia found herself pulling in the information quickly, as if she were reading a book. The pamphlet claimed that the big corporations, in conjunction with the government, were not only ignoring the environmental devastation on the ground, but actively profiting from it.

Environmental protections have been lifted under the guise of job development and revitalizing a broken economy. But what exactly do these abundant jobs create? A transient, underpaid workforce! Polluted air, water, and soil. Pipelines choked with oil, spilling out into our water supply! Thousands of BIRDS dead on the beach! Water levels rising, rising, RISING.

Our towns and streets are being washed away! And who comes to our rescue when such disasters STRIKE? The very same companies and government branches that have allowed these emergencies to happen in the first place with their policies! Our children are SICK from unclean drinking water and polluted air, and WHO sells us their overpriced medicine? WHO charges penalties when we cannot afford their insurance? WHO profits from the hospitals that house them as they die? Those SAME companies! By the hand of that SAME government.

When the ground is infertile, the air and water UN-CLEAN, where do we get our food, our water? Why, from the SAME companies that poisoned our land! They sell us protein bars and sterilized water and SHAME, telling us it is sick and immoral to grow our own food and drink from our own wells. We can only escape with our own DEATHS, shunting our bills over to our struggling families!

Our poverty is NOT simply a byproduct of the system. It is what the system was made to create. Our sickness, our disEASE, our emergencies, are meant to strip us of our power, our ability to fight for better. Now is the time to revolt! We must take to the skies and say, ENOUGH.

Claudia put the pamphlet down. There was nothing new in it. The most surprising aspect was why a call to action so clearly aimed at the lower tiers was being circulated Above. Suddenly Claudia was too tired for the world. She had lost her only friend at Felicity, and now she had no one to talk to. Of course the lower classes wanted to revolt against the companies. Of course the companies were taking advantage of them. Of course the government cared more about relationships with financial giants than the health and well-being of its citizens. Why, anything beyond that was just the promise of a politician. Idly, she turned the pamphlet over.

No longer will our lives and the lives of our children be poisoned by greed. Revolution is near. Stop Stecopo! Join us and rise!

At the bottom of the pamphlet there was a time and a date for a rally.

Meet us in the Middle!
Brothers and sisters from the Bastian, the Valley
Allies from the Middle and Above
Soon we come together as one!

The pamphlet promised the biggest rally the city had ever seen. Claudia threw it in the trash. She didn't feel too guilty; she couldn't attend, even if she wanted to. She and Martin had that thing on Saturday anyway. It had been in their calendar for weeks.

She heard the front door open. Claudia assumed it was Miguel, coming to clear the tray away.

"I said do not disturb!"

She walked back toward the main door, still in her gray robe. Sergio stood in the hallway, holding the trash can in his hands, a dark expression on his face.

"Get out of here," she said, cinching the robe around her. "I don't want to see you."

His face was a storm, his words a gale. "This is what you do with my love? You throw it in the garbage, for everyone to see? You reject my food at my place of work? I have to see these people around the clock, Claudia! I have to come here every day!" He looked at her expectantly. Then his eyes narrowed, and he made a sound of disgust in the back of his throat. "You don't even understand how insulting this is. You're just a Floater, blundering through life, offending people left and right, and you don't even realize." He threw the garbage can on the floor, its contents spraying out in a burst across the plush carpet. Claudia wrapped her arms protectively around herself. He paced around the foyer, eyes wild, starting to look like an animal. "Being upset with you doesn't even make sense. It's like yelling at a child!"

"How did you know?" she asked, barely audible. "How did you and Nessa guess?"

"How did I know?" he repeated. His voice had a mocking hardness to it. "How did I know? Because of everything, Claudia. A million little gestures. The way you take your tea. The way you forget to cover your mouth when you laugh. The way you look servants directly in the eye. The way you eat! All that chewing and swallowing. The way you look at your surroundings when you think you're not being observed. The way you carry your own shopping bags home from the store. The way you bite into a big piece of food and then let the rest of it hang there on the bloody goddamn fork, instead of cutting it into smaller pieces in the first place. Did you really think that you were passing through undetected this entire time? And obviously Martin knows—that's why he wants you. You're in his employ, like me and Nessa and everyone who's ever touched him!"

"Get out." Her voice was dead. A broken lightbulb, a carcass, a husk.

He knelt before her, his long limbs outstretched. Suddenly his bodily extensions seemed ghastly, arachnid. How could she ever have let those fingers massage her? And how had she not understood what that had meant?

"He'll never love you," he said, practically whining. She preferred him yelling. "You're his servant, not his equal. But I can love you—I do love you." His dexterous fingers began to claw at her robe. "You see?" he said, breathing heavily. He moved one hand to hold her side while the other wormed under her robe. She felt his fingers brush at her labia, clumsy and searching, as if he were trying to find a way to hold her in place rather than seduce her. She kneed him in the face, and he rolled to the floor, holding his bleeding nose.

"YOU DON'T KNOW ME AT ALL!" she screamed. He froze, and the room was silent for a moment.

"Leave," she whispered, furious. "If you have any idea what's good for you, you will never show your face here again."

Sergio scrambled up, raising his hands as if she had pulled out a gun, and fled.

The old pain was back, the phantom wound. Claudia reached down to touch her scar, as if by some magic she might have been shot again in the same place, bleeding out all over the carpet. But of course she wasn't. She had just been wrong again, so very wrong. Hands trembling, she cleaned up the garbage, ridding the apartment of any evidence of Sergio's violence. Claudia walked to the bathroom and splashed cold water on her face, breathing ragged. She could barely hear with the sound of blood roaring in her ears. She looked at her face in the mirror. But Claudia had disappeared, and it was Reiko who was staring back. She had the impulse to punch her, to smash her face in the glass. *Stupid, stupid girl. You were supposed to be smart. Not the prettiest, certainly not the kindest. That was the one thing you had that no one else had, the one thing that couldn't be bought or sold: your mind. And now look at you. You'll never get away from the ground, no matter how high you travel.*

Claudia collapsed on the cool tile, weeping. When she finally steadied her breath, she said her mantra a dozen times, a hundred, until the shaking stopped. She was lucky, truly, given how careless and lazy she had gotten.

"Aggie," she whispered into the floor. "It's not too late. There's still time to make it right."

———

Claudia paced, eating random snacks and day-drinking. Strawberries, corn chips, spicy peanuts, a tall can of light ale. These were the little treats that Sergio kept hidden for her in the back of the Beauty Broth™ fridge. In retrospect, this was another secret between them that had probably made Sergio imagine their affair. As she paced, Claudia couldn't decide if she was more upset about the people protesting whatever Martin was doing at work or about Sergio and the staff gossiping about her. It wasn't like she'd ever thought she was living with a saint. No one made their money by giving puppies to orphans and nuns. She'd be better off forgetting about the pamphlet entirely and carrying on with her life.

But no matter how she reasoned with herself, or however many breathing exercises she tried, she didn't feel better. So she turned to the other activity she used to calm her anxiety. Claudia stole money from Martin.

"Aggie, pirate mode: Martin checking to Claudia savings. *Shopping at Dahlia's: 2,000 ducats* and *Jewelry at Cesura's: 3,000 ducats*." She had modified her old program so it could create a unique charge instead of just duplicating small charges and funneling the money back into her account. Her magnificent Aggie could do almost anything.

Early in her relationship with Martin, she'd faked a minor surgical procedure, which he had gladly offered to pay for, depositing that money right into her account. That little cushion had allowed her to relax into this lifestyle she could never truly afford. Similarly Martin paid for two swimming lessons and one spa day per week at a luxury women's club that Claudia had made up. A thousand weekly ducats went right into her savings account, while Claudia used the spa and the pool at the high-rise for free whenever it suited her. She worried that Martin might push her to be more economical or chide her to use the amenities already included with their sumptuous apartment, but he never did. She could leave at any time and keep up her life in the air for another year or two, perhaps even three. But it wouldn't be enough to be truly independent, not permanently. This was what she hadn't understood before coming Above. Not even the Clarissa grift, if she had managed it, would have kept her in this life. It was never enough. Martin was from a prominent family, yet even their relationship to money was one of conquest, of titles and markets, of stocks and valuations. They were always grasping for more, more, more. No matter how high they climbed, it would never be enough. No one ever made it, even here. The chase, the hunt, had been so thrilling. Now it just made her tired.

There was a knock at the door. Heart pounding, she thought for a moment it might be Sergio, back to exact his revenge. But a woman in a red gown and red paper hat bowed low and entered, a bellboy pulling a massage table behind her. Claudia had forgotten about her standing bimonthly appointment—full-body wax, facial, massage. The bellboy set up the table in the middle of the parlor before he departed, and the woman put pleasing harp music on the speakers. Claudia tied up her hair, took off her clothes, lay on the table, and tried to relax. The woman began by scrubbing her face with a paste made from ground freshwater pearls. Claudia took pearls internally as well, each night in pill form. It truly did brighten her complexion, and apparently it was good for your bones. Some women, Claudia knew, also painted their nails with diamond dust and wore face masks made of gold, but that was really just because they could. The attendant removed the pearl paste with a warm towel before applying a gel of calendula and seaweed, followed by a pulsing laser to stimulate collagen production. She then waxed Claudia's legs, thighs, vulva, armpits, and chin before turning her over and doing the back side. During her deep-tissue massage, she thought of Sergio and burned anew with shame and fury. How could she have been so stupid? The woman's strong fingers worked the knots along her neck, her shoulders. She gently asked Claudia to turn onto her back.

"Miss, would you care for a meditation aid?"

Normally Claudia declined, but today she indulged. The woman squeezed clear jelly onto her labia and began rubbing in slow, circular motions. It wasn't Claudia's fault, she reasoned. Her life had been plenty hard, and at every turn, if she wasn't careful, there was someone like Sergio, waiting to drag her down. How glorious to think of herself as the wife of someone like Martin. She would pick out all their surrogates herself. They would be blond, like Nessa; Middle folk, like Sergio; like the kids she went to college with, who preferred fucking to studying because they never had far to fall. These women would lie on their backs for Martin, take in his sperm as servants, while Claudia was queen, her every demand obeyed—

She came with a shout and, when her breathing slowed, was surprised to find she had pushed the attendant's hand far inside her. The woman held still for a long moment, then slowly pulled it away. A blackness was blooming, dark and lovely, inside her mind.

"Inhale, one, two, three, four," murmured the woman. "Exhale, one, two, three, four."

In her meditative state, Claudia fell asleep. When she awoke, the woman was gone, and it was dark outside. And Claudia was hungry.

"Aggie, I want several things from different places. I'll name the food and you choose the best option. I don't want anyone coming inside, do you hear me? No one! Everything will be left outside the door in discreet packaging." She took a deep breath.

"I want beef that had a better childhood than I did.

"And a whole steamed lobster.

"Corn on the cob.

"Thick strands of pasta with tomato sauce.

"Spicy chips that turn my fingers red.

"A dairy-free ice cream sundae sprinkled with gold leaf and hot fudge.

"A bag of gummy candy.

"And some wine, but not fancy—like the kind we used to drink. The type from the jug. What was it called? Response mode, please."

The robot voice responded after a moment: "In the large yellow bottle? Caren Motto."

"Yes, with the bird on the label! We had so many nights with old Caren, didn't we? We used to call her our third roommate." Claudia let out a slow sigh. "I wish I could try sour pickle soup. Sometimes that feels like the only thing I'm hungry for."

The robotic voice returned. "There is a place that serves this dish, but they only accept dine-in customers. Would you like me to make you a reservation?"

———

Claudia ate the food on her palatial bathroom floor, in her robe, while watching makeup tutorials on her phone. She finished the sundae from the bathtub, soaking in bubbles until her fingers wrinkled into raisins. She loved these makeup videos, loved the way the women spoke softly to the camera as they transformed themselves into heavenly creatures. No look was too difficult to achieve, broken down into accessible steps. No mistake couldn't be corrected. Finally sated, Claudia got up from the bath and destroyed the evidence.

4.

When Martin came home, she was wearing his absolute favorite outfit—a short black plastic dress with a white leather collar and red thigh-high boots. Claudia found it tacky; Martin knew that. It had become quite the joke between them.

He saw her and laughed. "Do you have something you want to tell me?"

She blushed. "I spent too much today."

He sat down on the couch and took off his gold slippers. "How many ducats, my lovely?"

Claudia forced her fox smile. The pet name was too close to what Keith used to call her, and a wave of sadness crashed over her. She wished she weren't wearing this outfit. It was as if sex were already happening, even though it hadn't started. She didn't need to do it. Girlfriends got headaches, wives got headaches. She was allowed to say no. Yet she forged on. Claudia sat on the ottoman in front of him and affected a naughty-girl voice. "Two thousand on clothes and another three thousand on jewelry. Or maybe four? It all happened so fast. . . ."

"Were you so very bad today?" he teased.

Claudia cocked her head to the side. The motion, this play-acting, gave her power. "So bad."

Martin patted her breasts vaguely, as if they were friendly, familiar dogs. "Ah, that's nice," he said absently before clearing his throat. "Well, my bad girl, you should know something has changed."

"Oh?"

"I had my projections confirmed with accounting today. This merger isn't just an important deal for the company. It's a life-changing deal for us. That is to say, you and me." He smiled, a big, sweet smile, so genuinely full of love that Claudia felt that stirring of affection again. "I didn't want to tell you until I was certain. So don't worry your exquisite self about money, not anymore. No more asking before you buy yourself a perfectly lovely emerald collar like you're some nervous Middle housewife."

She went very still. "This is because of the Stecopo agreement?"

"It's always interesting to me to see what you're paying attention to. Yes, the Stecopo agreement." He stopped running his hands over her body and rubbed his own eyes. "Claudia, sit here." She went to sit in his lap, as he liked. "No, not like that. Next to me, please." He took her hands and held them. "Do you know how much you mean to me?" His voice was solemn. "These past two years have changed my life. I want you to understand—I think of this money as *our* money. Because before you, well, I wasn't the man I am now. I know you can't see that, you're just too close and too loving of all my imperfections. But before you, I wasn't closing these kinds of deals. I didn't have the confidence. Coming home to you every night has been a kind of miracle. Yet you remain a beautiful mystery to me. I never know quite what you're thinking, while you always have exactly the right thing to say." His fingers twitched. "Wait here," he said, glancing down the hall. "I have something for you."

Claudia's stomach flipped. This couldn't be it, could it? But Martin seemed so serious. He went down the hall to his study. She looked down at her body, at this ridiculous plastic outfit. This wasn't how she'd pictured a proposal at all.

"Martin?" she called. "Wait! Come back. I want to hear more about this agreement."

Martin returned to the front room, his left pocket bulging. Her stomach sank. Of course. He would propose to her like this, on their sofa, just because it had popped into his head. He was always adjacent to doing the right thing.

"You want to know about the deal?" he asked, absentmindedly patting his pocket. "It's a merger of sorts between my company and two other big companies."

"So you don't work for Rivirslow anymore?"

"Sorry, I'm not explaining this well. Basically, there's a situation below—a kind of crisis, you see, with flooding. A great many people will relocate to temporary housing owned by the third company in the merger. My company will supply the medical care. Housing, medicine, and food all from Stecopo and their associates. That's the agreement."

Claudia wrinkled her nose. That wasn't so bad. She thought back to the melodramatic pamphlet. Of course people were upset about the flooding. But no one, no matter how extreme in their beliefs, could blame Martin for that. The Bastian had been flooding since before she was born. "So, flood relief is keeping me in emeralds, is it?"

Martin laughed and pulled her back into his lap. No more

Mr. Serious. Relief mixed with disappointment washed through her. He wasn't going to propose, not today. But soon. She was so close.

"Imagine this: you set up a new town on the frontier," he explained. "A place with no infrastructure at all, no stores and shops. People need quite a few amenities, however basic, like shelter, electricity and plumbing, food and water, of course, and medicine for when they're sick. These new little communities will need all these things immediately. What the Stecopo agreement does, instead of setting up all these little shops separately, is streamline that whole process. So now the people who have been relocated will get their housing from the same people giving them water, electricity, lumber, supplements, and, yes, medical supplies. We'll provide them with everything at a price they can afford. Everyone wins."

"But how can they afford it? Haven't they just lost everything in the flood, including their jobs?"

Martin smiled with his glossy little mouth. "Very good, my dear. Yes, they will need jobs. And Stecopo will provide those too. The company will take care of everything."

Claudia felt a larger question forming on the edge of her mind but couldn't quite grasp it. "But what about people who can't work? People who are too old, or sick? Pregnant women? Mothers with babies?"

Martin nodded. "As long as one family member is working, the unit will be taken care of by the company. And if you want a job, we will find you a job. No matter your ability."

"That seems fair," said Claudia.

Martin slid his hand up her skirt, his voice pitched low and breathy against her ear. "And that's the genius that's going to buy us a whole new life, my love." He took out his wide pink penis and held it against her thigh. "The farmers who till the soil do so with

Stecopo seeds, which they'll need to buy back from us every year. To reuse a seed is now not only filthy, but illegal. Stecopo harvests the crops, made with Stecopo seeds and fertilizers, processes them in Stecopo factories into Stecopo bars and supplements, all to be sold back to those same mouths! That's the total vision of Stecopo, when your workforce funnels their earnings back into the products you make. It's perfect. The creation of a captive market."

She closed her eyes and tried to picture it as Martin kissed her neck. "But can't they choose to buy products from other companies?"

"Of course they can, but Stecopo products are cheaper than anything else. And why pay more, when you can get it for less? Until, that is," he said, turning her over and pulling down her underwear, "there is no more competition. Then you have complete market dominance, like Rivirslow does with our medications. Then you can charge whatever you wish, and your consumer must pay."

"You're creating an underclass of slaves," said Claudia, just as she was penetrated from behind. She imagined the little town in the middle of nowhere, on some plateau safe from the rising waters. Her face crushed into the couch, Claudia saw a small black box slide out of Martin's trousers and land on the carpet. A few tears leaked from her eyes. She couldn't let him see her cry! But how could he, her face pushed down into the sofa? He hadn't even noticed.

"God, you feel amazing," he said.

No one understood her. Certainly not this little man, about to ask her to marry him. He never truly heard a word she said. She was practically dead already, a ghost walking through her own life. What could her life have been, if she hadn't been scammed out of an education, if she'd never gotten involved with Keith, if he hadn't botched her grift and gotten her shot, if he hadn't scared her away from big jobs and real love and anything else that required risk? "I think Sergio, the concierge, is in love with me," said Claudia into the suede couch. Martin finished silently behind her, his thrusts becoming jerky and out of rhythm. She exhaled slowly, feeling the wetness spill out of her and onto the beautiful couch, now stained with semen and tears and whatever else. It was suddenly all ridiculous. The plastic dress, the overpriced couch, the people leaving their homes and everything they owned to move to higher ground. Claudia didn't know who or what she was crying for. Her mother? Her estranged sister? Her tiny, myopic life with no real friends, no real love, only Martin and his ugly associates, their ugly money, the brutal way they looked at the world as a resource to exploit? Her mind was a jumble of half-cooked metaphors running together as she slowed her breathing to stop the tears. Lions and lambs, the weak and the strong, the bottom and the top, dog eat dog, a million ways to say the same goddamn thing. Martin kissed the back of her neck before heading to the meditation turret to begin alternate-nostril breathing. She hadn't even pretended to climax. Claudia went to the bathroom and cleaned herself off. She let the water run as she looked at her face in the mirror. *I can't marry him,* she thought, looking into her own eyes. It was as though she were coming out of a trance. Steadied by her own reflection, she made her decision. She would never marry Martin. This couldn't be her life, the Mrs. to a banal architect of suffering. What a shame. She had wasted so much of her beauty on Martin, but perhaps there was still time.

Claudia peeled off the stupid dress and let it lie on the floor in a dense heap, like shed skin. Wrapping her gray robe around her, she went to the small Beauty Broth™ refrigerator, pulled out a bottle, and started sipping. Her fingers itched to load more money into her account, but she resisted. She already had quite the cushion, and she knew she couldn't keep this lifestyle without Martin. She could move back to the Middle, somewhere far from Clarissa's house. Claudia saw the memory of Clarissa, bleeding out on the carpet, at the strangest times—in the shower, or right before falling asleep. Then she would feel the phantom pain in her side where the bullet had grazed her, the bullet that had then lodged in Clarissa's stomach and left her dying slowly on the ground. Hear the sounds of Sabrina screaming on the floor, inconsolable. Then feel Keith's rough hands grabbing her, dragging her out the door.

I won't leave Martin just yet, she thought. "Aggie, evening meal number six, please." The "high vibrations" smoothie made with exotic fruits, nuts, and a variety of sea vegetables. It was sweet and creamy, however, and apparently quite nutritious. Dessert would be a pudding made from avocados and raw cocoa—healthful, tasty, and toothless.

She'd amass more credit as her next step, cushion the cushion. Redecorating the apartment would be the perfect cover. Why, she could take a million ducats that way. "Aggie, design catalogues, paint samples, we need everything for a total remodel. And contact my antiques buyer—let's invest in some furniture." Then she'd leave him, go to a new place, a new name. It wouldn't be so bad out there, not like it was before. She'd do better than just survive. She wouldn't trade herself to any more businessmen. And she wouldn't fall for the trap of falling in love.

Martin opened his eyes in the tower, looking at Claudia from across the room with a lucid gaze. "Soon," said Martin, "we'll leave Felicity for good."

Claudia controlled her face. "But where would we go?"

"Well," he said, "we'll have our own habitation bubble in the Upper Ring, with a personal chef and a serving staff, all for you and me. No more sharing, no more placing our own orders with the kitchen, no more virtual assistant. A whole castle in the sky for us. Would you like that?"

Claudia didn't have to manufacture her surprise. "Like the prime minister! Or . . . or a celebrity!"

Martin sniffed. "Well, not just *any* celebrity. Only the A-listers. We'd be above it all." He gazed at her lovingly. "My sky princess."

"Yes," she heard herself say. "I would like that very much."

"Tomorrow," said Martin as he stood and crossed toward her, "I must go oversee some aspects of this new merger. I might even be away a day or two. Will you manage by yourself?"

Claudia kissed his smooth cheek. "I'll be very lonely."

"When I come back, we'll go out for that special celebration dinner. We have some things to discuss." He looked at her in mock seriousness. "You'll have to buy a sky princess dress for the occasion."

Claudia laughed. "I can certainly manage that."

"I bet you can." He tilted his head, looking at her as if weighing something. "I always imagined Sergio was a poofter."

Claudia blinked. "Pardon?"

"I can tell you're upset, sweetheart." She flashed back to Sergio throwing the garbage on the floor, saying all those nasty words. His clumsy clawing at her crotch. He deserved whatever was coming to him. "What exactly did he say?"

Claudia needed to choose her next words carefully. Her entire future could be thrown away because of her misunderstood nonaffair with that useless fop. "I'm ashamed to even tell you. I fear that I didn't understand what he was aiming for, until things went too far." She shrugged. "He asked if he could brush my hair. I said no, obviously. I wasn't sure what he was getting at. But then another day, when he was bringing me food, he watched me eat it. I felt very uncomfortable, like I had done something wrong." Martin's face was perfectly expressionless. Claudia put the nail in the coffin. "And then yesterday, he asked me what kind of food my family ate. He said that he'd prepare it for me if I'd let him watch me enjoy it, but that I mustn't tell you about it." She looked at the floor. "I know that I'm not very experienced with men. But it seemed . . . incredibly inappropriate. Did I do the right thing by telling him not to come here anymore?"

His voice was breathy and low. "The only thing you did wrong, my love, is not telling me sooner." Martin's eyes were kind. "I'm so sorry that happened to you. Sergio's behavior is completely unacceptable." He frowned. "Did he touch you?"

Claudia watched his fingers twitching, the intensity of his gaze. She calculated. "Yes," she said. "He asked to rub my feet, and I let him. He said all the upper-floor women at Felicity got private foot rubs."

Martin's round little face was flushed, his voice thick, caught between anger and desire. "And then?"

"He knelt down and rubbed my feet."

Martin looked as if he were holding his breath. "And then?"

She studied him, unsure of how far to push this. Something told her to be cautious. "That's all," she said finally. Now if Sergio said anything, about the foot rubs or the eating or the hair brushing, all of her bases would be covered. He would certainly be fired, and she wouldn't have to see him again. Claudia tried to seem brave but shaken. "I don't think he'll try to bother me anymore. We can place our orders with another staff member now." Then she flushed with pleasure. "Until we're living in the Upper Ring, of course!"

"Mmm," said Martin, fidgeting with his phone. Serge might be getting fired at this very moment. This man, *her* man, could fire someone with a tap of his fingers.

Claudia smiled her doe smile. "Darling, when *will* you stop working?"

He looked up at her from his screen, snapping the case shut. "You're quite right. You've shared me too much lately! Let's go out tonight, be a bit naughty and chew our dinners. What do you say? Not our grand evening—let's save that for when I get back. How about we take in a sound bath and get that salmon thing from Octavio's?"

Claudia felt herself go pink. He knew he owed her for last night. A light, delectable dinner would settle her stomach after the day's indulgences. Martin always did right by her; it just took him a while to get there.

He pulled his pants back on. "Then mango custard with crispy rice balls for dessert."

Someday she could learn to love him, in a full way, as everyone deserved to be loved. Claudia's voice grew husky. "Why, all three of my favorite things. Four, if we count you, stinky-butt."

———

At Octavio's, they had a brief tea ceremony before their meal. Martin and Claudia poured tea for each other into the long, narrow cups meant to hold the fragrance, then into the shorter cups meant for drinking. They each smelled the toasty, nutty scent from the now empty long cup, then sipped the tea from the shorter drinking cup. Claudia felt her chest grow warm. Something inside her was softening. She looked into Martin's plain, open face.

"Did you end up going to that restaurant in the Middle?" she asked. "Everyone seems to be talking about it."

He blushed. "Yes, but you know how those kinds of evenings go. We drank far too much before we even got there. And Nessa was in one of her moods, very pouty. The food was truly delightful. But it was all work, really, not play. We were sent there to try to buy them out."

Claudia laughed. "You didn't!" She drank more tea. "So do we own a restaurant now?"

He shook his head. "Not us, my love—Stecopo. And no, they turned it down."

Claudia's mind boggled. "These Middle cooks—they turned you down?" She raised an eyebrow. "Did you lowball them?"

Martin smiled. "No. It was a very good offer, which I then doubled. But they're rather headstrong."

"Oh dear!" She sipped her tea and considered. "I thought Stecopo was against restaurants. Why would they want to buy one?"

"No need to call it Stecopo, simply rebrand and dominate the market. I wouldn't be surprised if a whole slew of these 'underground restaurants' crop up all over sooner or later. It's just good business." He gestured to their private booth. "Say this was a Stecopo restaurant. Hire a chef named Octavio, call it Octavio's. Who would know who the checks are sent to?"

Claudia shivered. Was nothing what it seemed? Was everything Above a false veneer, with a second, secret face underneath?

Martin didn't notice her unease. "Muelber wouldn't eat, of course, too religious, but he drank enough for two. I wish I had time to take you there instead of him. But we'll get them eventually, one way or another." He paused, holding his teacup against his cheek. "You know, before you, I didn't have many lovers. I had sweethearts, of course, as a teenager. I had a sort of reverse adolescence—as I grew older, I became more and more self-conscious. Always picked last at sex parties, hovering around the refreshment table. The older I got, the worse it became. After a while, I stopped trying to date altogether. It all felt hopeless, and I began seeing nuns instead. Did I ever tell you this?"

Claudia shook her head. He continued. "They helped me, of course, with my release, and taught me about meditation. They helped me begin to feel lovable again. There was one in particular—I fell in love with her." He took a swallow of tea. "I love her still, actually. I'll probably love her until the day I die." He looked at Claudia. "Does that bother you?" She shook her head again, thinking about Keith. His face, his hands, his wonderful crooked smile. The easy way they would talk together, when she never rehearsed a reaction or planned what to say. Martin continued. "Nuns can't marry, you know. They're married to God; that is to say, they're married to all of us." He smiled. "Her name was Sister Emery. I thought that what we had was special, and for a time, when I realized that she created this special feeling with everyone she saw, I was so jealous. She wasn't young. She had some parishioners she saw for years and years. She wasn't even beautiful, not like you. She just had a very full presence. When I was with her, I felt the full fire of her attention. I realized later what I was feeling. That was God's love."

Octavio came out himself with the salmon cups next to small bowls of bone broth and seaweed and a sticky mound of rice. He bowed low and pulled the panels of their private booth shut. The restaurant was so quiet. Claudia smiled at this simple, elegant meal. The fresh, raw salmon was lightly tossed with avocado oil, ginger, and black sesame seeds. She placed a bit of the salmon on her rice bowl, accented with purple shiso leaves. She took a balanced bite of all three, holding the flavors in her mouth as she chewed. After swallowing, she cleansed her palate with a sip of bone broth. Today's was lamb. Claudia detected the smallest hint of anise. For a moment, they just ate together in appreciative silence. She looked at Martin with new eyes. Another man would have kept talking, forging ahead with his story, his mouth half-full. She really did enjoy their meals together.

After they meditated on the quality of the food and the pleasure it brought them, Claudia reached out to touch Martin's hand. "I've never been to see a nun before," she said. "We didn't do that in my family. But this woman sounds amazing. Shall we go see her together?"

He gazed at her lovingly. "That's not what I'm trying to say. I'm doing a sloppy job, of course. Be patient with me?" Claudia felt her eyes well. He took out a narrow black box, just about the length of Claudia's palm. "I'm trying to tell you, Claudia, that I've never experienced this kind of love before. I've had lovers, and I've experienced God's love through a special nun. But I've never had someone to share my world with, my most intimate hopes and desires." He gestured toward the box. "Go ahead, open it." She did and, seeing what lay inside, raised a hand to her mouth. "This is a placeholder. Very soon I plan to give you another jewelry box with a very different gift inside. For now, I hope you accept this as a token of what you mean to me. This is our money, Claudia. I want you to enjoy it."

Inside the box lay a card made of black diamond and trimmed with gold. It was an invitation-only credit card—a card with no limit. Similar to what Agata had owned all those years ago, but far more exclusive and powerful. Agata's card was a child's toy compared to this. The card came with a personal account manager, a private concierge who could arrange your transportation or whatever else your heart might desire. They looked at it together, sparkling on the table.

"Translator, courier, and butler services too, if you're interested," said Martin. "After all that unpleasantness with Sergio, it's time you had your own staff. Until we're above it all. Then there will be quite a few people to attend to us. I hope this doesn't overwhelm you—I know you like your private time." He went on, to talk about the demands of a habitation orb—the cooks, the gardeners, the maids, the airship drivers, the twenty-four-hour security detail. Did they want a wine cellar? Neither of them drank much at home. A saltwater pool would be lovely, and they'd actually use that. Did she play tennis? Would she want lessons? Claudia, half listening, turned the card this way and that to see it catch the light. It was perhaps the most beautiful thing she had ever seen.

———————

Rain came down outside, its sounds mixing with the young soprano's voice. She appeared to be around thirteen, lithe and majestic, a little fallen angel in white and gray linen. But the singer wasn't as young as she appeared—she had been Stunted, with carefully calculated nutrition from a young age to make her stay childlike. Martin and Claudia lay on the floor of the small carpeted room. The lights remained dim but slowly changed colors in progression with the music. The singer sang in harmony with her recorded self, a complex aria of voices, looping and layering over each other. Claudia and Martin attempted to feel the tones in different parts of their bodies, starting from the toes and traveling up.

Claudia thought about the girl singing along with the recording of herself as a metaphor for life. How we are in control of our choices but we have to sing in concert with the choices we've made in the past. How every person she had been had brought her to this moment on this plush carpet with Martin. She felt her heart open and expand. Martin was meant to be her partner.

The soprano sang a series of high, clear tones, to stimulate their throat centers. Next to her, Martin began to sob. She rolled over to him, cradling his face into her chest as he cried.

Martin clung to her like a child, dampening her dress with his tears. The sound of the rain outside grew louder. It was all the same. The tones, the tears, the raindrops. All of it was natural, fine, and as it should be. Martin was just as good or bad as any other person. They had chosen each other. In the act of choosing, there was wisdom, decisiveness, commitment. The sounds rang through her body like church bells. No more scheming, no more escaping into the future. *This is my life,* she thought as she held Martin tight. *This is my life. Now, forever.*

After the sound bath, the small audience clapped for an encore. The singer returned wearing street clothes and makeup. She looked older now, clearly in her twenties. She sang a pop song, narrow hips thrusting, and the audience sat up, clapping along to the beat. Martin smiled and wiped his eyes.

Outside, the rain had stopped. The streets were steamy and bright as they walked toward the Loop.

"Do you ever wonder?" started Martin.

"Wonder what?" asked Claudia.

"If you're doing the right thing," he said. "If you're living life..." Martin paused for a long moment. "In a good way?"

Claudia shook her head. "No. I know I'm in the right place, with the right people." She squeezed his hand.

He held her hand to his heart. "Is that what certainty feels like?"

"Yes," she said, leaning in to kiss him, then pulled back to look at him. "My mother's name was Rosemary. But everyone called her Wanda."

Martin raised his eyebrows. "There's a story there."

"There is." She made a decision. "I can tell you all about it, if you like."

Martin suggested they walk back to Felicity instead of taking the Loop.

"I was born in the Low Quake," began Claudia, as they walked hand in hand. "The very lowest part of the Bastian. I've heard that the street where I was born doesn't even exist anymore, swallowed by the sea. . . ."

———

Claudia and Martin got into bed together almost shyly, as if they hadn't lain down next to each other every night for two years. Claudia placed the credit card on her bedside table, then propped herself up on her elbows and leaned over his face. She kissed him on the forehead, cheeks, chin, and his round little lips. Claudia anointed Martin with kisses. As she kissed, she made each one a blessing, a benediction. Each kiss was forgiveness, for Martin and for herself.

"Can we try something new tonight?" asked Claudia.

"Yes," he whispered into her hair.

She took his hand and guided it to her pubic mound. "Press down. Light, but firm. A little lower. There. Now move, gently, up and down, up and down, up and down." She wrapped her arms around Martin as he touched her. He kissed her neck. Her mind floated to the familiar carousel of images, but she kept guiding it back to Martin. Martin's fingers. Martin's kiss. Martin's weight on top of her. She told him when to hurry and when to slow down. When she came, she wrapped her arms and legs around him so he could feel the strength of her shuddering, the energy moving up her spine. With her spasms still crashing around her, she let him enter. She squeezed him close, and they moved together. As he came inside her, she imagined that they were both filled with light.

"I love you," she said, and in that moment, it was true. "I love you."

Martin was asleep by the time her eyes became drowsy. She couldn't stop staring at the credit card on the nightstand. It was so beautiful. Martin had made his point very well. She could buy an apartment tomorrow, and he wouldn't blink. Tomorrow she'd step out into the world of unlimited credit. Claudia tried to relax her mind enough to sleep. *I am God, and God is me; I am God, and God is me,* she chanted again in her mind. But the prayer became jumbled. *God bless me, and I bless myself, because I am God.* She thought of lions and lambs. Did God feel sad when predators ate prey? Did the lion cry himself to sleep at night over the poor dead antelope? No, the lion did not. The lion slept, belly full and heart light.

5.

That night, Claudia had a dream. She dreamt she was standing over a toilet after having just used it. Instead of roses, she looked down into the toilet bowl full of her own feces. The feces bloomed outward, multiplying like cells, expanding into a thick floral ring around the toilet, like a coral reef. She'd let it grow too much. She couldn't flush it away. Claudia was embarrassed, not that everyone would know that she ate and shat, but that she couldn't hide it away, as was proper. *Aggie,* she cried, *help me! Clear it away!* But no one came.

Claudia woke from the dream thinking of every terrible thing she'd ever done, a litany of mean words, petty actions, cowardly silences. Stealing from Agata. Clarissa, bleeding out on the carpet. How the first thing she did with Martin's money was to hire someone to beat up Keith, to punish him for his stupidity, for making her love him, for ruining her plans.

Stole money from my best (and only) friend.
Paid someone to beat up my ex-boyfriend.

Inadvertently got an old woman murdered.
Let my family think I was dead.

She saw them in her mind like a poem. She didn't need to carry these burdens with her anymore. Claudia let the words evaporate, like fog.

In the morning, Martin left for the airship depot very early. As he kissed her awake, he whispered visions of the private airship they would soon own. "Just for you, my love," he murmured into her hair. "We're not very good at sharing, are we?"

Claudia touched herself to climax as Martin packed his belongings, punctuating her orgasm with cries of "My king, my king!" She was his Ijo, and he took care of her.

"Martin," she said, grinning from the silken sheets, "I have my eye on a tenth-century sofa. I'd like to bid on it. Would you like to look at it?"

He chuckled, buttoning his tunic. "Darling, get whatever you wish. A bed from the third century, a chest of drawers from the fifth. I mean it—don't ask! It would be very hard for you to spend all of our money. So why not try, at least a little bit?"

She leaned back on the pillows. "Shall I buy a villa before you return?"

He shrugged. "Property is always a good investment. Somewhere warm, please."

She tried to control her face, but she couldn't. "Really?"

"Go wild, okay? I'll see you in three days. I'll miss you so much." Then he left her with a kiss.

Claudia lay in the center of the large bed. The apartment suddenly seemed small, its furniture middlebrow and tasteless.

"Aggie, cancel the renovations. And put in a bid on that sofa. Don't stop until it's mine." It was just the kind of piece Ijo might have sat on. She would create a whole wing of their new house dedicated to the period.

I must do something celebratory, she thought. *For achieving my long-standing dream.* But what? All of her usual activities felt lackluster, ordinary. She didn't wish to merely go shopping or to the spa or visit a museum.

"Aggie? What do rich people do? What are their hobbies? Response mode, please."

"The most cited hobby of the ultra-wealthy is philanthropy," the robot voice replied.

Claudia tried not to laugh and failed.

Claudia dressed carefully in her black silk jumpsuit with pearl buttons. She used to save it for nicer occasions, but not anymore. From now on, her wardrobe would be only the very best. Anything she owned that wasn't up to standard would be given away.

She was supposed to use her new credit card concierge to arrange for an airship and whatever else she needed, but it didn't feel right. "Don't worry Aggie, I haven't forgotten you. Even when I'm all the way up in the sky, I won't leave you behind."

Then it came to her, clear and whole—every action of her life had been leading to this perfect, shining moment. Her destiny. Hands trembling, Claudia knelt on the floor. She took a deep, expansive breath, and merged the unlimited credit card with Aggie. All of her splendid, ingenious programs, all of her best tech, all of her covert channels to the dark web and black market, were now supercharged with an unlimited wellspring of money.

"That's better. Aggie," she said, standing and brushing off her legs, "arrange for a personal airship to meet me on the high-rise tarmac. Have the concierge procure envelopes of cash—a hundred thousand ducats in each, five in total."

During the short flight, she enjoyed a flavored water, lightly

laced with mood-enhancing and appetite-increasing drugs, as she
gazed at the ground below. She could see only gently curving
streets, children playing ball, faraway figures frotting together in
the sex parks. Everything looked normal. There had always been
flooding. Claudia could remember a summer when the rains got so
bad her family just couldn't keep up with the constant leaking; too
many things needed repairs. The unceasing dampness had created
a terrible mold throughout their house. It was so thick and black
on the lower floor that her parents and grandparents took to sleeping downstairs, giving the children their own beds upstairs just to
get them away from the spores.

When they landed in the Middle, the airman gave her the cash
she had requested, five slender envelopes bundled into a thicker
one, and offered to escort her on her errands, but Claudia decided
to walk alone. She was eager to move among the people by herself.
Soon all of this would be a distant memory. Perhaps she'd have a
security detail in the future, guarding her from potential kidnap-
pers and extortionists everywhere she went. She had only been to
a habitat orb once, for a very grand charity gala. The world she'd
observed from the window of that gala was a true heaven in the
clouds. There was no limit to what its citizens enjoyed. An enclosed dome that contained a pristine white sand beach, a red-
wood forest, lush jungles, and jagged mountains, thick with
ever-white snow—all man-made, of course, and astonishing in
their perfection, their raw, untouched beauty. Land that would
never be tainted by gas spills or flooding or landfills. Land untouched by the threat of nuclear disasters or even war. Pristine,
sealed off, contained. And it would stay that way, enjoyed by the
luckiest few.

Claudia found the small basement office building without
trouble. The woman in the shabby coat from outside the botanical

gardens wasn't there, but there was another woman of the same type, with poor teeth and rough skin, organizing placards and posters on the floor. The woman stood with a grunt and asked if she was coming to volunteer for tomorrow's event.

She shook her head. "I'm making a donation," Claudia said. "Anonymous."

"Thank you!" she said, accepting the envelope with a polite nod. "Everything helps." Claudia delighted to think of what a difference she was making, and how the woman's expression would change on seeing the donation, but she did not linger.

Her next stop was Sabrina, that poor girl who had witnessed her benefactor murdered by Keith's stupid accomplice. She hadn't decided what she was going to say. She went to the address Aggie had procured for her, this time in the proper Middle, with a view of the lake downtown. She was buzzed into a large housing complex, and a man with a beard shot through with gray opened the door of the apartment.

"You're . . . a friend of Sabrina's?" he asked incredulously, looking at her clothes.

"Patrick?" called a woman's voice. "Who's there?"

A stout woman appeared with a child at her hip. Claudia blinked. The eyes, the shape of her nose, the posture—why, it was Sabrina! An adult now, with a young child of her own. And yet she looked older than Claudia. Sabrina gazed at her with no sign of recognition.

She decided to lean on what she knew as a grifter—a version closest to the truth was always the most practical.

"I apologize for not calling ahead," said Claudia. "I'm here from the estate of the late Clarissa Hollister. For many years, her will was tied up in court proceedings." She passed the envelope into Sabrina's free hand. "Please accept this gift from your late benefactor. Her family would like to keep this quiet, as the will was greatly contested. So there's no need to declare it—just enjoy the gift and know that Clarissa thought of you."

Claudia left quickly, but she caught some of the screams as they peeked inside the envelope. She heard Sabrina and her husband calling for her, to come back, to explain, to stay for dinner, but she was back on the street in seconds.

For her next two marks, she paid a courier service a nominal fee to deliver the envelopes to the Bastian. She wasn't about to risk crossing paths with Elena or Keith. Claudia wasn't sure why she'd let her family think she had died. When she was shot all those years ago, the police had simply assumed she was dead, and she'd let them. In their eyes, she was just a Free-Wah maid from the Bastian—there was no grand investigation, no search party, all media coverage focused on the wealthy woman murdered in her own home during a botched robbery.

There was a great power in being dead. Nothing could hurt you.

After her public death, it had been so easy to sever ties to her origins completely. And with that, Claudia found herself floating higher and higher, like a ghost. And now Martin, of all people, would take her to the last step of her upward voyage.

It was the golden hour by the time she got to the restaurant, the special time of day that Ijo and Queen Janus would sit together in their later years, enjoying the sunset glow. She thought of their unlikely friendship as she knocked on the door and waited. She had one more envelope, which she was saving for providence. Maybe she would give it to someone sleeping out on the street, or a student studying in a library, or a tired mother chasing her kids in a park. She would let the fates decide.

A handsome Ahinga man leaning on crutches opened the door. Claudia blinked back her surprise—there were no visibly disabled people Above, and she had not seen an Ahinga face in many years. She said she was a friend of his uncle Walter's, as she had been told to do. He smiled warmly and guided her inside. She followed him down a long, dim hallway into a bright, warm dining room. It was still midafternoon, not quite dinner but well past lunch, so the restaurant was sparsely populated. How strange to see people eating together at their little tables like there was nothing to fuss about. She had never seen so many people eating together in public while wearing all of their clothes. She couldn't help but stare. As a young woman, she would have gotten a table in the middle of this large room and relished every moment. The warm, merry atmosphere—no artifice, no shame. Now the idea of sitting with such people made her flush. Claudia longed, just a little, for her former self, who didn't mind standing out. But it was safer, certainly, to fit in. Far less could go wrong.

Claudia motioned to the man who had guided her into the restaurant. "I called ahead," said Claudia. "I wish to have the chef's tasting menu. And a private room?"

"Our private rooms are for large parties, but if you'd like, we can serve your meal in the garden."

"That will be perfect. Thank you so much." She followed the man out into the yard.

They walked on a short, smooth concrete path. A cleverly constructed trellis laced with ivy blocked the yard from any neighbor's view. Leaning on one crutch, he gestured for her to enter the garden.

It was a wonderland. Beds popped with dense heads of cabbage, frilly kale, and floppy beet tops, interlaced with frothy rows of bright-green herbs. Sugar snap peas and brussels sprouts grew up and out, while profusions of tomato plants were held in place by stakes. Shiny, skinny eggplants and dozens of varieties of sweet and hot peppers nested together in wide, raised beds, across from sprawling tangles of squashes, melons, and sweet sugar pumpkins. Rows of blueberry bushes grew next to a stand of rhubarb. There was an enclosed partition where citrus trees grew under a profusion of lights, dappled with prized fig, avocado, and pomegranate trees. He motioned to a small round table with two chairs. It had been set for one.

"Your waiter will be with you in a moment," he said.

Claudia sat down in the wooden chair and waited.

6.

A burly Free-Wah man distinguished by a long, thick mustache and a florid suit entered, bringing a beverage course—slender glasses of different infusions and sodas presented as a tasting flight.

"Fennel-lavender soda, cold rose-hip tea sweetened with honey, and rhubarb shrub accented with ginger," he said, pointing to the various flutes. "Last, my favorite—a simple celery soda. It gets the appetite going!"

Claudia sipped delicately from the last glass, a long, light-green drink that bubbled effervescently. The taste was slightly grassy, yet not bitter, with a touch of mellow sweetness. She felt refreshed and energized by the infusions, her palate awakened, her stomach growling. Claudia was ready to eat. But this was no great feat; one could get a brightly colored herbal infusion at any water café in the city. She smiled like a statue and waited patiently to be dazzled.

After about ten minutes, the man returned with the second course.

"I'm particularly fond of this one! It's our take on a bread basket. The corn is milled here, and the final product finished with lime juice and Chef Beatrice's tomato jam. The cheese is by Chef Cedric, and Head Chef Margot toasted and dried the chilies. Our whole community in a little bite!"

"I'm dairy-free," said Claudia, patting her stomach. "Can't take it." She had already let them know about her allergy and was unimpressed with this inattentiveness to detail.

But the man only smiled. "Don't worry—the cheese is made from fermented nuts. Please enjoy!" He bowed slightly, then went back into the restaurant. It was a large corn muffin, plopped unceremoniously on a plate, topped with crumbly cheese and chili powder, finished with a squeeze of lime. It was cute, but certainly not revolutionary. And where was the tomato jam? Claudia bit into the muffin. She was surprised to find that it was only lightly sweet, with a stocky little crumb. Its mild flavor was highlighted nicely by the tangy, slightly smoky nut cheese. She took another bite. Why, there were whole roasted corn kernels flecked throughout. She bit again. At the center of the muffin was a dollop of thick tomato jam. Claudia considered. Was it overpowering? No—the little treasure of jam was small, yet significant. Like biting into a cherry tomato in the midday sun. The whole dish worked in such harmony: the sharp, crumbly cheese, the jolt of lime, the rich jam, the dense muffin. Claudia found herself smiling as she chewed. Very clever indeed. A "dinner roll" that was a complete experience in itself. She took another big bite. It was so thoughtful, so playful. Simple, lovely. She could eat this every day and be happy.

As she ate, a deep feeling of wellness overtook her, the spacious buzzing in her mind. The sound of two voices laughing together. A man's deep baritone breaking into song. Claudia was called back to her childhood. Balancing a spoon on the end of her nose. Helping Mama peel the onions so she wouldn't cry. Her whole family eating from one huge platter. Her hand, reaching for seconds. Reiko, praised for her appetite, their beloved growing girl. Her sister, laughing. Her father, singing. She looked down at the plate. It wasn't her fault she hadn't understood happiness until it was taken from her.

The man's voice was soft. "Is everything all right, miss?"

Claudia came back to the present. "Just rediscovering things I thought were lost." She looked up at her host. "Perhaps your chefs are actually magicians."

"You're very kind." He set down a platter with two small bowls of soup. "Two soups for you today: a smooth butternut squash purée, topped with fried slivers of sunchokes, toasted sunflower seeds, and grated pickled radish. Then sour pickle soup, with dill. Enjoy."

"May I meet the chef responsible for the sour pickle soup?" she asked.

"Of course. Just a moment, please."

———————

Chef Beatrice Bolano came out wearing a starched white apron and a plain cotton work shirt buttoned up to her chin. Her thick dark hair was tied back in a high bun with a bright floral scarf around her head, framing her round face. She didn't appear to be wearing makeup. But, as Claudia's grandmother liked to say, she had good eyebrows and color in her cheeks, so she didn't need any.

"Hello," she said. "I'm Beatrice. How are you enjoying your meal?"

"It's wonderful," Claudia said, blushing. "Pardon me . . . but if you aren't too busy, I'd be very honored if you'd sit and talk with me." Claudia reached up and lightly touched the inside of Beatrice's wrist. "But I don't want to create more work for you, Little Mother."

She went on, unsure if her meaning had been heard. "Some palates, I believe, crave a certain kind of complexity."

"Yes," replied Beatrice, locking eyes with her. "They need sourness, the intensity of strong flavors."

Claudia felt intoxicated to find someone who shared her secret obsession. "I'd rather eat sour pickle soup than rose petals. Wouldn't you?"

"You're like the rain after a drought!" Beatrice laughed. "Enjoy your soup. I'll come back as soon as I can—I'd be delighted to share a meal with you." She walked back inside.

First Claudia ate the butternut soup. It spread out on her tongue, its base velvety and sweet, balanced by the various toppings, each different in texture and density: the delicious little fried bits, pickled radish, black pepper. Then, hands trembling, she dipped her spoon into the sour pickle soup. Hot, tangy, creamy, sour. The pickle warmed her appetite, encouraged her to keep eating. A terrific coziness filled her belly, a sense of well-being she hadn't experienced in so long. It tasted just like she had always imagined.

When Beatrice returned, she was carrying a tray that held a long platter and two empty plates. The platter was divided into two sections. One side was mounded with thin spirals of lightly cooked zucchini, marinated in oil and vinegar until they were softened and unctuous. It was a play on a pasta course, the ribbons of zucchini topped with a rich, deep tomato sauce. Claudia nodded her approval. *Yes, very good.* A real pasta course, after the corn muffin and the squash soup, would be too much starch. On the other side of the platter was a dense heap of what appeared to be wild mushrooms.

"Pasta and meat, all created with vegetables," said Beatrice. "These mushrooms are foraged locally and prepared three different ways." She plated Claudia's meal as she spoke. "Slow-braised in tomato and various spices, grilled, and this one's been stuffed with artichoke hearts and then roasted. Dig in!" She made a little plate for herself as well and picked at it.

The "pasta" twirled around Claudia's fork, surprising yet familiar. This woman had found a way to serve her what was essentially a salad with all the warmth and coziness of a main dish.

"Quite delicious." Claudia bowed slightly toward her. "And it impressed me very much that you served a soup course. A bold statement—we get to enjoy all foods, even 'acceptable' smooth textures."

"It would be a shame to forgo something delicious just because it isn't forbidden." Beatrice looked at her levelly. "We are safe to speak here, to an extent, about Ijo's story."

"How did you discover it?" asked Claudia.

"From a woman in the Valley who was very kind to me. I was born and raised in Seagate. My life would be very different without her."

"Seagate? The cult?" Claudia drank her celery soda. "You must have broken with all of that."

"They've broken with me, that's for sure. And you? Where did you find it?"

Claudia surprised herself by telling the truth. "I was working as a maid in the Middle Hills. The lady of the house had a whole room of Free-Wah artifacts tucked away in a far wing like the world's saddest museum. I stole it."

The chef shook her head. "You *liberated* it."

Claudia leaned closer. "I've never met another person who's known about the book. I've read it so many times! I can recite whole passages by heart."

"I'm the same." Beatrice paused, considering her. "There are others, you know. Groups of people who read and study this text, and consider its implications."

"Have you met them?"

"Some. When you do what I do, like-minded people come out of the woodwork," said Beatrice. "I was so young, so sheltered when I found it—I had no idea what I was reading—not for several years. I relied on that book so much when I first left home. Like Ijo, I had traveled to parts unknown. Back then I thought my family would come back to me." She smiled ruefully. "That we would meet again over cups of tea, even a meal. I thought if my parents were forced to choose between a fat daughter or a dead one, they would choose me.

"But it turned out that by leaving Seagate, I had committed a form of suicide. In a way, I had done what Ijo did a thousand years ago when she petitioned the queen to grant her death—slain one version of herself so a truer version might live."

Claudia sat stone-still, shaken by looking at her own story in a funhouse mirror.

The burly Free-Wah man brought out a platter of vegetables. "Here we go—Cedric and Beatrice's garden party," he said in a jolly voice. "Whole roasted carrots with carrot-top pesto, and a simple salad of shaved celeriac, celery, and capers, completed by sliced white peaches and heirloom tomatoes. Summer on a plate. Enjoy!"

"I've never tasted a carrot that tastes . . . so much like a carrot," Claudia murmured, covering her mouth as she chewed.

Beatrice's face lit up. "Chef Cedric has greatly improved our gardening practices. He comes from a long line of Ahinga farmers."

"The man I met at the door?" Claudia asked.

Beatrice nodded, eyes bright. "We're extremely lucky."

She tilted her head with interest. "You're in love with him."

Beatrice's cheeks pinked, but she didn't deny it. "Tell me, what do you love about Ijo's story?"

"In a world where very little is mine, Ijo belonged to me," she said softly. She saw Beatrice glance down at her beautiful clothes, her handbag, her perfectly lacquered nails. She was growing quite full by the time a stocky woman with a buzz cut and a severe expression brought out dessert. She placed the food on the table and left without a word.

"Candied black walnut ice cream with strawberry rhubarb cobbler," said Beatrice. "And don't worry—the ice cream is made from the water we boiled our beans in!"

Claudia took a small bite of the warm cobbler, topped with crunchy, sweet streusel, and paired it with just a taste of the walnut ice cream. She let the flavors mingle on her tongue. The ice cream was fluffy, yet creamy and rich, with beautiful crunches of candied bitter walnut throughout—the perfect counterpart to the warm sweet-tart of the fruit cobbler. She became self-conscious and covered her hand with her mouth. "Pardon me!" she said. "Did you just say bean water?"

Beatrice laughed. "I've tried every version of ice cream under the sun over the years. My first year at the restaurant, I tried making it from potato. It was disgusting. Luckily, the starchy liquid you get from boiling beans is pretty magical. I use it in several of my dishes." She took a bite as well and considered. "Do you think Ijo should have stayed with the king?"

Claudia heard the question inside the question. "Maybe freedom is more important than love. No servants, no masters." They sat for a moment and listened to the sounds of the birds outside, the insects buzzing the garden, before Beatrice excused herself to return to her duties.

Claudia left the fifth envelope on the table, writing *For Beatrice* across the front in a firm hand. *May Ijo's work continue, long after we are both dead.*

———————

To Claudia's surprise, Martin was waiting outside the restaurant, standing right on the street in his business finery, holding a lovely bouquet of flowers and smoking a joint.

"Darling!" she exclaimed, running into his arms. "How did you know I was here?"

"I just flew back into town," he said. "I forgot we had that thing on Saturday! It's been on the calendar for weeks."

"Oh, my dummy!" She kissed him. "Don't feel bad. I forgot too." He pressed the bouquet into her hands. She wiggled her fingers to steal his joint. He laughed.

Claudia took a petite hit, inhaling the blend of cannabis, raspberry leaf, and sage. It was the perfect way to settle her stomach after such a big meal. "Yum, thank you."

"I got a call that someone was using my credit card, asking me to approve the charges from the Middle," said Martin. "I'll call them and fix that, my dear. The whole point is that I have no desire to approve your purchases. But it was fun to surprise you." He put a hand on her stomach. "I take it you don't want to go to dinner?"

She looped her arm through his, and they strolled slowly back toward the airfield. "You'll have to roll me home! But I'm happy to sit with you, darling. Where shall we go?"

"I'd rather just poke around in the larder," he said. "Let's go home." He waggled his eyebrows at her. "How was the dining room?"

She giggled. "You always think I'm such a prude! And I suppose you're right. I ate in the garden, actually. Just me and all my little plant friends, and it was beyond lovely. One of the chefs,

Beatrice, chatted with me awhile. It was an unforgettable experience."

Martin gave her a squeeze around her small waist. "I'm glad you got to experience it before they shut down." He held the joint out to her, and she inhaled from it delicately.

The world began to spin, then flattened out gently. Claudia looked up at the brightly colored buildings, and for a moment the Middle was just as beautiful and marvelous as it had been the first time she was fresh off the Loop. She'd forgotten about the laced water in the airship; with the addition of this little bit of cannabis, she was really floating. She wanted to ask why such an exceptional and popular restaurant might be going out of business, but then her whole body relaxed, the tension she had been carrying in her shoulders for days unknit. She took a deep breath of cool air and let go.

7.

Erek came over for breakfast the morning of the big rally. They hadn't seen him in what felt like ages since his latest promotion at the patisserie, but Beatrice suspected it was because things were getting serious with his new girlfriend, Isa. Walter cooked, which had become their new tradition in recent years, to give the hardworking chefs at Delany Lane a much-deserved rest on their precious day off. Walter could make fluffy pancakes or poached eggs with sautéed vegetables, but not much else. This morning he made copious amounts of both, with hot, strong coffee and fresh fruit.

Margot, Beatrice, Erek, Walter, and Cedric sat together in the dining room, passing platters and refilling cups.

"You must catch me up on all the gossip," said Erek, helping himself to more pancakes and syrup. "I'm terribly out of the loop."

"Well, here's a big bit of news—an Ahinga collective is starting a huge farm in the country," said Walter. "And our Cedric has been asked to join them."

"No mono crops, no pesticides, no overworking the land," said Cedric, grinning proudly. "A return to the old ways."

"I heard about that on the radio!" exclaimed Erek. His gray eyes widened. "But won't it be dangerous? You'll be Stecopo's public enemy number one."

"There's nothing I'd rather do," Cedric said simply.

"Good on you." Erek nodded. "But we'll certainly miss you! When are you planning to go?"

Cedric glanced to Beatrice. "Haven't worked that out yet."

"Will Isa be joining us today, Erek?" asked Walter, topping off his coffee. "I think she's just lovely."

"You and me both," Erek said, his mouth full of cantaloupe. "She'll come as soon as she gets off work. Oh, and Beatrice—she's bringing a friend. I told him all about you."

"Lest I forget," said Walter, handing Beatrice an envelope. "Someone left this for you at the restaurant yesterday."

Beatrice slipped the envelope into her purse. "That's sweet," she said to Erek. "But I'm not looking for dates at the moment."

"It's been almost a year since you broke up with that Melissa woman, hasn't it?" Erek clapped Cedric on the shoulder. "Almost exactly a year, I remember because we three went out and drank far too many beers in honor of your liberation! You don't have to go on a date with her friend, just say hello."

"I'll certainly say hello to anyone." Beatrice put down her fork. "But I'm actually seeing someone, and it's gotten rather serious."

"Oh-ho-ho!" cried Erek. "That's a story I need to hear."

Cedric got up from the table, unhooking his cane from the back of his chair. "I'm going to head out so I can be as slow as I please."

Beatrice passed him a basket of handmade garlands. Cedric donned a long chain of flowers, pink and red blossoms streaming across his chest.

"I'll join you," said Margot, pinning on a boutonniere of orange and white. "Walter, thank you for breakfast—leave the cleaning for us later."

"No time like the present," said Walter, selecting his own multicolored garland, then completing his ensemble with a voluminous plaid hat. "Today is a historic day!"

"Erek and I will catch up in a moment," said Beatrice, stacking plates. "You all go on ahead."

"That's right," said Erek. "I wasn't raised to leave a dirty dish."

He filled the sink with soapy water. "Just like old times, eh, Beatrice?"

She wrapped an arm around his shoulders, squeezing tight. "I'm glad you're home, little brother." She had barely begun, and she was already crying. "There's something I've been meaning to tell you. To tell everyone, in fact. This is a happy secret, so it shouldn't keep."

"Quick, like a bunny!" He grinned. "Is the secret that you love me the best?"

It felt so silly to cry that she started to laugh. Beatrice wished she could freeze time and hold on tight to these people she loved, to the place where she had become a chef. This in turn made her cry again. She blew her nose, then laughed. "You guessed it—I love you the best."

Beatrice and Erek, in matching crowns of yellow and pink flowers, entered the park by the statue of the horse and rider. The fruit trees circling the great green lawn were in bloom, their fragrances sweet and heady. Children ran around holding balloons, while their parents listened seriously to speeches on various stages dotting the grass. Everywhere Beatrice looked, people wore flowers in their hair, on their lapels, passing out bouquets, throwing petals. There were so many people! Mothers with babies, old people and young, Bastian folk mixing with Middlers who lived around the corner. Beatrice saw the woman who ran the water café down the street and gave her a tentative wave. She'd always imagined that the woman, in her infinite thinness, would judge someone like Beatrice. But she waved back, face friendly, holding a single rose in her other hand. Beatrice was also surprised to see several people who looked like Above citizens wandering about, accepting pamphlets and signing petitions.

"I guess we really are meeting in the Middle," Erek said, gesturing at a man all done up in business finery, gold shoes and all, reading intently about the climate crisis.

All around them, people held placards, waved banners, and carried signs. There were many familiar faces from the restaurant in the crowd. Erek was quickly pulled away by a friend Beatrice didn't know, with promises to meet up later back at the house. After standing for twenty minutes in the sun, Beatrice felt like she'd said hello to everyone she knew in the city.

There were loads more people she didn't know, holding all manner of signs. There were stupid slogans and smart ones, silly ones, and lots of food puns. Beatrice's favorites included STECOPO: QUIT EATING US FOR PROFIT and THOSE ABOVE ARE NO SAINTS. They brought her back to that impromptu marketing session in her parents' living room so many years ago. These slogans probably weren't pithy enough for her father and Georgina.

Beatrice ambled along the perimeter, enjoying the sunshine. There were so many booths, all advertising their own causes. She found herself under a sign that read STOP SEAGATE. The people seated at the table were already explaining to passing rallygoers how in recent years the town had grown extreme in its methods of control—mandatory appetite-suppressing implants, punishments for poor weigh-ins, public humiliation. It was chilling to imagine all of the people she grew up with living in such a place. She pushed her parents out of her mind.

The man at the table was talking to a tall woman with a wide sunhat as he handed Beatrice a pamphlet. He told the woman how those who left Seagate lost all their savings and possessions, then were hounded for years after, intimidated to come back into the fold. She turned the pamphlet over. It was a picture of her own face, young and thin, the Seagate girl, overlaid with an image of an emaciated corpse riddled with flies.

In front of a small stage, a nervous-looking man attempted to turn on a finicky microphone. A severe-looking blond woman came up from the grass below to help him. The nervous man began warbling into the microphone about the need for the government to disentangle itself from private companies. A few people clapped, but most appeared to be looking elsewhere.

Walter and Beatrice stood by the stage, listening intently, Walter pausing every so often to theatrically blow his nose. He had taken the news of her leaving pretty well, considering. On the podium, the man described what he called the "weather gap." How the storms constantly threatened the lives of those on the ground, while those floating above could telecommute, use a backup generator, or complain about the rain while never fearing drowning. Yet as she listened to the sensible speech, Beatrice found herself getting angry. No one had protested when Cedric was born with his spinal condition, his entire community drinking poisoned water. None of these people had made speeches or attended a rally when his sister died of cancer at five years old, or when his parents lost their farm nearly a decade later, still paying off her medical debts. The company had indentured entire populations, then left crumbling communities in its wake. But now that this wasn't just affecting the Ahinga people, it was something to protest. But it wasn't just the stark injustices faced by Cedric's community—the posters and the pamphlets and the petitions overwhelmed her. A thousand dead birds on a beach. Domesticated animals so modified they couldn't reproduce. Milk filled with pus. Chemicals in the air, in the water, in the earth. If she had a child, she would pass those chemicals to her baby through her breast milk. These problems were so big, and she was so small.

Beatrice sighed. "Do you really think this is the best way, Walter? Speeches, petitions, pamphlets?"

"How can things get better if we don't talk about them, my dear?" He turned to gaze out at the crowd: Free-Wah, ALGN, Middle, Bastian, parents with children on their shoulders, workers next to businessmen. Everyone standing together.

Beatrice noticed another WE ARE ALL IMMIGRANTS poster, her third sighting that day, this time held by an ALGN woman in a pink hat. "Case in point!" she said. "Your ancestors welcomed the ALGN people to their shores and paid dearly for it." Walter raised an eyebrow at her. "I'm just asking—how will things get better if we can't even agree what to put on a sign?"

He was quiet for a long moment. "Think of truth like a bell," he said, "in that you can hear it even from far away. From up close, you can really feel it. In your body, in your chest, it vibrates." He squeezed Beatrice's hand. "And when all these people feel it? They become bells too. Together, we make a great big sound." He swayed their hands back and forth, as if to the beat of a gong. "Can you hear it?"

Beatrice turned back toward the stage. The nervous man on-stage had relaxed into his speech, following his big points with grand gestures. His audience exploded in a loud cheer. It was infectious. Other pockets of people, all around the square, started to holler and spontaneously clap, not because of the one man's speech, but because of his crowd's response.

"I hear it," said Beatrice, wiping her eyes. "Hey, Walter. Thank you for saving my life."

"Go on now," he said, waving at her with his handkerchief. "You're going to get me started again."

———

At the edge of the rally, there was a small table with a Free-Wah family—a grandmother, mother, and a few grandchildren, from the looks of them—passing out skewers of grilled fish and vegetables. Beatrice approached them.

The middle-aged woman pressed her to try each kind and told her which sauces were spicy and mild. "This is what my family does when we all gather together. A little grilling, some fresh sauce—what could be better?"

Beatrice looked at the multiple generations of home cooks and felt a pang in her chest. "Nothing that I can think of." She bowed in gratitude. "Thank you for sharing your food with me."

She brought a skewer back to Margot, whom she found standing under a tree, drinking a lemonade.

"Never thought I'd live to see the day," remarked Margot, gazing hungrily at her halibut skewer before taking a big bite. "Did you try the green sauce? It's got a kick!"

Beatrice unbuttoned her collar, enjoying the sunshine on her neck. "Things may be worse than ever," she said. "But this does give me some hope."

"If things weren't so bad," replied Margot, "I don't think most of these people would be here." A man walked through the crowd holding up a huge poster with Beatrice's face, mouth stuffed with a cucumber, that read CHOKE ON THIS, SEAGATE BITCH. "Want me to go beat that guy up?"

"It's okay." She handed Margot the Seagate pamphlet, corpse side up. "Looks like that girl is dead."

Margot put a warm hand on her shoulder. "May she rest in peace."

"Gone, but not forgotten." Beatrice smiled. "You know, I keep thinking about that day I tried to seduce you in the kitchen. Do you remember? When you brought me those flyers from Seagate."

"All that ancient history?" She barked out her sharp little laugh. "What of it?"

"I've learned so much from you over the years, Margot." Beatrice looked at her old friend. "Thank you for teaching me about love."

Margot narrowed her eyes. "Why do you sound like you're saying good-bye?"

The sun disappeared and Beatrice grew chill. She looked up to see a state-of-the-art airship passing overhead, casting its massive shadow over them. Squinting, she could see the silhouettes of several people leaning over the balcony. They appeared to be toasting drink flutes over the crowd below.

Beatrice and Cedric walked together through the far end of the rally, stopping to sign a petition or greet a friend or listen to part of a speech. But soon enough, they wound their way to an exit.

"We don't have to hurry home on my account," said Cedric.

"You know my favorite part of going out is coming home," replied Beatrice with a smile.

"All right then." He yawned. "That was exhausting. I argued with this woman for what felt like ages. She had this sign—STECOPO'S CHEMICALS CAUSE BIRTH DEFECTS over a picture of a baby with a spine like mine."

"Oh." Beatrice wrinkled her nose. "I didn't see that one."

"I asked her to change it from birth defects to 'spina bifida.'"

"Did she?"

"She couldn't comprehend how I could both want the company to answer for their malice *and* not consider myself defective." Cedric shook his head. "She said I was muddying the message. I told her I am the message!" He pointed at his chest. "So it matters how I wish to be spoken about."

Beatrice and Cedric had spent many, many hours hypothesizing about the relationship between Stecopo's rigid beauty standards and the erasure of disabled people, with all its sinister implications. In Seagate, when someone was injured, they stayed home until the bone was mended or the wound healed over. Beatrice had never thought much about this until she'd met Cedric. There had to be babies born in Seagate with similar conditions to Cedric's. Where did they go?

As if conjured by her thoughts, a flash of familiar colors appeared—yellow, tan, cream. All around the perimeter of the farthest part of the park stood a thick blockade of counterprotestors—some wearing bird masks, all holding placards and chanting scriptures. A row of policemen with batons kept them separated. She did not scan the crowd to see if Georgina or her parents were among them, but she kept her head down as she passed.

They turned a corner, leaving the rally behind. The noise of the crowds diminished; Beatrice could hear birdsong again.

"Ah, that's better." Cedric pulled her close and kissed her. "Hi."

"Hi." She snaked her hands into his back pockets and squeezed.

His big brown eyes crinkled with his smile. "You always were a nuanced thinker."

"I told everyone about us."

"Ah. How did they take it?"

"Walter was upset, Margot barely responded, and Erek seemed happy for us. I mean, he moved on, and the moons didn't collide—things change!"

"You're allowed to want a new adventure *and* love the time you had at the restaurant." Cedric leaned his cane against a tree and held on to her thick hips with his muscular hands.

"It's just holding two concepts at once," she murmured. "This, and also that."

"You're going to make an excellent revolutionary," he said, pulling her in for another kiss, and she felt herself go warm all over.

They smelled it before they saw it. As they approached their row house on Delany Lane, chatting about future orchards and possible fermentation projects in their new country home, Beatrice and Cedric could see the flames licking out from the downstairs window—glass broken, door kicked in, potted plants in pieces on the dirt-strewn front stoop.

Beatrice, covering her nose and mouth with her shirt, ran inside and grabbed the fire extinguisher in the front hall on her way to the kitchen, where she aimed the nozzle at the lowest part of the fire. The white chemical spray quickly blanketed the flames.

Cedric entered the kitchen, and they embraced. "The back entry is secure, the garden is untouched."

"Thank God Margot has always been such a stickler for fire safety," she said, hands and arms still trembling. "I've never had to use that thing."

"You were marvelous." Cedric examined the blackened stove, the cast-iron pan splattered with ropy white spray. The countertop next to the stove was half-melted, the wall behind the burners blackened and flaking apart.

Beatrice tapped a piece of broken plate with her shoe. "This is more organized than the other attacks. If we hadn't come back early, there would be nothing left." Cabinets had been kicked in, the floor littered with glass and porcelain. Almost all of the dishes would need to be replaced.

They began by opening all the windows and turning on the fans. Cedric switched to his wheelchair. Using what he called his pincher, a cleverly modified plastic claw, he rolled around picking up the larger shards of dishes before sweeping up the smaller mess with a lightweight plastic broom. After an hour of work, it was still a mess, although most of the glass and debris was gone from the floor.

Cedric rolled to the sink and filled a large jar with water, using one of the few intact vessels. "Water break!"

She pulled up a chair next to his and gulped water gratefully.

"You think Stecopo did this?" She passed him the half-empty jar, and he finished it.

"Not through direct channels. But I'd put nothing past them." He caressed her cheek. "Erek is right, you know. We'll be making ourselves even more of a target at the farm. They'll be coming after us by both legal and illegal means. I'm not trying to scare you—just being honest."

She looked around the busted-up kitchen. "When I lived in Seagate, I dreamed of a place with the girl I loved—a place for her animals and my plants. We were describing a farm, but we didn't have the words. I wanted a place free from the company and every-thing that went with it. Now I know that's impossible—we're part of the world, whether we like it or not. But this life, my life now, is so much larger, so much grander than anything I had ever imagined for myself. I know Stecopo will always try to take what we have, if we make something of value." She brushed a lock of hair from his brow. "I'm going to build it anyway."

Cedric leaned in close and kissed her. Fully, tenderly. Each kiss with him was a voyage and a return. She pulled him back in for another, and then he went off to mop the now-clear floor.

She found another bucket to fill with hot soapy water and began to wash the smoke-stained walls. It was the golden hour, the sunlight falling down low. Tonight they'd go to sleep the same way they'd done for almost a year—in his bedroom on the first floor, tangled together under the light sheets. She could picture it in her mind, a sweet domestic scene. Her stack of half-read books on his bedside table, her robe on the back of his chair. Or maybe the moons would collide, ending all problems, big and small.

She heard Cedric enter the garden for the nighttime watering. Alone in the kitchen, Beatrice sharpened her chef's knife. They wouldn't leave until the restaurant was running again. But the place couldn't remain open until the larger damage was fixed, and Beatrice anticipated that the repairs would cost them dearly. *Ring, ring, ring, sing, sing, sing*—the metal vibrated against the stone. They would find a way forward. Even when things felt the most dire, help always found her—help that couldn't be premeditated or planned. Lina had taught her that, and Father A, and all her friends at Delany Lane.

Ring, ring, ring, sing, sing, sing. She put her knife away. Her lower back ached, and she was sweaty and footsore. When Walter came home, they'd survey the damage, board up the windows, make a plan to move forward. Maybe there was danger in their future. But there was love now. There was safety now. And that was enough. Absentmindedly, as if sifting through a pile of junk mail, Beatrice took out her purse and opened the envelope bearing her name.

8.

Claudia awoke on Saturday morning feeling refreshed, as if she had slept away her old life and opened her eyes in a new world— a world of unlimited spending and custom habitat orbs. There had been no time to shop. She examined her palatial closet for the most intimidating outfit she could muster that was still appropriate for a daytime soirée. She settled upon a white linen suit of the finest weave, trimmed in surprising brown leather. The pants were long and wide-legged, while the jacket was cut very narrow, accentuating her tiny ribcage. The neckline plunged down, down, down to almost her belly button. Claudia tied a light-rose scarf around her neck. She painted her lips coral, then blotted them off so only the barest trace of color remained. In her tall brown wedges and wide-brimmed hat, she looked like a regal, artistic society woman, ready for a garden party or a long liquid lunch. She blew a kiss to her own reflection.

Just before leaving the apartment, Claudia ground a whole ripe pear onto the counter, watching the juices spill out over the marble. Martin was already downstairs in the lobby, enjoying an espresso and the morning paper. She took out six raw quail eggs from the refrigerator and dropped them in a row on the floor, one by one. She considered her work laterally, then from above; the dripping pear juice interacting with the smashed yolks below. It was dynamic, colorful, temporary. By the time she returned, the kitchen would be pristine.

They met the Muelbers and the Petersons at a private airstrip around midday. Though Claudia and Martin had noted this social obligation in their calendar weeks ago, neither of them could quite remember now what the occasion was commemorating. A dog's birthday? The Petersons' return from a vacation? The women kissed hello and took turns exclaiming over Claudia's outfit, remarking how some women were just hat people, and others just weren't. Mrs. Muelber wore a sheer lilac jumpsuit from last season, while Mrs. Peterson the elder inexplicably wore a white fur despite the warm autumnal sun. The second Mrs. Peterson, the younger one, wore a clear shift dress. Claudia resisted the urge to roll her eyes; it had all the charm of a shower curtain and did her figure no favors. She couldn't wait to move to the habitat ring, away from Sweaty Neck (Mr. Muelber) and No Neck (Mr. Peterson.) Her talents were being wasted here. There was no competition for miles.

Claudia forced herself to make nice with Mr. Peterson, who kissed her cheek too long and hugged her too close. Mr. Muelber gave her a warm peck on the cheek, and she remembered why she liked him best. Then she pressed into Martin's side, and he gave her a squeeze. He would protect her from No Neck's wandering hands. Someone passed Claudia a glass of chilled bubbly, and she drank it gratefully.

As they boarded, she remembered the point of this party. The Petersons had just purchased a state-of-the-art airship, like the one Martin had promised her the other morning after closing the Stecopo agreement. The Petersons had opted for a glass bottom (which Claudia found tacky) and a wide, open-air veranda off the port side (which Claudia found quite elegant; she would insist on that for her airship).

They began their slow cruise around the city—too high to discern particular people, but the perfect height for taking in the view. Claudia sipped her drink and tried to look lively. She spent a good twenty minutes talking about her moving plans with Mrs. Muelber, which she enjoyed, while Mrs. Peterson the younger poured courses into little flutes. Then lunch was served, *bon appétit*. The first course was a rather timid gazpacho, finished with lime juice, followed by a cold cucumber yogurt (Claudia excused herself thankfully, citing her intolerance for dairy). Dessert, if one could call it that, was melon purée with a hint of mint; an anemic, tepid offering from a woman wearing a plastic shower curtain. Claudia pushed away her dessert glass, repulsed by the homogeneous textures. As a young girl, she'd never imagined the rich to be so tasteless. Chef Beatrice was probably serving up something that both defied and reshaped logic at this very moment. Claudia glanced at the glass floor, as if she could see the restaurant from here. Instead, she saw a huge mass of people gathered in the Middle, just heads and heads as far as the eye could see. The crowd extended so far, she couldn't see where it ended or began.

"Aha!" said Mr. Peterson. "This is what I wanted to show you. The main event! Come, come, let's all go outside."

"But, darling," Mrs. Peterson the elder protested. "We're still partaking in lunch!"

"Oh dear," said Mr. Peterson, smiling in a way that seemed rather cruel. Claudia wondered how many glasses he had imbibed. "I'm sorry, will it get cold?" The elder Mrs. Peterson let out a short breath but said nothing, while the younger whispered something in her ear. It was clear to Claudia that both wives had bonded in mutual distaste for their husband, which Claudia found rather sweet. Mrs. Muelber made a fuss about finding a shawl for her poor arms. Claudia took off her hat with a grin and tossed it inside the airship. They all squeezed together onto the veranda. High up in the brisk fall air, it really was chilly, despite the sun. Martin pulled Claudia in close, and she smiled up into his face.

Below there was a huge body of people in the largest park in the Middle. Claudia knew it well. There was the statue of the horse and rider, where she'd once spent that beautiful day with Keith, feeling so buoyant she thought she might float away from too much happiness. She waited for her throat to get tight or her eyes misty at the memory, but nothing happened. Claudia took a deep breath, in and out. That love-lost, mournful feeling never came. Keith was her history. She looked to Martin. This was her man, her future, her love who would take her up to her life in the clouds. She looked down again. Dotted throughout the crowd were little stages where dense clumps of people had gathered, listening to speeches or songs or stories, clapping and cheering and waving their arms. Around the perimeter of the park stood rows of little booths with people sitting behind tables, passing out leaflets and signing petitions while other people milled about, reading and chatting and enjoying the weather. Claudia squinted, but she couldn't read the banners.

"How nice!" said Mrs. Muelber. "Is this some kind of fair?" Then Claudia remembered the pamphlet. That all seemed like life-times ago: the whole mess with Sergio, her inner torture over whether she should stay with Martin or try to start a life on her own. All those worries seemed like a dream now, or a plot on television.

"It's for us!" exclaimed Mr. Peterson, hoisting his glass in the air. "They're protesting Stecopo. Cheers, mates!"

"Oh my!" giggled Mrs. Peterson the younger, raising her glass.

The elder Mrs. Peterson clicked her tongue. "Don't be vain, dear." She made a show of rubbing her shoulders, which wasn't very convincing due to the fur. "Well, I'm a bit chilly. I think I'll go inside. I have some nice brandy, if anyone would like something more warming than bubbly. Oh!" Her eyes brightened. "Shall we all go have sex?" Then she frowned, considering. "Or is it too soon after lunch?"

Martin shook his head. "We can't take it personally, old boy." He patted Mr. Peterson on the back. "These people are uneducated and confused. How easily they're convinced by a fiery speech or a poorly written leaflet. They don't even understand the systems they're railing against, much less the intricacies involved if we were to even consider some of their demands. They're like children, asking for sweets and a ride on a pony. If anything, we should pity them." Claudia felt herself nodding to his words, but there was a buzzing drone in her ears. Suddenly her mouth was very dry. She swallowed the rest of her glass.

"Oooh, good girl!" said Mrs. Peterson the elder. "I'll get you a refill. Unless you'd prefer the brandy? Or why don't we all go inside and get cozy? It's so windy out here! I can barely hear myself think." The men ignored her.

"Another glass would be lovely," said Claudia. Mrs. Peterson the younger rushed inside to get another bottle.

"Are you sure you can hold your liquor, dear?" asked Mr. Peterson in false solicitude. "We need you alert for this afternoon's activities."

Claudia prickled inwardly, but smiled wickedly. "Thank you for your concern! I don't hold my liquor well at all." She reached out and plucked his bubbly flute from his sweaty hands. "Perhaps I should try holding yours instead?" She drained the glass and gave it back to him with a wink. The little party cheered, and Martin squeezed her waist. She remembered a time when Martin's business associates intimidated her, and was glad. How silly she was to ever have thought this life was above her.

Mrs. Peterson the younger came back with the bottle and gave it to Mr. Peterson. He opened it, shooting the cork into the crowd of protestors below. "Oopsie-daisy!" A great surge of sound rose beneath them. For a moment Claudia thought it was because of the cork, but then she realized that was merely a coincidence. The crowd was chanting something in unison, but it was difficult to make out the words.

"What's that they're saying?" asked Mrs. Muelber, rubbing her arms. Claudia couldn't tell if the other women really were cold or if they just wanted to get away from the protestors or get on with the sex.

"It's so sad," said young Mrs. Peterson to Claudia. "Always protesting something, aren't they?" Her blue eyes were wide and serious. "True change only comes from self-reflection."

Mr. Peterson leaned over the veranda to better listen to the chanting. "Georgie!" shouted his elder wife, in a pantomime of concern.

"I'm fine, I'm fine," he said. "I think they're saying, 'Clean Water Is a Natural Right'? Huh. Not very catchy, is it?"

"If they're so thirsty," said Mrs. Muelber, who was three-quarters of the way to drunk, "they can have some." And she poured her flute out on the crowd below. Mr. Peterson chortled, while Mrs. Peterson the elder shrieked. Mr. Muelber wagged his finger at his wife but said nothing.

A concentration of shouts rang out as several people looked up and pointed. Claudia resisted the urge to duck and hide. They were making quite a stir, bystanders in a luxury airship hovering above a protest, sipping their drinks. Some folks below booed, while others chanted: "Join us! Join us!" Claudia leaned back, holding her flute delicately in her hand. A part of her enjoyed the chaos. It was all just so ridiculous. Nothing looked the way she'd thought it would as a girl. Certainly not being on this incredibly expensive, tacky airship with these stupid people. She would simply take pleasure in the ride.

One by one, the party meandered back inside the belly of the aircraft. The novelty of the protest had worn off, and the wives would be performing sex acts soon enough between rounds of drinks. Claudia kissed Martin on the cheek, then took a moment to stand on the veranda by herself. She thought about the gifts she had made to both the restaurant and the climate group. In a sense, she was at that rally even now, as she floated above it all. Her money was energy in motion—it traveled, even when she stood still.

A warm body leaned against Claudia's back, pressing her against the metal railing. She turned, thinking it was Martin. But it was Mr. Muelber, her favorite, the one she felt safe with, pressing an erection into her lower back. Claudia stiffened. She tried to find Martin in her periphery, but she couldn't see anything inside the airship but Mr. Peterson's broad back. Surely Martin would notice soon and come to her rescue.

Mr. Muelber murmured in her ear, his breath hot, his voice slurred with drink. She hadn't realized he'd had so much. "See anyone you recognize down there?"

Claudia heard her own voice grow very flat. "Excuse me?" Back in the airship, Mr. Peterson stepped to the side to reveal Martin sitting on a sofa while the older Mrs. Peterson knelt in front of him, sucking his cock. Mrs. Peterson the younger perched next to him on the sofa arm so he could fondle her breasts. Mr. Peterson watched over them, egging them on cheerily as if enjoying a balloon race.

Muelber pressed his body even more aggressively into hers, causing her knees to knock against the railing. "Or did your people not make it as far as the Middle?" Claudia stayed very still. She tried to think of a joke, a way to defuse or steer the conversation in another direction, but her mind roared with blankness. He probably wouldn't remember this tomorrow, but she would.

"Come now," he said. "It will be our secret. You know someone down there. An old lover, a brother, or perhaps a cousin? You people," he said. "You always have so many cousins."

And just like that, his weight was gone. Mr. Muelber leaned on the railing beside her and smiled, showing even white teeth. "Well, Claudia," he said. "It's always so good to see you." His voice was now sober and friendly and light. The change was frightening, as if his drunkenness had been a pretext to molest her. "I like this outfit very much," he said, lightly fingering her sleeve. "You have such a flair for the dramatic." He went back inside the airship.

As Claudia rose higher and higher, she watched the crowd recede into the distance. They were now just a darkened smudge against the horizon. Maybe if she looked hard enough, she'd see Ijo out there in her cottage by the sea.

She raised her glass to her lips, drained it, and dropped it off the edge of the railing. Claudia watched it fall down, down, down to the earth below. She couldn't tell if it shattered on impact, but she knew it could not remain whole. She made a decision.

"Aggie," she whispered, as land flowed under the airship like water. "Find the document *The Kitchen Girl*. I want you to send a copy from an untraceable address to everyone who fits the following criteria."

She listed them off, one by one:

"All members of the press.

All restaurant owners and operators.

All Free-Wah churches and temples.

Every resident of Seagate.

Every member of parliament.

Every official in the Flesh Martyr Church.

Any group associated with the fight against Stecopo, including the free land movement, Ahinga, and Free-Wah liberation.

All college and university religion scholars."

She paused, gazing out toward the sea.

"And classic literature majors."

Soon everyone would know what Claudia and Beatrice knew—all tenets of Flesh Martyrdom, everything they held to be true, that had imprisoned generations, was about to be proven false by Ijo's immortal words. The list read like a poem. But what was a poem, really? Not decorative, empty words, but a match to set the world alight.

EPILOGUE

I was born by the sea and I will die by the sea. In my little house overlooking the cliffs, the waves sing to keep me company. I tend my garden. I pickle vegetables.

How very different from my years at Castle Mora as the royal surrogate. Sometimes pregnant, other times nursing, I spent my days organizing moongazing parties at pavilions designed for my pleasure, or crafting ornamental gardens in honor of one particular bloom. I added water features to our sumptuous grounds—ponds and fountains, grottoes and springs. Some of my whimsy was practical—a stand of chestnut trees, a cranberry bog. I oversaw a great many laborers and craftsmen, standing with my hands on my hips, considering samples of tile and shapes of sconces. I thought I had died and been reborn into a better life.

Yet when I remember this period, I am filled with shame. I was not my kindest. I let my new power get the best of me, encouraged cliques and infighting amongst my ladies-in-waiting. Please remember, I had suffered the majority of my teenage years at the hands of the old cook. I knew no better. Henray was gracious during this second adolescence as I paraded around in gowns and jewels, often carrying a small dog and overindulging in food and wine till I became sick. Eventually I grew tired of the frivolous projects, and the viciousness of castle life—the women waiting for favors, their words like knives behind my back.

During this early period I worried constantly that the queen would resent the attention I received in court, and no amount of assurances from Henray could ease my mind. I did my best to avoid her—a low bow in passing, polite words at dinner, nothing more. Only later did I realize that she cherished my presence. It removed her from the spotlight so she could live as she pleased. Later, she would return the favor.

Those busy years took their toll. Exhausted from childbearing, tired of garden parties, puffy and malcontent from rich food and wine, I began to observe the queen with new eyes. She would sit in meditation each day in one of the garden pavilions I'd had built with a particularly beautiful view of the setting sun. One day she invited me to join her in contemplation.

By then I was no longer scared of her, but I found sitting in stillness terribly irritating, even frightening at times. I couldn't wait to get up and move about. It took a long time for the healing elixir of silence to work its way through me. Eventually I grew to deeply treasure these afternoon sessions. This recounting makes it seem like this was a quick process, from boredom to bliss. I assure you, it was not.

We would come together in the golden hour, when the sun slowly fell down amongst the hills, and the moons rose in its place. What a relief it was to be with someone who had no wish to garner my favor. Nor did she position herself to use me for political gain. The queen seemed to want nothing, other than copious time for silence. She said little, but her presence was very large. I softened miraculously in those early months of sitting. Slowly, slowly, for the first time since leaving my village as a girl, I knew a taste of true ease, not creature comforts masking the abyss underneath.

The queen gained a following for these afternoon sitting sessions. I missed our intimacy as her audience grew. Powerful advisers and those wishing to climb in court tried to gain her favor there, but how do you barter with a woman who requires nothing?

Perhaps she had been waiting for an audience. She began to speak, in those group sessions, when she felt so moved—telling brief, poetic stories of various unnamed kings and peasants, or sometimes parables from the natural world. Or she would sit in her usual silence, and allow the group to ask her questions. Once she came wearing a bird mask, as a joke and a plea. She implored her ardent followers to understand that she was not a deity, that her birthright was one we all shared as people—to sit in stillness and receive the grace of God. But she never came at things directly. Only when asked if her acolytes should don bird masks too did she smile gently and say, "I am pointing at the moons, my friends, and you are staring at my finger."

I have not lived in the castle for many years now, but when I see in writing, or hear in verse, a supposed quote from Queen Janus, I know it to be counterfeit. There are those who would have you believe she never ate, as if she were a living miracle! Of course she ate, plainly yet regularly, and at our royal table, with her constituents dining all around her. Likewise, Queen Janus never spoke of the glory of nations or loyalty to an empire. She did not judge or preach. She never asked anyone for penance or to confess to a sin. And she certainly never beat the drums of war.

Eventually, the queen gave me my ultimate gift—she gave me my death.

I made my request to the queen while Henray was away. We were in her atrium, where she kept her songbirds. Her hawk rested in a special cage, far from the others in her glass-walled garden.

I asked for my public death and the freedom to live as I chose, away from court life. I asked for our children to be told that I had died. The request felt bitter on my tongue, but these kinds of secrets do not keep. I could fade politely from my children's lives—the two princes and the princess, having survived nearly to adolescence, had another mother and scores of adults to care for them, teach them, guide them.

The king belonged to the people, but Henray belonged only to me.

The queen listened a long time and was silent for even longer. I expected her to respond with one of her many parables. I knew all of them by heart, but often discovered a new meaning upon each recitation. I have included recollections of her parables following the conclusion of this text—"The Story of the Unbaked Bread," "Seven Strangers at the Wedding," "The Tree Which Would Not Bloom," "Two Fishwives Discover a Lost Purse," and many more. But for once, Queen Janus did not respond in story, or answer my question with another question. She only kissed me briefly on the lips, as was the custom of her homeland, and said that she would miss me.

I wondered if she was ever homesick. She'd been quite young when she flew to our shores, a treaty in the form of a person.

And so, I died in my eighth childbirth, or so the castle records have written. And then I was free.

Henray visited my secret kingdom once. He rode in like a knight on the dusty road. I was pumping water from the well, dirty and sweaty and glorious. Those middle years were my favorite—the vigor of forty, of fifty. Old enough to know my mind and young enough to do something about it. We met, for the first time in our long partnership, as equals. Never had I experienced such a feeling as serving us stew from my own hearth, his boots by my door. We spent a season this way, days working the fields, nights in each other's arms. Each plot of land contained myriad questions that we asked together. *What should we do with the azaleas? Where is the best light for pumpkins?*

Such musings are the joy of gardeners. We planted trees we would never see mature, and this satisfied us all the more.

Then he returned to the world of duty. But Henray never visited the grove he planted. He died later that same year, not even sixty, from unexpected heart failure. Or so they say. News of his death plagued me with worries greater than grief. Henray, dead, who outmatched me each day chopping wood and carrying water? Henray, who hauled a stump that might have been carried by two men together? Sometimes, late at night, I even feared for my children. But the good queen outlived him by many years, and she was a patient and fair ruler. My first son became king, and our lands grew all the more prosperous. Now everyone of my generation is gone, and when this account is found, I will be dead too.

Luckily, I am a gardener. I understand that some projects bear fruit quickly, while others take many years. I am planting for the future. When I die, this knowledge cannot die with me. I have written my story because books, like trees, are not always for the living.

During my years in Castle Mora, I sometimes felt that to be a woman means to never be sovereign over one's own body. After my seventh pregnancy, I knew I would use the old ways to prevent myself from ever conceiving again. I kept to my quiet life for many years on the cliff's edge and kept my medicinal gardens, making the same herbal tinctures my aunt taught me in my childhood village.

Under the cover of night, women would visit my cottage, looking for tonics to give them back control over their bodies. That was how the rumors started: people warned to stay away from my land, that I would try to steal their children and use their body parts in my evil brews. But they were warning women away from knowledge and independence, their birthright. I fear my death will not stop that struggle.

They named me the Night Witch—a frightening, lonely figure.

But when we understand nature's kingdom and work within its seasons, we are never afraid and never alone. The land and the sea are my mother, the sky my loving father, and I their devoted child, making my brews at the hearth. So I remain, humbly, the Kitchen Girl.

MENU FOR A LIBERATED SPIRIT

Well water

Fresh vegetables, fruit trees

The sea and her offerings

Each morning, ask yourself:
If I too am mostly water,
In which direction shall I flow?

Ijo, 987.

ACKNOWLEDGMENTS

My incredible editor, Amara Hoshijo, who embraced my vision and contributed so much to the manuscript: I'm so honored to be creating another book with you. Sarah Bolling, my wonderful agent—you saw the potential in this book back in 2017 and helped me dig deep, stay true, and keep going. I owe you so much. The gorgeous cover art by Aykut Aydoğdu. Huge thanks to my all-star PR and marketing team Kayleigh Webb, Bianca Ducasse, and Tyrinne Lewis; copyeditor Joal Hetherington; proofreader M.L. Liu; managing and production editors Emily Arzeno, Caroline Pallotta, and Laura Jarrett; designer Davina Mock-Maniscalco; Joe Monti, Jéla Lewter, and the entire Saga team for welcoming me so warmly into the fold. You make my dreams come true.

RACK writing group—Katharine Duckett, Ashley Bloom, and Rouxi Chen—your thoughtful notes greatly improved Beatrice's journey.

The independent booksellers and librarians that keep art accessible and in our communities: thank you for the life-changing work you do.

The teens of the Octavia Project, who inspire me to dream bigger every day.

My community: Eri Nox, for all the love and sour pickle soup. Lauren Monroe. Dinah Grossman—inspiring chef, baker, and dear friend who taught me how to use butter as a radical act of self-love. Agnes Borinsky, for the deep reading and vegan pizza nights. Levi Bentley, for their insightful edits. Sarah Einspanier. ray ferreira. Perel. Krzysztof Sadlej. Kate Watson-Wallace. Aviva Rubin. Delia Gable. Josephine Stewart. Meghan McNamara. Dave Hartunian. Rohan Chander. Eliza Bagg. JD Rocchio. Stefanie Abel Horowitz. Collen Eng. Chris Rountree. Ben Cassorla. Priya Swaminathan. Craig Lucas. Harmon. Adam Greenfield. Laura Lamb. China Miéville. Claire MacDonald. Ann and Jeff VanderMeer. Claire Kiechel. Ashley Tata. Steven Bradshaw. Tara Ahmadinejad. Andrew Lynch. Susan Bernfield. James Dean Palmer. Myah Shein. Patricia Black. Cass Vincent. Thank you for all the love and care from my first draft in 2016 until now.

The staff, cooks, librarians, and administrators of MacDowell, my creative home. You replenish and feed me, body, mind, and soul. All of the amazing artists I met at MacDowell from 2017 to 2021—thank for you sharing your gifts with me!

My wonderful brother, Matt Porter. My father, Steven Porter, who believed in the value of my art long before the world did. My mother, Susan Porter, to whom this book is dedicated—for everything. My grandmother, Lorraine Shulman, who sewed socks by the gross as a little girl. You showed me love with food when you couldn't say it with words.

Ted Hearne, my love—for your rigor, expansive vision, and your unwavering belief in my art. Calder, Simone, and Venda—olive juice more than I can say. Thank you for making my life so fun.

All That Is—thank you for the message, the patience, the detours, the needle, the thread. I am grateful.